Generally Recognized as Safe

LM Foster

This is a work of fiction. Names, characters, places and incidents are products of the author's imagination. Any resemblance to actual events, locales, organizations, or persons, either living or dead, is entirely coincidental.

9th Street Press
www.9thstreetpress.com

Corruption begins when knowledge of how things work is intentionally used to exploit those who have no idea they are being exploited.

NATE

My phone lit up. It was Wiley. I sighed. I didn't really have time for Wiley at the moment. Graduation loomed and I had one more exam to take, and I was trying to study. But what the hell. Wiley was my best friend. I pushed the button and said hello.

"Brendee's pregnant," he said without preamble.

"What?" Like it was scripted. "Is she sure?"

"I don't know. She hasn't said anything to me about it yet."

"Then how do you–"

"Who are you talking to, Nate? Let me read some of her recent browsing history to you."

"Does she know you read her browsing history, Wiley? Isn't she curious to know why you're looking at her computer when you have one – more than one – of your own?"

"I don't have to look at her computer, Nate. I wrote an app that replicates the important parts of hers on my phone. It's really very simple, actually, all you have to do is–"

"It's still none of your business, Wiley."

"If she doesn't want me to see it, all she's gotta do is erase where she's been. I'm not interested in it enough to resurrect it. Even though I could."

"But she hasn't a clue that you can see it, Wiley," I insisted. "It's . . . dishonest, somehow."

Wiley ignored my ethics. "Listen to these searches, Nate. *Symptoms of Pregnancy; When should I take a pregnancy test; How accurate are home pregnancy tests; When should I tell my boyfriend I'm pregnant.* She's not thinking about vacationing in the south of France."

"Don't you . . .? Isn't she on . . .?" But all that didn't matter anymore, did it? Wiley was right: his girlfriend's search conditions said it all. I couldn't imagine what I would do in his place. I wasn't ready for such a thing. I was about to graduate from college, as were Wiley and Brendee. Brendee already had a great part-time job, and

Wiley had a bright future in electronics . . . But Deneen and I would be lucky to find a good job with the rest of the glut of graduates. A baby wasn't for us. Was it for Wiley? "What are you going to do?" I finally asked.

I could hear Wiley's smile through the phone. "Something perfectly apt, I assure you. I always give Brendee what she wants. I'll call you back later and tell you what she says."

"Wiley, what're you gonna–" But he'd already ended the call.

BRENDEE

It'd been two days since the first test showed positive; I'd taken another one before I went to school this morning. It was positive, too.

I'd tried to have a fish pond once, when I was a kid, but it kept getting choked with algae. The fish kept dying. I researched it on the internet, read all the articles about how it was impossible to control the algae without flowing water and plants, just like in nature. If you only have water and sun, you're gonna get algae, despite all the unnatural precautions like algaecides and water changes. *Life will find a way,* the internet told me.

And it looked like that was one of those Truths, with a capital T. Despite all my chemical precautions, life had found a way. Almost to graduation, all ready to start law school, I was pregnant.

I didn't worry about school or career. My mom and dad had four kids – neither one of them was a lawyer. My dad sold real estate, and my mother had a well-paying-enough government job. I'd only planned on a law career because nothing else stood in the way of such a thing. I'd already completed the certification program and worked part-time as a paralegal – if law school had to be put on hold for a while, I wouldn't starve. And if I never became a lawyer, well . . . I was going to be a mom, and it had always been the proudest thing my mother had ever been.

And Wiley . . . In the modern world, Wiley's knowledge made him able to turn a buck as easily as members of the oldest profession. People might not be willing to pay for *that,* but they'd surely pay to get their electronics fixed. And Wiley could fix them all.

I believed that Wiley and I were in love. We'd been together since our senior year in high school. And other than a little doubt on my part at the beginning, for the last five years, everything between us had been as smooth as glass. We'd met through rather odd circumstances – well, really *all* the circumstances hadn't been odd. Just some of them. He needed a math tutor, and my friend Nate had suggested me.

Wiley and I were strangers when we met, even though his parents and my parents were old friends. His family had moved away when he was ten. When they moved back to town, my mom kept talking about my *Aunt Amy* and my *Uncle Alex* and their son – Mom kept saying his name was *Willie* – but I couldn't place them. My mom and dad were both only children – who were these people she kept talking about? We weren't blood relations it turned out, but apparently my brother and I and Cousin Willie had all played together as kids, had called each other's parents *aunt* and *uncle.* But I couldn't remember them at all.

And all that wasn't even the odd part.

The family history went that once upon a time, my mother had been quite enamored of a local singer. She and Aunt Amy and their friends had gone to see him every weekend at some dive bar, long since torn down and replaced with a *Baker's.* Mom and her friends were positively gaga over this guy – *he was the best looking man I'd ever seen,* Mom told me.

Mom and all of her friends longed for this guy – his name was Wes Thomerville – all of them, so the legend went, except for Aunt Amy. He was married, older than them, unattainable; and Aunt Amy just couldn't understand why they were all so obsessed with him. But Fate, not being without a sense of humor, decreed that Aunt Amy would marry a man that looked just like Wes Thomerville.

None of these facts would've mattered to me – tales of my parents' youth had always bored me to tears – if it hadn't been for a Friday afternoon, right before I finished my junior year in high school. Aunt Amy had called to tell my mother that she and her family were moving back to town, and this had caused Mom to want to reminisce. She went looking for her high school yearbook – I don't know if she ever found it. What she did find, what she showed me that put me right around the bend, was a video of the aforementioned Wes Thomerville and his band, singing some poppy tune about revenge.

My mom would never know – *no one would ever know* – but I had to agree with her: Wes Thomerville was the best looking man I'd ever seen, too, and his inane little video from before I was born was the sexiest three minutes and thirty-five seconds *ever.* I felt as though I'd lost my mind – I made a little ritual out of watching it on my laptop, every Friday night, all through the summer after eleventh grade, through the fall when senior year started, through the spring.

In April I met my cousin – his name wasn't *Willie* at all. His name was *Wiley,* son of Alex, my unremembered aunt's husband, he that had looked just like Wes Thomerville in his youth. I couldn't remember any of them, past perhaps a few visits to a family with a yappy, black-haired kid when I was little.

4

But my, how Cousin Wiley had grown. Like his daddy before him (or so it was told), Wiley was the walking, talking embodiment of Wes Thomerville, a man in his thirties. A man in his thirties before I was born. But Wiley was only thirteen months older than me, and because of an injury when he was sixteen, he was still a senior in high school. And he wasn't going to graduate unless he passed math, and he was an idiot at math. So he needed my help.

This is the part where things got a little odd. Wiley was, and continues to be, and electronics genius. He can fix a wet cell phone, a rolling television, a busted tablet, an infected laptop. He wrote an app that allowed people to surreptitiously watch others through the webcams on their computers, and he sent me a copy of it, right after he'd inadvertently showed me his IP address, the first day we met.

I watched Wiley while I tutored him; because of his undeniable resemblance to Wes, he was incredibly attractive to me. But he didn't respond to any flirting I tried; I decided he was shy. But from the moment I saw him, I'd become obsessed with him, so I loaded the app he gave me onto my computer, typed in his IP address, and went right ahead and watched him through his webcam, when he didn't know I was watching him, like it was a perfectly natural thing to do.

But Wiley *did* know I was watching him; at least he knew the second time. I never asked him how he knew — I figured it must've been some kind of security trace or something — someone who could write such apps would undoubtedly know how to detect them. When he figured out that I was spying on him, he held up a sign — there wasn't any sound to the app — a sign that said, *I know what you want.* Then another one that said, *Come get me.*

I never asked him how he knew. It somehow seemed romantic to me to not know the details. We've been inseparable ever since. He's a demon between the sheets, and through the coincidence of genetics and a dumb old video of an unknown singer, no one in the world will ever be more attractive to me than Wiley. He's also an arrogant son of a bitch, but I love him, probably way more than he loves me. But he does love me. I'm pretty sure of it, most days.

But now things were about to get complicated. I was gonna have Wiley's baby — flawless, black-haired, blue-eyed Wiley. All the clichés fit — he was the only man I'd ever loved; he was amazing; he was awesomely intelligent, hilariously funny; he was beautiful. How could his baby be otherwise? How could I not love his baby as much as I loved him?

The adolescent infatuation of high school and college sweetheart-dom was about to become the reality of a family and instant adulthood, however. I wasn't sure how he was gonna take it. I realized that, at its most base, this was really my problem. Wiley would always be Wiley, whatever degree of responsibility he chose or did not choose to shoulder, for this, our mutual mistake. Regardless, it would be up to me to take care of our baby.

I decided that there was no sense in waiting any longer. It was time to drop this most commonplace of bombs, and hope that the damage wasn't insurmountable.

I was sitting in the living room of our little apartment, waiting for him. He'd texted that he'd be a few minutes late coming home – he had an errand to run. He didn't specify what it was, and I knew he wouldn't, not unless I asked him. It wasn't that he was secretive; he just didn't offer explanations for everything he did. He'd tell me if I asked him, but really, I had bigger fish to fry at the moment than wondering about what was going to keep him for an extra half hour.

Finally, he walked in, and feeling like I was reenacting a scene that had played over and over, worldwide, since the dawn of civilization, I said, "Wiley, there's something I need to discuss with you."

"Wait!" he said, and held up his hand. "Me first. Whatever you have to tell me cannot be nearly as important as what I have to ask you."

There was that old Wiley superiority. Always in control was Wiley Royce. *Boy, are you gonna be surprised this time,* I thought.

He crossed the room in a few long strides, then gracefully dropped to his knees in front of where I sat on the couch. Before I could even as much as *flinch* to react, he was holding up a little black velvet box with a ring in it. "Will you marry me, Brendee?" he said, and again, the thought crossed my mind that here was another scene that had been enacted over and over again throughout history. But the ordinariness of it didn't matter, because it was happening to me. Wiley, my beloved Wiley, was asking *me* to marry him, and I just hugged him to me, speechless.

"I'll take that as a yes," he said smugly. But it was all right that he was smug. I would always be his most willing slave – he knew it and I knew it, so his confidence about it was okay with me.

He sat on the couch beside me and put the ring with its little diamond on my finger. Then he kissed me, just the way I liked it, and one thing led to another, and my even more momentous news was

6

forgotten for a moment, in glorious surrender to Wiley's touch. *Oh, how I love him!* I thought, like a school girl. *He always knows exactly what I want.*

While we were still curled up on the couch together, Wiley's phone beeped. He found his shirt in the pile of clothes on the floor, looked at it, smiled. "It's Nate. Do you want to let him and Deneen know, or shall I?" When I didn't answer immediately, he glanced over at me. "I almost forgot – you said something earlier – what did you want to tell me, Brendee?"

"I'm gonna have a baby," I said, and twisted the ring on my finger. "You're timing, as always, is perfect."

He blinked at me in surprise, his eyes just as blue as a summer day, then he hugged me again, and as always, the feel of his bare skin against mine made me shiver. "That's wonderful, Brendee," he stated simply. "That's the best news I've heard all day . . . It's the best news I've ever heard!" He kissed me. "When?"

"I've got a doctor's appointment tomorrow. I'm sure I'll get all the whens and wherefores then."

****

The whens and wherefores of being pregnant, I would discover almost immediately, were awful. I don't know how Deneen's mother did it twice, my own mother a staggering *four* times. I almost missed graduation because of morning sickness. Graduation was in the afternoon, but my morning sickness lasted all day.

I complained to the doctor about it. She said, "They say if you're sick a lot, it means you're gonna have a healthy baby."

What kind of insane logic was that? "Then I'm gonna have the healthiest baby ever born," I snapped.

She prescribed some drug to help with the morning sickness; but she wouldn't refill the prescription when I went back, because she said I was taking too many of them. It was just as well, because when Wiley Googled the compound, he said there was the possibility of it causing some irreversible movement disorder. Of course, the doctor hadn't mentioned *that,* but on the other hand, she probably hadn't thought I would over-medicate myself with the stuff. It wasn't like it worked that well, anyway. I was still sick all the time. Wiley and the doctor both gently suggested soda crackers and flat ginger ale. Right. I had a few suggestions for them.

7

Wiley was offered a position at a fairly prestigious data security company, immediately after graduation. It was a huge step for him: Wiley had never worked a day in his life, at least not like other people. Friends, relatives, strangers had brought their indispensable electronics to him, and he'd made them all better, quite profitably. That had always been enough before.

But now – for me, for his baby – he got a haircut, bought a couple of suits, and went to work for *Securi-Comp.* I stayed on at the firm for a little while, but then decided to take the rest of the time off, since they told me that my position would be waiting for me after the baby was born. They graciously told me that it could be part time again if I decided to go to law school, or full time if I wanted to continue as just a paralegal.

I was glad to not have to work. I was sick, I was moody. If it rained, I cried. If it didn't rain, I cried. I felt fat. I felt sorry for myself, out of sorts, a different person. I woke up in the middle of the night with agonizing Charley-horses in my calves. Wiley would gently knead them until the pain subsided. He patiently observed the changes I was going through, and would occasionally offer me gentle, internet-gleaned advice. But he didn't coddle me, didn't become an accessory to my misery. He just watched me, told me frequently how much he loved me, how happy he was.

I was not happy. I was miserable, though I realized the thing was only temporary. But I didn't always tell him that I loved him back. I didn't love anything right then. Not myself, not the parasite sucking the life from me, not the man that had put it there. I was fat, uncomfortable, bitchy, suddenly a crybaby, something I'd never before been. I often told Wiley that there weren't going to be any more, and he said that was fine with him. An only child's life is the best, he said – an only child never has to wonder who the favorite is.

"I was always the favorite," I said defensively.

"Are you sure?" he asked with a grin.

"Of course, I'm sure," I retorted, not sure at all.

"Of course you are," he repeated back to me, the way he would speak to a child, or to someone he thought was stupid. He talked to Nate's girlfriend Deneen that way sometimes.

It was just as well that Wiley didn't want any more children. He could've said he wanted ten, and no matter how much I loved him, it wouldn't've changed my mind. On one of the visits to the obstetrician, I signed the papers to get sterilized. That's how much I hated being pregnant.

8

Wiley and I enrolled in a Lamaze class, and I immediately discovered that the theory of natural childbirth, not to put too fine a point on it, is a mind-fuck. I despised the hippie-dippie earth-mother types that ran the classes. I despised the absurd ideas they spouted – one tenet was that I was supposed to bring a teddy bear or a picture of something beloved with me to the death chamber – I mean, the delivery room. I was supposed to pant and breathe and concentrate on this object to help diffuse the pain.

"I'm going to concentrate on that needle," I said to Wiley under my breath. One of the instructors heard me and frowned.

I was very frightened of the pain. The two things in life that I could never withstand, I always maintained, were pain and temptation. Present either, and I would roll over every time.

On the ride home, I railed to Wiley about the insanity of it. "I drive to work in an air-conditioned car, I sit in an air conditioned office. I get my information and entertainment from a million electronic devices–"

"All solid state," Wiley commented, apropos of nothing.

I glared at him. "And they expect me to squat down and have a baby like a caveman! With nothing for the pain!"

"It's not supposed to be good for the–" he dared.

"My mother had painkillers! We all turned out all right!"

"You ask for whatever you need, Brendee," Wiley soothed. "It's completely up to you."

The final straw came later in the course. I was six months pregnant by then, and the morning sickness had finally stopped. But I still felt like an uncomfortable, annoyed bear most of the time. We were sitting in class, Wiley silently observing all the mothers and fathers-to-be. Even Wiley's capacity for silent observation was beginning to annoy me.

We practiced our ludicrous huffing and puffing, and then the instructor told us we were going to watch a video. It showed the experiences of two young mothers in the throes of the miracle of birth, she said, as she dimmed the lights. The first unfortunate wailed unceasingly between pants; she shook like someone with a palsy; she sweated, she cried. The second one kept slapping her husband's hand away as he tried to pat her comfortingly on the head. Mercifully, the entire labors were not depicted, but it was still awful enough.

I looked over at the mother-to-be sitting a few chairs to my right. She was very young, maybe only sixteen or seventeen. The father wasn't there; her own mother was her Lamaze coach. The girl had blanched as white as snow at what they'd just shown us, and I said to her mom, "If that was supposed to engender the maternal instinct, it failed." Mom just shook her head. Like my own mom, I bet she'd had painkillers.

The instructor asked if there were any questions, and I raised my hand high, defiantly. Wiley put his face in his own hand, shook his head. The instructor ignored me, but as there were no other questions, she eventually had to pick me.

"Yes, Mrs. Royce?"

I was Mrs. Royce by that time. We'd had a simple civil ceremony, because I was just not in the mood for a big wedding. I had Wiley, and I was gonna have his baby – what did I need with a big wedding? Nate was his best man. We had a huge party afterwards. That was celebration enough for me.

I looked over at the pale young girl, then said to the instructor, "Could you tell us, at what point in the movie the moms received their pain medication?"

The instructor sighed. "This is natural childbirth, Mrs. Royce. We've been telling you all along: there is no pain medication."

"That's what I thought." I stood up with as much dignity as I could muster, seeing as how I was as ungainly as a snake that had swallowed a watermelon. Wiley dragged his hand across his face, looked up at me. He smiled. I smiled back at him. "Fuck this," I said, and waddled out of the classroom. He shrugged at the shocked sheep – *"Baa,"* I bleated from the hall – and he followed after me. I later received a full refund for Lamaze. It was insane.

I didn't get to have the whole *Honey, it's time* scenario, another chestnut of time immemorial, as it turned out, anyway. When I was already eighteen days past my due date – I'd been pregnant since the Jurassic period, and it seemed as though I would be pregnant until the last trump; I was huge – when I sat around the house, I sat *around the house* – my obstetrician suggested that it might be time to induce labor.

That lasted for two miserable days. I listened to the natural childbirth women screaming in agony around me in the maternity ward. I caught a cold, felt sick and snuffly. The result of the induction of labor was no labor at all – only one entire contraction – and I didn't like that one, not one bit. The doctor wrote *Failure to progress* on my chart and recommended a Caesarian section. When he asked me what kind of anesthesia I'd prefer, I said, "Just knock

10

me out." I wasn't going to have to go through it after all, and that was fine with me. "And don't forget my sterilization," I said.

****

When I came out of the anesthesia, my mom was standing beside the bed with my husband. I didn't wonder if I'd given birth to a boy or a girl, if it was healthy, if it had ten fingers and toes – I was lying on my stomach for the first time in nine months, and all I could do was thank God that it was finally over.

"They'll only let us in two at time, Brendee," Mom said. "But everybody's waiting to congratulate you."

I blinked at her and her incomprehensibility and looked at Wiley. "It's a boy," he said.

My mother grinned with grandmotherly pride. She said, "He looks just like–"

"Wes?" I asked.

"– his father," Mom concluded. She frowned for a second, then gave me a beatific smile – Mom had been the biggest, the *original* Wes Thomerville fan. She looked at my baby's father, so I looked at his father, too, my beloved Wiley. But Wiley frowned. Wiley never frowned. Wiley looked crestfallen. Wiley never looked crestfallen.

"Of course he does," I said. Why had Wes Thomerville, unthought of since I'd met Wiley, suddenly roared into my mind? It was some bizarre drugged logic of anesthesia that had spilled out of my mouth: Wiley looked like Wes, so his son would look like Wes . . . It was an abominable thing to say. "I'm sorry, Wiley."

"It's okay, Brend." He only called me *Brend* when he was annoyed with me or when he was annoyed at my interruption of something else that annoyed him. "We already filled the paper work out."

He handed me a birth certificate, which informed me that my son's name was *Wes Royce*. It sounded ridiculous, like an undercard boxer. No son of Wiley's would ever box. He might be a Tai Chi practicing, ninja assassin, but never a boxer.

Wes Royce – not *Wesley Royce*. That would've been too effeminate. No son of Wiley's would ever be effeminate, unless he was gay, and then his father would have the best friend in the world – someone that liked men that wasn't a woman. Someone who, besides a different sexual orientation, thought just like him. Imagine

11

all the insights he could learn about what was deemed attractive in the male animal! Think of how he could use it all on me!

But either name was awful.

"I'm so glad you picked it!" my mother cried out and hugged me.

Wiley left the room.

I said his name and opened my eyes. Wiley and my mother were standing beside the bed. It was all an anesthesia-induced dream. A hallucination. Maybe.

"They'll only let us in two at time, Brendee," Mom said. "But everybody's waiting to congratulate you."

I blinked at her and her incomprehensibility and looked at Wiley. "It's a boy," he said.

"He looks just like his father," my mother said.

I looked at his father and he smiled gleefully. I'd never seen him so happy, and seeing him so happy made me happy. Then a mudspatter of doubt, a big dollop of fear, splotched my joyous thoughts. "What's his name?"

"I thought we'd agreed we'd name him *William Tiberius Royce.*" Wiley grinned in pride. "Junior. We can call him *Willie.*"

My son, *Willie.* How completely awful was that?

"I don't remember that conversation," I told the proud papa. "We'll pick a name when the anesthesia wears off."

Wiley grinned. He didn't really want to name our son *Willie.* He was fucking with me, even when I was drugged. *Goddamn, I love you,* I thought. "You're a son of a bitch, Wiley," I said as I started to drift off.

"Aw, don't blame my mom, Brendee. She's a grand ol gal. She's waiting out in the hall to see you."

"Later," I said, and slipped back to sleep.

It was a hallucination; the product of the drugs, and my own jangled thoughts. Wiley didn't even *know* about my onetime addiction to that old video of Wes Thomerville, any more than my mother did. When she'd shown it to me, I'd given her the impression that I didn't like it, then had copied it on the down-low and put it on my computer. Once I'd started going with Wiley – I'd never watched it again since. The reality of Wiley was so much sweeter than any fantasy I'd ever had of Wes. There was no comparison.

Wiley had seen the video once, when my dad had showed it to him on *YouTube.* I wasn't the only one (secretly) that had noticed his resemblance to Wes, and they were all kidding my mom about her old crush, and her daughter's new boyfriend, who looked just like his dad, who'd also looked just like Wes. My opinion was asked, and I shrugged, saying that I didn't see that much of a resemblance. Wiley didn't know anything about my one-time obsession with Wes Thomerville and his stupid little video. No one did.

****

In the end, we named our son Benjamin Oliver, after his grandfather. We called him Bo, just like everyone called my dad.

The morning after he was born, I wasn't permitted to see him, because they said I had a fever. My mother made a nuisance of herself until they found me a wheelchair, and she pushed me down the hall to where he was. They were keeping him with the sick babies – that was another trope that I didn't get to experience – there wasn't a nursery full of healthy babies anymore. My mom said it hadn't even been like that when we were all born. They left your baby in the room with you then and nowadays, if he was healthy and you were healthy.

My mom wheeled me up to the window, and I stood up. It hurt very much, but I couldn't see him otherwise. Another woman was staring through the window at a tiny baby in an incubator – he was hooked up to myriad tubes and wires.

"Here's Bo," my mother said, as a smiling nurse brought him over to the window and held him up. He was big and pink and healthy, with a thatch of black hair, just like his father. The woman standing next to me said, "He's beautiful. Congratulations."

My mother said, "He looks just like his father."

I thanked the woman for her praise; then I suddenly felt guilty that Bo was so healthy, when the tiny baby in the incubator obviously wasn't. "Is he yours?" I asked gently.

"My sister's," she said.

"I hope he'll be okay," I said.

"Me, too," she agreed.

I wanted to get out of there then, go back to my room, away from the poor, sick little spark of struggling life, away from his sad aunt. I sat back in the wheelchair and my mother pushed me down the hall.

Later in the day, my fever broke, and they brought Bo in to me for the first time. Wiley wasn't off work yet, and my mother had gone to get something to eat, so I got to look at him for the first time, all by myself. He was perfect – I touched his tiny pink fingers and toes, kissed his black hair.

The nurse had said that I should try to feed him, so I did. It was very uncomfortable to perch him on my belly; the incision still hurt. I tried to get him to nurse, but he just didn't want to latch on. He didn't cry, but whatever way I turned him, it just didn't seem to work. I became frustrated, began to wonder if there was something wrong with him – maybe the anesthesia that I had insisted upon had damaged him in some way – I began to cry.

The nurse came back in to check on me. "What's the matter, honey?" she said.

I snuffled back my tears and tried to compose myself. "I can't get him to nurse," I said, as calmly as I could.

She looked at Bo, then looked at me again, then back at Bo. "He's asleep, honey. You have to wake him up."

She went into the bathroom, and returned with a wet washcloth. And then, I kid you not, ladies and gentlemen of the jury, she smacked my newborn baby right between the eyes with it, like playful boys snapping towels in the locker room.

("It couldn't have been as bad as all that," Wiley would say when I told him about it later.)

But I swear, that's what she did. Bo opened his eyes, and then his mouth. He took in a mighty breath and then started to wail. "He's awake now," the nurse said with a grin. "Try it again."

She waited until I got him situated, and then left us.

After his meal, Bo went back to sleep, and I looked at him some more. I noticed a tiny cut on his heel – I knew it was from a blood test they'd given him right after birth. Wiley had read about it to me from the internet, along with the APGAR test, something else they gave him the moment he was born. So that was okay. I found a little S-shaped cut in his scalp – that was from where they'd stuck a monitor into him, after they'd broken my water, in preparation for the C-section. The nurse had explained that one. Still, I was appalled: here was my precious baby, not even twenty-four hours old, and he was already cut up in two places. It was barbaric.

That was when I noticed the dried blood in his ear. I tried not to panic. I thought panicking wouldn't solve anything. If I became hysterical, I wouldn't be able to communicate to them that Bo was bleeding from his ear! I gently laid him in his little plastic box, and climbed gingerly out of bed. This was too important to wait for the washcloth-snapping nurse to answer my call.

14

I walked slowly out to the nurses' station, and calmly told her, "My baby has blood in his ear."

She came around the counter, none too quickly, I might add, given the gravity of the situation, and waited while I walked slowly back to my room. I pointed at him.

The nurse examined his poor little ear, then smiled. "That's your blood. From the procedure. You gotta relax, honey. He's fine. Get back in bed now. It's time for your injection."

My injection was morphine, or some derivative; to help with the pain. It was welcome. I needed it. I got back in bed and rolled ponderously onto my side, and the nurse administered the syringe full of bliss.

When next I woke up, there was a tray of food in front of me, and Wiley was sitting in a chair, holding his son. He smiled at me, and I smiled back. Words weren't necessary.

Wiley's mom and dad came in and they passed Bo back and forth between them, chatting happily, while I ate my breakfast. I remembered drinking coffee, then the next thing I knew, I felt a warmness on my chest, and Wiley and Aunt Amy and Uncle Alex were hovering worriedly over me.

"What happened, Brendee?" Aunt Amy asked. "You dropped your coffee."

Sure enough, I had spilled it all over myself, and I didn't remember doing it. Wiley went out and reported it to the nurse, and not long after, the neurologist showed up. He shined a light in my eyes, and had me follow his finger, back and forth, up and down. He wrote something on my chart and left, without making a diagnosis.

"Do I have brain damage?" I asked my husband and my in-laws.

Uncle Alex grinned. "It's the morphine, Brendee," he said. "Wiley was the same way after the surgery on his leg. He'd be talking to us, then he'd just nod out like a junkie. I'm sure you'll be okay, as soon as they take you off the morphine."

What kind of a slipshod operation were they running here? I thought. If it was the morphine, why had they sent for the neurologist? The nurse came in, and I asked her what he'd said. "You're fine," she assured me.

"How long do I get the morphine?" I asked. I didn't want to be nodding out and spilling coffee on Bo.

"Only for twelve hours," she said. "You can have another one in a little while."

15

Whenever it was time for my shot, I made all visitors go out in the hall. My mom and dad, my brothers and sister, Nate and Deneen, well-wishers from work, even my husband. Couldn't miss my morphine. They were only gonna give it to me for twelve hours. No sense wasting it.

Still I was miserable. I had dodged the bullet of labor, but I had bad dreams. I called Wiley in the middle of the night, told him that I'd dreamed that the nursing staff were stuffing all the babies into drawers, that the doctor had come in and started slapping me. He tried very hard not to laugh, but failed.

I was in the hospital for three days after Bo was born, and I hated every second of it. They had some concern about a recurring fever – but the tests came out negative, so finally they cut me loose.

****

On a Saturday, three weeks after Bo was born, I went in for a check-up. I still felt miserable. The incision was healed, but it still hurt to move, to breathe. Coughing was a nightmare. My back hurt. I asked the doctor if I could go see a chiropractor.

This was the man who had delivered Bo. My regular doctor, the one that I had seen throughout my pregnancy, *the woman,* had not been on duty that day. I didn't like male ob-gyns. I couldn't understand why a man would want to specialize in such a discipline. No matter how educated he was, it seemed to me, he still just couldn't relate.

He looked at me blankly for a moment, then said, "Well, you might think that you just had a baby, and maybe your pelvis is going back to where it was. That might cause a little lower back discomfort."

Was he kidding? I sincerely didn't like this guy, and I was in a bad mood anyway. I felt cranky and hot, and it seemed like I hadn't had a wink of sleep since Bo was born. He was colicky, and wasn't sleeping through the night yet. In fact, he slept all day, like a tiny, little, blue-eyed vampire, and like a vampire, he was up all night. Wiley had the new job, so he was gone during the day. He took as much care of Bo as he could at night, but I still had to nurse him. The lack of sleep didn't seem to affect Wiley at all: he was always as fresh as a daisy when he got up in the morning, put on his shirt and tie and left me alone with his son. My mom came by and helped out, but she wasn't a coddler either. She had not one scintilla of pity for

16

my backaches and feverishness and whining. "I was confined to bed for two weeks after you were born, and Gary was still in diapers," she told me with a superior sniff. "This is nothing."

Now, at my three-week appointment, lying on the examining table, I snapped at the smarmy doctor. "Well," I said, "it's not my pelvis that hurts, but my back. Can I go see a chiropractor?"

He considered me for another moment. "If you want." He nodded at the screen beside the table, at the record of my travails. "Everything looks good." I bent my knee up and grabbed onto it to pull myself up, and he looked at me curiously. "Why do you do that?"

"Because it hurts, Doctor," I snapped again. "I can't sit up any other way."

Now he looked concerned, and told me to lie back down. He pushed and prodded my abdomen and asked me if it hurt. It did.

"We're going to have to re-admit you," he said.

So much for *Everything looks good.*

He called a nurse in and she took my temperature; I had a fever of a hundred and four degrees. They put me in a wheelchair, and as they wheeled me from the examining room, the doctor said brightly, "It seems that you either have a uterine infection or an appendicitis."

"I'm gonna die then," I told him, "'cause I'm not gonna let you people cut on me again." I wasn't feeling nearly as bright as he was, but then he didn't have a raging fever, did he? He hadn't been filleted like a fish less than a month ago, had he?

I asked the nurse to please call my husband and tell him that I'd been re-admitted. Let her explain it to him. I wasn't in the mood. He left the baby with his mom and hurried to the hospital. While my mom loved Bo, of course, she'd had four of her own, and Wiley's mom was much more delighted with him. By the time Wiley arrived, the tests confirmed that more surgery wouldn't be necessary: it was indeed a uterine infection.

"Apparently, someone didn't wash their hands before surgery," Wiley commented darkly.

They didn't put me back on the maternity ward – it would've been bad press, I imagined. They didn't want me telling the new moms that my baby wasn't even a month old yet, and here I was, back in the hospital, due to their botched operation. They put me in a room with two elderly ladies. The one to my left, closest to the door, had a broken hip and mostly moaned under sedation. The one on my right, closest to the bathroom – I never did find out what was wrong with her. Whatever it was, it was fatal.

I'd been in the room probably three hours, and was dozing. I awoke to the sound of her gasping, unable to catch her breath. I was hooked up to an IV, and was still in pain; besides, what was I gonna do for her? I couldn't see her, because the curtain was drawn between our beds, but I could hear her, and I desperately pushed the call button. After what seemed like a lifetime – it was indeed the rest of the old lady's life – a nurse came in. I pointed at the next bed, and she went over there slowly. Didn't she care that it was a life and death situation?

There was no Code Blue, no crash cart, no rushing, scurrying personnel. The old lady had died, and to my astonished horror, they just left her there.

The nurse's name was Madonna, and I couldn't think of a less appropriate name. I found not one thing nurturing about her: she was very pretty, wore lots of make-up, and to my continued amazement, she had long, brightly painted fingernails. Maybe I was being unfair, but she looked nothing like I expected a nurse to look.

She came up to my bed and asked me if I was all right.

I glared at her. "Why do you ask?"

She checked the tubes to my IV – it was full of antibiotics, to combat the infection. *The infection that they had caused,* I thought. She said, "Sometimes young people have a little trouble coping when someone dies." She patted my shoulder. "Don't worry, Mrs. Royce. You're not going to die. You're gonna be fine." The thought that I was gonna die had not entered my mind, but it was there now. Madonna looked at the curtain. "She was old. It was her time."

I was speechless with anger. *Maybe it wouldn't've been her time if you people would've come in here a little bit quicker,* I thought, but I didn't dare say it. I thought that if I started to speak, I'd start to scream at her, and then they'd sedate me, too, like the poor lady in the next bed. I had an irrational fear that they'd sedate me if I complained too much. But since she stood there, expecting me to say something, I croaked, "I'm okay."

Madonna the beautiful nurse smiled brightly. "I'm glad," she said. "Someone will be in here to change your IV in a little while." She patted me on the shoulder again, and left the room.

It seemed like they left the poor old lady there for hours. Finally, when I couldn't wait any longer, I got out of the bed, and pushing my wheeled IV stand in front of me, I went to the bathroom.

I had to pass by her bed to get to it. *I just won't look at her,* I told myself, and I didn't. But some primitive part of my brain told me that I could smell her, even though that was ridiculous. She hadn't been gone that long.

The whole situation was just horrible.

They brought me a fresh IV, and a breast pump to express my milk. It couldn't be saved, Madonna told me – something about the antibiotics in it would stain the teeth Bo didn't even have yet, if we fed it to him. "A little formula won't hurt him," she assured me with a smile.

She paused at the foot of my bed and wrote something on my chart. At that moment, Wiley called. I said hello to him, and watched as a gentleman, perhaps fifty, came into the room. They still hadn't removed the old lady's body – she'd lain there for probably two or three hours – and I watched as Madonna stopped him before he could go around the curtain.

"Hold on, Wiley," I said. Madonna said a few words to the man, and he hung his head. I couldn't hear what they were saying, because Wiley, not holding on, was talking in my ear. After a moment, Madonna escorted the grieving man from the room.

"Oh, my God, Wiley, you gotta get me out of here!" I told him what had happened. "What if the poor man had come in when the nurse wasn't here? What if he walked in and found his mother's body? What kind of hellhole is this hospital?"

I was in there for two days, that time. All in all, I estimated that they put thirty bottles of antibiotics through my arm. I hoped that the next time I was in the hospital, it would be when I was old like the poor lady beside me – that it would be when it was *my time.*

If I thought pregnancy had been bad, the whole dirty-fingernailed surgery and its infectious aftermath had been much worse. I loved my baby and I loved his father, but there was no force in heaven or earth that could ever make me go through this again. I was glad that they'd done the sterilization at the same time as the C-section.

****

Bo was a handful. My mother insisted that he was not, that he was just a little fussy, but he was a handful to me. It seemed like he cried all the time. I'd change his diaper or try to feed him or rock him, but sometimes he just kept crying. If Wiley was there, he'd walk around with him, bouncing him gently, or put him in his car seat and drive him around the block. That always worked. But Wiley wasn't always there, and when he wasn't, sometimes I'd look into Bo's little blue eyes and ask despondently, "What do you want? I can't wait 'til you can tell me what you want!"

I understood at that moment why some women bash their babies' heads to the wall. When I told Wiley this, he just raised his eyebrows mildly and didn't comment. Sure, he could get by without saying anything; he didn't understand. He didn't feel miserable and feverish and still fat; he didn't have a scar as big as the equator; Bo always stopped crying for him.

Of course, I loved Bo, and I wasn't going to bash his brains in. But I understood why it happened. Some women probably just didn't encompass as much love and humanity and self-control as I did. I knew that all these musings were anathema to the maternal instinct, so I didn't mention any of them to my mother. She'd loved everything about being pregnant, loved babies and all their crying and spitting up. She didn't even mind changing diapers. She would be shocked to discover that I hated damn near every aspect of the motherhood experience.

But Wiley knew me better than she did; Wiley knew me completely. Except for the whole Wes Thomerville thing, I'd always shared my innermost thoughts with Wiley, even though he didn't do the same with me. But that was okay. It was part of his mystery, just another thing I loved about him.

Wiley's parents and my dad, and my brothers and sister, and Deneen and Nate, all wanted to visit, but I told Wiley to tell them all that I was still sick. I was not in the mood. My mother said to nap when the baby napped, so that's what I did. I slept and fed him, bathed him and played with him. I didn't do much else at all for the first three months of his life. Sometimes the wonder of him – that Wiley and I had produced something so perfect – would overwhelm me, and I would burst into tears of joy. But I couldn't wait until he could communicate.

Wiley was a prince. I could tell that he didn't like the new job – I'd hear him bitching to Nate on the phone about it – but he never took it out on me. He always had a smile and a kiss for me when he walked in the door, and the very second he was home, all my responsibilities would evaporate. Wiley would cook dinner; Wiley would take care of the baby. Most days, I took a nap as soon as he got home.

He'd put Bo down for the night and climb softly into bed with me, trying not to wake me up. I'd wrap my arms around him, and hug his lean, flawless form to me like a body pillow, tell him I loved him. I was too tired for anything else but this weak show of affection and gratitude, and Wiley, being Wiley, never made so much as a gesture to me that anything was lacking. It wasn't like him. Wiley always waited for me to come to him. But I was still just too tired.

By the time Bo was four months old, I was feeling myself enough to feel embarrassed that I'd shunned my family, and pretty much my husband, and Deneen and Nate. We had a little dinner party for our best friends – Wiley again cooked – and Deneen cooed and clucked over Bo like the mother hen of renown.

"I want one," she told Nate firmly, and I could tell that she wasn't kidding. "Think how nice it would be if they could grow up together! We could all be aunts and uncles to them, just like Wiley and Brendee's parents!"

I watched Wiley and Nate exchange a glance. It didn't say, *Yeah, doesn't that sound like a great idea?* Wiley hadn't mentioned it, but I was a different person right then: a cold, bitchy, sarcastic, unloving person. I know he noticed it, because I noticed it. I hated myself for it, but it was just who I was for the moment. New motherhood was taking it out of me.

I drank a little wine, thinking a little bit wouldn't hurt Bo, and maybe it might relax me and put me in the mood. I missed Wiley terribly, but I was just exhausted. The wine didn't help. After Deneen and Nate went home, I passed right out.

****

When our boy was six months old, I at last felt well enough and deserving enough to reach for my husband when he came to bed. But now it was Wiley's turn to be bitchy and out of sorts. It was the job – he hated *Securi-Comp,* and had brought his problems home with him, to bed with him. He wasn't in the mood, not even after all the months of deprivation. I'd just have to be satisfied with merely holding him, telling him I loved him. When Wiley wasn't in the mood, he was simply *not in the mood,* couldn't be budged any more than the most steadfast virgin. I'd never seen him so pensive, and while he'd turned me down in the past, it had always been to heighten the tease for later. Not now. Wiley was agitated, unhappy.

21

"Quit the damn job," I told him. "I'm going back to work next week, anyway."

So he did. But it didn't make him as happy as I thought it would. For the first week, he would bring Bo in at lunch time so I could feed him. But he felt the eyes of my co-workers upon him, their accusing stares. Why wasn't he working? Why was I, the new mom, the breadwinner? What was wrong with him? What kind of a lazy-ass deadbeat was he?

If it'd just been the people at work, maybe he wouldn't have let it get to him. Nobody cared less about the opinions of others more than Wiley. But his own parents couldn't hide their dismay that he'd quit his job, hadn't even given two weeks' notice. He still brought in plenty of money: he made more than half of what he was pulling down at *Securi-Comp,* just from fixing people's electronics, through nothing more than word of mouth. But his parents' disapproval ate at him. He frowned more. He was silent more. His only joy at times seemed to be his son.

"My dad," he'd say, and shake his head. "It's enough *to mark the full-fraught man and best indued with some suspicion."*

Wiley had spent a long period of convalescence in a farmhouse attic with a lot of books after he'd shattered his leg as a teen. He was always making obscure quotations. He'd wait for us to get the reference, and when we didn't, he'd just shrug. If we didn't ask for an explanation, he wouldn't supply one. It was just how he was, how he thought. But I knew he enjoyed explaining, so I asked him what he meant this time.

He said, "I'm becoming paranoid. I think everybody's ashamed of me." *Even you,* was left unsaid.

Wiley's superiority was his enemy in the workaday world. He thought – no, *he knew* – that he was smarter than everybody else. He'd never wanted for money, because he could fix anything electronic, and electronics have enslaved the modern world. And his self-taught knowledge of classical literature, all the ancient music and movies he'd consumed as a teen, made him feel above a generation not known for its readership or appreciation of history. "They're gonna take over this country without firing a shot," he'd often tell me in disgust, when confronted with some new public disgrace.

Wiley would tell his best friend – his only friend – that he was dumb, right to his face. Wiley didn't really think that Nate was dumb – just uneducated about what he considered the finer things in life:

art and history, poetry, literature, old movies and music. He felt the same way about me, although he'd never come right out and told me that I was dumb. Except for his friends and family, Wiley considered the rest of his fellow men to be nothing but ignorant sheep. *Baa.*

But I wasn't gonna lie to him. I wasn't ashamed of him, but despite his arrogance, he'd have to get a real job someday. He was a husband and father now, and such a thing was what was done. So I just told him I loved him, and went to work. I was patient. He'd always come through before, and I knew he would this time also.

When his father stopped bringing Bo in at lunch time to be fed, I just slowly weaned my son off the breast. He was six months old. It was time. Besides, I wanted to have a drink, eat some spicy food. It was time for Bo to be his own little person, at least as far as eating was concerned.

Wiley was happier once he quit *Securi-Comp*, but he remained distant. His parents' disapprobation weighed on him. I was still a little tired, still not feeling my normal ravishing self – I didn't think that it would do my recovering self-esteem any good to have my husband turn me down again, so I didn't ask. He knew I'd come back around eventually: Wiley was the sexiest man I'd ever seen, and somehow, it was a little fun to wait. I thought about it frequently, and I figured that when I couldn't wait another second – he'd frequently made me wait when we were still sneaking around behind our parents' backs in high school – it would be all the sweeter.

It wouldn't be too much longer now. I was starting to have dreams about him. In them, he was wearing a black leather jacket and playing a black guitar, singing to me; as always, looking just like Wes Thomerville in that old video. It wouldn't be long now. But I savored my growing desire. I could wait a bit more.

.

NATE

Wiley stopped by to have lunch with me, since he didn't have anything else to do. I'd been fortunate enough to land an entry-level, low-ranking management position with the County – Deneen already worked as a secretary for a different department on the fifth floor. She talked constantly about starting a family, now that we both had good jobs. But I wasn't ready.

I met Wiley in the cafeteria, and he set the baby carrier on the table, then took the baby out of it, bounced him gently on his knee.

"I saw Wes Thomerville on the internet this morning," I said, taking a bite out of my sandwich.

Wiley looked at me in surprise. "Did he die?"

"That's not very nice, Wiley," I replied with my mouth full. "If it wasn't for Wes Thomerville, you wouldn't be . . ." He waited for me to tell him what he wouldn't be. I chewed and considered. What wouldn't he be? Married? Unemployed? A father? "You wouldn't be the happy man you are today," I said at last.

Wiley shrugged, not willing to comment on his happiness or lack thereof at the moment. He kissed Bo on the top of his black-haired head. The kid looked just like him. I tried to imagine what that would be like, to be responsible for a little human being that looked just like me. I failed.

"Did he die?" Wiley repeated.

"No. It wasn't really even about him. It was on the *Press-Enterprise's* website."

"Ah. The yellow *Press-Enterprise.*"

I ignored this remark. "Did you know that Jason Whitsun, the guy that directed *Eileen's Mother,* is from Riverside?"

Wiley shook his head, let the baby gnaw on his finger.

"Well, he is. He also directed a little unknown project called *Rolling Blackout's Hometown Debut,* featuring the video to *My Disgrace.*"

Wiley squinted at me. "Really."

I nodded. "That's where I saw Wes Thomerville. They were interviewing Whitsun, and they showed a clip from the video. I guess it was his first production, from film school. The interviewer asked if he'd ever directed any other music videos, and he said, 'I filmed another one of Rolling Blackout's songs. There was going to be another video, but it never made it past the rough cut. I was more interested in the documentary aspects of filming a band; I wasn't much for making music videos.'

"He said that he only did the video to *My Disgrace* so he could do the documentary – he said he kinda had a crush on Thomerville's girlfriend – she wanted a video, he wanted a documentary – Thomerville didn't care either way – and Whitsun wanted to make her happy, so they shot *My Disgrace,* and a lot of material for another video.

"I guess the interviewer figured that enough has been said about *Eileen's Mother.* It's great, it won the Oscar, enough already. I think he thought he was covering some new ground, talking about Whitsun's early stuff, so he said, 'What happened with that? We'd all like to see another music video made by an Oscar-winning director, from film school.'

"The director laughed. 'It might be on the internet somewhere still. I had the whole shoot of it posted at one time, all the umpteen boring hours of it, so my crew and costumer could look at it, suggest ideas for how we'd edit it. But a rough cut was all that ever got done.'

"The interviewer said something about how much fun it would be to find an Oscar-winning director's unedited footage online, and told us all to search for it."

"I'm thrilled," Wiley said, not thrilled at all. "More incentives from the media for people to waste their time online. You're never gonna waste your time online, are you, Bo?" he said to his son. Bo gurgled and smiled.

"What's wrong with you, Wiley?"

Wiley shrugged. "Nothing's wrong with me, Nate. It's just bizarre to hear you mention Brendee's old boyfriend–"

"Old boyfriend?" I said in surprise. "Is that how you think of him? *As her old boyfriend?* Now that's bizarre."

Again Wiley shrugged. "You remember that clip I used to have of her, from her webcam? Remember how turned on she used to get from watching him?"

"But she forgot all about him when she saw you. The way she used to look at you . . ."

I wondered if there was trouble in paradise, if maybe what Wiley had always feared had come to pass, if maybe Brendee didn't look at him like that anymore. Maybe she was bored with him, what with the baby and all. People change, life goes on. I looked at Wiley and saw that old fear reflected in his eyes – Brendee wasn't bored with him yet, but maybe he thought it was starting to happen.

"Does she ever . . ." *Oh shit, did I really just say that out loud?* Yes, I did, and since it was half out, I thought I might as well finish it. "Does she ever watch it?"

Wiley grinned. "I deleted it. Mommy has no Memory Lane to stroll down anymore, does she?" he said to Bo.

"Fuck, Wiley!" I said in astonishment, not even considering the baby's tender ears, or those of my co-workers at the tables around us. "Really? Why?"

"It was an accident. I was doing a little maintenance on her laptop . . ." He looked at me to see if I was believing him. I wasn't. "Wouldn't I have been surprised to find such a thing on there, after all these years? How would she explain that? Didn't she tell you that she'd only seen it once?

"Besides, it's still on *YouTube.*" He took his finger out of the baby's mouth and studied it. "I think he's getting another tooth." He looked at me. "The video's probably getting a million hits, now that people know that Jason Whitsun directed it." I still looked at him in amazement. "She hasn't even looked for it," he said.

"How do you know?"

"Who are you talking to, Nate?"

"Not someone who accidentally erases things."

Wiley shrugged. "If she goes to look for it and can't find it, she can always watch it on *YouTube.* And when she does, I'll know about it."

I was speechless. If Wiley thought Brendee was getting bored with him, he would know the minute it happened. The minute she went to watch Wes again.

He looked a little guilty about what he'd done, I thought, and maybe at my judgment of it. *"The best mirror is an old friend,"* he said and sighed. "This is an aspect about women I don't know anything about, Nate. How they are after they have a baby, what they become after they become mothers. This is new ground for me. I'm inexperienced."

And inexperience produces doubt, I thought, and Wiley didn't like being doubtful. It was foreign, unknown to him. But here it was, tapping him on the shoulder, whispering in his ear. I thought that his doubt was making him a trifle bitter, maybe. *Welcome to the real world of us non-supermen, Wiley,* I thought. *Welcome to a world where you're not always quite so sure what your woman wants. Welcome to doubt.*

He put Bo back in his car seat. He wiped his wet finger on the baby's onesie and then took his phone out of his pocket. "Since I'm such a bad guy, maybe I should just find this lost Wes Thomerville classic for her." He typed on his phone, and scrolled through it for a minute. "The only thing I'm getting for *Jason Whitsun music video* is a link to *My Disgrace*. I told you it was still on *YouTube.*" After another minute, he sighed. "I'm not much for internet searches."

"Really?"

"I'm a programmer, for Christ's sake, Nate," he said, with a rare trace of annoyance.

"You *were* a programmer. Until you quit."

"I'll always be a programmer. I've been one since I was a kid. And the things I've programmed haven't always been the most upstanding apps. You know that. *Securi-Comp* really wasn't the best place for an old hacker such as myself. They're a bunch of squeaky-clean, goody-two-shoes, out to protect the world from people that think just like me. But they can't see the forest for the trees. How can you call yourself a data security company, and not have one shred of the Dark Side about you?"

"Maybe that's why they hired you, right out of college. For your . . . darkness."

"My darkness doesn't show on a resume. What were they gonna do, purify me?" I shrugged, and he looked at his phone again. "Hold on, I've got an idea." He pushed a button. "Hello, Dad," he said. "Didn't you tell me that you knew a guy that specializes in finding things on the internet?" Pause. "Yes, he's right here." Wiley pushed another button, and held up the phone so his dad could see his grandson. Bo reached for the phone, and Wiley pulled it back, pushed another button. "He wants to eat the phone, Dad. He's teething. What's this guy's name?" Pause. *"Morry's Books?* Ok. Thanks. Bye."

Wiley disconnected the call and frowned. "Dad's not too happy about me quitting *Securi-Comp.* What kind of a name is that, anyway?"

"It was a great job, Wiley–"

"Fuck 'em if they can't take a joke." He smiled at his son. "Isn't that right, Bo?" Bo gurgled. Wiley looked back at me. "The internet search guru owns a bookstore."

"Do they still have bookstores?"

"I've been in there a few times. You want to swing by with me after work? It's only a few blocks from here."

"Sure, Wiley. But why do you want to—"

"Maybe she'll like it," he said, and tickled his baby.

****

Morry's Books was dim. While there was plenty of light coming in through the windows, they were dirty, and the towering bookshelves seemed to block the sunlight; almost diffuse it. I noticed that two of the overhead lights were out, which also lent a murkiness to the place.

Wiley took a deep breath. "Smell that, Nate? That's knowledge."

"Knowledge smells like mildew, then," I said. "I much prefer the smell of *Radio Shack*. All those new electronics . . ." I grinned at him. "Are you gonna apply for the job?"

When he and I dropped Bo off at home with Brendee, she'd mentioned something about a management job that she'd seen advertised at the electronics giant.

He sighed. "I dunno, Nate. Four years of college to run a *Radio Shack*. It hardly seems worth the money."

"Well, if you hadn't quit *Securi-Comp—*"

"I swear to *Christ,* if you people don't stop nagging me about that fucking job . . ." He let the thought die. *"Securi-Comp* was beneath me, Nate."

"And *Radio Shack* isn't?"

Wiley frowned. *"Better to reign in hell than serve in heaven.* Let's see if this guy can help us."

An old party was sitting behind the counter, staring intently at a laptop. He had the whole mad-scientist vibe going on: the gray hair was shaggy, disarrayed; he wore a slightly rumpled, collared shirt.

"Excuse me," Wiley said politely. "Is Tom Bastion here?"

"A piece of him," the old guy replied, not looking up.

Wiley grinned. "My dad tells me that you're good at finding things on the internet—"

"A box without hinges, key, or lid, yet golden treasure inside is hid."

"He said you're a Google expert," Wiley repeated, then looked at me. *"And how does one say it? Obtainer of rare antiquities."* He paused. I could tell he was quoting something, waiting to see if this stranger would get the reference, just like he always did with us.

Now the old guy looked up and smiled. *"That's one way of saying it. Why don't you sit down, you'll be more comfortable."*

There were no chairs.

"Yes, you're a man of many talents," Wiley continued.

The old guy stood up and offered his hand. "Who *are* you, kid?" he said in admiration. "Who's your dad?"

"My name's Wiley. This is my friend, Nate."

He introduced himself as Tom Bastion, the guy we were looking for, and we all shook hands.

"My dad's Alex Royce."

"We are advertis'd by our loving friends."

Again Wiley smiled. "He said you found him some–"

"Manuals for an old Cobol system. I remember. Are you looking for ancient, dead computer languages, too?"

"I am seeking for the bridge which leans from the visible to the invisible through reality. I'm looking for a rough cut of a video from a local band. From 2011 or 2012."

"Next to the Word of God, the noble art of music is the greatest treasure in the world."

Wiley grinned. "I have no doubt that this is neither noble nor a treasure. The songwriting style – *it reminds me of a string of wet sponges; it reminds me of tattered washing on the line; it reminds me of stale bean soup, of college yells, of dogs barking idiotically through endless nights. It is so bad that a sort of grandeur creeps into it. It drags itself out of the dark abysm of pish, and crawls insanely up the topmost pinnacle of posh. It is rumble and bumble. It is flap and doodle. It is balder and dash."*

Tom grinned gleefully. "I'm assuming that you're not looking for this for yourself then?"

"It's for his wife," I spoke up.

"Age cannot wither her, nor custom stale her infinite variety," Wiley said. "But her taste in music is . . . dubious."

"It's not her taste in music, Wiley," I told him. "It's her taste in singers."

"I am above the weakness of seeking to establish a sequence of cause and effect, between the disaster and the atrocity," he replied. Tom's eyebrows went up. "Edgar Allan Poe," Wiley supplied.

"Is this singer really that bad?" Tom asked.

Wiley shrugged. "She doesn't think so. And since *there is nothing either good or bad, but thinking makes it so . . .* It's a long story."

"An honest tale speeds best, being plainly told," Tom prompted.

Again Wiley smiled. "You tell it, Nate. *I'm not going to tell you the story the way it happened. I'm going to tell it the way I remember it."*

"All right," I said. "When we were in high school, Wiley wrote an app that allowed him to watch people through their webcams, and—"

"No, no! The adventures first, explanations take such a dreadful time." When I blinked stupidly at him, Tom said, "I'm just kidding. Please continue."

This guy was another babbler of obscure bullshit, just like Wiley. *Jesus wept,* I thought. *How's that for a quote for ya?* I looked at Wiley, and he nodded for me to go on. "Anyway, he'd gotten into the computer of this girl I knew – we'd gone to grade school together – and he showed me a clip he'd recorded of her. In it, this girl – Brendee – was watching some music video. It's not the one he's looking for now, but it's from the same band. A local band."

"And earthquakes are to a girl's guitar, they're just another good vibration," Tom said.

"And tidal waves couldn't save the world from Californication." Wiley smiled. "More local than that. From right here in Riverside. And not even remotely as famous."

"They called themselves Rolling Blackout," I said. For a change Tom just looked at me blankly, in silence. "Ever heard of them?" I asked, even though I knew by his expression that he hadn't. He shook his head.

"Not many people have," Wiley supplied.

"Anyway, in this clip Wiley had, Brendee is obviously enjoying herself very much." I paused, and Wiley leered at Tom. He grinned back in surprise. "At the time, I had a thing for Brendee—"

"We begin by coveting what we see every day," Wiley interrupted.

"Do you want me to tell this story or not?" I asked him in exasperation.

"Please. Proceed."

"So I asked him to find out what she was watching, what it was that turned her on so much. It was this Rolling Blackout video.

30

Apparently, Brendee had quite the thing for the singer, this old guy named Wes Thomerville. To make a long story short, Wiley looked just like him. The first time Brendee saw him–"

"Who ever loved that loved not at first sight?" Wiley said and grinned wickedly.

"And they lived happily ever after," I concluded, tired of being interrupted.

"Something like that." Wiley paused, frowned slightly. Maybe there really *was* trouble in paradise.

"Brevity is the soul of wit," Tom observed.

"Have you heard of Jason Whitsun, Tom?" Wiley asked. The old guy shook his head. "He directed *Eileen's Mother*. It just won an Oscar."

"I didn't see it."

"Me either. But it turns out that Jason Whitsun also directed the video that my beloved Brendee used to like so much."

"Before she met you?" Tom asked.

Wiley nodded, but didn't grin, as I would've expected him to.

I said, "I just saw an interview clip with him, and he talked about film school, and this music video he directed. They showed part of it, and it got me thinking about the old days . . . Then he mentioned that he was gonna make another video of the same band, but it never happened. But he said that the rough cut of them performing used to be on the internet."

"We want you to find it," Wiley said. "Legend has it that once something's on the internet, it's there forever."

Tom considered us in silence for a moment, then he said, "Let me get this straight. You want me to find the rough cut of a video that was never produced? From . . ."

"2011 or 2012," Wiley said.

"You want me to find the rough cut of a video that was never commercially produced, from twenty-six or seven years ago." He looked from one of us to the other and we nodded. "So you can give it to your wife, who you used to watch through her webcam, while she watched this band. When you were high school sweethearts. I'm assuming that she knows that you watched her? That's why you're gonna give her a copy of the other video?"

"Though I am not naturally honest, I am so sometimes by chance," Wiley replied. "But not in this particular case."

31

"So she doesn't know that you watched her?" When Wiley shook his head, Tom said in amazement, "That's a pretty fucked up state of affairs, my son."

Wiley's grin returned at this use of his favorite expression. *"I am not bound to please thee with my answers. Besides, they say, best men are molded out of faults, and, for the most, become much more the better for being a little bad."*

Tom also grinned. "So . . . how will this work? If I find this video, how will you give it to her without her knowing that you know about her fondness for the other one?"

"Her mom was a big fan, too," I said. *"A big fan."*

"I'll just tell her I got it for her mom," Wiley agreed.

"If thou canst mutine in a matron's bones . . ."

"Seriously," Wiley said. *"A good man came to me, never seen eyes so blue . . ."* Wiley batted his blue eyes.

"Now I'm curious," Tom said.

Wiley gestured at the laptop. *"Action is eloquence,"* he suggested.

"Later," Tom said. "I don't want you guys breathing down my neck while I'm looking for this thing."

"How much is it gonna cost me?"

"Did you already look for it?"

Wiley shrugged. "I couldn't even find the clip of Jason Whitsun that he's talking about."

"It's on the *Press-Enterprise* website," I told him.

"They wanted me to pay for it, or sign up or something. I never sign up for anything online, if I can help it." He looked at Tom again. "How much?"

"Profits on the exchange are the treasures of goblins."

Now Wiley looked at him curiously. I needed to write this down, the day somebody stumped Wiley on a quotation. "Lope de Vega. Sixteenth century Spanish playwright."

"Do you speak Spanish, Tom?" Wiley asked.

"I do." Tom smiled. "Finding this ancient shit will be a challenge, Wiley. *The greater the obstacle, the more glory in overcoming it.* Don't worry about the fee."

"Life is either a daring adventure or nothing at all."

"Who *are* you, kid?" Tom asked again.

"When the Day of Judgment dawns and the great conquerors and lawyers and statesmen come to receive their rewards—their crowns, their laurels, their names carved indelibly upon

imperishable marble—the Almighty will turn to Peter and will say, not without a certain envy when he sees us coming with our books under our arms, 'Look, these need no reward. We have nothing to give them here. They have loved reading.'" He gestured at the bookshelves. "I am Wiley Royce. Reader. *And your most obedient subject."*

Tom smiled. *"Art thou, indeed?"*

"Prove me, my gracious sovereign."

"You've proved yourself, Wiley. Most people your age don't know the classics. Nor are they familiar with their grandparents' music, or the popular culture of yesteryear."

"All the people in this world haven't had the advantages that I've had." Wiley smiled smugly.

"Hereafter, in a better world than this, I shall desire more love and knowledge of you." Tom looked at me. "What about you, Nate? Are you a reader like Wiley, or do you just put up with his gibberish because you're his friend?"

"A hit, a very palpable hit!" Wiley said.

"That's about the size of it, Mr. Bastion."

"Please, call me Tom. Especially since you guys are about to drag me into your little game." He tilted his head and looked curiously at Wiley. *"I thank God I am as honest as any man living that is an old man and no honester than I,"* he said, "but I wonder at your motivations for looking for this clip for your wife." He looked at me. "Some video of another man."

"Shit, Tom," Wiley said, "the guy's got to be your age, at least, by now. It's not like she's gonna run out and track him down. It was never like that. He was before our time. It was just a fantasy she had. *Love looks not with the eyes, but with the mind.* I look just like this guy, so I thought it might remind her–"

"Strong reasons make strong actions," Tom cut him off. "You don't have to explain it all at once. I don't think I can understand it all at once. I've been hunting up things for people for a long time, but this has got to be one of the strangest requests ever." He looked over his shoulder at an old-fashioned exposed-gear clock on the wall behind the counter; I noticed that there were cobwebs in the works. Beside it was a framed drawing of intricate gears and cogs, like an Escher. It was fascinating, and I studied it until Tom said, "It's six o'clock. I'm done not selling anything for today. Are you gentlemen hungry? The place down the street has the best steaks in three

33

counties. *One cannot think well, love well, sleep well, if one has not dined well.* My treat."

I rolled my eyes, thinking that I didn't want to sit through dinner, listening to them exchange lines from literature and ancient songs and movies, none of which I'd ever read or heard or watched. "I kinda have to be getting home, and Wiley's a vegetarian."

Tom's eyebrows went up. "Is he now?"

"He is not," Wiley said. "Not when someone mentions *the best steaks in three counties* and *my treat* in the same breath." Wiley squinted at me. "Didn't you say that Deneen was having dinner at her parents' tonight? I'll text Brendee, tell her I'll be home later."

Damn you, Wiley, I thought. He always remembered little details like that, where my girlfriend was having dinner. It was an amazing trait for someone who was so self-absorbed. He was also a mind reader, because the next thing he said was, "I promise we'll cease the King's English and allow you to take part in the conversation."

I looked at Tom, eyebrows raised hopefully. I nodded.

****

The restaurant to which Tom led us was just a few blocks from his bookstore. It was called *Tartare.* Wiley rolled his eyes at the name. "Like I'm going to eat any raw meat served in Riverside."

"Concerned about what might be in your food, are you, Wiley?" Tom asked with interest, as he opened the door.

Wiley shrugged. "My mom's a nutritionist. I'm mostly a vegetarian, but I do appreciate a good steak now and then. But I'm not eating any raw meat in this town. God only knows where it came from."

"God only knows where the cooked meat came from," Tom commented. "But we can't live our lives without a little risk." The waitress smiled and called Tom by name, showed us to a table. "This place has had about twelve different titles over the last twenty-five years, but I think they've kept the same chef. Their steaks are always the same." He made the little French finger-kissing gesture. *"Magnifique."*

The waitress asked if Tom would have the usual, and he nodded. She looked at Wiley. "I'll have whatever Tom's having."

I could tell Wiley liked this old guy immensely, already. He didn't take to people very well; it was because of his overweening

34

feeling of superiority. We'd been best friends since high school, and he loved Brendee and his parents. He talked to Deneen like she was nine, but she didn't notice, so I didn't object. The rest of humanity was just below him. But I could tell he was uncharacteristically impressed with Tom. Where else was he gonna find someone that spouted the same cryptic bullshit that he did?

The waitress looked at me, and I said, "The same, please."

The waitress paused and looked at Tom again. "You boys want a drink?" he said.

"I'm driving," I said.

"I'm not much of a drinker," Wiley said. "But . . . Why the hell not?"

Tom held up two fingers. Apparently the waitress knew what he drank, too.

"The usual is just a big grilled T-bone," Tom said. "If you want any vegetables or bread or anything else with your steak, you'll have to order it separately."

"I don't eat a lot of bread. I tend to be a little Paleo."

"Aw, Paleo's bullshit, Wiley," Tom said. "You don't seem the type to fall for that kind of sheepish trend."

Wiley's eyebrows went up in surprise at the use of his favorite expression. *"Baa!"* he bleated gleefully. "I said I'm just a little Paleo."

"It's still bullshit, Wiley," Tom insisted.

Wiley looked at me. "What Tom is dissing so thoroughly is the Caveman Diet, Nate." He took his phone out of his pocket, typed, then read the *Wikipedia* entry to me. *"The Paleolithic diet is a modern nutritional plan based on the presumed diet of Paleolithic humans.*

"The Paleolithic diet consists mainly of fish–" I was surprised to see Tom shudder in disgust, *"grass-fed, pasture-raised meats, eggs, vegetables, fruit, fungi, roots, and nuts, and excludes what are perceived to be agricultural products; grains, legumes, dairy products, potatoes, refined salt, refined sugar, and processed oils. More than seventy percent of the total daily energy consumed by all people in the United States comes from foods such as cereals, dairy products, refined sugars, refined vegetable oils, and alcohol."* Tom smiled as the waitress set down his and Wiley's drinks. He slammed half of his in one gulp.

"Advocates of the Paleolithic diet assert these foods contributed little or none of the energy in the typical pre-agricultural hominid

diet and argue that excessive consumption of these novel Neolithic and industrial-era foods is responsible for the current epidemic levels of cancer, cardiovascular disease, high blood pressure, obesity, osteoporosis, and type 2 diabetes in the US and other contemporary Western populations."

"The so-called *diseases of affluence,* Nate." Tom took out his own phone. "You're glossing over the most important part, Wiley. It says it right here on *Wikipedia. One of the most frequent criticisms of the Paleolithic diet is that it is unlikely that pre-agricultural foragers suffered from the diseases of modern civilization simply because they did not live long enough to develop these illnesses, which are typically associated with old age."* Tom paused, scrolled, continued. *"Critics further contend that food energy excess, rather than the consumption of specific novel foods, such as grains and dairy products, underlies the diseases of affluence. The health problems facing industrial societies stem not from deviations from a specific ancestral diet but from an imbalance between calories consumed and calories burned, a state of energy excess uncharacteristic of ancestral lifestyles."*

"That's why I said I'm only a little Paleo. *You know, 'Carbs are the enemy,' eh?"*

Tom grinned merrily and slammed the rest of his drink. He signaled the waitress for another one. Wiley looked at his, stirred it with the thin straw. "What is this?" he asked.

"It's a gin and tonic, my son," Tom said. "Puts hair on your chest. Helps you to forget your troubles." At the mention of troubles, Wiley frowned. He gulped some of the gin. I watched his eyes water, but he didn't cough. Just like he'd said, he wasn't much of a drinker.

Tom smiled. "It's not the carbs or the fat that lead to diseases of affluence, Wiley, at least not directly. It's the chemicals, the additives. You would not believe the shit that's in our food." I must've looked surprised at this remark, because he said, "You agree that there are chemicals all around us, right, Nate? In the air, in the ground. But there are so many more, so many extra things that they put in the food. Stuff that simply should not be there. Not only the fertilizers and the insecticides and the preservatives and the hormones. There's also all the additives that they put in there to make it look good and taste good. For texture and color. So it doesn't melt. So it *does* melt. That's what kills you."

"That's why I'm a vegetarian. Most of the time," Wiley added as the waitress set down a sizzling steak in front of each of us. She returned a moment later with Tom's second drink. She was a great waitress. I wondered if the service was always this good at *Tartare*, or if it was only because Tom was a regular.

Tom waited while we cut and took a bite of our steaks. "How is it? Isn't it the best steak you've ever had?" We nodded and murmured appreciatively, chewing. Tom looked down at his own T-bone. "Ah, decadence!"

We ate our steaks in silence for a moment, then Tom said, "Strict vegetarians aren't generally very healthy. Neither are strict Paleos." He shook his head. "You need some carbs. Nothing's better for you than a little enriched, fortified bread every now and then."

Wiley stopped chewing, then resumed quickly and swallowed. "You've got to be kidding, Tom. Bread's the worst for you. All that processed flour? My mom bakes her own bread."

"Processed flour's gotten a bad rep," Tom said. He laughed softly. "You know, I had almost this same conversation with my wife, the first time we went out to lunch together. It was at this same place, but it was called *Smiley's* then." He looked at his steak, half-devoured. "I was probably eating this cow's great-great-grandmother."

Wiley smiled. "Is your wife as well-read as you? Or does she just put up with your gibberish?"

Tom smiled ruefully. "She was. She did. She's passed on now."

Wiley again stopped chewing, blanched, swallowed hard. "Oh, my God, Tom, I'm so sorry."

"A wound will perhaps become tolerable with length of time; but wounds which are raw shudder at the touch of the hands." He shrugged. "It's okay, Wiley. She's been gone for fifteen years. I no longer shudder about it."

"You'll have to tell us about her sometime, then," Wiley said softly.

"Indeed!" Tom said, attempting to clear the sudden sadness. "Like I said, we had a similar conversation, about chemicals in our food. And I'm telling you that processed flour's gotten a bad rep."

He started cutting up the rest of his steak. He asked with a sly smile, "You know why you're so healthy, Wiley?"

"Diet and exercise." Wiley also smiled, relieved that Tom was again cheerful. "And a happy outlook on life."

Tom shook his head. *"You've been living in a dream world, Neo."*

Wiley grinned. *"There is no spoon."*

37

"You're a healthy young man, not because of the choices you make, but because of the choices that've been made for you, my son. For you, for your parents, your grandparents. Hell, your great-grandparents. Have you ever heard of pellagra, my healthy young men, straight and true?"

We shook our heads.

"Since we're in the middle of this fine meal, I won't go into gory detail. Suffice it to say that pellagra killed you, and fucked you up before you died. At the turn of the last century, it was endemic in the poor, rural south. Through many years of dedicated research, it was discovered that it was not contagious, not hereditary. It was strictly, one hundred percent dietary. Pellagra was caused by the mechanization of the processing of corn. The modern method took all the niacin out of it. So did they go back to processing corn like the Indians did? No.

"When all the farm boys answered the call to war in the 1940s, the armed forces discovered, to their dismay, that their fighting men were an unhealthy lot. There was still pellagra, as well as rickets, beriberi, scurvy, goiter. Committees were convened, more research done. They couldn't be sending their boys over there to die so diseased.

"The upshot of this was food fortification. You're so healthy now, you've never heard of these scourges, because they put niacin in your food to prevent pellagra. Thiamine, so you won't get beriberi. Iodine in your salt to prevent goiters, to prevent iodine-deficiency mental retardation. Vitamin D is put in margarine and those vegetable oils that your Paleo buddies won't eat, Wiley, and of course, in milk. A Vitamin D deficiency can give you rickets, give you heart disease, high blood pressure, type 2 diabetes. It can make you fat.

"Added calcium gives you those strong bones. Vitamin A for your eyes and your immune system; Vitamin C so you don't get scurvy. Riboflavin and all the B2s help to covert those evil carbs to energy; they're also good for our livers, and God knows I can use that." Tom took a swallow from his drink. "They allow you to have that shiny black hair, Wiley, your nice skin. You might get enough riboflavin from the broccoli you eat, being a vegetarian, or the Brussels sprouts or the spinach. Big spinach fan are you, Nate?"

I shook my head.

"No. But you're just as healthy as Wiley, are you not? Fucking-A, Skippy, you are. You never have to eat a single Brussels sprout to get enough riboflavin. You never have to eat spinach to get enough iron. Why? Because they put it in your food. You have good, strong teeth because they put fluoride in your water. The put folic acid in stuff so our babies aren't born with neural tube defects."

"They gave that to Brendee when she was pregnant," Wiley said.

While he had talked about vitamin fortification in our food, Tom had seemed rather glum. Now his smile bloomed again. "You have a baby, Wiley?"

"Fucking-A, Skippy, I do." Grinning with pride, he called up a picture of his son on his phone and showed it to Tom. "His name's Bo. He's six months old."

"O brave new world, that has such people in't!" Tom said and smiled in delight at the picture.

At last one I recognized! Wiley had made me read Huxley once, and I recognized the quotation as being from Shakespeare's *The Tempest.* I hadn't ever read *that,* but I knew it was where Huxley had gotten the title to his book.

Tom handed Wiley his phone back. "You live in the greatest country in the world, gentlemen, at the greatest period in its history. You're part of a population that's the healthiest that's *ever lived in the tide of times."*

Tom paused, and we waited. At last Wiley said, "To paraphrase Marc Anthony, how do you prophesy over our wounds, Tom? What *curse shall light upon the limbs of men* because of all this health?"

Tom smiled faintly. "The old curses have been cured. Gone are pellagra and polio, whooping cough, measles, tuberculosis, tetanus, smallpox, diphtheria, typhoid, and the Black Death. At least in the first world. Your darling boy won't even get chicken pox – you didn't either.

"You're healthier than any populace ever in the history of this planet. Yet heart disease, high blood pressure, diabetes, cancer, obesity are rampant in this country. The treatments for these things are a multi-fucking-kabillion dollar a year industry."

Again Tom paused, and again Wiley prompted him, much more simply this time. "And?"

With his fork, Tom toyed with the bone on his plate. "Once upon a time, I told my wife that I didn't worry about the chemicals in our food. 'If you worry about them, you'll go crazy,' I told her. Since then . . ." Tom shook his head, shrugged. "It doesn't matter anymore. There's nothing I can do about it. What's past is past."

"What's past is prologue," Wiley disagreed.

Tom tilted his head and looked at my friend intently. "I can't dump all my insanity on you at once, Wiley. It's not fair. It's not nice. It's not polite. *I could a tale unfold whose lightest word would harrow up thy soul, freeze thy young blood . . .* Fuck, boys. I'm sure you'll get it all out of me eventually." He nodded at Wiley. "Finish your drink. I'm sure you want to get home to your wife and son."

****

As soon as we stepped out on the sidewalk, Tom lit a cigarette. Wiley stared at him.

Tom grinned at the shocked look on his face. *"And be it indeed that I have erred, mine error remaineth with myself."* Tom was just the slightest bit drunk, I observed. "We're outside, Wiley. You're safe from second-hand smoke."

Wiley shrugged. "I don't see how you can be so worried about chemicals in what you eat if you smoke," he said, with more than a little touch of righteousness.

"Five to one, baby, one in five," Tom sang in a low, raspy voice. *"No one he-ere gets out alive, now."*

Wiley grinned. How did he recognize this shit? "I'm just saying . . . Your credibility suffers."

"I got your credibility right here, Wiley."

So not only did this old guy quote stuff like Wiley, he also talked shit, *just like Wiley.* They grinned at each other.

Tom took the cigarettes out of his pocket. "It says right here: *Surgeon General's Warning. Smoking by pregnant women may result in fetal injury, premature birth and low birth weight.* I'm not a pregnant woman, so I have not a fucking thing to worry about." He winked and put the pack back in his pocket. "If I want to damage myself, I've been warned. It's still a free country, up to a point. Now if I offered little Bo a cigarette, I might get put in jail. But nobody's gonna blink twice if you offer him a *Happy Meal."*

"I wouldn't feed that shit to my kid, Tom," Wiley said, offended.

"The buns are fortified."

"Still—"

"There aren't any *Surgeon General's Warnings* on them, though, are there? Nobody warns the masses about the poison in a *Happy Meal.* You know because your mom's a nutritionist, and

40

you're smarter than the average bear." Another one that I'd heard Wiley say before; if you didn't believe Wiley was smarter than the average bear, all you had to do was ask him. "But your plebe on the street – nobody's warning him. Nobody but a bunch of whiny hippies on the internet."

"Are you a hippie, Tom?" I asked.

"You want a cigarette, Nate? You're of age." When I shook my head, he grinned. "Email me tomorrow, Wiley. I'll let you know if I found anything."

"What's your–"

"Google it, my son. *Morry's Books.*" He waved, then turned and started walking away.

"Thanks for dinner, Tom!" I called after him.

"Anytime, Nate!" he replied over his shoulder.

****

When I got home, my girlfriend Deneen was waiting for me, wearing nothing but the pink silk mandarin robe that Wiley had given her for Christmas a few years back. To a stranger, it might've seemed like an inappropriate gift for a guy to give to his buddy's girlfriend; but Wiley had one just like it, except his was black, and so did his wife, except hers was green. It was smooth and slick and felt good against your skin, but I drew the line at such girlish accoutrements. I thought such a thing would look ridiculous on me, just like Wiley's looked ridiculous on him. But it sure looked good on my Denny.

She leapt up into my arms, wrapped her legs around me. She was tiny; only about a hundred and twenty pounds. She had enthusiastically cultivated anorexia in high school – *it's my body and I'll do what I want to it,* and all that bullshit – but she'd giving up actively starving herself when we started going together. She was still tiny and thin, but – I thought of Tom and his description of Americans – she wasn't unhealthy.

"Let's try again, Nate," she said and bit my neck. "Right now."

"I dunno, Denny, we're not even married yet . . ." It was understood that we were engaged, but details of a date for an actual wedding and all that hadn't ever really been discussed. We'd just started new jobs, moved to a bigger place . . .

41

"I don't care about that. We can always get married later. It's 2038, for God's sake, Nate. No one cares about that sort of thing anymore. Least of all me."

I wasn't turning her down to tease her, like I knew Wiley did to Brendee. It was all part of his philosophy: women appreciated us better if we made them wait for it, if we let them think it was always their idea, according to him. I thought it was all bullshit, but it seemed to have worked for them for the last five years.

Until now. Now Wiley seemed melancholy and a little distracted, things he never was. Wiley was always happy and focused, always in control. It came from being convinced that he could fix anything that was handed to him; it came from believing he was smarter and better educated than his fellow man; it came from knowing that his wife continued to be thrilled by his very glance.

But maybe that part – the most important part – was starting to fade. The fact that he'd erased Brendee's secretly most favorite video of all time, the fact that he was monitoring whether she was looking for it again – that was strangely distressing. Wiley had always worked very hard to keep his relationship with Brendee perpetually exciting: it was his chiefest joy and hobby in life, or so he'd told me. And it had always been easy for him, because she'd worshipped him from the moment she'd seen him.

Brendee didn't have the slightest idea that Wiley knew exactly why she'd been instantaneously attracted to him. She didn't know that he'd once spied on her through the webcam on her computer, had recorded a clip of her while she watched that horrible old video of Wes Thomerville and his band, while she'd been all alone and obviously enjoying to the utmost what she was viewing.

Wiley hadn't targeted Brendee specifically as an object of this deplorable practice. He'd written the app, so he had to test it – Brendee's clip was just one of perhaps twenty that he'd recorded. It wasn't something that he did all the time: when we were in high school, he much more preferred watching girls when *they knew* he was watching them. He liked to study them, observe them – clinically, almost; like lab rats.

He'd told me the story about how he'd broken his leg – *snapped all three bones, like kindling,* he'd said – and then how he'd had the most accommodating of physical therapists. Kitana, who was twenty to Wiley's seventeen, had helped him regain his range of motion through the most outrageous of sexual means, or so he'd told me. She'd taught him Tai Chi and yoga – Wiley could still do impressive, acrobatic handstands – and she'd also visited myriad porn sites with him and helped him build a trapeze, of all unbelievable things. I knew that, before Bo was born, he and Brendee had occasionally gone back to his parents' house when they weren't home and made use of it.

Kitana had also told him all the secrets of the female mind, according to Wiley, and he still used all the knowledge he'd learned to bind Brendee, all unknowing about any of his secrets, to him.

At first I'd thought that it was all just another brick in the giant castle of his giant ego – I thought that he toyed with Brendee just because he could, just because he wanted to see how the experiment would turn out. But I knew that he'd grown to love her almost as much as she loved him – as much as he could love anybody. I'd never seen him happier than his wedding day, except for maybe the day that Bo was born.

But Brendee was no longer the girl he'd captured through these less than honorable means. I guess that wasn't really fair – Wiley would've gotten Brendee even if he hadn't already known that she'd fall for him. He looked just like this guy she fantasized about. But it hadn't hurt that he'd known all about it ahead of time.

But now she was a wife, a mother, a full-time worker bee – not a high school girl secretly watching her fantasy come to life through the webcam on his TV. And the fact that she was watching him hadn't been a secret to Wiley. He'd known all about it; he'd planned it, caused it to occur. Brendee was a different person now. And what was her husband but the same old Wiley?

It wasn't as if she was gonna leave him. Brendee loved Wiley, heart, mind, body, and soul. It really couldn't have turned out any other way. But maybe he wasn't the be all and end all of her existence so much anymore. There was her job, and there was Bo. I knew that she'd had a rough time – some woman had died in the same room with her when she was in the hospital, and I thought it would take anyone a while to get over that. Wiley had told me with no bitterness whatsoever that there wouldn't be any more kids. One was enough for him, and it was unquestionably enough for her.

But maybe Brendee had changed behind it. Maybe Wiley thought he was losing that spark. This whole deal about searching for Wes's lost video – maybe it was his idea of rekindling what he thought he was losing. I didn't know if it was the best idea – like Tom had said, what was past was past – high school, Brendee's one-time obsession with Wes – maybe that was all best left behind.

Maybe Wiley should be working on the future, on his new role as husband and father.

"I want a baby," Denny said and pouted prettily.

And that was why I was tending to turn her down right at the moment. Wiley's baby had changed his life, had changed his woman, and the jury was still out on whether it was for the better or not. I didn't know if I wanted to take that risk in my own relationship.

But then Denny kissed me, and I knew that I was powerless to not give her whatever she wanted.

The only reason Wiley had shown me that clip he had of Brendee was because I'd had a thing for her at the time. I'd had a thing for her, really, since I'd met her in grade school. But Brendee hadn't ever been interested in me, and once she saw Wiley, after a few weeks of torturing myself about it, I realized that she never would be. In high school, Deneen looked at me just the way Brendee looked at Wiley, and I decided that there wasn't much more a guy could ask for in life than that. And she still looked at me that way.

"Okay," I told her. "We can try again."

BRENDEE

Wiley asked me to pick him up after work at some place called *Morry's Books*. The night before, he'd told me he'd made a new friend, and he wanted me to meet the guy. "He even bought me a drink," Wiley had said happily. Wiley didn't drink with just anybody.

A bell tinkled over the door when I walked in. The place was almost empty, although a few old professorly types, heads bent over thick books, were standing around beside the bookshelves. A gray-haired older gentleman sat behind the counter, staring fixedly at a laptop. I saw Bo's car seat on a little side table beneath the window. Next to it, his diaper bag yawned open, empty. I sighed. Wiley had been here a while if he'd had time to take everything out of Bo's diaper bag. Maybe he'd been here all day.

The man behind the counter looked up and smiled at me. "Welcome," he said, standing up. "How may I help you?"

"I'm looking for–"

"Romance? Adventure? Classical literature? Quaint old encyclopedias?" he interrupted hopefully.

"Actually–"

"History? Intrigue? Philosophy?"

There was a doorway in the wall behind the counter; there was probably an office behind it, I thought. Wiley stepped through it, carrying a freshly-diapered Bo, onesie still unsnapped. I nodded at him, and the man looked over his shoulder.

"Ah!" he cried. "You must be the inestimable Mrs. Royce!" He came around the counter and shook my hand, then just went right ahead and gave me a hug. "I've heard so much about you!"

So Wiley *had* been there all day.

Wiley came around the counter and introduced us. Bo said, "Goo!" and held his arms out to me. I took him and told Mr. Bastion that it was nice to meet him.

"That remains to be seen," he said. He had the friendliest, winningest smile I'd ever encountered. Even more so than Wiley, whose smile was almost always tempered by his lofty, conceited confidence. "Please, Mrs. Royce. Call me Tom."

"If you'll call me Brendee," I said, feeling like a character in an old-timey movie. But he was charming, so I was charmed, even if I did detect a little hint of alcohol about him. Wiley kissed me on the cheek, and I smelled it on him, too. "Have you been drinking?" I asked in amazement, before I could stop myself.

"Oops," Tom said, and looked down at the floor. *"Drink not the third glass, which thou canst not tame, when once it is within thee."* He grinned at Wiley, who promptly grinned back. "I'm sorry, Mrs. – Brendee. I'm afraid I'm a bad influence on your young husband."

I also grinned, in surprise. "Wiley's not easily influenced, Tom," I said, looking curiously at him.

"The sun *is* over the yardarm," he said. Whatever that meant. Sometimes listening to Wiley talk was akin to hearing a devout, speaking in tongues. It was English – Wiley had never put that always observing, always clicking mind to a study of languages – but sometimes it just didn't make any sense.

"Tom's invited us to dinner, Brendee," he continued. "If you didn't have plans."

There was the Wiley I knew. He would be having dinner with his new friend, and probably taking Bo with him – whether I went along or not.

"It's the monthly gathering of the clan," Tom said. "Maxine and her husband Sam, and their daughter Janae."

"Janae Rossmore?" Wiley said with a suddenly-interested smile.

"Yeah," Tom said. "Do you know her?"

Wiley shrugged. "No, not really. But I know *of* her. I went to high school with her."

Tom looked at him in alarm. "You don't have any–"

"No," Wiley said, equally alarmed. Then they grinned at each other again. "Are you her grandfather?"

"No, not by blood. I'm an orphan in this world. But her mother adopted me, or I adopted her, not long after I arrived here. When she was about your age."

"Thanks, Tom," I said. "Dinner sounds great."

"It's so nice to meet you," he reiterated. "Let me get rid of these people." He walked down the aisle and spoke to the first professor.

I looked at Wiley, who was making faces at his son. A thin, sharp wire of jealousy whipped through me. Who was this Janae person that he knew from high school? Why did Tom ask if he had any – any what?

I kissed him, spontaneously, and now he looked at *me* with sudden interest. We had yet to resume marital relations, but it would be soon, perhaps even tonight. He was my husband, my beautiful, talented, impeccable, blue-eyed Wiley – and now I was having bouts of jealousy because he'd mentioned some girl from high school. *Yes,* I decided. *It would be tonight. As soon as we got through dinner with this odd old man and his adopted family, as soon as we put Bo down to sleep.* "I love you," I told him.

"And I love you."

"Goo!" Bo said, and we had a little family hug.

Wiley picked up the empty diaper bag, and I followed him as he began to gather up Bo's things, scattered throughout the front of the store. His bottle was behind the counter, as was his little jacket and hat. Wiley tossed one shoe in the bag, and I looked down and noticed that Bo still had the other one on. Bo said, "Gaa!" when Wiley picked up his rattle, also behind the counter, so his dad handed it to him. He stuck it in his mouth.

"He's getting another tooth," Wiley said absently, looking around for more of his stuff. "Ah!" he said, and went into the office. I watched him from the doorway, as he swept a small pile of diapers into the bag, from where they sat on the corner of a cluttered desk. The middle of it was clear – Wiley had been using it for a changing table. There was a small refrigerator next to it, and he reached into it and stuffed three empty bottles and two full ones into the diaper bag. He had come prepared. He had *intended* to be here all day.

Wiley's phone beeped. He took it out of his pocket and said, "Hello, Dad, how are you this lovely evening?" Uncle Alex said something and Wiley's smile faltered. "No, I didn't. I didn't think that you paid for four years of college for me to be running a *Radio Shack.*"

I cringed. That had been my un-thought-out suggestion. I'd been looking at my email the night before, while Wiley was putting Bo in his playpen, and Nate was standing there making small talk with me. I'd clicked on an ad that said *Tech Jobs in Riverside,* and quite without thinking about just to whom I was speaking, I said, "They're looking for a manager at *Radio Shack,* Wiley."

Nate looked over his shoulder, waiting for his friend's reaction to *this* suggestion. Wiley grinned and said, "Maybe I'll meet another Bradley." Nate rolled his eyes. I didn't know who Bradley was, and from Nate's expression, I didn't think I wanted to know.

Wiley hadn't commented further on applying at *Radio Shack,* but somehow his dad knew about it. Maybe he'd mentioned it jokingly, and Uncle Alex had thought he was serious about it. Or that he *should be* serious about it.

"I'm twenty-four years old, Dad, don't you think it's a little late for you to start asking me what I did all day?"

I blinked in shock at the annoyed tone of this remark. Bo dropped his rattle, but I caught it before it could clatter to the floor. I didn't think that Wiley would particularly want me to be listening in on this conversation.

"No, Dad, to tell you the truth, I really haven't been looking."

I felt rather than saw Tom come up and stand beside me in the doorway. I was embarrassed for Wiley. It wasn't really a conversation that this stranger needed to be overhearing either.

"I make enough money." Pause. "There are more important things in life than *a steady, reliable income* right now, Dad," Wiley said with a bitter sarcasm. "I'm taking care of Bo. Maybe when he starts school—"

There was a burst of angry words from the other side of the call at that. I couldn't blame Uncle Alex. Bo was six months old; he wouldn't be starting school until he was *five*. Did Wiley really intend on remaining unemployed until then?

"Fuck you, Dad," Wiley said, almost conversationally, and hung up. I was stunned. It wasn't so much what he'd said, although that was certainly bad enough. I'd never heard Wiley speak in such a manner to his father; I'd never heard of Wiley ever having any kind of a disagreement at all with his parents. He'd always maintained that they were the best parents a guy could have, that he'd had the best childhood ever.

It was his tone: the soft, growling, defeated contempt to it. I'd never heard such a tone come out of Wiley; there was disgust in it, and dislike. An ominous kind of rebellion.

Tom frowned. "Something wrong, Wiley?"

He saw us standing in the doorway, and his expression turned to one of guilt. Petulance. "My dad says I'm a poor father."

"Oh, Wiley," I protested immediately, "that's not true! You're the best father—"

Wiley held up his hand, shook his head. "I should be out chasing the almighty dollar. I should leave my kid with strangers. *Baa,*" he bleated angrily. Wiley was never angry.

"You looking for a job, Wiley?" Tom asked. He crossed the room and moved stacks of books and papers around on the desk. He opened one of its drawers, then another one. At last, he pulled a wrinkled *Help Wanted* sign out of it. He blew the dust off of it and handed it to my husband. "I just happen to be hiring."

Wiley grinned sadly, and his sorrow cut me. "Thanks a lot, Tom. But I've been here all day–" he glanced guiltily at me, "– and you haven't had more than three or four customers."

"And they didn't buy anything," Tom said merrily. "Don't worry about it, Wiley. It's not like I have to do anything but pay the light bill. I own the building. It's been in the family for a long time."

"Still, Tom, I don't see how you could pay me–"

"Did you worry about how *Securi-Comp* was gonna pay you?" Tom replied, feigning offence. Wiley shook his head. "I've been thinking about putting some cameras in. Didn't you say you know something about surveillance?"

Did he know something about surveillance? It was the first I'd ever heard about it. "Yeah. I could install some security for you. I'd need tools, though. Do you have any tools?"

"What kind of tools?"

Wiley squinted up at the ceiling of the office. Like the few turn-of-the century buildings still left standing downtown, it had a plaster ceiling: cracked and bumpy; a few exposed beams, exposed pipes.

"I dunno, maybe some screwdrivers; an electric drill. That kind of thing. To hang the hardware."

"There's a roll-around upstairs." Wiley blinked uncertainly. "A *tool box,* my son," Tom explained.

OMG. Not someone else that used that expression. Wiley called everyone he knew *my son,* mostly when he was pointing out their mistakes. I'd heard Nate threaten him over it – *if you call me* my son *one more time, Wiley, I'm gonna cut you.* It was just another expression of his condescension to the rest of humanity.

"I'm sure all you need'll be in there," Tom continued. "I used to work on auto engines, once upon a time."

"Really?" Wiley marveled. "Fuel cells and all that? Electric ones?"

Tom shook his head. "No. Nothing that modern. The older, the better, in fact. Pre-fuel injection, even. Carburetors." Wiley blinked again. He had no idea what Tom was talking about, any more than I did. Wiley Royce, boy genius, knew absolutely nothing about cars.

Then he brightened, thinking about what he *did* know about. "Yeah, I could make this place as secure as Fort Knox. Hook the cameras right into your laptop. You could even see what was going on from your house, your phone, and–"

"Great!" Tom said and slapped him on the back. "You never know when a roving band of rogue librarians might escape from the old folks' home and decide to make a midnight raid. I'll take you on as a consultant."

"What do you think, Brendee?" My husband looked blankly at me – not hopefully, not defiantly. My decision wouldn't be a reaction to his, because he wouldn't show me a reaction. But he still wanted to know what I thought.

"Tom's money's green," I said. Maybe this undertaking, simple and temporary as it might be, would brighten him up a little bit.

"You're hired," Tom said. He took the *Help Wanted* sign from Wiley and stuck it back in the drawer.

"Thanks, Tom," my husband said. His voice held more gratitude than I'd ever heard in it. He crossed the small room and took his son from me. "I'll have to bring Bo with me. He writes the subroutines."

"Of course," Tom said. "I wouldn't have it any other way. You should see how the ladies make over him, Brendee. He's gonna be a heartbreaker."

"I told that redhead that you were his grandpa," Wiley said. He frowned for a second, probably thinking about what he'd just said to Bo's real grandfather. Then he shrugged, and I knew it was forgotten. If Uncle Alex would be expecting an apology, I thought he might not want to hold his breath. "I almost got you a date."

"You're single, Tom?" I asked in surprise. He was a little rumpled, but he was tall and lean, not unlike Wiley, with the same blue eyes. He was quite attractive for his age. And he had that killer smile.

He said he was a widower, and when I went to say I was sorry, he held up his hand. "You're as compassionate as your husband," he said. I looked at Wiley curiously. He was not known for his compassion. "It's been a long time. The bulk of my grief has passed."

"That's why I'm gonna find you a date," Wiley said.

Tom smiled at the floor, shook his head.

"Don't worry," I told him. "From what I've heard, Wiley wasn't ever much for even finding *himself* a date."

From what I'd heard, there'd just been one other besides me – his physical therapist. I'd heard about it from Deneen, who'd heard about it from Nate. Just that one, but she'd been enough. She'd been the one that had showed Wiley how to use a trapeze, of all fantastic things. I often mentally thanked her, and profusely, for everything she'd taught him, and thanked God just as profusely that she lived in another country now. Wiley had never mentioned her, and I'd always felt it prudent not to bring her up. He probably thought that I believed, like his parents did, that I'd been his one and only girlfriend. He probably thought that I believed that his marvelous ability to always know exactly what I wanted was just something that he'd come by on his own, without any . . . training.

"Janae tries to fix me up, too," Tom said. "She's done it all her life. She's always dragging her teachers in here to meet me, telling me I should read poetry to them."

"But they don't want that, do they, Tom?" Wiley grinned wickedly.

Tom endeavored to look embarrassed. "No. No, they don't. But I'm not really interested in any kind of casual . . . Although . . ." He stammered to a stop. *"The hey-day in the blood is tame, it's humble, and waits upon the judgment."*

"And I'm a Chinese jet pilot," Wiley said. "What was that story you told me, about you and your uncle in Las Vegas? About the showgirls?"

Tom endeavored to look embarrassed again. "That was a long time ago, Wiley. Before you were born."

"Ah, before I was born! The days they saw, the adventures they encompassed, before we were born, eh, Brendee?"

You have no idea, Wiley, my son, I thought, remembering Wes's video, which was from before we were born.

"When men were men, and women were . . . What were women before I was born, Tom?"

"Younger," he said.

****

Tom lived in another big, old, rambling Craftsman-style two-story, just like Wiley's parents. Tom introduced us to Maxine, his more or less adopted daughter – it was her turn to cook the feast, he said. She was about my mother's age, I guessed, but she was a bit more kicked-back than my mother: she had a ring in her nose, and her hair was dyed a shade of platinum that did not occur in nature. She hugged Tom and gave him a big sloppy kiss when we entered the house, and only waited to be introduced before taking Bo from Wiley and squeezing him. He squawked in surprise, but then just laughed.

"Would he like an avocado? Or a banana?" she asked, kissing him on the forehead. "Maybe some *Cheerios?*"

51

"They're fortified," Tom said, and grinned at Wiley.

"Ah . . . He's never had . . . Sure," I said. Bo had just started on the gamut of baby foods, but avocados didn't come in a jar, and why would these people have baby food?

"Will you make him a plate, Tom?"

"A plate?" Wiley and I said in unison.

Maxine blinked her tan eyes at us. "You guys don't let him . . . I'm sorry. It's been a long time since I've been around any babies. When Janae was his age, we'd just make her a plate and let her feed herself. It's messy, but babies are messy."

"That sounds great, Maxine," Wiley said. "I'll go get the tray-thing."

The *tray-thing* was a high-chair accessory that fit onto Bo's car seat for times just like this, when he needed to be fed and there was no high chair available. My mom had bought it for me, to go with the car seat that my parents had given us.

Babies were old hat to my mom, and she'd advised me to buy what I needed, as I needed it. Aunt Amy, on the other hand, was completely enamored with grandmotherhood. She'd gotten us a crib and a high chair and a stroller and a changing table and a playpen – every piece of baby equipment imaginable – the day after Wiley told her I was pregnant. So my mom's utilitarian little add-on was still in its box in the trunk of the car. I was surprised that Wiley even remembered it was there.

Maxine's husband Sam came in while Tom and Wiley were figuring out how to attach the tray to Bo's car seat. He was not quite as tall as Tom, rail thin; with enormous brown eyes, and reddish-brown hair, graying at the temples. Maxine introduced us, then told him that she was gonna kidnap Bo. He smiled fondly, then said, "Can I make you a drink, Tom? Wiley? Brendee?"

"No thanks," I said. "I'm driving."

Tom and Wiley, brain trust that they were, were still flummoxed by the *tray-thing*. They had the car seat sitting at the head of the dining room table. "Gin for both of us," Tom told him. "I think it's just supposed to snap on here, but it doesn't seem to want to go on," he said to Wiley. "I'm afraid it'll break if I force it." Wiley feebly pushed on the plastic; he didn't want to break it, either.

Sam went out to the kitchen to make drinks.

"Dinner's almost ready," Maxine said, and handed Bo back to me. I asked her if she needed any help, and she smiled and said that she needed lots of help, always, but not with dinner. She told me to just sit right there on the couch and relax.

Sam came back out of the kitchen with three drinks; Tom and Wiley each relieved him of one of them. He looked at what puzzled them so much for a moment, then shook his head and set his drink down. He snapped the tray onto the high chair and looked at them like they were lame.

Wiley shrugged. "I'm not much for anything that isn't . . . electrified in some way."

"I'm not much for anything made out of plastic," Tom said. "It's my upbringing. No plastic where I'm from." He grinned widely at Sam; Sam gulped his drink and didn't grin back.

Wiley opened his mouth to say something, perhaps to ask Tom where he was from that didn't have plastic, when Maxine trilled, "Here're some treats for Bo!" and came back out into the dining room with a plate of cubed avocado and sliced banana, with a light dusting of *Cheerios*.

Sam unsnapped the tray again, and I put my boy into the car seat. Wiley gestured with his drink; Sam snapped the tray back in place again. Maxine put the plate in front of Bo. He'd never fed himself before, past trying to grab the spoon from me, and I was curious to see what he'd do.

Maxine held a chunk of the avocado out to him; he grasped it, crushed it, dropped it back on the tray, looked down and tried to retrieve it. Maxine gave him a piece of banana – it was a little firmer, and she was able to guide his hand to his mouth. He goo-ed and kicked in delight at the taste, and after a few minutes was stuffing avocado and banana and *Cheerios* into his mouth, when he wasn't rubbing them in his hair, and on his onesie, and dropping them over the side of the car seat onto the table.

"He's gonna be left-handed," Maxine predicted. I didn't see it – he was using both hands.

"Stellar!" Tom said. "I come from a long line of lefties." He again grinned at Sam. "My whole tribe, as a matter of fact, were southpaws." Again Sam didn't grin back.

Maxine went out to the kitchen and brought me a couple of wash cloths for Bo, then returned and started bringing out the food. I insisted on helping her with this, and asked Wiley to wipe up his boy as best he could.

"What do you do for a living, Wiley?" I heard Sam ask him.

"He's working for me," Tom said.

I looked over at Sam as I set down a big bowl of peas. He paused with his drink halfway to his mouth. *"At the bookstore?"* he said in amazement.

"I'm gonna put security cameras in for him." Wiley tried to scrape matted avocado out of Bo's hair.

"At the bookstore." It was a statement now, I noticed, as I set down a mouth-watering looking pork roast.

"Wiley's an electronics genius," Tom said. "Or so he tells me."

"So he tells everyone," I said *sotto voce*. Wiley winked at me.

"And you're gonna wire the bookstore."

"The cameras are actually wireless–"

"Maybe the house, too," Tom said. "You never know when they might come to take me away." I watched him raise his glass to his mouth, holding Sam's gaze. He didn't grin this time. I detected some unpleasant undercurrent between them, but I couldn't imagine what it was.

Maxine invited us to sit and eat. Wiley gave Bo his rattle, and he goo-ed and laughed and kicked and watched us enjoy her delicious meal.

"Where's Janae?" Tom asked.

"She's running a little late," her mother said. "Something to do with school. But she'll be here, or die trying. You know she'd never miss dinner with you."

But this Janae person did miss dinner, and dessert, too. I helped Maxine to clean up, to put all the leftovers away, to load the dishwasher. Then she and her husband told us that it had been nice meeting us; she gave Tom another big, sloppy kiss goodbye. I noticed that Sam was not as demonstrative to Tom in his leave-taking. He barely even nodded in his direction. As they left, I again wondered what the trouble between them could be.

Tom asked us to sit on his porch with him for a minute, while he had a cigarette and Wiley finished an unprecedented third drink. It was the third since we'd arrived for dinner; God only knew how many he'd had at the store with Tom. Bo was snug in his car seat, fast asleep, worn out from all the new sights and sounds and foods and people. I hoped that he would sleep through the night – if he did, it would be the third night in a row – so I could at long last amuse myself with his father.

I was anxious to go home and pursue these activities, but Wiley liked this old guy, and wanted to sit around and talk to him some more. After a few moments, a stunningly beautiful, strawberry-blonde woman, our age, strode up the walk. I heard Wiley say, *"Soft you now! The fair* Janae!*"* to himself, and I was so surprised that I turned around to look at him. He didn't notice me: he watched her approach, a thoughtful little grin on his face.

Tom had gotten up from his chair, walked down the steps, and was hugging her. She smiled up at him, her dark green eyes alive with adoration. "Sorry I'm late, Tommy," she said. "I got caught up at school."

"I heard," Tom said. He put his arm around her shoulders and turned back to us. "Janae, I'd like you to meet–"

"Wiley Royce," she said. *"I always knew some day you'd come walking back through my door. I never doubted that. Something made it inevitable. So, what are you doing here* at Tommy's house?"

You could've knocked me over with a feather. Wiley might've only known *of* this beautiful creature, but she obviously knew him. My amazement must've shown on my face, because Wiley said, "It's from a movie, Brendee." He beamed his irresistible Wiley smile at her. "I wasn't aware that we'd ever been formally introduced, Janae. I–"

"Well, it wasn't exactly a formal introduction. I remember – I was looking for something in the bottom of my locker, and you looked around the door and said, 'Hey, if you've lost your virginity, could I have the box it came in?'"

Tom's eyebrows went up; I looked over at Wiley. I hadn't gone to the same high school as Nate and Wiley and Deneen, and this vision; but I'd heard from Deneen that none of the girls had liked Wiley, because he was known to say the filthiest, most embarrassing things. Anything filthy he'd ever said to me had been behind closed doors, so I'd never been embarrassed.

I looked back at Janae. She didn't seem embarrassed now. She was simply waiting, a little haughtily, I noted, for Wiley to say something else. Haughtiness was not always the best stance to take with Wiley. Especially in discussing something he'd said. If she thought he'd been filthy and embarrassing in high school, he was liable to show her that he was still just as –

He closed one eye and squinted at her. "Well," he said, "I'd say that I–"

"I'd like to apologize for my husband's sense of humor," I said. I arose, walked down the steps and extended my hand. "I'm Brendee Royce."

Her mouth dropped open; she was dumbstruck for the span of perhaps five seconds, then she recovered, shook my hand, and introduced herself. I looked over my shoulder at Wiley, still seated; he returned my glance innocently. I looked back at Janae. Was it really so hard for her to believe that Wiley was married?

Bo woke up and started to cry, and Wiley unhooked him and picked him up.

"This is my son," he said to Janae. "His name's Bo."

She came up the steps and smiled – of course, Wiley's son had immediately stopped crying as soon as his father picked him up – and she said, "He looks just like you."

And you're not the first one that's remarked on it, sister, I thought uncharitably. I gave Wiley the *It's time to go now* look, and for a change he acknowledged it. He put Bo back in his car seat and drained his drink.

Tom caught my look and said to Wiley, *"Come to my office tomorrow morning. We'll do everything businesslike."*

Wiley replied, *"We'll be there at six!"*

Janae said, "He'll *be there at ten."* They all grinned at each other.

Wiley noticed me, not grinning, and said, "It's from *Casablanca,* Brendee." That was twice in one conversation that he'd had to enlighten me about what was being said. And apparently no such elucidation was necessary for Janae – she understood, participated, *initiated.* Apparently she, and Tom, too, were ancient movie buffs, just like Wiley. Wasn't that cute?

"Seriously, Tom," Wiley said, endeavoring to be serious. It was difficult, because he was drunk. I'd seen Wiley smashed probably only once or twice a year since I'd known him, usually on New Year's Eve, and the Fourth of July, when our parents threw a giant drunken barbeque. He wasn't much different – Wiley didn't have any demons hiding inside him that only showed themselves when he'd been drinking. He was just a little more playful, maybe a little bit louder. But it was still unusual for him – this drinking – an unexpected, new aspect to his personality. "What time do you want me to be there?"

"Nine's fine."

"Okay." Wiley told Janae it was *so nice* to see her again.

I noticed that she didn't comment on seeing him again, that it was nice or otherwise. She just kind of nodded at him, like her father had done to Tom earlier. But she turned and smiled graciously at me. "It was nice to meet you, Brendee. Your baby is adorable."

"Thank you," I said. "I'm sure I'll see you again. Thanks for dinner, Tom."

Tom said anytime, and I said goodnight. Wiley followed.

I was mostly silent on the short drive home – I wanted to ask what, if anything else, had ever passed between my husband and the lovely red-blonde Janae in high school, but I didn't really want to know, and I surely didn't want to seem even curious. He just sat there with a slightly unfocused, musing smile on his face. If he was thinking about her, I vowed to make him think about *me*, for the first time since – God, I couldn't even remember how long it had been. Had it really been since our wedding night? I'd had morning sickness, almost from the day I'd found out I was pregnant . . . Surely it hadn't been that long. But each encounter with Wiley was an event, and I couldn't recall another one since our wedding night. It had been way too long. It would be tonight, as soon as we got home, as soon as Bo was asleep.

We Rochambeau-ed for who would give Bo a bath, like we always did. The task fell on me this time, so I got into the tub with him, and washed the avocados out of his hair, and the bananas out of his ears; I found a *Cheerio* stuck to the bottom of his chin. I wasn't so sure about Maxine's baby-feeding regimen – it was *really* messy. But he'd seemed to enjoy himself.

Wiley plucked him out of the bath and dried him off and whisked him away. I stood up and took a shower, washed my hair; then got out and primped and perfumed, all the things one does in anticipation of returning to the man one loves, after a prolonged absence. I looked at myself in the full-length mirror on the back of the bathroom door – I thought that all signs of carrying and bearing Bo had faded – even the scar from the procedure wasn't very noticeable. And it surely wouldn't be noticeable in the dark . . .

I took my green robe off the back of the door beside the mirror; it had gone unworn for more than a year. But I relished the slick feel of the silk on my skin, relished the thought of once again joining the ranks of the sexually active. And now, I didn't even have to worry about getting pregnant anymore. *Watch out, Wiley, you glorious, blue-eyed tomcat; ready or not, here I come!*

But Wiley was most assuredly not ready. He was sound asleep, lying on his back, his arms wrapped around Bo. My son, on the other hand, was not asleep. "Goo!" he said when he saw me, and struggled

57

to crawl out of his dad's grasp. I took him from Wiley's arms. He didn't wake up, but mumbled something in his sleep and turned over. I was pretty sure it wasn't *Janae*. But I wasn't entirely sure.

JANAE

I went back into the house with Tommy. I sat on the couch and he tossed me his cigarettes. For all his healthiness – Tommy had a vegetable garden in the back yard that had been featured in magazines – he understood the finer aspects of a little vice. Since he'd first caught me sneaking one of his cigarettes when I was sixteen, we'd been having a smoke together. It was our little secret.

I was glad to have Tommy all to myself – he was the most important person in the world to me. Sure, I loved my parents – my mom loved Tommy almost as much as I did, but my dad – my dad had grown colder to him over the years. I knew that they'd had a huge fight, around the time that Tommy's wife had died. I was only eight years old then, so I didn't know the particulars of it, but it had reverberated through the years of my life, leaving devastation like an earthquake.

We'd once been one big happy family: Liz and Tom, Mom and Dad, and me. There was nothing but love and joy and fun. Then there was sadness; I didn't understand why everyone was so sad – they told me that Liz was sick – I got sick sometimes, and everyone didn't get so sad about me.

Then Liz was gone. I was sad then, too. She had always been kind and fun and sweet to me.

Then there was anger, a thick cloud of it, between Dad and Tommy; and over the last fifteen years, I'd come to understand that their friendship had been wounded by events surrounding Liz's death, and in the interim, it had withered. I didn't think it was possible for it to die away completely, because my mom and I loved them both. But I also understood that the complete brother-like alliance that they'd once shared existed now as only the shadow of courtesy between them.

Tommy was always cheerful and funny, clever and optimistic when he was around my mom and me, but when my dad was there, it was all tempered with a kind of watchful contempt. Tommy monitored himself when my dad was there. So I was glad to have him all to myself.

All my life, Tommy had brought strangers to have dinner with us: bikers and bankers, punks and pols, artists and actuaries. There weren't too many readers of actual books anymore, so he had plenty of time to talk to anyone who walked into his store. He remembered their names and their stories, whether they bought anything or not, and he occasionally befriended one of them enough to bring him home for our monthly family dinner. He had hundreds, maybe thousands, of acquaintances, but not a single close friend beyond my parents and myself. My mother had told me once that he'd lost his best friend – as had she – when Liz died. And he'd never been much inclined to try to find another one.

"Under what rock did you uncover Wiley Royce?" I asked.

"He came into the store – he wants me to try to find some old clip for him on the internet." Tom grinned at me. "How can you not like Wiley? He's the only person your age I've ever met that's as intelligent and as well-read as you. *We'll be there at six!* I bet you can't name five of your peers that've even seen *Casablanca,* nonetheless can quote lines from it."

"He was an asshole in high school, Tommy. He used to say the filthiest things."

High school had been a sea of less than mediocrity to me, an ocean of near-maddening idiocy. I was Tom Bastion's granddaughter, in fact if not in blood – he was the most brilliant person I'd even known, and his brilliance was augmented with a curiosity and a delight in the world around him that was almost childlike. The things he showed me – fairy tales and books and websites with glossy pictures of animals and far-away places when I was a little girl, then classical literature when I was about eleven, then old movies and music after that – it was like he was discovering each new thing for the first time, along with me. He showed me old-fashioned picture albums of all the places to which he and Liz had traveled, and from the cheerful commentary, you'd never know that their love had been cut so tragically short. They'd only had ten years together.

No one I knew in high school had ever been interested in anything that Tommy had taught me. It was always who was screwing whom, and where was the party, where were we gonna get drunk this weekend. I liked to drink with them – they seemed less like mindless, selfie-taking cattle to me when I was drunk. I wasn't the shy, bookish girl, hiding in the corner. How could I be, with the likes of Tom Bastion for a grandfather? I drank and smoked, did the occasional drug with my friends; I was one of the crowd. I never let any of them know that I thought that they were all just so damned *stupid . . .*

60

Tommy was always my solace. When I'd get frustrated with the constant pettinesses of high school, he'd make fun of them with me, remind me, *this too shall pass.* He'd remind me that high school was mandatory – there wouldn't be as many idiots in college, he'd say. They had to pay for college. He was still paying for mine. I couldn't quite decide what I wanted to be, and since he never objected to paying for it, I just kept going.

One Saturday morning when I was about sixteen, not long after he'd caught me sneaking one of his smokes, I'd shown up at Tommy's house; we were going to put that year's tomatoes into the garden. I had a raging hangover; I was wearing the blackest pair of shades that I could find, even though the sun had been playing hide and seek with the clouds all morning. Tommy had tilted his head and looked at me curiously. "Dig the holes," he instructed. "I'll be right back."

He returned a few minutes later with a tall glass of something green that smelled like grass clippings. He told me to drink it, told me it would make me feel better. I drank it, and as always, Tommy was right. I felt immediately better. "What is this?" I asked.

"It's a hangover cure," he told me. "You look like you need it." I couldn't hide anything from him. He knew that a lecture wouldn't do any good. Tommy had always treated me like an adult – lecturing me was my dad's job; his *avocation,* actually.

A few weeks later, I came back for another visit, to see how the tomatoes were growing. I was a little anxious to depart: there was another party in the offing. Out of the blue, without comment, Tommy made me a little watered down gin and tonic, just like it was routine to be feeding your granddaughter liquor. He handed it to me without comment. I sat down to drink it and started talking to him, just like I had for my entire life.

The upshot of it was, I didn't go to the party. I stopped going to drunken teenage parties on Friday nights after that and hung out with Tommy instead. His conversation was galaxies more amusing than that of my ignorant peers. I didn't get nearly as drunk with him as I did at those same parties, and I never got into the kind of trouble that such parties facilitate – the kind of trouble such parties are thrown *in order* to facilitate. I never got in any trouble at all.

It was still totally inappropriate; he knew it, and I knew it, and my dad would've *had a small litter of carnivorous kittens* – one of Tommy's favorite expressions – if he'd ever found out that Tommy was giving his innocent, impressionable daughter alcohol. But I was neither completely innocent nor overly impressionable, and since I liked to drink anyway, drinking with Tommy kept me from drinking with people that didn't have my best interests at heart. Tommy always called me a cab home, even though I lived within walking distance. I even took a grounding from Dad once – I'd staggered in smelling like gin and when he demanded to know where I'd been and who I'd been with, I told him I'd been at a party with my friends from school. There was much posturing and threats about turning in the party-thrower's parents for contributing to the delinquency of a minor, but nothing ever came of it. Dad hadn't asked for any specific whos or wheres – but if he had, I would've made something up. Pain of death wouldn't have made me let him know with whom I'd really been drinking.

Throughout high school, I hung out with Tommy, had a few drinks. We watched old movies, listened to old music, screened and re-screened Olivier's *Hamlet* and Welles's *Macbeth* and *Citizen Kane,* and a million lesser-known flicks, not all of them classics, but all of them fun. Any question that I had about anything – all I had to do was ask Tommy. If he didn't already know the answer, he'd rub his hands together and say, *"Let's find out!"* and consult the web. Thus was I able to make it through high school without a single teenage misstep. I learned about anything that interested me from a wiser and kinder source, instead of from my ill-informed peers.

School itself was a haze of boredom, and at the start of my senior year, into the midst of its day-to-day inanity waltzed Wiley Royce. He'd materialized out of nowhere; I found out that he'd just moved here.

I didn't have any classes with him, and probably wouldn't have noticed him at all, if it hadn't been for the fact that he always sat in the cafeteria by himself, *reading.* I thought I was the only one that did that – and I only did it until called upon by my friends to conform, to gossip, to consult our phones about the latest meaningless piece of flotsam flying across the world. I'd grown up in a bookstore; that was as foreign to my peers as growing up in a lighthouse or aboard ship. They couldn't relate. They knew how to read, but just didn't; nothing past their friends' texts, and whatever was required of them to pass in school. But there was that black-haired, blue-eyed kid, sitting in the corner of the cafeteria, all by himself; eating baby carrots out of a plastic bag and *reading for pleasure.*

Once, I was sitting a few tables over from him, when some guy came up and asked, "Do you think you can fix my phone?"

Wiley said, *"My name is Ozymandias, king of kings: Look on my works, ye mighty, and despair!"* I turned around and stared at him. I'd never heard Shelley spoken aloud in my entire life. When the kid blinked stupidly at him, Wiley just shook his head and said, "Lemme see it." The kid handed him his phone.

"Who *is* that?" I asked the girl sitting across from me.

She told me his name and told me not to go near him, not to speak to him – he'd say some off-color, dirty remark if I did, she warned me. So I never spoke to Wiley Royce – what would I say? *Gee, I noticed you're just as smart as I am. Wanna chat?*

He used to say the filthiest, cleverest *things,* I should've told Tommy. The intelligence that Wiley possessed, that Tommy had just now discovered – I'd known about it back then. I'd watched him, listened to him if he was within earshot; but mostly, just like my girlfriends said, all he ever said was some dirty comment. They were almost always on the mark, though, and ingenious. Even if they were sometimes a little cruel.

I'd never spoken to Wiley, but eventually, he'd spoken to me. I'd looked up to see him standing there, long and lean and blue-eyed – and when he made his obscene comment, I'd thought, *Maybe you could have my virginity* and *the box it came in if you'd just recite some more Shelley.* But of course I didn't say that – I didn't say anything. What was I gonna say to classless, brilliant Wiley Royce? I just blinked expressionlessly at him and he walked away.

The next time I saw him, he was sitting at a table in the lunchroom with big, quiet Nate Osbourne. Wiley had a fat lip and Nate had four bloody knuckles. There'd obviously been a fight. Again, I probably wouldn't have noticed them, if I hadn't heard Wiley say, *"What a piece of work is a man! How noble in reason! How infinite in faculty!"* It wasn't like I had a crush on him or anything. It's just not often that you hear *Hamlet* in a high school cafeteria.

After that, I seldom saw Wiley alone at school anymore: Nate was always with him. Then I heard that he was dating some private school girl. The Talking-to-Wiley-Royce-Train had left the station. My chance, whatever it might've been, had passed. But really, what would I have said to him?

Now here he'd been, sitting on Tommy's porch, drinking Tommy's liquor, with his adorable little baby and his breathtaking wife.

"Well, his wife sure is pretty," Tommy said innocently.

"What am I now, a homewrecker?" I asked archly.

"You're allowed to notice," Tommy said.

Oh, I'd noticed all right.

The virginity that Wiley had asked after in high school had been surrendered without ceremony, not long after college began. Boris was a Russian exchange student and he had dark hair and black, brooding eyes and his accent was amazing. But I didn't think I loved him or anything as melodramatic as that. I was just curious about him and all his dark foreignness; and I was curious about the whole sex thing in general. So that was close enough.

I brought Boris over to meet Tommy; they'd had almost an entire conversation in Russian. Then Tommy had laughed and told Boris that these few words were the extent of his skills. But then they'd talked in English about Russian literature and poetry and cinema.

After Boris, I'd met a girl who called herself Jaycee. She saw me sitting in the quad, reading the label on a small bottle of orange juice, and said, "Hey, Curious. What'cha reading?"

By the next morning, Jaycee and her soft mouth and hard, toned body were one less thing I was curious about. I brought Jaycee over to meet Tommy, too. She was not nearly as impressed as Boris had been.

After she left, Tommy tilted his head curiously at me – it was his trademark gesture. "You know, where I come from . . ."

Just where Tommy was from was a matter of some conjecture. For my whole life, whenever I'd asked him, he'd always avoided the question, telling me that it was a long story that required a lot of boring explanation. Something about agriculture. He said he'd tell me all about it someday. When I'd asked my mother, she'd just said, "He'll tell you when he's ready." Dad had said, "Whatever he tells you, don't believe any of it."

"Where I come from, bisexuality is virtually unknown."

"Is that a fact?" I said and smiled blankly. "You've got fifty percent more of a chance of getting a date on a Saturday night."

"You'll have to tell me about it sometime."

It was nice to be acknowledged without judgment.

I continued to bring the parade of momentary boyfriends and girlfriends by to meet Tommy. I'd discovered that I just couldn't pick a side. I liked girls – maybe that's why I'd been so willing to hang out with them in high school, even if they *had* been a gaggle of silly geese. But I also liked guys – usually I preferred them strong and masculine, but quiet. Maybe that's why I'd found all the yappy, entirely too eager boys in high school too stupid to let them do anything more than kiss me. Except for Wiley. I'd often thought that Wiley would've been smart enough for me to let him do anything he'd wanted, if he'd ever asked me.

But none of my – for lack of a better word – *relationships* ever lasted. They were always looking for something more, something additional, something continuing. I was just Curious. I wasn't looking for love.

I guess a shrink would've had a field day with me. I was in love with Tommy – I'd been so all my life. I'd always felt him to be my soul-mate, in everything but the physical sense, of course – I'd never desired Tommy – he was my grandfather, for God's sake. But still I loved him, in a different, deeper way than I loved my dad.

But since the physical was necessary, I indulged myself with any of the boys and girls that piqued my interest. But I'd never sought a relationship with them, not companionship and conversation, not anything that was supposed to lead to love, marriage, continuation of the species. If I wanted to laugh, to be entertained, to think, to discuss – I had Tommy for all that. None of them had ever been even on the same planet when it came to these things, compared to him.

Now Wiley Royce, the most intelligent, filthiest-mouthed smart-ass that I'd never really known, was married to one of the most beautiful women I'd ever seen. And they were my beloved Tommy's new buddies.

"I imagine," I told him, "that if someone put you and Wiley in a bag and shook you, you'd fall out side by side."

"You know, I've Googled that expression several times. I come up empty every time. Completely fucking empty."

"Did you put quotes around it?"

Tommy grinned. "What exactly does it mean again?"

"It means, I bet you and Wiley are the same. Birds of a feather. Peas in a pod."

Again he tilted his head curiously. "What makes you say that?"

I grinned back at him. "Wiley's an asshole, Tommy. He's a foul-mouthed, very well-read, exceptionally superior son of a bitch. Who does that sound like?"

"I'm not superior," he protested.

"Of course you are," I said. "I wouldn't have you any other way."

NATE

It was Saturday morning. Once upon a time, I got to sleep in on Saturday mornings. When I was a kid, when I was in high school . . . Right up until the time I became friends with Wiley. Sleeping in was a waste of time to Wiley. "I'll sleep when I'm dead," he told me. He got up at the crack of dawn, did his Tai-Chi, practiced his yoga, and invariably called me before seven.

Deneen was another early riser. This morning she and Brendee were going shopping, and she woke me up – nicely – to get another baby-making attempt out of the way before she went out into the world.

Not that I'm complaining – who would complain about such things? But it was beginning to feel a little bit scripted – some of the magic was starting to wear off of it. I'd been sucked into this whole family endeavor against my better judgment; was I really ready to be a father? Wasn't it something that should just happen when it happened? But Deneen was ready, and I loved her, so I was as ready as I was ever gonna be. I could see myself with no other woman but Denny, and if she wanted a baby, everything else, including getting married, would just have to follow on her timeline.

Sometimes, I thought that maybe Denny didn't want to get married now, because if there was some problem, if, for some reason, I failed to produce this heir she wanted so badly, then maybe she'd be glad that we weren't married. Then she could more easily find a more fertile someone else.

But that was just ridiculous, just self-doubt. Denny wanted a baby because she loved her little sister, because she loved me, because she thought it was time. She wanted to have a baby because her best friend Brendee had one – a tiny, little, gurgling clone of his dad. Denny wanted a tiny, little, gurgling copy of me, or of herself.

When Wiley and Brendee and Bo arrived, Deneen was already up and dressed, sitting at the dining room table, once again reviewing how-to-get-pregnant websites on her tablet. While we used to languish in bed in each other's arms for a while – the thing was for a purpose now, and since it was concluded for the moment, Denny wanted to get in a few minutes of study before our friends arrived. Denny had never been much for study before, but now she even had a little pad and pen and took notes.

When Denny read, her lips moved. I'd watched Wiley watch her once, and had expected him to make some derisive comment about it – Wiley didn't think Denny was the sharpest tool in the shed – and I was surprised when he didn't. He must've caught my puzzled expression because he said to me, "At least she's reading *something*. I'll never make fun of her for that."

It was almost nine when they arrived. Late for Wiley, and it didn't take me long to figure out why. He was pale, and wore giant black *Ray-Bans;* he was uncharacteristically quiet. Wiley had a hangover.

"We went to Tom Bastion's for dinner last night," Brendee explained, when Wiley flopped down on the couch like a sack of flour. He sighed, ran his hand through his hair – I noticed it was getting long and curly again. He was gonna have to get another haircut pretty soon if he wanted to look presentable for job interviews. "Tom's quite the drinker. Wiley tried to keep up."

Brendee smiled and handed the baby to him. Wiley remained silent. Bo reached for his sunglasses, and Wiley took them off and put them on him. He grinned at his boy's cool new look. Nothing could dull Wiley's appreciation for Bo, not even the effects of too much liquor. Maybe this kid-having thing wasn't so bad after all.

"Are you ready, Deneen?" Brendee asked.

"Yes." She set her tablet down and smiled at me. "I'll be back in time for our afternoon–"

"I'll be here," I said quickly. It had become an appointment. An appointment that she didn't feel embarrassed about mentioning in front of our friends. But I still believed that talking about it in front of them was TMI. It was something that should be kept private. But just like Wiley had always told me, girls discussed such things just as much as we did. He'd hacked damn near everybody's cell phone in high school, including Deneen's and Brendee's. Some of their conversations didn't bear repeating.

I gave her a kiss; Brendee kissed Wiley and her boy on their respective foreheads. They departed for the mall.

"What time is it?" Wiley asked. Bo was now chewing on the stem to his shades and he gently took them away from him and put them in his pocket.

I looked at my phone. "It's 8:45." I wondered why he didn't just look at his own phone; but then I realized that Wiley was pretty beat to shit from this unaccustomed drinking with his new buddy.

Removing his phone from his pocket, dodging Bo when he made a grab for it – it was all just a little beyond Wiley at the moment.

He sighed again. "I gotta go to work."

"What? Where? With Bo?"

"I was gonna leave him here with you. For practice." Wiley grinned when my mouth dropped open. "I'm just kidding, Nate."

"Where did you? *What?"*

"Tom gave me a job." He tossed Bo on the couch and then caught him again when he bounced. Bo squealed in delight. "He wants me to install some security cameras for him. Although I don't know how much I'm up for today. You wanna come with us?"

What else did I have to do?

When we got downstairs to their car, Wiley strapped Bo into his car seat, then walked around and crawled into the backseat beside him. "You drive," he said, slouching down in the small space. He stuck his hand with the keys in it through the window. "Has the sun always been this bright?" He fumbled for his shades, put them back on.

I grinned. He was a mess. It tickled me to see always cheerful, always *downright perky* Wiley brought so low by something as conventional as a hangover.

I parked in the lot behind the bookstore, and Wiley allowed me the privilege of carrying his boy. "For practice," he said – while he carried the car seat.

The bell above the door tinkled. Tom looked up at us from behind the counter and smiled. I noticed that he wasn't hung over, and wondered – quite unkindly – if he was an alcoholic, if whatever he and Wiley had consumed the night before was a regular measure for him, if maybe he'd had a little hair of the dog already.

"Good morning, friends," he said.

"That's your story," Wiley said. He set the car seat on a side table beneath the window. "You got any aspirin, Tom?"

"A pill for every ill," Tom said. "I've got just the ticket for you, Wiley." He tossed him a bottle of water.

"I need more than this, Tom. I feel like my head is gonna detonate at any minute."

"Good for what ails ya, boy. If you've got a headache, drink some water. If you're tired, drink some water. If you're angry . . . *Aqua vitae,* and all. The stuff of life."

"Do you have any aspirin?" Wiley repeated.

"Look in the fridge. There's some of *Tom Bastion's Always-Effective Hangover Cure* in there. I made it just for you. It's in a Tupperware bottle-contrivance." Tom shuddered. "Something that Max must've left at my house. Tupperware is poisonous. The chemicals in the plastic leach into the food. But I didn't have anything else to bring it in."

Wiley was down for any relief at the moment. He went into the office. Tom smiled at me and asked how I was. I said I was fine.

"The green stuff?" Wiley said from the other room.

"Yup," Tom replied.

I heard shuffling noises, the door to the fridge closing; then Wiley returned with a shot glass full of something that looked like dark green salad dressing.

"A smoothie?" I said.

"Something like that." Tom looked at the little cup. *"You're gonna need a bigger boat."* Wiley grinned. "Trust me, my son. Down a couple of those and you'll be good as new. Right as rain. The bees' knees."

"All right, all right," Wiley said, but still he hesitated.

"The real deal. Top drawer. The cat's meow."

Wiley winced and swallowed the smoothie in one quick gulp, like it actually was a shot of liquor. He blinked. "It's not bad."

"Have another one. Maybe three."

Wiley poured himself another shot of the potion. He downed it, then poured himself another. The more of it he consumed, the better-tasting it seemed to get to him.

"I have a surprise for you," Tom told him.

The surprise turned out to be a brand new playpen for Bo, still in the box. Tom dragged it out of the office and said to me, "I'm so glad you're here, Nate. If it has a camshaft, I can usually put it back together, but . . . Wiley and I had a little trouble with the *tray-thing* on Bo's car seat yesterday. And since Maxine's husband isn't here to supervise . . ."

"He's about a rude bitch," Wiley, seemingly fully recovered, said as he opened the box to the playpen and peered inside it. "He was as surprised as hell that I'd wanna work for Tom," he continued. "He was kind of an ass about it."

"He's kind of an ass, all around," Tom said.

I was a little surprised myself. Not so much that Wiley would want to work for Tom: Wiley was just like Tom, and Tom was just like Wiley – I figured they could sit around and trade quotations all day. But I was surprised that Wiley would agree to it when it was obvious that this relic of a bookstore couldn't possibly make any money. How, exactly, did Tom intend to pay him? But I thought that any kind of a job, even if it was a temporary one, might ease Wiley's troubles with his dad. Might make Brendee stop suggesting *Radio Shack* positions to him.

Tom seemed to read my mind. "I'll admit that the old place isn't a cash cow. But like I told Wiley, I own the building. I just have to pay the light bill."

"Still–" Wiley began, a guilty look on his face.

Tom held up his hand. "I'm kinda getting tired of your bitching already, my son." He grinned widely. "So I'll let you in on a little secret. My extended family has been turning a tidy profit on this rock for a long time. *Centuries,* to be exact. I am what you would call independently wealthy, and I'm the last one left, that I know of. So if I wanna hire–"

"A smart-mouthed know-it-all," I said.

"Exactly. If I wanna hire a smart-mouthed know-it-all, I will. So shut the fuck up about it, Wiley." Tom's gleeful grin widened further. "What's the going rate, anyway?"

"For what?" Wiley asked.

"For smart-mouthed know-it-alls," Tom and I said in unison.

"What the market will allow, Rich Man," Wiley replied with a grin.

****

By the time we got the playpen assembled, Bo was hungry. I didn't know how Wiley knew this – the baby just whimpered a little bit, like he did sometimes. Wiley said I would figure it out when I had one of my own. He took a jar of baby food out of the diaper bag and was about to open it when Tom said, "You're not really gonna feed him that, are you?"

"I don't have any *Cheerios,* Tom." He looked at me. "They're fortified."

Tom sighed. "It's called *the industrialization of the palate,* Wiley. It all starts with the first things you're fed. You think you like *Cheetos,* because you like *Cheetos?* "

"I don't eat *Cheetos,* for Christ's sake, Tom. And I surely wouldn't give *Cheetos* to–"

71

"Then why give him these?" Tom took the jar from him and looked at the label. "*Bananas.* Right. Why not just give him a banana?"

"These are awesome, Tom," Wiley said with enthusiasm. He dug around it the diaper bag and found another tiny jar of bananas. "That one's for Bo. This one's for me. *They're grrreat!*"

"I'm sure you wouldn't give him Frosted Flakes, either."

"No," Wiley agreed. "Not hardly."

"Then why give him these?" Tom repeated.

"It's just bananas, Tom."

"Does it taste like bananas? Really? Even a little bit?" He twisted the lid off of the jar and held it out to me. "Taste it, Nate. Tell me if it tastes like bananas to you."

I frowned. "I don't want any baby food, Tom. Seriously. Yuck."

Wiley found a spoon in Bo's diaper bag. "Go ahead, Nate. They're awesome. I dare ya."

"All right." I took the spoon from him and the jar from Tom, and without as much hesitation as Wiley had given to the miracle green hangover cure, I sampled Bo's baby food. I was pleasantly surprised. It was smooth and sweet, delicious – Wiley was right. It was awesome. But Tom was right, too. I didn't taste like bananas.

Tom smiled. "The plums are even better. But they don't taste like real plums."

I read the label. "*Ingredients: Fully Ripened Bananas, Citric Acid, Ascorbic Acid (Vitamin C).*" I looked at Tom for explanation.

"Vitamin C's good for you. There's that fortification, sponsored by our benevolent government. Always looking out for us, is our government. Citric acid is something that they put in ice cream, sherbet, candy, fruit juice. It's a flavoring. Probably not harmful, per se . . ."

"However . . ." Wiley said suspiciously.

"It doesn't taste like bananas," Tom insisted. "If you, as a grown, thinking adult, had a choice between that jar of baby food and a real banana, which would you choose? Based solely on taste?"

I ate another spoonful of it and grinned.

"There's my point right there, Wiley. You're teaching Bo that this is what bananas taste like. No. This is what *citric acid* tastes like. You're teaching him to like that taste – it's not difficult. *It tastes good.* A whole lot of very educated men spent a lot of time and money to make it taste good. But it's not real. It's a chemical.

72

"Bananas are the perfect food. Every part of a banana can be cooked and eaten. You can't say that about anything else. Bananas are so perfect for human consumption, it's been rumored that they're extraterrestrial." Tom winked. "But when Bo gets a little bit older, and you give him a real banana, it's gonna taste bland to him. Not sweet enough, because he's been eating this shit all his life. He doesn't want a banana. He wants some citric acid.

"You've been raised from birth to eat what is most readily available here in the first world: packaged, quick and easy to prepare foods. Your palate has been industrialized, just like the foods themselves. You're not educated in school about nutrition, at least not very thoroughly. You're trained from birth to not rise above what is right there on the supermarket shelves. Convenient. Inexpensive. *Baa–*"

"I think I eat pretty damn well," Wiley countered, offended. "No *Cheetos*," he continued, as if he was talking about garbage, "no fast food–"

"You don't eat *Cheetos* because your mama the nutritionist has taught you to read the labels." Tom grinned and took out his phone. "The whole label thing – the guy was named Wiley, just like you, but it was his last name. Dr. Harvey W. Wiley, in the 1890's. He was the first one to come out against some of the preservatives that they used in food then. Terrible stuff.

"It's all here on the FDA's website – they used to use borax, formaldehyde. *Wiley and the public became convinced that chemical preservatives should be used in food only when necessary; that the burden of proving safety should fall on the producer; and that none should be used without informing the consumer on the label – basic principles of today's law and regulations.*" Tom scrolled his phone up. "You know what's in your food because of our friends at the FDA; but our friends at the FDA have screwed the pooch in modern times. I imagine that Dr. Wiley is turning over in his grave." Tom sighed and put his phone back in his pocket.

"You don't eat *Cheetos* because you read that label. You see all the fat, the sodium, the sugar. *Cheetos* are like cigarettes, in a way. Thanks to the FDA, the label is warning you that they're not good for you.

"But I'm telling you, Wiley. You don't read far enough down on the label." He nodded at the baby food. "You see fully ripened bananas, you see Vitamin C. You don't see fat or sugar or sodium, so since you never learned in school what citric acid is, you overlook it.

73

It's gotta be okay, 'cause the FDA lets 'em put it in there. For your baby."

He nodded at me; I had finished the whole jar and was licking the spoon. "But here's our guinea pig. That baby food tastes good to Nate, and you, and anyone else that eats it – because you've been eating that citric acid your whole life. Since you were a baby."

"You said it's probably not harmful–"

"*Per se,*" Tom stressed. "But it teaches Bo that this is what bananas taste like. And that's a damned, unhealthy lie."

Wiley looked at the baby food jar he still held, then at Bo, waiting patiently for his chemical-laced bananas. He put it back in the bag. Tom went into the office and returned a minute later with a real banana. The way he peeled it was amazing: he inserted his fingernail just below the stem and gave it a little shake, then extracted the insides, unbroken, after only putting a single split in the peel. He tossed the peel into the trash, then brought a worn Swiss Army knife out of his pocket, opened it with one hand, which was also amazing. He cut a slice of the banana and handed it to Bo.

"He's gonna make a mess again," Wiley began.

Tom gave him a withering glance – was cleaning up a mess too high a price to pay for his child's nutrition? "There's an apartment upstairs. Right after I inherited this place, I used to live there. I just use it for storage now. It's tiny, but it's got all the comforts of home. There's a sink in the kitchen and a bathtub – I'll give you a break schedule from your tasks." Tom looked around the store. Not a single task, whatever they were going to be, had been performed. He grinned. "You can give him all the baths he needs." Tom gave Bo another slice of banana.

I tossed the baby food jar into the trash. Wiley glared at me.

"You don't have a recycle bin?" he said to Tom.

"A what?"

"A recycle bin. That glass . . ." He looked at Tom a trifle incredulously. "You don't recycle? Jesus, Tom, you have to recycle."

Tom grinned. "I don't have to do anything but die, Wiley. And live until I die."

"But . . . You're so concerned with what Bo eats; he's not gonna be able to live on top of a landfill." Tom just blinked at him, unconvinced. "I'll get you a recycle bin."

"As long as you don't nag me about it, my son." He gave Bo another slice of banana. "I'm not here to save the planet. Shit, I can't even save myself."

I grinned at Wiley, licked the spoon one last time, and handed it to him. He didn't grin back, but looked pensively at the spoon, then at his boy. "Sure," he said, "it doesn't taste like bananas. But . . . Maybe it's because it's for babies?"

Tom gave Bo another slice, then cut one for himself. He looked at me. "Nate's a pretty big baby. He liked it. You like it." He tried to give Bo another slice, but he was done. Tom ate the rest of the banana, then considered us for a moment. "Since we don't seem to be doing a land office business today, let's try a little experiment. I'm gonna run around the corner to the grocery. I'll be right back." He wiped the knife on the leg of his pants, then closed it and put it back into his pocket.

"I located some panhead manuals for this guy named Josh." He nodded at a stack of three greasy, soft cover books on the corner of the counter.

"Panhead?" Wiley looked at me, like he thought that I might know what such a thing was. I did not.

"It's a type of motorcycle engine," Tom said. "A bona fide antique; they stopped making them in the 1960s. I tried to call Josh to tell him they're here, but he didn't answer. He's really looking forward to them though, so he'll probably come in anyway, just to check. If he shows up – the price is there on top. I'll be right back," he repeated, and after giving the baby a smile and a little pat on the head, he left the store.

Wiley found a wash cloth in the diaper bag. He disappeared into the office again – there was a little bathroom back there – then returned after a moment and wiped off Bo's face and hands. Then Wiley unhooked the strap on his car seat, and picked him up with one hand and his diaper bag with the other – it was changing time – and went back into the office again. *Damn,* I thought, *these babies require constant attention,* and again wondered if I was gonna be up to it.

The bell tinkled, and a man in his fifties entered. He had long hair, brown streaked with gray, which ran down his back in a braid. He was wearing a leather vest, a torn t-shirt and oil-stained jeans. His thick arms were covered from the fingers to the shoulders in tattoos. He was an in-the-flesh, biker cliché. This was obviously Josh.

He looked at me silently, unsmiling, for a moment, then finally said, "Where's Tom?"

"He stepped out for a moment," I said, trying to sound professional and businesslike.

The biker wasn't impressed. He just stood there, staring at me.

Wiley came out of the office, and handed Bo to me over the counter. "How can I help you?" he said.

"Where's Tom?" the guy repeated.

"He stepped out for a moment," Wiley repeated. The biker glared. Wiley smiled. He was used to dealing with people that were . . . How should I put it? Bad-asses? They didn't faze him in the least.

Wiley had once obtained a screen for my busted cell phone from a guy named Bradley, who'd been a dabbler in stolen goods and a dealer of some awful drug called Meow. He'd looked a lot like this guy, tatted-up and unsmiling. Wiley had installed security cameras for him, just like he was supposed to do for Tom.

I learned that Bradley had saved Wiley's ass once upon a time, so when he had to leave town in a hurry, Wiley had voluntarily given him five thousand dollars to help him get on his way at the first possible opportunity. It represented a lot of broken cell phones and infected computers, but Wiley had been glad to do it. They were friends.

And this guy was old, and didn't look half as mean as Bradley, although he did make me a little nervous.

"Is there something I can help you with?" Wiley asked.

"Tom was supposed to get some books for me. Repair manuals."

"For your panhead?" The biker nodded. "They're right here."

"Awesome!" He seemed to relax a little bit. He took his wallet out of his pocket – it was chained to his belt loop, I noticed – and handed Wiley a couple of greasy bills.

Wiley looked at the money, then looked at the cash register, then looked at me. "It's electronic," I said. "How hard can it be?"

The biker smiled. "Keep the change, sonny."

Wiley smiled back gratefully and stuck the money under the side of the cash register. "Can I ask you something?" he said, as Josh thumbed through the topmost ancient book.

"No, I won't take you for a ride," the biker replied, not looking up.

Wiley grinned at me. "It's just – isn't all that stuff on the internet? I mean, I understand the enjoyment of holding an actual book in your hand. Sometimes it's a pain to read from a device, but it's not like that's literature . . ."

76

Now Josh looked up in surprise. "I'm sure it's all online. Everything's online nowadays, isn't it? But that's not gonna do me a whole lot of good out in the garage."

"But . . . You can't just use your phone?"

Josh shook his head. He laid the book back on the counter, open, on top of the other ones. "I can put a wrench down on this, to hold my place. I can page back and forth in it, and it doesn't matter if my fingers are greasy. The print's big and easy to read. If I get mad, I can throw it across the room." He grinned, and I noticed that he was missing a couple teeth on one side. "That happens frequently when working on Harleys. My phone won't take that. Can I do any of that with my phone?"

"I guess not. I guess I never thought about it like that. The stuff I work on–"

"Lemme see your hands," Josh demanded.

Wiley held out his long-fingered, immaculate hands, palms up.

"That's what I thought. What do *you* work on, kid?"

Wiley blinked at his insolent tone. "I work on phones. Computers. Televisions."

"Security cameras," I added.

"Well, maybe it's just my lucky day, then. My manuals came in, and you fix phones." Josh took a battered model out of his back pocket. It looked like a black spider had been mashed into the top of the screen: it was starred, and grease was caked into the cracks. It wasn't on, I didn't think. He slid it across the counter to Wiley. "Can you fix that?"

"Yes," Wiley said, without even picking it up, without even really glancing at it.

"You didn't ask me what's wrong with it."

Wiley shrugged. "It doesn't matter. I can fix it, whatever's wrong with it. That's what I do."

Josh grinned. He told Wiley how much they wanted to fix it at the phone store. "And they said two weeks. Then the guy tried to sell me a new one."

"I'll do it for half. And you can pick it up . . . How's Tuesday sound?"

The bell over the door tinkled, and Tom walked in, carrying a grocery sack. "Hello, Josh," he said. "I expect you to bring that panhead in by the end of the month."

"Right. You know what they say: *expect* in one hand and shit in the other, and see which fills up faster." Josh continued to hold Wiley's gaze. "Can this kid really fix my phone by Tuesday, Tom?"

"If he says he can."

Josh stared at Wiley for another second. "Okay," he said at last. "If you vouch for him, I'll be back on Tuesday."

"On your panhead?" Wiley asked.

Josh grinned at Tom. "He doesn't know anything about bikes, does he, Tom?"

Tom shook his head. Josh gathered up his books and the two of them walked outside.

****

While Tom stood outside the store and smoked a cigarette with Josh, Wiley took a blanket out of the diaper bag and showed me how to put the now-sleeping Bo down for a nap in his new playpen. He had drooled on my shoulder. When Wiley moved to go back to the counter, I hesitated. "You're just gonna . . . leave him here? You don't have to . . . watch him?"

"He can't get out, Nate. I'm not going to Peru. When he wakes up, he'll let me know."

I shrugged, still unsure, feeling a little silly. Of course Bo didn't have to be watched while he was sleeping. "You're the dad."

"You'll find out."

"Not too soon, I hope."

Wiley looked at a non-existent watch on his wrist. "It'll be at least nine months."

When we went back out, Tom was standing by the counter. "Are you ready for our experiment?" We nodded cautiously. "You guys like rice pudding?" We nodded again. "Okay. Hold on just a second."

Tom disappeared into the office for a few minutes; there was the sound of drawers opening, closing. Then he reappeared with two paper plates, two plastic spoons.

"You really shouldn't use paper plates, Tom," Wiley started preaching again. "The landfill–"

"You're nagging, Wiley." There was a little scoop of rice pudding on each of the sinful, landfill-filling paper plates. Tom set them down on the counter and handed both of us an evil plastic spoon.

"Okay. One of these is sold as *organic rice pudding*. *Organic*, as I'm sure you know, is an advertising term that's been around for decades – you've heard it all your lives. It's supposed to denote something that's natural, right? And everything that's *natural* is good for you, right?" Tom shook his head. "It's a stupid concept. Cancer is organic. It's *natural*, or so they tell us.

"If something's called *organic*, you've been led to believe that it's good for you, that it doesn't have any additives or preservatives, right?" We nodded. "And so this is. Its ingredients are rice, sugar, milk.

"The other one doesn't call itself organic. It has no such pretensions. Its ingredient list goes all the way around the top of the lid. All chemicals." Tom paused. "Now, what I want you to do, is taste these two samples, and tell me which one you think is organic."

We complied. They both looked more or less the same: just lumpy ol' rice pudding. The first one was nice; sweet and rice-y, maybe a little chalky. But good. Good enough. But the second one was delicious, sweeter than the first sample, silky, smooth; there seemed to be more than a hint of cinnamon to it, although I couldn't see anything brown. The second one was *grrreat.*

Wiley looked at Tom. "The first one is the organic one."

"Why do you think so?" Tom asked, grinning.

"Because it's . . . Because it's bland. Tasteless, compared to the second one."

"Do you concur, Nate?" I nodded. "You are correct, my gourmands. Your tastebuds have made my point. The first one calls itself organic – the second one is basically organic, too – but they wouldn't dare try to market it that way, because in addition to the main ingredients of rice, sugar, and milk, it has a zillion other things in it. All chemicals. Modified corn starch to make it thicker; artificial flavors and colors to make it more palatable, more appetizing; calcium carbonate – you know that's used in taxidermy to remove the flesh from the hide, Wiley? In that pudding, it's used as a stabilizer, to keep all this stuff uniform. And of course, carrageenan, which is made from seaweed, to make it smooth; it also irritates your guts.

"None of these things are supposed to be in rice pudding, my boys. It's supposed to be rice, sugar, and milk, just like the first one. But the first one tastes like shit to your industrialized palates."

Tom looked at us for a moment. There was no arguing with what he said. The one with the chemicals in it tasted better.

"Here's a thought, gentlemen," he continued. "How healthy would Bo grow up to be, if he drank his fluoridated water; if he ate some chemical-free, fortified breads, and got any vitamins he might be lacking from them – and we do need those carbs, anyway, Wiley.

"But what if he ate this rice pudding–" Tom indicated the bland one, "instead of that one? What if he ate homegrown fruits and veggies, devoid of pesticides and herbicides, grown for the taste and the nutrition, instead of for the ease of mass harvesting? Maybe some eggs whose shells hadn't been bleached for appearance sake? What if he had the occasional steak for some good-tasting protein? Personally, I can't resist a good steak now and then, no matter what's in it. It's a taste I've most enthusiastically acquired since I arrived here." He grinned. "What if we fed Bo some chickens that hadn't been fed chemicals themselves? Maybe some–"

"Wild-caught fish?" Wiley suggested.

Tom shook his head resolutely. "No fish. Growing up, I ate enough fish to last for the rest of my entire life. No fish."

"But fish is good for you!" Wiley said in astonishment.

"Fish is good for *you*. *Variety* is good for me." He grinned again. "Bo can have some fish; it *is* good for you. I've just had more than my share.

"What if he ate a little sugar, a little fat, a little sodium – you need salt to live – but just a little bit of these things? Moderation in the key. But what if Bo ate nothing with more than two syllables to it?"

"Ri-bo-fla-vin." Wiley counted on his fingers.

"He'll get that from his veggies, naturally, the way he's supposed to get it, as well as from his fortified grains. How 'bout if I put it this way? What if Bo never ate anything that has an explanation after it: as a preservative, as a stabilizer, as an emulsifier; to prevent caking; to retain freshness; to retain color? How healthy would he grow up to be then? How many diseases of affluence would he avoid? How long might he live?"

The bell over the door tinkled, and as a man, we turned to see who had entered.

"Well, what d'ya know?" Wiley grinned brilliantly. "You remember Janae, don't ya, Nate?"

"Yes," I managed to say. I mostly certainly did remember Janae.

In high school, there had been three girls that had always been running through my mind, mostly naked, at least when I was alone. There had been Judy and Brendee. And there had been Janae.

Judy was blonde, brown-eyed, tall and curvy, what my dad called *a healthy, corn-fed, farm girl.* She'd been my girlfriend, ever since I'd made the varsity squad as a sophomore. She was head cheerleader, and I was starting wide receiver, so it only seemed right – we were a high school stereotype, a matched pair. She'd given her all to our relationship: Judy was phenomenal in her enthusiasm for giving her all, and I enjoyed every second of it.

But then I broke my hand right before practice started for senior year, and on the coach's advice, I quit football. I might've been a starter for *his* team, but there was never gonna be any kind of college or professional future in it for me. I knew it. Coach knew it.

I didn't miss football: not the heat, not the pain; and I missed my teammates least of all. They were assholes. That was how I met Wiley: three of them were going to kill him over some obscene remark he'd said about one of their sisters, and since it wasn't gonna be a fair fight, I'd jumped in and helped him out. It had felt good to sock Neal, the center, who was chief asshole of the bunch, even though I'd almost broken my hand again. They'd shunned me, called me *fag* and *quitter,* ever since I'd quit the team. I didn't miss any of them.

But Judy . . . Judy surely couldn't be seen about town with a non-team cripple, either. She'd been dry-eyed, annoyed, when she'd said, "I'm sorry, Nate." She wasn't sorry at all. "This just isn't working out." I didn't even get a consolation blow job. I didn't miss football, but I'd missed her a little bit.

Then there was Brendee. I'd had a thing for Brendee ever since grade school. She was tiny, like a little elf, blue-eyed, also blonde. *A spinner,* Wiley had said with a leer. She'd had a permanent residence in my head, even before Judy. I'd wanted Brendee since before I'd ever even known what *wanting* meant. But she'd gone to a private high school, and my chance had never materialized. When I met Wiley, and I found out that he needed a math tutor – I thought of her, thought we all might start hanging out together. I thought I might get a second chance. But once Brendee saw Wiley, there was never gonna be any chance for me. Or anyone else, for that matter. Wiley was all she'd ever wanted.

And then there was Janae. She was taller than Brendee, but not as curvy as Judy. She was willowy, lithe, with flashing green eyes and wavy, red-blonde hair. While I'd never got anywhere near Brendee, and had enjoyed Judy at my whim – at least until my athletic career ended – Janae had fallen in the middle of these extremes. I'd only *almost* had Janae. And that had served to keep her there, part of the trio of blondes in my mind.

It had been at a party, sometime before it came to be understood that Judy and I were a couple. We'd been talking, but . . . Janae had flat out made a pass at me, put her arm around my neck and whispered in my ear. "Do you want to see Carol's parents' etchings, Nate?" she'd asked. "They keep 'em in their bedroom." I didn't know what etchings were, but Janae Rossmore had said *bedroom* to me, and that was all I needed to hear. We were both only sixteen, but she seemed older somehow, calmer, less giggly than the other girls. And she was beautiful.

We went to Carol's parents' bedroom, and Janae, all initiator, all in control, locked the door and pushed me down on the bed. She climbed on top of me and started kissing me, aggressively, with none of the girlish shyness I'd always experienced before. *This is how girls ought to act,* I thought. It was awesome. I was just about to roll her over and take the lead in this dog and pony show, when her phone rang.

She sat up abruptly, still astride me, and took it out of her pocket. "I'm sorry, Nate," she said. "It's my mom. I have to take it." She answered the phone, simultaneously climbing off of me. She left the room, closing the door behind her.

I sat up, bewildered, more than a little frustrated. Couldn't she have called her mom back? It only would've taken a few minutes . . . I sat there, still ready to go, and waited for her to come back. I waited for her until my hard-on at last faded away, and then I just started to feel silly. She wasn't coming back. I left Carol's parents' bedroom, pausing to peek around the door to make sure no one would see me leaving it, all by myself.

Janae was standing on the patio, drinking a beer, chatting and laughing with Carol and a few other girls. She smiled blankly at me, and Carol turned around and gave me a knowing little smirk. Janae had never intended to come back, had no doubt told Carol that she'd left me high and dry in her parents' bedroom. They'd probably had a good little laugh about how long it'd taken me to figure it out. Janae had gotten all she wanted from me – a little hard-kissing, a little hair-pulling. Whatever else I'd wanted, whatever else I thought I was gonna get . . . That was all just my problem.

Janae was a tease.

Before I had too long to resentfully reflect on it, before I had too long to think about what an ass she'd made of me, Judy showed up at the party. I decided it was time to see just how far Judy was willing to go, and after that, like I say, we were a couple.

But like Brendee's never attained loveliness, and Judy's easily attained wonderfulness, Janae's forceful – though ultimately empty – kisses had remained in my mind. Yeah, I remembered Janae, all right.

"Hello, Nate!" she said now, cheerfully. But there was no hint of a memory of our truncated tryst in her eyes. She remembered me – we'd gone to school together – but that was all she remembered. The furtive little not-coupling that had occurred at Carol's house – which still stood out so clearly to me – Janae had no recollection of it. If she did, she wasn't gonna let on that she did.

"Hi, Janae," I replied. "Long time no see."

She nodded, glanced briefly at Wiley, then went around the counter and gave Tom a big hug and a kiss on the cheek. Baffled, I looked at Wiley for explanation.

"Janae is Tom's granddaughter," he supplied. "It's a small world after all, isn't it, Nate?"

He could've mentioned this to me earlier. But then, he didn't know about . . .

Wiley was always dropping *it's a small world after all* bombshells on me. When I'd first mentioned her as a math tutor for him, when we were still in high school, he hadn't let me know that Brendee's parents and his parents had once been close, that they'd considered their children to be cousins, before Wiley's family had moved away when he was ten. He hadn't seen Brendee since then – except online, and she hadn't seen him there – but he could've said something when I first mentioned her.

He'd let his mom drop that one on me: "I talked to your Aunt Darlene today," she'd said to him, to which he'd replied, *"Brendee's mom?"*

This was right after he'd shown me the clip he had of this crush of mine, his *cousin,* writhing around on her bed in ecstasy, while she screened that horrible old Wes Thomerville video. We didn't know what she was watching then – Wiley couldn't care less what the girls he'd taped were watching. "We're watching *them,* for Christ's sake!" he'd said to me. "Who cares what *they're* watching?"

But I wanted to know, so he'd found out for me. And that was another *it's a small world* incoming shell that Wiley had dropped in my lap, and watched gleefully as it exploded. The next day, after he'd hacked Brendee's laptop and discovered what she'd been watching, the little song that got her motor running so much – he'd already known that he looked just like Wes Thomerville. He'd already known that things would follow just the way that they did, that Brendee would fall for him the moment she saw him, that she would never give me a second look.

But it had been Wiley who'd fixed me up with Deneen, and I was happy with her. I hadn't thought about Judy or Janae again after I'd started going with Deneen. And Brendee – Brendee had become a cold, bitchy, sarcastic whiner while she was pregnant, and I wasn't so sure that the old Brendee had come back yet. I wasn't so sure that she'd ever come back. I thanked God more than once that I'd not been given the opportunity to take that path. Denny was the girl for me. We were gonna start a family, get married, live happily ever after . . .

But here was Janae, and she was Wiley's new buddy's granddaughter. It *was* a small world after all.

JANAE

Ah, Nate! I remembered Nate. He was just the kind of guy I liked, strong and masculine and quiet. I'd had a little go at Nate in high school, but in the middle of it, I'd changed my mind. I wasn't ready then, wouldn't be ready, as it turned out, until I met brooding Boris some years later.

Nate was a big boy and he was enthusiastic . . . I hadn't wanted to lead him too far down the garden path and then have to tell him no. That was a dangerous pastime, could get a girl hurt. I didn't think Nate was the type that would've tried to force me, but I didn't know him, and . . . You never know. People do things in the throes of passion, so, I'd just reached into my pocket and pushed a button on my phone. He surely hadn't noticed. I told him my mom was calling and cut it short before it could go too far.

He'd never tried again, had never really spoken to me after that. He wasn't mad, I didn't think – we just didn't have any classes together, and slutty, beautiful Judy had kept him on a short leash. And well she should've. Nate was cute. Then he'd taken up with Wiley . . . Ah, Wiley!

I looked at him, and discovered that he was looking at me. Wiley wasn't as bulky as Nate, but he was just as tall, lean. And Wiley had that sparkle of devious intelligence in his dark blue eyes, just like Tommy did. It wasn't that Nate was dumb, at least I didn't think so. He was friends with Wiley, after all, so he couldn't be too dumb. But I didn't know Nate. I didn't know Wiley, either, but I liked that little gleam of evil that danced in his eyes. I'd liked it since high school. *"Well, well, well, well, if it isn't little* Wiley. *Long time no viddy, droog. How goes?"* I asked, and Wiley's grin widened. He got the reference.

"No time for the old in-out, love, I've just come to read the meter," he replied, another line from *A Clockwork Orange.*

"To what do I owe the extreme pleasure of this surprising visit?" Tom added further, and we all smiled at each other. Except for Nate. He had not a clue. *Just stand there and look pretty,* Nate, I thought. *That's what you're for.*

"I was just in the neighborhood," I said to Tommy. "Thought you might have something in that I hadn't read before." Tommy grinned at that. "What's you're excuse, Nate?"

"I'm helping Wiley," he said.

"Helping Wiley what? Surely he already knows how to read?" Wiley smirked at me.

"Wiley's gonna wire the store. With security cameras," Tommy said.

"They're actually wireless, my son," Wiley corrected. Always superior Wiley. Damn, I liked that.

"Has there been a break in?" I asked with sudden concern. If something was to happen to Tommy . . .

"No," he said with a chuckle. "What would they steal? Wiley needed a job, I needed a tax write-off–"

"Is that all I am to you, Tom? A tax write-off?" Wiley replied, feigning injury.

"Look at it this way, Wiley, and you won't pout so much. I have a little extra funds; you need a little extra funds. Call it a job, call it a tax write-off, and we're both getting one over on the IRS."

Wiley grinned. "And it'll keep my dad and my wife off my back."

I heard a baby cry then, and Wiley ducked into the office. A moment later, he returned with his darling little boy. His hair was matted from sleep, black curly ringlets pushed up into a faux-hawk. He was adorable. He looked just like his dad, who, while not quite what I'd call adorable – he was too smart for that – his dad was undeniably intriguing.

I held out my arms, and Wiley handed the baby to me. He blinked sleepily, and considered me solemnly for a minute – I wasn't his mama. He reached out his little chubby hand and grasped my hair. Then he smiled. I wasn't his mama, but I was all right. I looked up to find all three of them watching me, so for something to say, I said, "I might have to get me one of these someday."

Without missing a beat, Wiley replied, "I can show you how to make one."

I blinked and Tom blinked. Even Nate blinked. Wiley took his phone out of his pocket, consulted it. "Would you like graphics? Pictures? Video? Or just plain text?" He looked up at me innocently.

Ah, Wiley, you slick bastard, I thought. *Are you flirting with me, right here in front of Tommy and your buddy? Is that how you roll? What about your sexy little wife?*

"I think I'll know what to do when the opportunity presents itself," I said.

"Indeed," Tommy said, grinning, breaking the loaded moment. "I was just telling Wiley about the industrialization of the palate.

About how there's a world of corporations out there aiming to enslave his boy's tastebuds."

"Ah, Jesus, Tommy," I said, bouncing the baby a little bit, just to make him smile. "Not the food additives thing again."

He sobered suddenly, just like I knew he would. "They killed Liz, Janae."

"Cancer killed Liz, Tommy," I said gently.

A lifetime of pity for him rushed back upon me. I'd heard this story before, over and over, from the day when I was ten years old, and Tommy had smacked a *Coke* out of my hand. "If I ever see you drinking one of those again, I'm gonna beat you to death," he'd said, eyes blazing, as serious as a heart attack.

And then he'd read the riot act to me, about the additives, how they were killing us all, slowly, inexorably. How they fortified our food to make us healthy on the one hand, then incrementally murdered us with all this other shit, on the other hand. I was too young to understand it all, but I'd tearfully promised to never drink another soda. It was the only time in my life that he'd ever shown anger to me, the only time he'd ever raised his voice. Because I was just a child, it was devastating, frightening to me.

Over the years, he'd eventually explained the whole thing in his calm, analytical way. The food additives caused cancer, high blood pressure, heart disease, according to him. They exacerbated asthma and diabetes. They were the very devil in our midst. It hadn't just been a tragic deal of the cards that had given his beloved Liz cancer, had taken her from him at the insanely unfair age of forty-eight. It hadn't been just her tough luck, and his. It had been the food additives.

I thought that he'd had to blame something for his loss, or the tragedy of it would've driven him insane. Maybe it did make him crazy. Since Liz passed, when I was eight years old, I'd overheard my dad saying just that. Dad would never say it directly to me: he knew it was useless. I'd defend Tommy 'til my dying breath: he was everything to me. But I'd overheard Dad say it to my mom enough times: "Don't listen to him, Max. *He's nuts.*"

I looked at Wiley and Nate, who blinked somberly at Tom. They didn't seem shocked or surprised at his sudden seriousness, and I thought that he'd probably been haranguing them about his perceived food dangers at length already. He hadn't started in on my mom and dad about what they were feeding me until I was about nine. This was because, my mom told me, Tommy hadn't cared about the chemicals in our food too much before Liz died, before he'd decided that they were the cause of her cancer. But it became like an obsession to him for a few years after she was gone; I remembered him constantly reading labels, anxiously checking definitions on his phone, saying to my mom, "For Christ's sake, Max, don't let her eat that!"

The obsession had died down after a while. His grief had subsided, as I imagine it will. I've never lost anyone, so I can't say how it all works, but by the time I was fourteen or fifteen, Tommy seemed to have accepted that he wasn't going to be able to get me to read the label on every single thing I ate. He wasn't going to be able to convince me that I was poisoning myself. He'd started the tirade, the indoctrination, too late. My palate was already industrialized, and I just didn't buy all the bullshit he was trying to sell me.

But here were fresh victims for his theories. And they'd brought a baby with them. Someone whom Tommy could save from the food-borne evils of the first world. Here was a *tabula rasa*. He could instruct Wiley on how to protect his innocent boy, if only he could convince Wiley of the dangers.

In the ensuing silence, Wiley at last spoke. "No more jarred bananas, Tom. Or plums." Apparently Tommy was succeeding. Apparently Wiley was buying it.

"Atta boy, Wiley," he said, and it did my heart good to see him smile, just like it always did. "You can be taught."

"Indeed," Wiley said, and considered me thoughtfully for a moment. "I'm a very apt pupil."

From the sly look on his face, my first inclination was to ask him if that was a fact, to offer to teach him anything he thought he'd like to learn from me. But I wasn't going to fall for it a second time. If Wiley was flirting with me, he wasn't going to let it play out in front of Nate and Tommy. If I responded openly to this new veiled come-on, he'd just turn it into some other innocent remark. I'd have to wait for some time when we were alone to see exactly what it was that he was trying to communicate to me.

But I thought I had a pretty good idea. Maybe he was getting tired of his wife, no matter how sexy I thought she was. Maybe he wanted a change. It was a sinful thing to consider, but if cute lil' Brendee couldn't keep her husband at home – that wasn't my fault.

BRENDEE

The plan was simple enough. Deneen texted Nate and told him that she'd pick him up at the bookstore at two-thirty, so they could run home for their scheduled appointment. She tried to explain to me how it was supposed to be the peak time of her ovulation or something, and I really tried to listen, or at least tried to make her *think* I was listening. I tried to make her believe that I cared. But I couldn't possibly have cared less.

I loved Deneen, and wished her well in her attempts to conceive. Like she did, I thought it would be cool if our babies could grow up together, if they could be Aunt Denny and Uncle Nate to Bo, and we could be Aunt Brendee and Uncle Wiley to their baby. It would be just like my parents and Wiley's parents. But the clock was ticking – Bo and her baby were already going to be fifteen months apart, if she got knocked up today. It would still be okay – my brother and I were barely a year apart, and we'd always been the best of friends.

But all the procedures and timings and Deneen's constant discussion of them was wearing on me. I must've missed a pill, or maybe one of them was defective: my pregnancy had been totally unplanned, unsought; an accident, kismet, fate. No one in the world had been more surprised than me when the test came out positive. And since I wasn't gonna have any more – the smarmy ob-gyn that had delivered Bo had taken care of that at the time of my C-section, at my demand – I was just the tiniest bit disgusted with Deneen's constant descriptions of uteruses and endometria and placentas, fertilization and egg attachment. I wished it would just *happen already*. Then she'd get to find out how miserable being pregnant actually was, just as I'd found out.

So the plan was simple. Deneen told Nate that she'd pick him up and they'd go on home. She told me that she'd be back in a little while, and we could continue shopping. "It shouldn't take more than a half an hour," she said. I thought of poor Nate, reduced to stud. I'm sure he would've been embarrassed to hear Deneen discuss the brevity of it – she wasn't interested in passion and foreplay right at the moment, she'd told me, so she'd dispensed with it. It was all about the purpose at the moment, and the purpose didn't require a great expenditure of time. Poor Nate.

But when we arrived at *Morry's Books* at two o'clock, Nate wasn't there. Tom told us that he'd accompanied Wiley to the electronics place to buy security cameras and whatever accoutrements were required to *wire the store.* Wiley had told me that the cameras were wireless, but I think Tom just liked the expression.

Deneen stamped her foot in annoyance. "Damn it! Fucking Wiley! He's always stealing Nate away when I need him the most! I told him that it had to be at two-thirty!"

"I'm sure a few minutes couldn't make that much difference," I began, but stopped when Deneen glared at me. Her internet charts and graphs told her that it *did* make a difference. To take her mind off of the whole thing, I introduced her to Tom.

He'd been standing by the window when we came in, and when he came over to the counter and greeted frustrated Deneen with that killer smile, I saw Bo's car seat, empty on the table. If his car seat was here, and he wasn't in it – "Where's Bo?" I said.

Tom and Deneen had started off down the aisle between the bookshelves. Tom said, "Janae's changing his diaper," then smiled at Deneen, and listened attentively to whatever she was saying. *He must have some baby books to show her,* I thought, because that was the only thing she cared about at the moment. Like the rest of us – except for Wiley – Deneen had never been much of a reader. But if Tom was taking her to show her books now, and she was amenable to it, I was confident of the subject matter.

I frowned, unsure of just how I felt about Wiley leaving my son here with these strangers. I wasn't sure how I felt about this beautiful woman he'd talked dirty to in high school changing my baby's diaper. I surely wouldn't change *her* baby's diaper. She hadn't seemed the motherly type at our initial meeting, and I suspected some ulterior motive to her kindliness. She hadn't seemed overly friendly to Wiley, but such a tactic might be a play . . . Wiley was exceptional. She obviously knew it – I'd witnessed her smile at their cute little movie-quote exchange.

Wiley was exceptional in ways that Janae didn't know about – in ways that I longed to more than just *remember* – and I considered that maybe Janae thought she might like to sample a little bit of that action her own self. It was all ridiculous, of course, this jealousy: it was a product of my growing desire for my husband again. I thought everybody wanted him. I had no need for concern. It took two to tango, and I'd never doubted Wiley for a split-second; I'd never seen him even as much as look at another woman. I'd never heard him say anything but mocking remarks about any of them.

But he'd looked at Janae. I'd seen the appreciative smile on his face when he'd beheld her beauty – and she was beautiful – try as I might, I couldn't find a single flaw to her face or figure. She was taller than me, athletically built, with that luxurious reddish-blonde hair, and those gorgeous, dark green eyes. Wiley might've even said her name in his sleep last night, but that might've just been my hard-up paranoia. But here she was, changing Bo's diaper. If Wiley trusted her enough to leave his son in her care, I thought that she might be getting a little chummier with him than I cared for.

I went around the counter and paused in the doorway. Janae had just finished putting Bo's diaper on, and she tickled him. He kicked and gurgled in delight, and she impulsively kissed him on his tummy. I'd never for a moment cared who'd changed Bo's diaper in the past – that was just one more I didn't have to change. But when I saw this beautiful creature kiss his tummy, some groundswell of maternal instinct rose up in me – who was she that she thought she could be mommying *my* baby?

"Hey," I tried to say, but the word stuck. I cleared my throat. "Hey, Janae." She looked over at me, the happy smile that she'd been showing to Bo still on her face. I expected her expression to change, to become guilty, to reveal to me with a glance that she was using Bo to get at his father. But her expression didn't change, and his father wasn't even here. She was just a nice girl. She liked my baby, and didn't mind helping out while Wiley ran errands for her grandfather. I was just being insane.

"Hey, Brendee!" she said with enthusiasm. She picked Bo up and turned him around so he could see me. "Who's that?" she said and kissed the side of his face. Bo giggled. "Who's that? Is that your mama? Let's go see your mama!" She crossed the small room and handed him to me.

"Thanks for changing him, Janae," I said, gratitude returning to replace my crazy suspicious thoughts. She was okay.

"It's nothing," she said. "He's adorable!" She kissed Bo on the cheek again.

"Wiley's supposed to be–"

"Wiley's a great dad," Janae said, as if I hadn't even spoken. "I have to warn you that I think he's fallen under Tommy's influence, however."

"Wiley's not easily influenced–"

91

"Tommy is persuasive, though. He has the voice, the logic, the rhetoric of a zealot." She tickled Bo again, and when I didn't reply, she looked at me. "Let's just say that I don't think you're gonna be feeding him too much more jarred baby food."

"What?" I asked, totally confused. "What's wrong with his baby food?"

"Tommy has a vendetta against food additives. To make a long, sad story short, he's convinced that they led to his wife's cancer."

"What does that have to do with–"

"He's been preaching to Wiley all day. *The industrialization of the palate begins in infancy,"* Janae intoned.

"The industrial – what?"

Janae shook her head. "It's not important. I'm just warning you. He's been telling Wiley about the chemicals in the *Gerber,* and I wouldn't be surprised if Wiley decides to drop baby food like a bad habit, just for Tommy. He has that effect on people. He can be very convincing."

"Wiley's not easily convinced," I maintained, still wondering what the hell she was talking about. No baby food? Who *are* these people? I heard the bell over the door ring, and thought I might give Wiley a piece of my mind about leaving his son with a bunch of crazy-talking hippies. No baby food? *What the hell?*

Janae and Bo and I stepped out of the office. But it wasn't Wiley who had come in. It was a woman: I estimated her to be in her mid-fifties. She was tall, like Janae – sometimes I felt like the shortest woman in the world – everybody was taller than me. She was well proportioned, but trim, and she was wearing a plain blue t-shirt and jeans. She wasn't trying to show off her nice figure. She was pretty, but a trifle severe – she wasn't wearing make-up, her gray hair was done up in a tight bun, and she didn't smile at us. She just nodded and said evenly, "Janae."

Janae didn't smile either. "Dionne."

"Where's–"

"It's not my day to watch him," Janae said.

Dionne looked expectantly at me. "He's in the . . . the baby aisle," I said, figuring that she was asking after the proprietor.

"The what?"

"He's with a customer," Janae supplied.

"Right." Dionne turned her back on us and started down the aisle.

"She's got a crush on Tommy," Janae informed me under her breath. "But he's not interested." Just then, Tom and Deneen emerged from the other side of the store, neither of them empty-handed. "Dionne's looking for you," Janae told him.

"Is it too late to hide?" he whispered.

Janae nodded behind him. He took a deep breath, and turned around. He offered that killer smile to Dionne, and I thought, despite his and Janae's derision, he was not unhappy to see her. This impression was further reinforced when he gave her a big hug. Janae frowned.

"I'm gone for a few days and I come back to find you surrounded by beautiful young women," Dionne said coquettishly, as she and Tom came back to the counter, arm in arm. "Some of them not even related to you." She looked dubiously at Janae.

"All spoken for, unfortunately," Tom said. "I'd like you to meet Mrs. Royce, and the soon-to-be Mrs. Osbourne. And of course you already know Janae." He winked at his granddaughter. "This is my good friend–" I watched Janae's frown turn to a scowl, "– Dionne."

Dionne ignored Janae and shook our hands, and Deneen and I told her to call us by our first names. When I went to introduce Janae to Deneen, Janae said, "We know each other from high school. I talked to Nate this morning. He didn't mention that he was getting married. Isn't that just like a man? To let a single girl think she still has a chance? Congratulations!"

"We haven't set a date yet," Deneen said. "We're waiting until after . . ." but then she faltered in her always-ready story about trying to have a baby. Maybe she suddenly felt the same way I did, that she didn't want this *single girl* knowing too much about her business. Or Nate's. "We haven't set a date yet," Deneen repeated, and let it go at that.

The bell tinkled and Wiley and Nate came in, burdened by cardboard boxes, no doubt full of components with which to *wire the store*. My precocious boy kicked in delight, seemed to point at his dad. He said, "Goo!"

Wiley smiled and said, "Greetings, my son!" He never used baby talk, always spoke to Bo as he would to anyone else, as if he understood every word. Wiley set the box on the counter, and kissed Bo on the forehead. Then he said, "Greetings, my wife," and kissed me on the forehead, too.

Wiley was glad to see us, as he always was, but the look on Nate's face told a different story. He looked at Deneen, then at Janae

– guiltily, I thought – then back at Deneen. Now that was a curiosity – what did Nate have to be guilty about? But then I thought maybe I'd misread guilt for embarrassment. Maybe Nate assumed that Deneen had been regaling his old friend from high school with tales of their short, scheduled baby-making sessions, just like she did me.

Don't worry, Nate, I thought with a little smile. *We old married women are a little suspicious of* single girls, *even if their interest in our husbands might be innocent. Deneen kept her mouth shut for a change.*

"Thanks for letting me watch Bo, Brendee," the single girl said, and gave us a completely unexpected hug. Bo grabbed her beautiful hair, and she gently extracted it from his hand, and kissed him on his nose. Bo blinked and smiled. "It was nice seeing you again, Deneen. Nate. Wiley." I tried to detect something extra in her good-bye to my husband, but there was nothing there. "I have to study. But I'll see you guys soon!" She gave Tom a hug and a big sloppy kiss, just like her mother was wont to do. As an afterthought, she said, "Dionne."

"Janae."

We told Janae good-bye and she left the store.

"Look at the books Tom found for me, Nate," Deneen said, setting them on the counter. "There's Mr. Spock–"

"Doctor Spock, Denny," Tom corrected gently. Nate looked at him in surprise to hear him use his pet name for Deneen. Just like he had Wiley, it seemed that Tom had instantly befriended Deneen. He was just that charming.

"Really?" Deneen said. "Not the pointy-eared guy? My dad likes that ancient space show. That's where I thought I'd heard the name."

Tom shook his head. "Doctor Benjamin Spock. He was a household name in baby care, right up until he died."

"In . . .?" Nate said.

Tom took his phone out of his pocket, typed for a moment. "He died in 1998, aged ninety-four. He was *an American pediatrician whose book,* Baby and Child Care, *published in 1946, is one of the best-sellers of all time. Throughout its first fifty-two years,* Baby and Child Care *was the second-best-selling book, next to the Bible. Its message to mothers is that 'you know more than you think you do.'"* Tom smiled at Deneen. "It's a good one."

Nate thumbed through the dark-blue-covered hardback. "It says, *The Common Sense Book of Baby and Child Care,"* he noted.

94

"That was the original name," Tom said with a grin. "This is a used bookstore, Nate. That's practically a first edition."

Deneen showed a couple more baby care books to Nate, more modern ones. I noticed that she left a small, tattered, leather-bound one on the counter, and didn't point it out to him. "How much do I owe ya, Tom?" she asked, and covered it up with the others. It was odd behavior on Deneen's part, and I wondered what it was she was attempting to hide.

"Ten bucks oughta cover it," Tom replied.

"Show me how to work the cash register," Wiley requested, taking Deneen's credit card from her.

"I'm sure you can figure it out, Wiley," Tom said in surprise.

Dionne said to Deneen, "How can you, in good conscience, want to bring a baby into–"

"You don't have a dog in this fight, Dionne," Tom warned. Dionne shut up.

Wiley said, "Please sign the pad thing, Deneen." He'd figured the cash register out, just that quickly.

She complied, then said, "We've gotta go . . ." She smiled at Tom. "Last time, Tom. I promise." She took a bewildered Nate by the arm and quickly left the store.

We all looked at Tom for explanation. Even Bo. He grinned, looked sheepishly down at the counter for a moment. "That little black one? It's a spell book. Magic." He waved his hands to indicate spookiness. "I got it from *Mohini's House of Dreams,* over on Orange. The occult bookstore."

"The competition?" Wiley asked.

Tom shook his head. "That's *all* they sell, competition-wise. Spell books. Stuff about rituals. The history of witches and magic. They mostly sell robes and candles and incense.

"British journalist Malcom Muggeridge said, *One of the peculiar sins of the twentieth century which we've developed to a very high level is the sin of credulity. It has been said that when human beings stop believing in God they believe in nothing. The truth is much worse: they believe in anything.*

"I don't know if Denny believes in any of that shit. But I thought it might take her mind off of all these time tables. I thought that some magic might bring the *mood* back a little bit. Norman Mailer said, *Good fucks make good babies."* I blinked at the profanity and Tom grinned at me, not embarrassed at all. I had a beautiful baby, so it only followed that Wiley and I . . .

"Deneen's supposed to say a few words, light a few candles; don a diaphanous gown. All the better to invoke the spirits to aid in conception. I thought it might be a nice change for Nate, too."

"You are a piece of work," Dionne said and shook her head in amazement.

Tom grinned at her. "I found that cookbook for you." He opened a drawer behind the counter and brought out a thick, hardbound book. *"The Joy of Cooking. 1946 Edition."*

"Now I know *that's* online," Wiley said, apropos of nothing.

"Not this one, my friend," Dionne said.

"Probably not," Tom agreed. "This one shows you how to field dress game."

Wiley blanched. "I'm a vegetarian," he said defensively.

"In other words, he has someone else field dress his game," Tom told Dionne.

"No game, Tom." Wiley still looked pale, appalled. "Some cows and chickens, maybe–"

"It shows you how to clean those wild-caught fish, too," Tom said.

"No fish," Wiley said and they grinned at each other.

They're like twins, I thought. *Already. They have their own little language. What the hell are they talking about?*

"I was wondering if you'd like to have dinner at my house tonight, Tom?" Dionne asked, all coy.

"It's not that canned stuff again, is it?"

"You fed Tom *canned* food?" Wiley asked. Rudely, I thought.

"Dionne's a survivalist," Tom told us. "She's got a little place up in the mountains, all prepared for Armageddon."

"That's the word, Tom. *Prepared.* We don't call ourselves *survivalists* anymore. Now we're called *preppers.* "

Tom grinned at Wiley again. *"A rose by any other name . . ."* Wiley grinned back. Tom sighed. "That's why she wanted that ancient cookbook. She wants to know how to kill the fatted calf without *Oscar-Mayer's* help, once the crack of doom has sounded."

"You'll be sorry you don't know how to do it, when there aren't any supermarkets anymore," Dionne predicted ominously.

"My friend made me a fabulous dinner once," Tom told Wiley and me. "All from her survivalist – I apologize. All from her *prepper* stores. Just to show me how *good* it all tasted."

"Some of that stuff has a thirty year shelf life," Dionne said proudly.

96

"My point exactly." Tom looked at Wiley again, and Wiley rolled his eyes.

"But it tasted great," Dionne said. "Didn't it?"

Wiley looked shocked. "You ate it?"

"Of course I did, Wiley. Dionne spent all day re-hydrating it and warming it up for me. How could I refuse?"

"It's not all dehydrated, Tom," Dionne said.

Tom shrugged. "If Armageddon arrives and there's nothing left to eat but food with a thirty-year shelf life, then I'll just climb aboard that pale horse." He smiled kindly at her. "Why don't you let me take you out to dinner, Dionne?"

"That would be great, Tom!" she said in pleased surprise.

"Say six o'clock?"

"Okay! I'll be here at six!" Dionne practically skipped from the store.

Tom shook his head, sighed, looked down at the counter.

"Aw, don't be like that, Tom," Wiley said. "She likes you. She wants you to–"

"I know what she wants, Wiley."

"Well, what's wrong with that? She looks like she'd be a fun old gal!"

Tom tilted his head and looked at my husband thoughtfully for a moment. "Do you believe in an afterlife, Wiley?"

Wiley blinked. "You mean, like heaven and hell?"

Tom tilted his head back. "In its most rudimentary form, I guess. I don't believe in a white-bearded, be-sandled and robed deity, nor angels with wings and harps. What I believe . . . Where I come from, the prevalent belief is that when one dies, one's essence, one's energy, one's *spirit*, for lack of a better word, simply melds with the greater energy, the greater nothingness of all the others that have died before. There is no reward, no punishment, no heaven, no hell, no angels or demons. Just an anonymous blending of energy. Peaceful oblivion. I guess you could say that they believe that when you die, you simply become one with the universe, another particle in the great void.

"But since I came here, after I met Liz . . . Now I believe that there *is* a reward or punishment once we die, but it's not based on adherence to or violation of any prevailing morality of the moment. The only reward after death is to be reunited with the one we loved in life, in whatever form we might take, energy or light or whatever."

97

Tom paused, and we waited patiently for him to go on. "Liz is waiting for me, Wiley. I believe that. I have to believe it."

Wiley shook his head. "If you believe it, I'm happy for you. But all I see is a miserable, lonely old man."

"Wiley!" I hissed, stunned by his disrespect.

But he just went on. "How can you believe that any plane of existence was created – by whatever power you believe created it – so you'll be miserable here in anticipation of the next plane? What are you, Tom, an Untouchable? Do you believe you're gonna be reborn into a better life than this vale of tears, if you just suffer through it?"

"No, Wiley," Tom said quietly. "I said that I believe that Liz is waiting for me."

"How do you know? You don't know. It's *the undiscover'd country from whose bourn no traveler returns.*"

Wiley took in my shocked expression. How could he be so cruel? But still he continued. "I can only imagine the soul-crushing pain of her loss, Tom," he said seriously. It was more serious than I'd ever seen him. "I've never lost anyone, so I can only imagine, and it must be horrible. But even if she is waiting for you – do you think that she'd want you to be miserable and lonely for the rest of your life, until the time comes for you to join her? I'm sure she was a wonderful woman – I get that just from your sorrow at her loss. So I'm sure she wouldn't want you to be unhappy and lonely. I'm sure she'd like to see you have someone like Dionne for . . . company."

"It wouldn't be fair to Dionne, Wiley."

Wiley snorted. "You're ridiculous, Tom," he said harshly. "It wouldn't be fair to Dionne that you've decided that you're gonna meet Liz in heaven? After you *die?* Listen to yourself."

"Still–"

"Why don't you explain it to Dionne and let her decide? I don't think she's as metaphysical as all that. I don't think she cares about who you want to be with after you're dead. I think she cares about who you want to be with *now.* And she wants it to be her."

Tom smiled. He wasn't offended, but I was. Wiley's superiority was showing again – he didn't believe in an afterlife, and he wasn't averse to telling Tom what he should believe, either. It was just offensive. He didn't see anything wrong with belittling the man's grief, his hope.

"I asked her out to dinner, didn't I?"

"Are ya gonna go for it?" Wiley asked. When Tom hesitated, he said, "Will ya at least think about it?"

Tom shrugged. "Maybe you're right. Liz wouldn't want me to be lonely . . ."

"You can tell Dionne that if she wants to live long enough to see the apocalypse, she'd better stop eating all that preserved food." Wiley grinned and now Tom grinned, too. "Just think! Another convert!"

Bo began to whimper a little bit. It was time for him to eat, and I was reminded of Janae's cryptic comments about his baby food. "Bo's hungry, Wiley," I said cautiously. "Did you feed him his bananas yet today?"

Wiley shook his head. "Not today." He looked at his hungry boy. "He had a real banana. No more bananas in jars."

Tom smiled. "Take the rest of the day off, Wiley. Go visit the produce aisle."

"Thanks, Tom. Same time tomorrow?"

Tom nodded. "Don't go nuts – I've got plenty of stuff growing at home. Google *How to make your own baby food*. Do you have a blender?"

****

I wasn't quite prepared to address this *making your own baby food* issue just yet. I'd thought for a moment that Wiley was going to suggest that I go back to nursing Bo. I knew all the pediatricians recommended it for a year, but I was done. Bo was old enough for his own food. I was relieved that Wiley hadn't suggested that insane alternative – he hadn't said anything yet – and making our own baby food didn't seem so bad in the face of the idea of going back to all that earth-mother absurdity. But still, the idea of making one's own baby food seemed unnecessarily difficult to me, yet here we were on our way to the grocery store. I just got groceries. Wiley wasn't ready to discuss it yet, and I thought it best to just let it ride until he let me know what was on his mind. Making our own baby food. What were we, cavemen?

I said, "Maybe Tom just isn't thrilled with Dionne."

Wiley smiled. "She looks like she'd be fun. She looks like a tough ol' gal."

I considered. Who did I know that was Tom's age? I figured him to be in his late fifties. I mentally went through all the older

99

ladies at work; but none of them qualified. They were all either married, or . . . uptight. I thought it would take a special lady to appreciate Tom. He was one minute *high-falutin'*, like my grandmother used to say, trading obscure movie quotations with Wiley and discussing the afterlife. The next he was quite down to earth, attempting to help poor Nate enjoy getting laid again. I didn't think any of the older ladies at the firm would get Tom.

My grandmother was a widow. My grandfather had passed suddenly, right before I was born, and Grandma Corrine had never remarried. But she'd always seemed rather a stick-in-the mud to me, severe, also uptight, not overly happily. She would never do for Tom.

And then I thought of my Great-aunt Rae, my grandmother's sister. In contrast, she was a jolly, happy old lady. She wasn't married – she'd been divorced since before I was born. She'd never had a boyfriend that I ever saw, growing up. Her only companion was a tall, blonde, purple-eyed woman named Iris. My dad had once wondered aloud to my mom if perhaps Great-aunt Rae and Iris were lesbians, and my mom had had a laughing fit at that one. "Not only is Rae not gay," she'd said, "we have similar tastes in men." She'd kissed my dad on the cheek and spoke no more about it. Apparently, he knew what she was talking about.

For as long as I could remember, Great-aunt Rae had never forgotten our birthdays; she'd never missed a Christmas; she'd always been there with presents for us. And despite being single and not a lesbian, she'd always had a smile on her face. No one in my life had every seemed more happy to me than my Great-aunt Rae. I thought she'd be a perfect match for Tom.

I said as much to Wiley, and he grinned. He had his own reasons for liking Great-aunt Rae. They were akin to why he was so fond of my mom.

I called Rae, and when she answered, the first thing I said was, "I've found the perfect man for you."

She giggled. "Not again, Brendee! You're just like your mom. Always trying to fix me up. I'm old. I don't need a man. *The hey-day in the blood is tame, it's humble, and waits upon the judgment.*"

I blinked. "That's just what he said," I told her. "See? You even think alike." I reminded myself to ask Wiley what that was from.

Aunt Rae sighed. "Who is this guy, Brendee?"

"He's very bright, Rae. He owns a bookstore, over there on–"
"Morry's Books?"

"Yes." I wasn't surprised that she knew of it. It was the only bookstore in town.

"Are you trying to fix me up with Tom Bastion, Brendee?"

Again I blinked. "You know Tom?"

"Not well," Aunt Rae said, laughing. "We went out to dinner once. Years before you were born. He was quite the looker back then – he had black hair and big, blue eyes. But we didn't seem to have too much to say to each other during dinner. Then his daughter came into the restaurant – she had purple hair – and Tom had to give her all the money in his wallet to get her to leave. She even took his doggie bag.

"He explained that she was staying with him – I guess he lived above the bookstore. He said she was just out of rehab or something. He said she had friends that came by at all hours of the night. I wasn't really anxious to get involved with any of that, Brendee. I'd just gotten divorced myself. And since we didn't seem to have too much in common – even though he was cute – nothing ever came of it. I used to go in *Morry's* every now and then to say hi, to see if his daughter had moved out yet. But he always said she was still there, still in trouble. He never asked me out to dinner again."

"His daughter's all grown up now, Rae. She has her own daughter, my age."

"Thanks, Brendee. But no thanks."

"He's so smart, though!" I insisted. "Very spiritual. He was telling Wiley how he believes his wife is waiting for him in heaven."

"We all have someone waiting for us in heaven, Brendee. That's one of the reasons why I'm not interested in . . . How is Wiley, by the way?"

Ah, yes. *How is Wiley, by the way?* Aunt Rae asked after Wiley the same way my mother did, with an entirely inappropriate, entirely unconscious wistfulness to it.

My mother had gaped open-mouthed at Wiley, the first time she'd met him. She'd been amazed, astounded, and probably more than a little aroused by his resemblance to Wes Thomerville. My mom had been Wes's biggest fan, or so the legend went. The man she married – my dad – had blue eyes like Wes, had once been a musician like Wes; but there was nothing else that they had in common. But the man her friend Amy had married *had looked just like Wes,* and their son, to my continuing, daily joy, also looked just like him.

My mother had dragged Aunt Rae out to see Wes's band, weekly, according to family history, and she had also been quite impressed with him, despite the fact that she was old enough to be his . . . *his mother's baby sister,* she used to say. I often wondered what it must've been like, to see Wes live; to see him perform something else besides the three thirty-five of *My Disgrace.* That was incredible enough, but to see him in person, to talk to him . . . That must've been awesome.

How is Wiley, by the way?

"He's fine," I said. Wiley grinned at me.

"He most certainly is," Aunt Rae said, and giggled like a school girl.

Aunt Rae, who was not his mother-in-law, who was old enough to be his grandmother, was thereby a little more acknowledging of Wiley's attractiveness than my mom, who pretended, unsuccessfully, to ignore it. She tried to maintain her dignity around him. But they both asked after him the same way, with that little sigh. Wiley loved it.

"So you're not interested in Tom?" I said.

"Not in this world or the next," she said. "But thanks for thinking of me."

I told her that I thought about her all the time, that I loved her, and said good-bye.

****

I carried Bo through the grocery store, and Wiley pushed the cart. If it was just the two of us, I'd put him in the little seat, but I preferred to carry him otherwise. I thought it was more comfortable for him than the metal cart.

Wiley went down the baby food aisle first, and for a moment I actually believed that he'd given up this whole *making your own baby food* idea. It was 2038, for God's sake – nobody made their own baby food anymore. Had anybody *ever* made their own baby food? I knew my mom hadn't. Maybe platinum-blonde Maxine – once purple-haired and a delinquent, according to Aunt Rae – maybe she'd been hippie enough to waste her time with such activities when Janae was a baby. But my mother had had four, the first two very close together, and she hadn't had time for such foolishness. *Gerber* had been good enough for us – we'd all turned out all right.

102

But Wiley didn't put any jars in the cart. *Gerber* had conveniently divided up what they peddled by age: Bo was old enough for food from this section, but wouldn't be old enough for the selections from that section until he was a year old, then a toddler, and so on. Wiley was just checking what he could have now. He was all right with *Gerber's* recommendations – he just, all of a sudden, wasn't all right with their products.

I watched Wiley scan the labels. There were sweet potatoes, apples, pears, green beans, carrots, peas, bananas, plums on the first foods shelf. Bo loved all of those, except for the peas. He tended to spit those out. The next row were the second foods – I had already tried a few of those, too: the same ones as the first foods, only in bigger jars, plus apple-strawberry-banana blend, garden vegetables, mixed vegetables, squash, apples and cherries, potatoes and corn.

They also had what they called *Nutritious Dinners:* vegetable chicken, vegetable beef, chicken noodle. And meats: chicken, beef, ham and turkey, each in its own gravy. But Wiley was mostly a vegetarian, and wouldn't eat gravy, even on stuffing. And Bo was just starting to eat on his own, so I hadn't bothered with the nutritious dinners and the meats yet.

Wiley plucked a jar off the second foods self and looked accusingly at me. *"Mac and Cheese and Vegetables?* Really? You haven't give him–"

"No," I said. Wiley wouldn't eat mac and cheese any more than he'd eat gravy, so I wasn't going to feed it to his son. "But it says it's organic," I pointed out to him.

"Cancer's organic," he replied, mostly to himself.

He pushed the cart out of the baby food aisle without making a single choice, and it was then that I realized that he intended on going through with this *making your own baby food* ridiculousness. I followed him silently to the produce aisle, and watched him put bananas and avocados in the cart; apples, peaches, pears. Carrots. Potatoes. He considered the rest of the vegetables for a moment, then looked at Bo, as if Bo was gonna tell him what he wanted. "Skip the peas, Dad," I said for him. "I don't like peas."

I smiled at Wiley, but he didn't smile back. "He doesn't like *baby food* peas," he said darkly, then glanced around at the produce. "They don't sell fresh peas, anyway. We'll have to get frozen . . ." Wiley took out his phone, pushed buttons. "Do you grow peas?" Pause. "Okay. I'll see you tomorrow." He looked at me again. "Tom has peas. Those ones from dinner the other night were from his garden."

Wiley was talking to me – but he really wasn't. He was really just talking *at* me, not waiting for a reply. He was single-minded in this shopping trip, preoccupied. He didn't care to discuss it with me yet. "Let's get him some *Cheerios.*"

There were about nine different kinds of *Cheerios*. Wiley picked up the simplest box and looked at the ingredients, then took out his phone and called Tom again. "What's a tocopherol?" Pause. "Okay. Thanks." Wiley hung up and threw the box into the basket.

Since it seemed like he wasn't going to enlighten me on his own, I asked, "What's a tocopherol?"

"Tom says it's Vitamin E." He looked at the basket full of fruits and vegetables, and one box of *Cheerios*. "Do we need anything else?"

"I just went to the store, Wiley. We have everything we need, already." *Including a shelf full of baby food,* I thought.

I waited until we went through the line, paid, went out to the car, were on our way home. Then I asked, "What's going on, anyway?"

He hadn't clued me to anything. He didn't know that Janae had said something to me about baby food, about Tom's paranoia concerning food additives.

"No more bananas in jars." That's all Wiley had said to me.

He considered me silently for a minute. At last he said, "Who's the smartest person you know, Brendee?" I just looked at him and he smiled. "I've always thought that I eat pretty well. No fast food, no junk food. Just chicken, veggies, fruits. *Fish.*" He grinned to himself. It had to be some kind of inside joke between him and Tom.

"But I found out today that I'm just as much of a sheep as Deneen."

"Baa," I said.

"Baa," Bo said from his car seat.

I turned around and looked at him; Wiley looked at him in the rearview mirror. *"Baa,"* he said.

"Goo!" Bo said. It was just a coincidence, just a baby sound. My son had not just *baa-ed* at me, like his father was always doing, whenever he wanted to point out my conformity, and his lack of it.

"My mother always taught me to read the labels on food," Wiley continued.

Here it comes, I thought. *Janae was right.*

"She taught me that sodium and sugar, fat – they were all bad for me. But Tom says that she didn't teach me to read far enough down the labels." He looked over at me again. "Did you ever taste Bo's bananas, Brendee?"

"No, Wiley. Bo's almost always out of bananas. You're always eating them."

"That's 'cause *they're grrreat.*"

"Then why don't you want him to have them anymore?"

"You've been living in a dream world, Neo." Wiley had made me sit through *that* one, more than once. Some dumb old movie, where all of reality was just a construct of a computer. "Bo's bananas aren't real, Brendee."

"What are you talking about, Wiley?" I asked. Sometimes listening to him was like trying to build a conversation out of crossword puzzle clues. Sometimes, I wished he'd just get to the point.

"I'm always trying to get you to eat better, right? You'll eat a salad if you can put some Ranch on it; you'll eat your peas and carrots if you can put some butter on them. Nothing's tastier than candied yams to you, or a big baked potato, smothered in sour cream."

"And? So?"

"You know why you don't like vegetables by themselves, Brendee?"

"Will you just get to the point, Wiley, for Christ's sake?" I snapped. I was beginning to get annoyed. I found that I'd been becoming easily annoyed with him lately.

He reacted to my impatience, something that he usually didn't do. Wiley liked to build up to his conclusions, to pad them with obscure proofs; and if we became bored waiting for him to explain what he was getting at, that was just one more demonstration of our sheepish ignorance. Fuck us if we couldn't take a joke. It was just how he was.

But now he looked over and frowned at my peevishness. "Here's the point," he snapped back. "They put chemicals in our food to make it taste good. So we learn to like the taste, and we avoid real, nutritious foods in favor of those artificial flavors. Bo's bananas don't taste like bananas; I don't want him eating that shit anymore. He can eat real bananas."

"And this is all just because Tom said? You've never been so easily led before, Wiley. You've never been such a . . ."

105

He looked over at me again, almost daring me to say it. Were we having an argument? We'd never had an argument before. We'd had disagreements – Wiley had subjected me to his withering sarcasm and rapier wit enough times, when he found my thoughts on something to run differently than his. And usually, I would come around to his way of thinking, because he was usually right, usually more logical than me.

But now he was just making me angry. He wanted to change my son's routine because some hippie stranger he'd just met had told him about some off-the-wall conspiracy about poisoned baby food? This just wasn't like Wiley. I was shocked, dismayed, angry, all at once, that he was buying this bullshit wholesale. What was he gonna do next, suggest that we move back to his grandpa's farm?

"That's just what I'm telling you, Brendee. I *have* been a sheep. We all have. But not anymore. Not me, and not my son. It's called *industrialization–*"

"*Of the palate.* I know. Janae told me." He looked over at me in surprise. "She also said that Tom's been preaching this crap to you all day. That he's very persuasive. She said that Tom's convinced that food additives killed his wife, gave her cancer." I softened a little bit. "I'm sure that gives him some comfort, Wiley. But every day, you hear that something else causes cancer. The truth is, they *don't know what causes cancer.* And just because your new friend has imprinted on food additives as the cause – I'm telling you – it ain't necessarily so."

Wiley pulled up in front of our apartment building. He shut off the car and looked at me. "You don't understand, Brend."

Ah. There was that expression, the one that infuriated me whenever he said it. I could break it down, diagram it, just like we'd done in English class. *You.* That was the subject of the sentence: me. Me, apart from him, less than him, beneath him. Akin to a racist's *you people.* In fact, if he was talking down to Nate and Deneen and me, instead of just me, he'd use just that term: *you people don't understand.*

And then there was the verb, and the idea that it was negated: you *don't* understand. I was too stupid, incapable of the same high realms of cognitive thought as the inimitable Wiley Royce. And to underline that this was what he meant with the first three words, he'd always tack on *Brend.* He only called me *Brend* when he was annoyed with me.

106

Those four words pushed my angry button, and I doubted if Wiley even knew it. He didn't say them to me very often, but when he did . . .

I glared at him. "What don't I understand this time, Wiley?"

"I don't want Bo eating that shit anymore. I'm not kidding." He told me about the rice pudding experiment, and I just shook my head. I didn't think he was being very logical this time.

"Did Tom tell you how much they cost? Maybe the non-organic one was more expensive. Of a higher quality. Maybe that's why it tasted better."

Wiley shook his head, disgusted with my stupidity, and got out of the car. He took the groceries and Bo's diaper bag out of the trunk and went up the steps, leaving me and his son sitting in the car.

****

I stood in the doorway with the baby and watched him while he put the fruits and vegetables and *Cheerios* away. Then he turned around. "Look, Brend," he began. There was that shortening of my name again, and this time it was coupled with *Look*. It was another expression of his that I didn't like. Anytime Wiley said *Look* to me, I wasn't going to like what he was gonna show me. I wasn't gonna like whatever he said next.

"You can give him the rest of what we have. I've got something I have to take care of, and I'm not in the mood to Google *How to make your own baby food* right now. But I don't want him having any more of it. It's not about cancer. It's about being led by the nose and being too stupid to realize it."

Just who the fuck do you think you are, Wiley? I thought. *Telling me what you don't want my son to have, as if I wasn't his mother? As if I didn't have any say in it?*

I'd often thought of how Wiley and I had snuck around behind his parents' backs in high school. We'd engaged in a marathon sex escapade for nearly four days, our first, when they'd been out of town. But when they came back, even after he'd announced that we were going together, Wiley wouldn't kiss me, wouldn't even hold my hand in front of them. He wanted them to think he was still their good little boy with his very first girlfriend, when he was in reality a quite accomplished lover, a glorious, ravening beast. His parents hadn't known about what went on between him and the physical therapist.

I'd always figured that our first argument about what Bo was and wasn't going to be allowed to do would've come no sooner than high school. I thought that I wouldn't believe my blue-eyed son when he told me that he was just innocently watching movies with his girlfriends. Just like Tom had said, he was gonna be a heartbreaker. How could he be otherwise? He looked just like his dad.

I figured that Wiley would want to believe him, and we might've had a disagreement over that, maybe even an argument. I didn't think it would start so soon. *Over baby food.*

"What is it you have to take care of?" I asked.

"I told this guy that came into the store that I'd fix his phone for him. I left it there. I need to go get it, figure out what's wrong with it."

"Tom's got a date, Wiley–"

"I've got a key." He kissed Bo on the forehead. "I'll be back later."

Then he turned and walked out.

It *was* our first argument.

NATE

Wiley called and asked me if I wanted to go back to the electronics store with him before it closed. I asked Deneen if I had to service the cause at any particular time this evening – she'd been a little pissed that I'd been late getting back to the store, and the whole thing had been even more rushed than usual. But she smiled at me now, ran her hand across my back. "Just don't be too late," she said. "I have a surprise for you when you come back."

"Are you?" I said. "You're not?"

"Not yet," she said. "Go on, now. Just don't let Wiley keep you out too late."

I told Wiley I'd meet him downstairs. Wiley was not one to be staying out all night anyway. He had a wife and son waiting for him at home.

But we didn't go to the electronics store. We went back to *Morry's*. The place was closed – I figured that Tom made his own hours – and Wiley let himself in with his key. He retrieved Josh's phone from the drawer in the counter, put it in his pocket. Then he took his own phone out of his other pocket, typed on it, scrolled, waited. He typed some more, scrolled some more, waited again. I was just about to say something, to ask him what the hell he was doing, when he looked up at me and smiled. He held up his finger, pushed the *Call* button on his phone.

"Hey, Janae. This is Wiley." Pause. "Tom gave it to me." Wiley winked at me, and I realized he'd just that moment searched for and found Janae's number by some other, probably illegal, means – Tom had most certainly *not* given it to him.

"Are you busy?" Wiley was saying. "I wondered if I might come over and talk to you for a minute." Pause. Wiley plucked a pen from the counter, and wrote Janae's address down on a little pad beside the cash register. "Thanks. I'll be right there."

Wiley turned off the lights, locked the door, and we went back out to his car. He looked at me over its roof. "Brendee and I just had a little fight, Nate," he said. "I told her that I didn't want Bo eating jarred baby food anymore, and she called me a sheep for just following along with what Tom told me. She said that Janae said that Tom blamed food additives for his wife's cancer."

"We heard him say that to her, Wiley."

"But he didn't say that to us, did he? He just talked about how Bo wasn't going to like good food if he ate all this shit now." Wiley shook his head. "It makes sense to me, but Brendee intimated that maybe it was Tom's grief and not any basis in fact that makes him so adamant about it.

"But what he's talked about so far . . . It's not about getting cancer. It's about getting hoodwinked. *If the old dog barks, he gives counsel.* Still . . . Maybe Tom *abuses me to damn me: I'll have grounds more relative than this.* Let's go see what Janae's take on it is."

****

Janae's smile faltered when she opened the door and saw me standing behind Wiley. I immediately got the impression that she'd believed that he was gonna show up alone, and that she was more than a little disappointed that he hadn't. The idea of where she hoped *that* scenario would've led surprised me, but then I figured it was Wiley's own fault. He *had* said a few flirtatious things to her. But Janae was barking up the wrong tree. There was only one woman for Wiley. At least that's what he'd always told me.

Janae invited us into the house, and introduced me to her dad, who was sitting on the couch, watching TV. He turned it off, and invited us to sit. I watched Janae frown when Wiley plopped down in a chair. I took the other chair, and after a moment's hesitation, Janae sat on the couch next to her dad.

"I wanted to ask you guys something about Tom," Wiley began. "He told me about this food additives thing today."

"The industrialization of the palate," Janae supplied.

"Yeah. It made a lot of sense to me. But my wife said that you told her it's just some kind of obsession with him, that he blames it for his wife's death . . ."

"Tom's crazy, Wiley," Sam – Janae's dad – said softly. "He's delusional. Maybe even schizophrenic. We got him to talk to a professional once, after . . . They tried to give him anti-psychotics, but he wouldn't take them. He wouldn't talk to the shrink again, either." Sam paused, his eyes full of pain.

"I'm not going to sit here and listen to you bad-mouth Tommy, Dad." Janae rose. "There is not one thing crazy about him. I'm the second door on the left, Wiley. Come get me when my dad's done smearing my grandfather."

110

"He's not your grandfather, Janae," Sam said. But she'd already left the room. Sam waited for the door to slam, then continued. "Tom's delusional," he said again. "And it doesn't have anything to do with food additives. It's much worse than that. He thinks he's—"

"Napoleon?" Wiley said and grinned. He looked down the empty hall after Janae.

Sam shook his head. "I said he was crazy, Wiley, not illogical. Napoleon is dead. Tom's delusion goes beyond thinking he's some historical figure, whose life and death could be demonstrated to him. It's much worse than that. The Federales—"

"Federales?" Wiley ceased peering down the hall and looked back at Sam.

He nodded. "About two months before she died, Tom took his wife to Mapimi, Mexico. He got into an argument with an old man that lived on a ranch there – an actual fist fight, essentially. Details are sketchy, but I guess they restrained Tom on the ranch and called the law. Apparently Tom knew this old guy that he attempted to assault – Martin – and he took pity on Tom. He figured that this irrational behavior was all over Liz's illness.

"Martin and the Federales got in touch with us – my wife speaks a little Spanish – and the upshot of it was that they escorted him to the border and we took possession of him in San Diego. Martin refused to press charges, even though I guess the assault was pretty bad, and there was also some property damage; Tom caused some kind of fire. I guess they'd been friends once, and Martin didn't want to see Tom thrown in a Mexican jail when his wife was dying."

"What was the fight about?" I asked.

Sam looked at me, then back at Wiley – Tom's new best friend. His face was the picture of pity, of sadness. "Tom's the cleverest, most intelligent man I've ever known, Wiley. My daughter worships him, over and above her mere mortal, blood parents and grandparents. But she's young, like you are, and it's easy to overlook what you don't want to see when you're young and you love somebody. My wife and I have known him since we were your age.

"But even Maxine, who's also always worshipped him – even she couldn't ignore it, after we had to go all the way to San Diego to pick him up. I guess he'd driven his car into the side of the barn at Martin's ranch . . ."

Wiley exchanged a glance with me, then repeated what I'd asked. "What was the fight about?"

Sam sighed. "Like I say, details are sketchy, but it shakes out like this. Tom attacked his old friend Martin, burned his barn to the ground, because Martin refused to help him return to his *home world. To the planet Sirius.* If he could get Liz back to Sirius – that's *where he's from,* you see – then they'd cure her cancer."

"So you're telling us that Tom thinks he's–" I began.

"An alien. An extraterrestrial. From the planet Sirius."

Wiley raised his eyebrows mildly. *"Your tale, sir, would cure deafness."* But then he shrugged. Tom's delusion didn't seem to bother him overly. He surely wasn't shocked by it. "Is that all? There are worse things to believe you are than an alien," he observed. "A righteous man. Your brother's keeper."

Frowning, Sam glared at Wiley. "Liz was *dying,* and Tom dragged her all the way to the middle of Mexico for nothing. Through twelve hundred miles of heat and the dust. *For nothing.* He dragged her all the way to Mexico, because *he's nuts."*

Wiley shrugged. He remained unconvinced.

"Tom attacked Martin when he couldn't help him with this delusion, couldn't help him return to Sirius to save his wife. He had to be restrained. Money – *ransom almost* – was exchanged, and like I say, the Policia brought them to us at the border. Liz looked like a ghost, and Tom looked like a lunatic. Since none of it was on any kind of a record here, no one could compel him to seek any kind of professional help. He went once, for Maxine, but he never went back. He didn't like what the guy told him, I guess."

"Does he still talk about being from another planet?" I asked.

Sam shook his head. "No. Except for little oblique references that he makes, as digs at me. *No plastic on Sirius.* Max said he'd only mentioned it once before – Liz's cable was on the fritz on Christmas Eve, the first year they were together, and to amuse them, Tom told them this alien story. Max believed he was joking – it was just a yarn he told them when there was no TV. What else could she believe?

"But she told me that it had been a fully formed delusion, even then. He had histories and cultures made up for this planet he was from, ideologies, stories of wars with lizards and excursions to Earth. Explanations for every aspect of all that ancient aliens' bullshit.

"I'd never heard anything about it before the . . . *incident.* And since then . . . He didn't flesh it out for me. Maxine did. Tom and I don't talk the way we used to. He doesn't trust me anymore. I kinda flipped out on him for what he did. Like you can yell the crazy out of a person."

After a pause, Wiley said, "I appreciate the insight, Sam," and said no more.

Sam nodded. "I thought you should know. Before you take anything he says too seriously."

Wiley also nodded, rose. "Tell Janae thanks," he said.

****

We walked back out and got into the car. I waited. At last Wiley said, "Do you think Tom's delusional, Nate?"

I shrugged. "Sometimes I think *you're* delusional."

Wiley grinned gleefully. "Sometimes I think I'm from another planet, that's for damn sure." He sobered. "I mean, about the food additives. I don't care about the alien thing. Do you think it's all something he dreamt up? In grief, to find something to blame?"

"He didn't dream up that thing with the rice pudding," I said. "The one with no additives was awful. And the baby food . . . It didn't taste like bananas. He didn't preach to us about them causing cancer. He just talked about taste." I paused. Then I said, "Why don't you just ask him, Wiley? He seems like a logical person. If it's all a product of his grief . . . Maybe no one's ever pointed it out to him before. And if it's not . . ."

"If it's not, I'm just gonna have to learn to make my own baby food. By the time Bo's old enough to eat a steak, I'll have learned what all this shit really is, learned what not to eat . . . And he'll have learned to not eat it, too." We drove in silence for a while, then he said, "Brendee's pissed at me."

"Has that ever been a problem before?"

"She's never been pissed at me before. Not like this. She's never been big on me telling her what to eat, but she goes along with it, because I do most of the cooking. It was hard for her to give up all those boxed rices and pastas and cereals, though. Eat a bowl of strawberries instead of a bowl of *Cap'n Crunch,* for God's sake. That shit is all just too much carbs. We're not farmers, Nate, not ditch-diggers. We don't need as much food as we eat, no matter what's in it."

He'd been preaching this line to me since high school. I'd made the mistake of giving him a bologna sandwich once, and that's what started it. He'd told me that I ate too much, that I didn't need all the carbs and red meat. "It sticks in your guts. It makes you tired," he'd said. "Makes you slow. Maybe a little fish or chicken, lots of veggies, a few whole grains. That's really all you need."

And now Tom Bastion, perhaps delusional, had given Wiley another reason to watch what he ate, what little there was of it. And if he was watching what he ate, then Brendee and Bo were going to have to, also.

I thought it was a stupid thing for Brendee to want to argue with him about. Were they not all healthy, based on Wiley's food choices? But then again, I remembered what Tom had said – none of us were really unhealthy, no matter what we ate, until we got fat or got cancer . . . I shook my head. I didn't know if I was buying into this whole thing as much as Wiley was. I tended to believe it, but I'd need a little more proof of any danger. Sure, chemicals made stuff taste better. What was wrong with that?

But then I considered that maybe Brendee's anger with Wiley over this new thing was just the tip of the iceberg. Maybe there was something else she was pissed at him about – the job, maybe. Women are strange. They get pissed about the weirdest things sometimes.

Wiley pulled up in front of my building, and I sighed. I looked up at my apartment: it was dark, except for a little glimmering coming from the bedroom. Deneen was probably on her tablet, researching. I sighed again. Yes. Women are strange.

"I'm gonna start hanging the cameras in the store tomorrow," Wiley said. "You wanna supervise?"

I looked up at my apartment again. "If it fits in with Deneen's schedule."

Wiley slapped me on the back. "At least you're gettin' some, my son."

I looked at him in surprise and he tapped the side of his head. "All part of my plan."

But somehow, he didn't sound as sure, as confident, as he usually did. Maybe there *was* trouble in paradise.

****

When I unlocked the door, I was surprised to see splotches of color on the carpet, made visible by the pale glow from the streetlight outside. I flipped on the light and discovered that they were flowers: I recognized some daisies, and a couple Black-eyed Susans. Rose petals; red, white and yellow. There were some sprays of baby's breath, and various greenery. It looked like a bouquet had exploded all over the floor. Interspersed with the flowers, I noticed little slips of paper with arrows on them. I went in the direction they pointed.

Denny was standing in the doorway to the bedroom, wearing some filmy, purple, see-through thing. She had a garland of flowers in her hair, and was backlit by candlelight. She jumped up into my arms like she always did, and I saw over her shoulder that the room was ablaze with candles – there were some on the night stands, on the dresser, reflected by the mirror. Short, fat ones; tall, thin ones. Denny had been busy while I was gone.

I was just thinking about the danger of fire when she said, "Maybe we've been rushing this, Nate. I wanna do it slowly this time. Naturally."

And then she kissed me, and I didn't worry about the fire hazard, didn't worry about Wiley and Brendee and their problems, didn't debate whether Tom was delusional or not. "Slowly," Denny said again, and everything was forgotten except for her.

BRENDEE

It wasn't late when Wiley came home, but I was already in bed. I was feeling unusually tired. I figured that I was just worn out from walking around in the mall all day, listening to Deneen prattle on about ovulation. I was tired from arguing with Wiley.

He was quiet – Wiley was as graceful as a cat – and through the open door of our bedroom, I watched him pad softly down the short hall and check in on Bo. When he came back out, he paused in the shaft of light from the bathroom, and peered through the darkness in my direction. I knew he couldn't see me – if he wanted to find out if I was awake, he'd have to enter the room.

But I could see him. I noticed that his black hair was getting long again, curling behind his ears and along the side of his neck. I loved to wrap those curls around my fingers. Just like my mother and Aunt Rae had observed, Wiley was fine.

He took off his shirt and threw it in the hamper in the bathroom, then he took off his shoes, and set them neatly by the door. I thought about the first time I'd watched him through his webcam: he'd been shirtless then, too. Barefoot, like he almost always was. Wearing only a pair of white sweatpants, he'd let a trapeze that I hadn't even known existed down from the ceiling, and then proceeded to do the most amazing exercises on it; I remembered thinking how *strong* he must be. I was pretty sure he hadn't known I'd been watching him that first time.

The second time I watched him, he was again half-dressed, wearing only those phenomenal white sweats – and he'd practiced his Tai Chi, there in his dim bedroom. All the slow, graceful movements – it was the sexiest thing I'd ever seen. *He* was the sexiest thing I'd even seen.

Wiley knew I was watching him the second time, had called me to him.

Now, as he paused in the light from the bathroom, I sent the same message telepathically to him: *You know what I want, Wiley. Come get me. All is forgiven, you can feed Bo whatever you want, just . . .*

But he didn't know I was watching him this time, probably thought I was asleep. He wasn't attuned to my signal now. Wiley could always anticipate my desire; he always knew when I wanted him to make the first move, sometimes when I wasn't even aware of it myself. But not tonight. Maybe it had been too long; maybe his incredible instincts had gone dormant. Sex with Wiley had always been transcendental – why had I waited so long?

I watched him turn and go back out into the living room, and after a few minutes of hoping he'd come back, quite against my will, I drifted off to sleep.

****

Wiley's note said, *Wanted to get an early start. Come by the store and see us, if you'd like. Love you.*

I smiled. My first thought was what a great dad he was. His boy was his best friend, even though he wasn't much of a conversationalist yet. Then an acrid wisp of resentment floated across my mind, and my smile evaporated. I went out to the kitchen. Two of the avocados were gone, and two of the pears. But all the baby food was still there, in neat little rows on the shelf.

Maybe it wasn't love or responsibility that had motivated Wiley so much this time; maybe he'd been so anxious to take Bo along because he wanted to make sure that his evil mother didn't give him any poisoned baby food today. Whatever. I still felt a little tired, so I went back to bed.

NATE

We went to the electronics place to get parts for Josh's phone first, and we still beat Tom to the store by a good ten minutes. When he arrived, Wiley was sitting at the desk in the back, disassembling Josh's phone. I was holding Bo and watching his dad work.

Tom came into the office and said, "What *are* you doing here so early? *Six days shalt thou labor, and shalt do all thy works. But on the seventh day is the Sabbath of the Lord thy God: thou shalt do no work on it, thou nor thy son.*" He ruffled Bo's hair. Wiley looked dubiously at him. "Okay. How 'bout, *all work and no play makes Jack a dull boy?*"

"How 'bout, *hoes gotta eat?*" They grinned at each other. "Besides, I'm not working for you yet, today. I'm fixing Josh's phone. I need a ladder to work for you."

"There's one upstairs." He tossed Wiley his keys. "The blue one opens the security door; the black one opens the door to the apartment."

Wiley put them in his pocket, and went back to examining the insides of Josh's phone. He took a few little tidbits out of the bag from the electronics store; he removed a few little things from Josh's phone, stuck a few little things in. I really couldn't follow what he was doing. He attached a new, unstarred screen, then quickly put it back together. He pushed the power button and it came on; he scrolled the screen around and then looked up and smiled at us. "Voila! It's fixed. You can call Josh and tell him he can come pick it up, if you'd like, Tom. Two days early." He set Josh's phone on the desk.

Then he said, "Let's light this candle," and stood up. He took Bo from me and sat him down in his playpen. We went upstairs to fetch the ladder.

The apartment above *Morry's Books* was indeed tiny, just one oblong room, and a bathroom, plus a kitchenette with a stove with only two burners, and a hotel room sized refrigerator. There was a tiny balcony, and a nook with a brocade curtain around it, behind which I assumed was the bed. It had to be a huge bed, however, because it was a long curtain.

Against one wall were two large aquariums, empty. And across from them were two bookcases, also empty. Between the bookcases was an Egyptian mummy case; a marlin sailed above them on the wall. "Do you think those are real?" I asked Wiley. He shrugged.

In the middle of the room were various things one might put in storage: A mop and bucket, a stack of boxes: two said *XMAS* and one *Halloween* on the side. There was a big box fan, and a tall, rickety-looking wooden ladder. And a giant three-tiered tool box. Everything was coated with a thin layer of dust. Wiley opened the drawers to the tool box, one after another; he found a battery-powered drill and its charger; a hammer; assorted screwdrivers. He found a ratchet and swung it around by the socket on the end, just to hear the noise it made, like a little kid. He grinned at me.

I peeked behind the curtain around the bed – there was a wooden shelf for a headboard with a few books on it. The bed was neatly made, as if someone would be returning soon for their rest. But no one had slept here in a long time.

"What a cool little space!" Wiley marveled. "It reminds me of the attic at the farm. Very cozy. Very . . . private." He ran his finger through the dust on one of the shelves. "A little cleaning up, and who knows what a body could get up to in a little place like this." He wiggled his eyebrows at me. He put the tools in the bucket on the floor and went to fold up the ladder.

****

We re-entered the store through the side door. Tom had put Bo in his car seat, in its regular place under the window, and was handing him a bottle.

"What's in–" Wiley began.

"Water," Tom replied.

"Not from the–"

"No, not from the hundred and forty year old tap. Bottled. The plastic's not great for you, but Christ only knows what those pipes are made of."

Wiley looked up at the ceiling, then had me help him set up the ladder directly beneath a beam, in front of the counter by about fifteen feet. The beam ran parallel to an exposed pipe. He opened up the cardboard box full of components and extracted one of the cameras, still in a plastic bag. It was maybe three or four inches long, black, cylindrical, with a little rubber-covered antenna-looking thing on one side, and a round bracket with three holes for mounting screws. Wiley took off his shoes – Tom's eyebrows went up at that.

119

"Better to grip the rungs with, my son," Wiley said.

"Actually, he's just a monkey. He tries to never wear shoes."

"Are you a hippie, Wiley?" Tom asked.

Wiley snorted. "Hardly."

"A barefoot recycler, out to save the planet?" Tom insisted.

"What did you say, Tom? *I'm not here to save the planet. Shit, I can't even save myself.* I'm just trying to save a little ground for Bo to live on. Let me give you some landfill statistics sometime. I don't care about saving the planet. But I do recycle. And Nate's right. I like to be barefoot."

Wiley climbed up the ladder with the camera, then asked me to hand the drill up to him. He held the bracket against the beam, at the same time wrapping his fingers around it. He put a screw on the magnetic bit, went to drive it into the beam. But the drill was dead.

"Shit," Wiley said, and handed the drill back to me. He set the camera on top of the ladder, then looked at his fingers. They were positively black with dirt already, just from him wrapping his hand around the ancient beam. "Shit," he said again, as he climbed back down the ladder. "When was the last time someone cleaned up there, Tom?" He rubbed his gritty, filthy fingers together.

"World War I, maybe? Never, perhaps? Just think. This building's been here since at least 1900. That dust might have Spanish Flu spoor in it; radiation blown in from White Sands; Malathion – they used to spray that shit everywhere around here, trying to kill the Mediterranean fruit fly, in the late 1980s. Gotta protect that orange crop."

"How long have you owned this place, Tom?" I asked, while Wiley, without comment, went back into the office to wash his hands. I plugged the drill charger into an outlet built into the counter, and put the battery in it for him.

"The place has been in my family since it was built, but I've only been here since 2011. Before that, I was . . . somewhere else. But I'm a history buff, Nate. The story of your little town is fascinating. Did you know that the founders of Riverside intended it to be a sort of utopia?"

"Didn't the founders of every place intend it to be some kind of utopia?" Wiley asked.

"Dionne thinks she'll have utopia, up there in the mountains, after the bombs fall, or the social unrest burns civilization to its foundations, or however it's all supposed to end. She thinks she's gonna live like our forefathers again, all agriculture and fresh air. No electricity, no internet. The first thing I'd build would be a generator."

"And then a web server."

"After the tomatoes, the first thing I'd plant would be some tobacco." Tom grinned.

Wiley squinted at me quickly, then said, "Did I ever tell you that I grew up on a farm, Tom? From the time I was ten, 'til I was eighteen."

"Really? Me, too. A whole great, big agricultural community. But I was in my forties before I got away from it."

"Around here nearby somewhere, was it?" Wiley blinked innocently at him.

Tom shook his head. "No, as a matter of fact, it's rather a long way from here."

"Light years, maybe?"

Tom tilted his head and considered us for a moment. "You've been talking to Sam."

"Yup," Wiley said. "I was checking up on you."

"Why is that, Wiley?" Tom said, a trifle suspiciously. I couldn't blame him. No one likes to hear they're being checked on.

"Well, here's the deal. I've kinda fallen for your whole citric acid, tastebud-hijacking conspiracy; hook, line, and sinker. Got in an argument with my wife about it, when I told her that I didn't want Bo *eating his bananas* anymore. She suggested that maybe this theory of yours was a product of your sadness over the loss of your wife." Wiley paused, then said, "I figured that was possible. I imagine that someone who is grieving might look for something to blame for his grief. His terrible loss.

"So I went over to Janae's last night, to ask her what she thought about it. I asked her and Sam if they thought that this might be the case – that maybe you just needed to find a cause, a place to lay the blame . . . But before Janae could say anything about chemicals in our food, Sam said you were delusional, and she left the room."

"She said she wasn't going to listen to him bad-mouth you," I added.

"Janae's my biggest fan. That's *her* delusion." Tom smiled fondly. "You know, I really owe my life, such as it is, to Janae. When Liz died, I was paralyzed. I was unfamiliar with the customs here." He grinned humorlessly at us. "Maxine took care of all of it for me.

121

"After the empty, meaningless little ceremony, I went home and laid down in our bed; I tried to find Liz's scent in the sheets. But she'd been in the hospital for a week before she . . . died, and her smell was gone.

"What did Alex say in *A Clockwork Orange? Suddenly, I viddied what I had to do, and what I had wanted to do, and that was to do myself in; to snuff it, to blast off for ever out of this wicked, cruel world. One moment of pain perhaps and, then, sleep for ever, and ever and ever.* The only woman I would ever love was gone.

"The doctors had prescribed painkillers for her; she was in a lot of pain at the end. It was morphine – not phenobarbital like the Heaven's Gate people. Are you familiar with that story?" We shook our heads. "It was a religious sect. They committed mass suicide in 1997. They swallowed barbiturates with a vodka chaser, put plastic bags over their heads to ensure that there were no kind of survival slip-ups. The leader convinced them that they were going to catch a space ship that was trailing the Hale-Bopp comet. *As if.*" Again, Tom grinned without any humor.

"The morphine would've done it for me. But I thought the plastic bag was a good touch, so I had one ready. I didn't write a note. Words weren't necessary. Max would understand, and I couldn't possibly care less what Sam thought. I sat there on the bed that I'd shared for so long with Liz – my true love, my soul mate. I had a big tumbler full of gin – no vodka – I've always been a gin drinker, ever since I'd met Liz. It was her favorite. I had a whole bottle of morphine pills. I was just sitting there, smoking a final cigarette. I wasn't considering it – I'd already made up my mind. I was gonna do it, as soon as I finished that cigarette.

"But then the doorbell rang. Some flash of humor spiked through my head: I couldn't off myself before I answered the door. I'd read a story once where this guy thinks he's the only person left in New York City. He wanders around for days – nobody. So he decides to jump off a building; and on the way down he hears a telephone ringing. Who knew what could be waiting for me on the porch?

"Whoever they were, they weren't going to bring Liz back. But just like you said, Wiley – she was a wonderful person. She wouldn't want me to be lonely these days, and she wouldn't have wanted me to off myself over her then, in the first place, and she certainly wouldn't have wanted me to off myself before I found out who was at the door.

122

"So I staggered downstairs. I was quite drunk already – who commits suicide sober? I opened the door. It was Janae. She was only eight years old then, so I looked around for Max or Sam, figuring that one of them had brought her over. But I didn't see them. They only live a couple of blocks away, but she was too young to be walking over there by herself. I looked for their car. Max would've come up with her, but Sam wasn't talking to me. I figured maybe he was waiting until he saw that I'd opened the door, before driving away.

"But there was no car. 'Where's your mom, Janae?' I asked her.

"'I'm running away from home, Tommy,' she informed me, matter-of-factly. I noticed that she was carrying a little pink plastic suitcase. Minnie Mouse smiled up at me from the side of it.

"'Where are you running to?' I asked her.

"'I heard Daddy say, "If it was up to me, the men in the white coats would be taking Tom's crazy ass away, like yesterday."' She blinked up at me. 'So I asked, "Why do you want Tommy to go away, Daddy?" And they just looked at me. Like they looked at me that time I said the bad word.'

"That was also my fault," Tom said, and grinned a little sheepishly. "I'd been looking at something online, and had exclaimed, 'What the fuck is that?' Janae overheard me, and the very next time she saw something that confused her, she said, 'What the fuck is that?' in front of her mom and dad, which necessitated a little speech from them, something to the tune of, *Nice little girls don't say that, Janae. That's a bad word.*

"Janae told me that her mother said, 'Tommy is very sad because Liz went to heaven. He might have to go away for a while.'

"'I asked them where you were going, but they wouldn't tell me,' she went on. 'They told me not to worry about it. But I am worried about it. I'm sad, too, because Liz went to heaven. If you're going somewhere, I want to go with you. We can be sad together.'"

Tom paused. "I picked her up and gave her a hug. I told her we could be sad together, right here. We didn't have to go anywhere. I told her that we didn't have to be sad too long, because Liz wouldn't want us to be sad. I took her into the house, and called Maxine and told her where she was. She hadn't even missed her yet, thought she was out playing in the backyard.

"I made her a little snack and we watched TV. Maxine eventually came over to pick her up, and after Janae skipped out to get into the car with her little Minnie Mouse suitcase, I told her

123

mother, 'Tell Sam I said not to send the men in the white coats just yet. And after you tell him that, you can tell him I said he can fuck right off.'

"'You're drunk, Tom," she said. 'He's just worried about you. We both are.' Or some other meaningless platitude like that.

"I told her thanks for her concern, but I'd be all right. She gave me a hug and took her daughter back home. I went upstairs and dumped the gin out, flushed the morphine down the toilet. I've never considered *snuffing it* again. I've been sad sometimes, and I've wished my time would come, but even though Liz is gone, I realized then that I still have Janae. I have to stick around for her."

"She wouldn't listen to her ol' man talk shit on you," I reiterated.

Tom sighed. *"The loss of a friend is like that of a limb; time may heal the anguish of the wound, but the loss cannot be repaired."*

"Fuck him if he can't take a joke," Wiley said. Tom smiled. "So if Janae would never listen to her dad about you, then she doesn't know about . . . the Sirius thing?"

Tom shrugged. "I don't have any kids of my own, Wiley, but I have learned one thing. Adults – their parents, their parents' friends – we forget that they're there." He gestured at Bo in his car seat: he was sucking on his bottle, watching us.

"And up until they *stop* listening to us – before that, they listen all the time. Keenly. I'm sure Janae could recite entire conversations that her parents have had, when they didn't realize she was listening. She might not've understood what they were talking about at the time, but she remembered what they said until she did understand it. I'm sure she's heard Max and Sam discuss it." He shrugged again. "I don't know what she's heard. She's never mentioned it to me."

Wiley glanced quickly at me, then he said, *"Are* you from Sirius, Tom? Sam said you got in a fist fight with some guy in Mexico because he wouldn't help you get back to–"

"I was misled on that. Forget about Sirius for a minute – let's just say that I'm not from around here, okay?" We nodded. "Let's just say that, in order to get back to where I'm from, I had to get in touch with Martin, there in Mapimi. So I did. There'd never been any trouble with going back before – like I told you, Wiley, my . . . for lack of a better word, my *uncle,* Morry – he went back. We had a big party in Vegas, then I drove him to Mapimi, and Martin sent him back home.

"Then I came back here, and I met Liz . . .

124

"When she was first diagnosed, I got in touch with Martin. It took about a month for him to get back to me. Communication is not the best between here and Mapimi – I had to talk to one guy, then he had to talk to another guy, then they had to go out to the ranch and talk to Martin. It's still the third world down there, for Christ's sake. But eventually the messages were exchanged: I said I wanted to go back to . . . to go back *home,* and he said he'd make the proper arrangements. I knew that they could cure Liz there."

Wiley exchanged another glance with me.

"But when we arrived, Martin said that he hadn't realized that I wanted to take Liz with me. *'Usted ha dicho nada acerca de traer a esta mujer extranjera. Ninguna persona que haya nacido aquí es bienvenida allí,'* he told me indignantly. *'You said nothing about bringing this foreign woman. No person who is born here is welcome there.'*

"Like he knew what the fuck he was talking about. He'd never been there. He's nothing but a meet-and-greet, someone who plucks us out of the desert, gives us some clothes, some money, then sends us on our way. Out of gratitude for his simple services, I put his fucking granddaughter through college, for Christ's sake." Tom looked at us for a moment, guiltily, as if he'd said too much. He sighed. "I insisted. Martin felt sorry for me, sorry for Liz. He sent another message to . . . he sent another message *home.* Communications are slow–"

"It's some distance," Wiley opined.

Tom grinned humorlessly. "Indeed. We stayed at the ranch, ate good, additive-free Mexican food for a week. But the answer came back the same. *Nadie que nació aquí. No one who was born here.*"

"So you drove your car into the side of his barn . . ."

"Is that what Sam told you?"

Wiley nodded.

"No. That's not what happened. Something must've gotten lost in translation. My car was *inside* the barn. So was the communication device, and the . . . *apparatus* for sending us back." Tom waited for us to look dubious. We must've, because he grinned. "It wasn't a transporter, like from *Star Trek,* gentlemen, at least not to anyone looking at it. It just looked like one of those big, old-fashioned satellite dishes, with a bunch of car batteries hooked up to it in some kind of sequence. Very third world-looking. We're not too big on electrical contrivances . . . where I'm from, and there's not exactly a spring-break-in-Cancun rush to go back. Once we're here, we tend to stay here. It's great here.

"But I'm no engineer – I didn't know exactly how it worked. Holding Martin at gunpoint," Tom looked down at the counter, "I tried to hook it up. But I didn't know what I was doing. There was a little humming noise, then the thing burst into flames. The hay and the old wood caught immediately, and when we fled the barn, some of the ranch hands were waiting for us. They jumped me, tied me up, dragged me back to the house.

"Martin said he was sorry, over and over again. There was nothing he could do, nothing I could do. So I gave up. I can never go home again, my friends, but it really doesn't matter. This place is my home now." Tom sighed. "I told Martin how to get in touch with Maxine, and he had the authorities take us all the way back to the border. Sometimes the truth is least believed, so . . ." Tom took out his phone, typed on it, handed it to Wiley.

Wiley read the *Wikipedia* entry. *"The Mapimi Silent Zone is the subject of an urban myth that claims it is an area where radio signals cannot be received. In July 1970, an Athena test missile launched from a U.S. military base near Green River, Utah toward White Sands Missile Range lost control and fell in the Mapimi Desert region. The rocket was carrying two small containers of cobalt 57, a radioactive element. Immediately, a team of specialists arrived to find the fallen rocket. The aerial search lasted three weeks. Finally, when the rocket was found, a road was built to transport the wreckage, along with a small amount of contaminated top soil. As a result of the U.S. Air Force recovery operations there, a number of myths and stories relating to the area arose, including strange magnetic anomalies that prevent radio transmission, mutations of flora and fauna, and extraterrestrial visitations."*

"Martin had the official tell Maxine and Sam that I'd lost my mind, that I believed I could return to Sirius from Mapimi. The official was stern, telling her that they didn't like gringos coming down there, disturbing the peace, setting fires, riling up the locals, talking about aliens. They'd give us back, seeing how Liz was sick . . . Seeing how she was dying, and they knew she could get better treatment back in the States, blah, blah, blah. Martin said he was sorry, the official said he was sorry, and they delivered us at the border to Sam and Max, like some kind of hostage exchange.

"Sam didn't say a word to me all the way home. He didn't say a word, in fact, until after Liz passed. Then he screamed at me, telling me that I was nuts, that I'd hastened her death with my insanity. Max just cried. Mercifully, they'd left Janae with relatives, so she didn't have to witness it.

"Max begged me to go see a shrink, so I did, for her. I told him that it was all a big misunderstanding. I told him I'd heard about healing springs in Mexico, or some such bullshit. There aren't any springs in Mapimi. It's the fucking desert.

"But there was no official report from Mexico; I hadn't hurt anyone. Liz was gone. I passed all the are-you-a-nutball? tests the shrink administered, so he had no choice but to let me go on my merry way. With a prescription for scopolamine. Or lithium, or *Prozac,* or something. I didn't even get it filled."

Tom considered us for a minute, then smiled. "Believe whatever you want on that score, gentlemen. Believe I'm an alien, believe I'm delusional. You can't prove it one way or another, any more than I can. Our DNA is indistinguishable."

How convenient, I thought.

"But where I'm from – even where I might *think* I'm from – it doesn't have any bearing whatsoever on what they're putting in our food. In what they're putting in what you give to Bo."

"How did you get interested in the food additive stuff?" Wiley asked.

"Where I come from – for the sake of argument, let's just say it's a big, agricultural community – there's no such thing as food additives. There's never been any large meat sources – we're all a bunch of left-handed, fish-eating vegetarians. Buy me a drink sometime, and I'll tell you the whole story, my son. If you care to hear it." Tom grinned. Wiley grinned back. I wasn't so sure.

"The whole draw of *here* is to get away from all that natural goodness, *there.* Have a drink, smoke a cigarette. Eat a steak. Drive a car. Literature, art, movies. *Dirty* movies. The thrilling saga of the history of mankind's struggle to tame this unhospitable place. We've never known anything but peace and prosperity, except for one war . . . But that's a story for another day.

"So I never worried about the chemicals here. I was aware that they existed – or thought I was – and avoided them where possible, but I always figured that it was just a part of modern life. Can't make food appetizing to a bazillion people in the first world without adding a little citric acid, a little Red Dye 40.

"But one day, a year or so after I'd buried my one true love, when I was minding my own business on the internet, I came upon an article about the links between a food additive called BHT and cancer, asthma, and all around nuttiness in children. In food, it's used as an antioxidant."

"Which is?" I asked.

Tom smiled and took his phone out of his pocket again. He typed; then said, "According to *dictionary.com,* in chemistry, an antioxidant *is any substance that inhibits oxidation, as a substance that inhibits oxidative deterioration of gasoline, rubbers, plastics, soaps, etc.* In biochemistry, it is *an enzyme or other organic substance, as vitamin E or beta carotene, that is capable of counteracting the damaging effects of oxidation in animal tissues."* Tom looked at me; shrugged. "Gobbledygook, right? BHT is put in our food to keep it from rotting, but we're told that it's also good for us; it's available as a pill, marketed as a vitamin." Tom consulted his phone again. "It's also used *in cosmetics, pharmaceuticals, rubber, electrical transformer oil and embalming fluid; hydraulic fluids, turbine and gear oils, and jet fuels.*

"I thought, *This is not a good thing to be in our food."* Tom grinned. "But the research was contradictory – some findings said it increased cancer and asthma and behavioral risks; some research said it decreased them." He shrugged. "But I was intrigued. I come from a much simpler place. Effect is easily deduced from cause. The good doctors here told me on more than one occasion that they don't really know what causes cancer."

"That's what my wife said," Wiley commented.

"If thou couldst, doctor, cast the water of my land, find her disease, and purge it to a sound and pristine health, I would applaud thee to the very echo, that should applaud again."

"Throw physic to the dogs," Wiley said. *"I'll none of it."*

Tom smiled. "Like I say, I was intrigued. They might not know what causes cancer here – but cancer is unknown where I come from. Nor any of the diseases of affluence. No diabetes, no hypertension, no heart disease." Tom paused. "Maybe they couldn't have cured Liz," he said, mostly to himself. Then he sighed. "We live for a very long time. We die of old age . . . We simply wear out." Tom looked at us. "How old would you say I am, Wiley? Nate? I know the young aren't very good at gauging the elderly, but give it a shot."

"Let's see. My dad's fifty; he's bald, a little paunchy." Wiley squinted at Tom. "You pass yourself off as Janae's grandpa, but there's no way you're old enough to be her mom's dad."

"Maxine's forty-eight," Tom said.

"So . . . I'd say, you can't be a day over . . . Maybe fifty-five, fifty-six." Wiley looked at me for confirmation. I nodded.

Tom took his wallet out of his pocket, showed us his driver license. He was born April 30, 1971. He was sixty-seven.

"No way," Wiley said, nonplussed.

"And I've probably got another good couple three decades in me," Tom said. "I'll make you a bet, Wiley – I'll be there to dance at Bo's wedding."

"Why would you want to leave such a healthy place – a place of such . . . longevity?" Wiley asked in astonishment.

"It's unbelievably, unrelentingly, boring. Here, like I say, is vice. Sin." Tom grinned wickedly. "I came here to have fun. That's why we all come here. I was fortunate enough to find so much more than just that, but then it was taken from me. Too soon. Liz was the same age as Maxine is now." Tom paused. "So my discovery of this possible BHT/cancer link interested me.

"It was too late to save Liz, but . . . What else did I have to do? The internet has always been my playground. I believe the sum of all human knowledge can be found on the internet. All the science, all the art . . . all the madness. If you just know where to look for it. *How* to look for it. It just takes a little digging, a little intuition. More than just a Google search for *Cancer and food additive links.*" Tom grinned. "I got a bite on your lost Wes Thomerville video, by the way."

Wiley said, "Really. What did you find out?"

"Be innocent of the knowledge, dearest chuck, 'til thou applaud the deed. It's just a bite. I'll let you know when I have something more substantial."

"Awesome," Wiley replied, with zero enthusiasm. I thought that maybe he was regretting this search down Memory Lane. He'd just had an argument with Brendee, over their son; a concern from the here and now. I looked over at Bo. He was asleep. Maybe Wiley wasn't so anxious to remind his mother of those carefree days of yesteryear so much anymore.

"Anyway," Tom said, "one search led to another, and I found out about GRAS. It's an acronym that stands for *generally recognized as safe.* To paraphrase Macbeth, GRAS is like the Prince of Cumberland, Wiley. It is a step on which we must fall down, or else o'erleap, for in our way it lies." When I just looked at him blankly, Tom laughed. "Let's do a little role-playing, shall we, Nate?

You like role-playing, don'tcha?" Tom winked at Wiley. "Of course you do!

"Let's say that you are a big ol' food conglomerate. You want to put something in your food – a stabilizer, an emulsifier. How 'bout an anticaking agent? Let's say you want to add a little sodium aluminosilicate to your new brand of powdered coffee creamer."

Wiley took out his phone, typed. *"Sodium aluminosilicate is an acid salt comprising sodium, aluminum, silicon and oxygen. The FDA has as of April 1, 2012 approved sodium aluminosilicate for direct contact with consumable items under . . .* a bunch of numbers and letters." Wiley scrolled. *"It is encountered as an additive in food where it acts as an anticaking (free flow) agent."*

"Don't ignore those letters and numbers, my son. Those are FDA regulations." Tom took out his own phone once again. "Let's see. *Under 21 CFR 170.30(c) and 170.3(f), general recognition of safety through experience based on common use in foods requires a substantial history of consumption for food use by a significant number of consumers."* Tom blinked at me. "More regulatory gobbledygook.

"What it shakes out as, is this – they've been using aluminosilicate since 2012 – its common use in foods has had a substantial history. Twenty-six years. Since before you were born. So it must be okay, right? So it is GRAS – generally recognized as safe.

"And here's the killing part, my friends, literally and figuratively. Nate doesn't have to go through any testing to put this in his new creamer. It's already in use in existing ones. All he has to say is, *Hey, FDA! We here at Nate's Foods think this stuff is safe. Sure, it's nothing but sand – but we say it's okey-dokey.*

"And what does the FDA say? *You go right on ahead and put it in there! If you guys at Nate's Foods say it's safe, why that's okey-dokey with us, too!"*

Tom let all that sink in for a minute, then he said, "The inmates are running the asylum, my sons. The FDA has neither the funding, nor the staff, the time, nor even the inclination to test out all the new shit they're putting in our food. And the old shit . . . Well, it already *has a substantial history of consumption.* So the FDA trusts the manufacturer's judgment. The manufacturer, who's going to make money off of it."

I shook my head. "But if something already has a substantial history of consumption, maybe it *is* okay." I smelled a government conspiracy theory coming, and it stunk already. "Maybe a little sand won't hurt us."

Tom grinned. "Allow me to give you just *one example* of the safety of a substantial history of consumption." Tom looked at his phone again, typed. "From our indispensable friends at *Wikipedia: In the late 1920s, Lysol disinfectant began being marketed as a feminine hygiene product. It was claimed vaginal douching with a diluted Lysol solution prevented infections and vaginal odor, and thereby preserved youth and marital bliss. This Lysol solution was also used as a birth control agent, as post-coital douching was a popular method of preventing pregnancy at that time.*"

Wiley blanched. *"Lysol? The cleaning stuff? Really?"*

Tom held up his phone. There was a picture of an ad: A statuesque, dark-haired woman in a shiny gown looked thoughtfully off-camera. The larger caption read, *The Poise that Knowledge Gives.* Wiley took Tom's phone, enlarged the picture, read the small print. *"Lysol is safe. Every modern woman should know the facts about feminine hygiene. So much of beauty, charm, and self-confidence is lost to the woman who remains ignorant of these facts so vital to her well-being. To make these facts available to every woman, the makers of Lysol Disinfectant have prepared a booklet on feminine hygiene, which contains important statements by three eminent women doctors."* Wiley handed the phone back to Tom. He was still pale. *"Lysol? Really?"*

"Wouldn't be a whole lot of fun to stick your nose in *that,* would it?" Tom grinned wickedly. "This product was used in this manner for years. *It had a significant history of consumption.* Then women slowly discovered how awful it really was for them. But *three eminent women doctors* surely wouldn't lie, would they? And neither would Nate and his food company. That sand's safe because he says it is. The FDA believes him. Why shouldn't we?"

The bell over the door tinkled, and Josh entered, followed by three other bikers: a short one, a fat one, and a skinny one. Tom's eyebrows went up at this crew, and he smiled.

Wiley also smiled. "I'll get it for you, Josh." Wiley disappeared around the counter, and returned a moment later. He handed Josh's phone to him. "Good as new," he proclaimed.

Josh turned it on, scrolled. "Thanks, kid." He extracted his chained wallet from his pocket, handed Wiley several wrinkled bills. "You fix other electronic stuff, right?" Wiley nodded. "Let me introduce you to my friends. This is Johnny."

The short biker stepped forward. He showed Wiley a tablet; it looked brand new, except for the diagonal crack from corner to corner. "I got in a little fight with my girlfriend. His sister." Johnny nodded over his shoulder at the fat biker. "She threw it across the room. So I threw her phone across the room."

"Then they made up," the fat biker said.

"It still comes on," Johnny said. "But it just makes those little dots in a circle, and says–"

"Preparing automatic repair," Wiley supplied.

"Can you–"

"Of course," Wiley said. "You've probably just unseated the . . . It doesn't matter. I can fix it."

"Here's Candie's phone," the fat biker said, and handed Wiley a darkened phone in a pink and rhinestone-bejeweled cover. "It won't even turn on."

"I can fix it," Wiley repeated. He looked expectantly at the skinny biker.

He shook his head. "I'm good," he said. "I just gave Josh a ride."

Wiley quoted them insanely reasonable prices, then said, "How 'bout . . ." He looked at the destroyed tablet. "Next Sunday?"

Johnny smiled, nodded, shook Wiley's hand. Josh, already talking to someone on his resurrected phone, also shook Wiley's hand. The bikers departed.

"Another satisfied customer," Tom said.

Wiley grinned. "It's what I do."

BRENDEE

I blinked at the clock on the nightstand. It was two o'clock in the afternoon. I'd slept all damn day, and I still felt tired. I didn't want to get up, but then I had to – I ran to the bathroom and threw up. It wasn't much: I hadn't eaten since lunch at the mall yesterday. What with arguing with Wiley and all, I'd skipped dinner.

I remembered when I'd had morning sickness – almost every day for six months. I hadn't been ill since. The thought didn't cross my mind that I might be pregnant. There was the operation and . . . the last time such an event had occurred, there'd been a star in the east. If I was pregnant, it would've had to be via a second immaculate conception. I must've picked up a bug.

I sent Wiley a text, asking him to get me some *Pepto* on his way home. He didn't respond; I figured he must be busy *wiring the store.* He'd read it soon enough. It wasn't like I wanted him to rush right home, anyway. I wasn't in the mood for him right then, didn't want to risk him or Bo catching whatever I had. I went back to bed.

NATE

When Janae walked into the store, I was holding the bottom of the ladder. I turned to look at her; at the same time, Wiley shifted his weight, and the ladder tottered for a moment.

"Careful, Wiley," she said, grinning up at him. "Just one slip–"

And you'd be gone for good, not one single chance, I thought, the lyrics to Wes Thomerville's stupid old song coming into my mind from I knew not where. I'd only seen the video to it once. How bizarre it was that I would remember the dumb lyrics.

"– and it'll be, *Good night sweet prince: and flights of angels sing thee to thy rest,"* Janae concluded.

Wiley set the drill down on the top of the ladder. In one fluid motion, he leapt from it, grabbing onto the exposed pipe that ran beside the beam. He pointed his toes, swung back and forth for a moment, then dropped gracefully to the floor, directly in front of Janae. He put his hand fondly on her cheek, leaving a black, dusty handprint. *"Adieu, adieu! Remember me!"*

"I could never forget you, Wiley," she said softly, holding his gaze.

"Jesus Christ, Wiley!" Tom said, looking up at the ceiling. "You almost brought a hundred and forty years of bad plumbing down on our heads!"

Still looking at Janae, he said, "It's sturdy enough." He nodded at her. *"There's blood on thy face."*

Janae rubbed her cheek, and tearing her eyes from Wiley's for a split-second, she looked at the dirt on her hand. She grinned at him. *"'Tis Banquo's then."*

"Go get some water, and wash this filthy witness from your hand."

Janae took Wiley's hand, turned it over. *"My hands are of your color; but I shame to wear a heart so white."* Wiley grinned wickedly at that one. Janae playfully swiped some of the dirt from her own fingers onto his face. *"When shall we meet again,"* she said, *"in thunder, lightning, or in rain?"*

Wiley smirked. *"When the hurlyburly's done, when the battle's lost and won."*

"That will be ere the set of sun," Tom said. When they turned to look at them, breaking their little tête-à-tête, he tilted his head curiously, grinned.

Wiley turned, and batting his baby blues guilelessly at me, he climbed back up the ladder.

"Who wants pizza?" Tom said. Janae blinked rapidly for a moment, then went into the office. To *wash the filthy witness from her hand,* I imagined. And her face. Where did they get this stuff?

"Pizza?" Wiley said. "That's gotta be full of–"

"From *Georgina's,*" Tom said. "Down the street. They tout themselves as organic. So it'll only half kill you." When Wiley still looked dubious, he said, *"Hoes gotta eat,* Wiley. They're hippies, just like you. They use as few chemicals as you're gonna get, unless you make it yourself. They don't even deliver. Don't want to pollute the air by driving it over to you."

"They could walk it to us," I said.

Tom shook his head. "They don't deliver anywhere. In addition to saving the atmosphere, it cuts back on their overhead. Don't have to employ delivery people. Very trendy, very shrewd." He looked thoughtfully over his shoulder as Janae emerged from the back, clean-scrubbed. "People think something's better if they have to go out of their way to get it. Down for some *Georgina's,* Janae?"

"I don't know if I have the time, Tommy–"

"Do you have the inclination?" Wiley called from atop the ladder. "Do you think you have the energy?"

Janae ignored him. "I only stopped in for a minute. I've gotta study."

"You can study upstairs," Wiley suggested. "I can help you, as long as it's not math. There's a big bed–"

"I know," Janae said, looking up at him again. "I used to play up there when I was a kid."

"It's Sunday," Tom said. "You're supposed to relax on Sundays. Have a pizza with us."

Janae looked back at Tom, but I watched her consider Wiley out of the corner of her eye. She relented immediately. "Okay. I'm never one to pass up a free meal."

"I'm never one to pass up a free anything," Wiley commented.

"I'll bet," Janae said. "I don't know about *Georgina's,* though," she said to Tom. "Maybe something from *Tartare?"*

"Tartare's closed on Sundays."

"I don't know, Tommy," Janae insisted. "The girl that runs the place doesn't shave her armpits. Ewww."

"If I flip a coin, what are my chances of getting head?" Wiley said. When I looked up at him, he said, "I mean, *heads.*" He grinned. Same ol' filthy-mouthed Wiley.

Tom said, *"They're probably foreigners with ways different than our own. They may do some more . . . folk dancing."*

Wiley grinned, then burst into song, in a weird falsetto. *"Toucha toucha toucha touch me, I wanna be dirrrrty!"*

"Shut up, Wiley," Janae said. She might've blushed.

"We'll be right back," Tom said.

"Don't hurry on my account," Wiley said.

Tom and Janae left the store. Wiley finished screwing the camera into the beam and climbed down from the ladder. He started dragging it toward the back of the store.

"Why do you talk to her like that, Wiley?" I asked, conversationally enough. "What if Brendee–"

Wiley stopped pulling the ladder, turned and looked pointedly at me. "Who's gonna tell Brendee? Her? Tom? *You?*" There was an unexpected shade of meanness in Wiley's tone, a defensiveness, an accusation.

"What are you doing, Wiley?" I asked, not in response to his words but to his tone.

"I'm not doing anything, Nate," he replied, still uncharacteristically defensive. "It's not like I'm . . . I'm not gonna–"

"What?" I asked. Now it was my turn to be accusatory. "You're not gonna *what?*"

He looked steadily at me, but his blue eyes were unreadable. "I'm just having a little fun. It's not like I'm . . ." he repeated, but he still couldn't say it. *It's not like I'm gonna fuck Janae.* Because that's what was on the table for consideration, wasn't it? They flirted with each other shamelessly – in front of me, in front of Tom.

Maybe it wasn't very macho of me, but it made me uncomfortable. Brendee was my friend. And Janae was . . . Janae was a tease in high school, and now she thought she was teasing Wiley. But she was a grown woman now, and I doubted that she suddenly got important phone calls at critical moments anymore. I doubted if she'd hesitate for a minute if Wiley put a *clean* hand on her face.

And Wiley, who'd studied the minds and motivations of girls like lab rats; who was quite sure he knew exactly what they wanted; he was teasing her right back. And he was much more proficient at it, much more in control.

136

I remembered an ancient, awful old movie that Wiley had made me sit through once: *Hannibal Rising*. There was a scene in which the bad guys think they're gonna kill Hannibal; but they have no idea how evil he is, how completely and utterly unafraid. He's already a far worse monster than they are. I thought that Janae's teasing Wiley was like trying to murder Hannibal: he was immune to her charms. He believed that he knew what she wanted, as much, if not more than she knew it. Study women was what he did, and I'd heard from Brendee, via Deneen, and from Wiley himself, that he was a *consummate* tease. Janae had no idea who she was toying with.

But I thought it was still a dangerous game, especially for him. Janae had nothing to lose; *she* was the one that was just having a little fun. But Wiley would lose it all. He'd lose Brendee and his baby. And he'd lose me, because I wouldn't be able to look at him anymore, if he hurt the woman that loved him so much.

"It's harmless," Wiley said. "I'm just keepin' sharp. It's fun to have someone look at *me,* for a change, Nate. To have someone really look at me – because I'm me, not because I look like–"

"I'm not gonna listen to that excuse, Wiley," I told him. "That's bullshit, directly from the bull. You're not gonna whine to me that you want to cheat on Brendee because you think that she's been pretending that you're Wes Thomerville all these years."

He winced when I said the word *cheat,* but he didn't look guilty. "Like Caesar's wife, I am above reproach, Nate." I frowned angrily at him. "It means – I haven't done anything wrong. I've made no promises, told no lies. I'm just telling you, it's nice to know that some girl likes me for me–"

"I'm not buying that bullshit, Wiley," I repeated. "You just like it because she responds to you – it strokes your ego–"

"And what's wrong with that?" he demanded, again with an uncharacteristic defensiveness.

"If you can't see what's wrong with it – whatever blows your skirt, Wiley."

"An intriguing turn of phrase, my son." He grinned, then shook his head. "I'm not gonna do anything with her, Nate," he assured me. But I wasn't assured. "Just because I know what she wants, doesn't mean I'm gonna give it to her." He grinned again. "Trust me. I'm just fucking around." When I still looked skeptical, he said, "Okay. I'll tell Brendee what Janae said just now. What I said. I doubt she'll understand that there was anything inappropriate to it, but – will that make you feel better?"

"Fuck you, Wiley. It's not about me."

I wanted to believe him, that he'd never betray Brendee, the mother of his son, *the only girl for him,* as he'd often said. But I knew Wiley, and I knew he'd go right up to the glass partition of what was done and what was not done. He'd smile at Janae; he'd put his hands on the glass, and invite her to put her hands on it, from the other side. I wanted to believe he'd go no further, no *closer* than that.

Wiley wouldn't betray Brendee, not physically, not actually. I knew him. But psychologically? Wiley, the studier, the connoisseur of women's motivations? Wiley, who believed that he knew what they wanted? I thought he would betray Brendee enough – he'd let Janae believe that he was thinking about it. Considering it. What else could she think, the way he flirted with her? And somehow, to me – that just wasn't right either.

BRENDEE

Wiley brought me *Pepto,* and soda crackers, and evil of all evils – clear soda; the same things that the doctor had recommended for morning sickness. Wiley knew it wasn't that, as much as I did, but threat of torture couldn't have made him bring it up for discussion. In that area, Wiley wasn't a talker. He was a doer. He wouldn't say, "I think I wanna . . ." He'd just do it.

But there was no doing it now. He let me kiss my son, but then he quickly took him away from me and gave him a bath. Then he fed him some mashed-up apples, and gave him *another* bath. Wiley was a little bit of a germ-phobe, I thought, though I knew he'd never admit it.

When he came to bed, he scooted way over to one side. He didn't object when I hugged his back – he wouldn't dare *object,* I thought – but I didn't think he'd turn over and kiss me, or anything else, even if I begged him. No exchange of fluids tonight. Wiley didn't want to catch what I had, any more than he wanted me to give it to Bo. I'd never known Wiley to be sick a day in his life, and he wasn't gonna start catching stuff now.

It didn't matter. I wasn't hardly in the mood, anyway.

I called in sick on Monday, because I still felt like *Death eating a tea-cake,* as my grandmother used to say. Wiley made me a bowl of chicken soup, cut me up a pear, and brought it in to me on a tray with some soda crackers and a *Sprite.* With ice. I wanted to tell him – Wiley Royce, who knew everything – that chicken soup was for a cold, not a stomach bug. But it was sweet of him. He was a good man, a good father, a good husband; and I reminded myself again that it was past time for me to show him my gratitude for his being all these things. As soon as I felt a little better.

I had just drifted back to sleep when my phone rang. It was Deneen. "Oh, my God, Brendee!" she squealed. "Oh, my God, oh, my God, oh, my God! The test! It's positive!"

I looked at the clock. It was nine-fifteen. "Where are you, Deneen?"

"I'm at work! I always take my test at work, except on the weekends! I can't go when I know Nate is standing outside the door, waiting. So I don't take it 'til I get here. Oh, my God, Brendee! I'm pregnant!"

"I'm so happy for you!" I was happy for me, too. I wouldn't have to hear about uteruses and endometria anymore. But then I sighed to myself. Now I'd have to hear about gestation and pre-natal nutrition and folic acid, turning and dropping, methods of delivery. At least Nate would have to be the one holding her hair back while she threw up every day for six months. It would be Nate that accompanied her to the mind-fuck of Lamaze class.

"I'm gonna make a doctor's appointment for today. Just to make sure. Do you want to come with me?"

"Oh, Deneen! I'm home sick. You don't want me to be around you right now. Wiley's petrified to even kiss me. You don't want to catch it. It wouldn't be good for the–"

"Okay, Brendee. I'm sorry you're sick. Feel better!"

"It's just a little stomach flu."

"I have to call Nate! I'll tell you what the doctor says!"

It touched me that she had called me before she'd called the father-to-be. "I love you, Deneen. I'm so happy for you."

"Thanks, Brendee. I'm happy, too!"

She hung up and I called Wiley. "Bust out the cigars, my son," I told him. "Deneen's pregnant."

"Finally! How are you feeling?"

"Better. I think I'll go back to work tomorrow."

"I'm so glad. I love you, Brendee."

"I love you, too, Wiley." And a wave of love for him hit me, so strong that I wanted to reach through the phone and *squeeze* him.

"I'll see you after work."

"Okay. Bye."

"Maybe we can . . ." But he'd already hung up.

****

I got up, took a long, hot shower. I was still feeling weak, but the water served to revive me a great deal. I made myself a peanut butter sandwich – no jelly. Wiley never ate jelly. "It's just sugar and dye and horses' hooves," he always said. "Somebody whispers *fruit* over it, and they call it jelly." And that was even before this food additive craziness. I picked the sunflower seeds out of the bread – Wiley always insisted on this multigrain brand, with all sorts of different seeds interspersed in it. "If you have to eat bread, it might as well be good for you," he said. My husband was a hippie. A fucking barefoot hippie. Whoever heard of sunflower seeds in bread?

But I loved him. I put on my green silk robe, and climbed back into bed with my laptop. No sense in over-exerting myself. I still felt a little wrung out, but I was getting better, and thinking about Wiley . . . That always made me feel better. I looked at all our old pictures – from high school, from college. *Hot damn,* he was cute! And we were cute together.

I thought that some people probably lost a lot of their pictures – computers crashed. But not mine. My husband was an electronics genius. I had the same laptop that I'd had in high school. The software had been updated, of course. But all the old memories were intact.

I had one folder called *Old Stuff.* It really should've been called *Old Stuff, Before Wiley* – that's how I thought of it. Here were some pictures from grade school, a copy of a report I'd given in tenth grade that had been particularly well-received by my English teacher. Here was a picture of me and Dave: he'd been my boyfriend, but I'd summarily dumped him within days of meeting Wiley. The picture was from a dance at school. I'd only kept it because I thought I looked exceptionally good in the dress I'd been wearing.

My phone beeped. "I can't get into the doctor today!" Deneen wailed.

I looked at the picture of Dave, and it stirred another memory. "Go to *Planned Parenthood,*" I told her. They had been my source for birth control pills when I'd still been in high school. Dave and I had enjoyed a little tumble, every Thursday afternoon. We'd both had study hall, and we'd sneak home to do the deed while the rest of my family was still out in the world. I'd enjoyed myself very much with Dave – he was what my mother called *a big, strapping, healthy boy.* Just like Nate. It wasn't like I'd ever loved him, though, I thought in retrospect. But I did like him a lot, and I certainly liked what we did together.

But eventually, after I saw Wes Thomerville's incredible sexiness, making love with Dave became as boring to me as watching paint dry; I began to close my eyes and pretend Dave was not a big, strapping, brown-eyed redhead with freckles. I began to pretend he was a tall, lean, black-haired guitar-player with blue eyes. And then I met a tall, lean, black-haired guy with blue eyes. He didn't play the guitar, but he looked just like Wes . . .

I blinked, realized that Deneen had said something. "They're over there off of Central," I said. "They'll get you in and give you another test right away." Yeah, *Planned Parenthood* had never steered me wrong. They'd never given me any bunk birth control pills, like I'd obviously gotten toward the end of college.

"Okay," Deneen said. "I'll let you know what they say."

I disconnected, and scrolled through my *Other Stuff* folder. That's where my copy of Wes's video was. It had been *so long* . . . I wondered if it would have the same effect on me as it used to. After all, I was a grown woman now, a wife, a mom. Not a high school girl who became incredibly turned on from watching three minutes and thirty-five seconds of an unknown singer from before she was born.

But it wasn't there. I did a search of the entire computer. There were plenty of videos: Wiley and me at the beach, our little wedding ceremony, the raucous party afterward. Hours of Bo. But no Wes. No *My Disgrace.*

I couldn't imagine what had happened to it. But unlike my pictures and home movies, which were irreplaceable – I'm sure Wiley had them backed up somewhere – my memory of Wes was there on the internet, for public consumption. I just called up - *YouTube,* and typed *Rolling Blackout* into the search box. And there was Wes.

NATE

I went to *Morry's Books* after work to share the good news with my best friend. But Wiley wasn't there, and the news had arrived before me. Tom gave me a slap on the back, and told me congratulations. I took three cigars, wrapped in cellophane, out of a paper bag. I handed one to Tom.

"What's this?"

"It's a cigar, Tom. It's traditional."

"I'm aware of the tradition, Nate. But this isn't a cigar. This is an abomination, masquerading as a cigar." He grinned at me. "Where the fuck did you get it, anyway?"

"At the liquor store. Where's Wiley?"

"Wiley's at the liquor store. We've been celebrating a little, in anticipation of your arrival. I don't know how you missed him."

I went over and looked at Bo, asleep in his car seat, like I was seeing him for the first time. Before long, *before I knew it,* I was gonna have one of my own. It was amazing, exciting, incredible. More than a little scary.

"You want a drink?" Tom asked. "There's a little left."

"I'm driving," I said. "Actually, I thought we might all go over to my place and celebrate. I haven't seen Denny yet."

"That sounds good. That'll give me an excuse to drive Wiley and Bo. He's already a little bit–"

"You know how to drive, Tom?" As far as I knew, he didn't even own a car. And he called Wiley a hippie.

"What do you think I am, Nate? From another planet?" He grinned. "Of course I know how to drive. I'm just close enough to everything to walk, so I don't. If you must know, I've got a 911 Porsche. In storage. Practically an antique. My Uncle Morry gave it to me, before he went back to . . . before he went home." Tom sobered a little bit, changed the subject. "Wiley hasn't been his normal cheerful self today. Do you know if something's bothering him?"

"His wife's sick."

"I heard. But I don't think that's it. I heard him talking to her this morning – she told him your good news – and everything seemed okay. Then a couple hours later . . . his phone beeped. It actually went *Ta-da!* He looked at it; then he got quiet. He went in the back and started working on our biker friends' stuff. I actually had a few customers, and didn't miss him. When I went back to talk to him later, he was staring at the wall. He looked at me blankly and said, 'I think we should celebrate Nate's happiness.'

"I said, 'Shouldn't we wait for Nate?' It was only about three o'clock.

"'I think I want a drink,' he replied. 'You got any of that gin left?'

"So we killed the rest of the gin I had in the desk, in celebration of your good news. At least that was the excuse. But Wiley didn't seem in a very celebratory mood, and I didn't have much to drink. Wiley's already had about three, however, and he insisted on walking over to the liquor store to get another bottle."

The man himself walked in then. Unexpectedly, he gave me a big hug. "Congratulations, Nate! Are you hoping for a boy or a girl?"

I was amazed to see that his enthusiasm was forced. "Just ten fingers and ten toes, Wiley," I told him. "Boy or girl, it doesn't matter to me, as long as it's healthy."

I watched him go over and look at Bo. He seemed sad, almost sentimental, as he touched his baby's curly hair, his little chubby fist.

"Here, my son," I told him cheerfully. "Have a cigar."

"I told you, Nate," Tom said. "That's not a cigar. Hold on a minute." He went back into the office.

"What's wrong, Wiley?"

He ceased looking at Bo. "Nothing's wrong, Nate. How could anything be wrong, on this, one of the happiest days of your life?"

"I'm not talking about me. I'm talking about you."

"It's nothing, Nate. You want a drink?"

"You've had enough to drink, Wiley."

"I'm thinking about taking it up. As my new hobby." He sighed. "Brendee finally took that walk down Memory Lane today."

"Tom found the video?" I imagined that Wiley must've given it to her, and apparently he didn't like her reaction to it.

Wiley shook his head. "No. Not yet. She doesn't need anything new. She looked up the old one."

"Oh, for Christ's sake, Wiley! Is that all? You're crying in your beer about that?"

"It's been a long time, Nate. Maybe she doesn't want me anymore. Maybe she's decided that Wes is good enough–"

"You've become a regular bullshit factory lately, you know that? First you tell me that you're making time with Janae because she wants you for you. It's all the same in the dark, Wiley. Once you get her there, she's not gonna care who you are." He seemed a little startled that I would lay it out for him as starkly as that.

"I'm not gonna–"

"Now you're pouting because Brendee watched that stupid fucking video. For the first time in years. Maybe she *is* lonely. You said you haven't . . . Maybe you should rethink your *plan*, Wiley."

"I pray thee cease thy counsel, which falls into mine ears as profitless as water in a sieve," he said evenly. *"Do not mistake my deception for a character flaw,* Nate. *It is philosophical choice, a profound understanding of the universe. It is a way of life."*

I shook my head. He was resolute. Brendee would get what she was so obviously wanting again, but only when Wiley was ready to give it to her, when he thought it was time, when he thought it would be to his utmost advantage. "Byron?" I asked him.

Wiley had once told me that he was *mad, bad, and dangerous to know,* and then told me that's what they'd said about Lord Bryon, the poet. "You're no poet, Wiley," I'd told him. But whenever he quoted things to me that I'd never heard of, which was damn near all of the time, I always asked him if it was Byron. It was our little joke. It was never Byron.

"The first part was Shakespeare, my son. The second . . . *Lost in Space.* A very old, very bad movie."

Tom came out of the office. "Did someone say Byron? Here's some Byron for you, Nate: *Though sages may pour out their wisdom's treasure, there is no sterner moralist than pleasure.* And this–" he held up a dusty glass tube, "– *this* is a cigar! Rolled on the soft brown thighs of Cuban virgins!"

"A Cuban cigar? Aren't they–"

"Banned and contraband, once upon a time, my son." He grinned at us. "Seeing how you guys don't smoke, I don't see how you'd properly enjoy it." He disappeared into the back again, then returned, the end cut off of the cigar. "You can smoke those domestic atrocities." Tom found a box of matches in the counter drawer and commenced to lighting his cigar.

"You're not going to smoke it in here?"

"No, Wiley. I'm not going to illegally smoke my illegal cigar in celebration of Nate's illegitimate baby." Tom winked at me. "Nor have I been illicitly drinking with you all afternoon in my un-liquor-licensed place of business."

"I meant . . . because of Bo."

145

"Oh, shit!" Tom said. "I forgot about Bo. Lock up, Wiley. I'll wait for you guys outside."

I texted Denny. *I'm bringing two drunks over to celebrate. They may pass out on the floor.*

It's ok. I'm at my mom's. We're looking at baby pictures. She's telling stories.

I'm calling in sick 2morrow, so we can celebrate.

I will 2. I luv u.

I luv u 2.

BRENDEE

When I heard Wiley's key in the lock, I jumped up. I was looking forward to seeing him, had been thinking about him all day. He opened the door, empty-handed.

"Where's–"

Nate came in behind him, carrying my sleeping son and his diaper bag.

"We're going over to Nate's," Wiley told me. "We're gonna celebrate." I noticed that he slurred the *gonna* a little bit. He'd been celebrating already.

I pulled my green silk robe up around my neck a little bit. He hadn't even noticed that I was wearing it. "I have to go to work tomorrow, Wiley. I thought we might celebrate on Friday."

"Tom's waiting for us downstairs," he said. He went to take Bo from Nate, thought better of it. "You take him, Brendee. I'll see you . . ."

"Tomorrow," Nate said. "I'll put him up in the spare room."

"The nursery!" Wiley said with drunken enthusiasm.

Nate handed the baby to me, set down his diaper bag, looked at me sheepishly. "Don't worry, Brendee. He didn't drive over here . . . like this. Tom drove."

Tom probably didn't come up because he didn't want me giving him a dirty look for getting my husband drunk again. I didn't imagine that he was in much better shape than Wiley, but on the other hand, I thought that Tom was probably a much more experienced drinker. And apparently Wiley was trying to make up for lost time, all those years of claiming that drinking *defiled the temple of the spirit.* In the past, Wiley had claimed that he only drank when he had something to celebrate.

He certainly had something to celebrate now. But I was still a little upset about him doing it while Bo was with him, and . . . I'd hoped we might celebrate a little ourselves tonight . . .

Wiley gave me a sloppy kiss; he missed my mouth, landed it mostly on my chin. "I'm *so* glad you're feeling better." He patted Bo on the head. "Come on, Nate. That gin isn't gonna drink itself!" He staggered out the still-open door.

"Goodnight, Brendee," Nate said, looking embarrassed for his friend.

"Congratulations," I told him.

"Thanks. I'll take care of him. We'll have a better celebration on Friday."

I nodded and told him goodnight again.

I put my son in his crib and wondered suddenly if I should be worried about Wiley. Right after we'd gotten married, he'd bought a bumper sticker that said, *Yes, I'm afraid it's true. I've fallen in with the wrong crowd.* He wouldn't lower himself to be so common as to actually stick it on his bumper, but it had amused him, and it was still on the refrigerator, held it place by magnets.

It had been a little, playful dig at me: the great Wiley Royce, already married and gonna have a baby, before he was even twenty-five. What feats might he have accomplished, what statesmen and philosophers might he have befriended, if only . . . But it was just a joke. He'd asked me to marry him before he'd even known I was pregnant, so it wasn't as if his instantaneous domesticity was the result of societal pressure, as was his dad's bitching at him to get a real job. Wiley loved us. He wouldn't have it any other way.

But I wondered if he'd fallen in with a *different* wrong crowd now. A bunch of drunken, baby-food-despising hippies. I shook my head. I was just being silly. Wiley just wanted to celebrate his friend's long-sought good news. He was allowed.

But when I tried to picture the future of my marriage, now that my husband had this new friend, this new *drinking buddy,* the scene was strangely dark. Soon Nate would be busy with his own family, leaving Wiley and Tom to bond further. I sighed and went to bed. It would turn out the way it turned out. Worrying about it wouldn't do any good.

It was the first night Wiley and I had been apart since we'd moved in together, right after high school, other than when I'd been in the hospital. The bed seemed cold and huge without him there with me. But he'd be home tomorrow. I'd have another chance tomorrow.

****

I was gonna be late for work – I'd forgotten how much time and thought went into getting Bo ready to go, getting his food and clothes together, making sure there were enough diapers to last him for the day. Wiley always took care of all that.

I found the four of them sitting in folding chairs in front of the counter at the bookstore. See No Evil, Speak No Evil, Hear No Evil, and Drank Too Much.

Deneen smiled at me and immediately rose, took Bo from me. She had a little air of entitlement to her about it, as if now, by being pregnant, she'd already been admitted to that most common, most exclusive of clubs: motherhood. It was okay. It wasn't like Deneen didn't know anything about taking care of babies, once they were here. I'd helped my mom a little bit with Hal and Jen, but I was only five years older than Jen and seven years older than my baby brother, and Mom had mostly taken care of them herself. She loved babies. But Deneen was thirteen years older than her little sister – Delia had been quite the surprise to her parents – so it wasn't as if she didn't know how to take care of a baby. I'd much rather hand Bo to her than to Janae.

Wiley was wearing his black *Ray-Bans* again, even though the sun was barely up, and he was inside. He looked over them at me, and I noticed that his blue eyes were bloodshot. "Sorry I got drunk, Brendee," he said. But he didn't elaborate further, nor did he get up and hug me.

"You're allowed," I told him.

I looked at them, feeling a little left out that they were all playing hooky, while I had to go to work. Tom was again staring intently at his laptop; Nate was reading a more modern version of *Baby and Child Care;* Deneen was bouncing Bo and telling him about how he was going to have a little cousin soon. Bo smiled as if he understood, and touched her face. Wiley stared at a spot on the floor in front of him.

"Well," I said, and they all looked at me. "You truants enjoy your day off. I have to go to work."

"Call me for lunch," Deneen said brightly. "I'll bring Bo. I'll bring everybody."

I set his car seat and his diaper bag on the table under the window, considered Tom and Wiley and Nate. "If they're up for it."

Tom grinned; Nate waved absently, absorbed with Dr. Spock; Wiley continued to look at the floor. I sighed. I kissed him on the forehead – he reached for me, delayed, after I'd already moved away.

He dropped his hands back in his lap, and looked at the floor again. Drinking was definitely not for Wiley, I thought. It turned him into a zombie the next day. I kissed my son, thanked Deneen for watching him today – Wiley was obviously not going to be much of a babysitter – and went to work.

NATE

"Let's go to *IHOP* for breakfast," Tom suggested.

Wiley looked at him as if he'd suggested that we *field dress some game* for breakfast. "You've got to be kidding. I've never been in an *IHOP* in my life." Wiley sniffed. "All that fat and sugar." He looked pointedly at Tom. "All those chemicals."

"You don't know what you're missing, my son. I'd have to go home to make another batch of hangover medicine. The next best cure is a huge, sugary, fattening pancake breakfast."

"There's still some in the fridge," Wiley said.

Tom shook his head. "It's too old. Oxidized." He winked at me. "Not to mention, the plastic . . . Come on, Wiley. Live a little."

Wiley frowned. "How can you talk about chemicals and then want to go to *IHOP?* I'm confused."

"What have I been telling you, Wiley? Chemicals *taste good.* They are . . . ubiquitous. You can't just give them up overnight. It's gonna take a little work. Phase 'em out slowly."

"But *IHOP?* That seems like going in the opposite direction."

"I am in blood stepp'd in so far that, should I wade no more, returning were as tedious as go o'er." Tom grinned. "I came here to your little burg to have a good time, Wiley. I'm no hippie, no ascetic. *IHOP* tastes good," he said again.

"I had forty years of healthy living before I came here. I'm way ahead of the curve. A couple of pancakes aren't going to hurt me, and life's not worth living without bacon." When Wiley remained silent, Tom continued. "I have more to tell you about the whole food additive thing–"

"Food additive thing?" Deneen said.

"You would not believe what's in our food, Deneen," Wiley said. "Citric acid. *Sand–*"

"You haven't heard the half of it yet," Tom said. "But here's the deal, Wiley. You can teach Bo. But unless you move to . . . another planet, you're never gonna be able to keep it all away from him. And the rest of us–"

"I *can* keep it all away from him," Wiley said willfully. "I'll make his baby food–"

"He's not gonna be a baby forever. He's gonna have to live in his culture, just like you do. What I make at home – it's as chemical-free as it can possibly be, and it's the bulk of what I eat. But a little

IHOP is like barebackin' it, my son." Tom grinned wickedly when I blinked in surprise. "It's dangerous, it's bad for you – but it's a lot of fun."

Wiley was not amused. "So, in other words: if you can't beat 'em, join 'em."

Tom's grin widened. "You can't beat 'em, Wiley."

"Then why did you tell me about all this?"

"It's just like *The Matrix.* If you stick with me, I'll show you how deep the rabbit hole goes."

"You didn't give me a choice between the red and the blue pill," Wiley said crossly. "You just started to tell me about this shit–"

"It's cumulative, Wiley. A little excess every now and then isn't going to hurt you. You can't give up a lifetime's worth of–"

"Sure I can."

Tom sighed. "Do you know what *Frito-Lay's* slogan is?"

Wiley brightened. "Do you know what you call eating corn chips and having sex at the same time? A *Frito-Lay!*" Deneen rolled her eyes, tried to pretend that she didn't think it was funny.

Tom grinned. "Their slogan is, *Food for the fun of it.* You live in a culture that thinks like that, that a basic human need is, and *should be,* a playground. It's like saying, *Air for the fun of it.*"

"Food's not for fun," Deneen spoke up. "Food is . . . the enemy."

Tom looked at her in surprise, then back at Wiley. "Have you been polluting Denny's mind with my hysterical obsession already?"

Wiley shook his head. *"Quod me nutrit me destruit."*

"That's right," she said defensively.

"My Latin's a little rusty–"

"It means, *What nourishes me also destroys me,*" I told Tom. It was all the Latin I knew, the mantra of the anorexia freaks Denny used to follow online.

Wiley, God love him, had been able to get her to quit starving herself with just one observation. While I'd never admit it to him, on pain of torture, I thought my friend was brilliant, and this particular time, his logic had been ironclad, immutable. Denny had started in on that whole *It's my body and I'll do with it what I choose* spiel, which had its own brand of righteousness to it, if not a whole lot of logic.

Wiley had shrugged; he wouldn't argue with her zeal. "What, according to the Bible, is the root of all evil, Deneen?"

Deneen, who hadn't read the Bible any more than I had, was still not unfamiliar with the proverb. "Money."

"No!" Wiley said fiercely, making us all jump. "The *love* of money is the root of all evil. And so it should be with you people that wanna starve yourselves. It's not food that's your problem. You need food to live, Deneen, and especially to live well. It's *the love of food* that's the problem. The big, sloppy, disgusting, stuffing-your-fat-face philosophy that surrounds us. I can tell you what to eat, to be healthy. It's not too much."

And just like that, just as easily and completely as Wiley had fallen for Tom's food-story, Denny had fallen for Wiley's. He taught her what was good for her: fruits, veggies, a little chicken, a little fish; and Deneen ate it, in small, mostly bland portions, just like he did. She particularly liked celery, because Wiley had told her it had negative calories. "So it cancels out a little peanut butter on there, which is good for you."

I thought that the tiny portions were what Deneen appreciated about Wiley's theories, more than the nutritional aspects: everything he ate was always just *a little bit.* She liked that Wiley *didn't eat very much.* She didn't necessarily care for Wiley overly as a person: she thought he was a smart-mouthed, confusing know-it-all, most of the time. But she did go along with his dietary advice.

Like we were traitorous, adulterous lovers, Brendee and I would have lunch together, once or twice a week. We'd have bread and pasta, go to *The Cheesecake Factory,* or *Sizzler,* or sin of all sins – may God have mercy on our souls – every now and then, we'd even hit *McDonald's.* Guiltlessly. It wasn't as secretive as all that – our spouses knew that we had to get away from their relentless, little, tiny, *healthy* meals sometimes.

"Food is *not* the enemy," Tom said. "The enemy is ignorance, complacency, and those who would perpetuate it, who would capitalize on it . . . They're a bunch of bastards, indeed.

"But *the fault is not in our stars, but in ourselves, that we are underlings.*" He nodded at his laptop. "The truth is all right here. All we've got to do is look for it, read it, believe it."

"Then how can you wanna go to *IHOP?*"

"Excess ain't rebellion, Wiley."

Wiley glared at him. "But *you're drinkin' what they're sellin',* Tom. Not me."

"Asceticism is excess, too, my son. Eighteenth century Anglican clergyman Laurence Sterne said, *'People who are always*

153

taking care of their health are like misers, who are hoarding a treasure which they have never spirit enough to enjoy.' And that was long before the FDA or food additives or childhood obesity or the Paleo diet.

"Denying yourself a few simple pleasures just because you're smart enough to know they're not good for you . . . You're gonna lose your mind, Wiley. *It is a course of impious stubbornness."* Tom grinned. "Your self-denial *doesn't hurt them, your chaos won't convert them.* A little bit isn't gonna hurt you, and it'll help with that hangover."

"I'm not going," Wiley said stubbornly. "It'll just make me feel dull and sleepy. Slow. Fat."

"I'm not going either," Deneen agreed. "Come on, Wiley," she said, and I looked at her in astonishment. *Come on, Wiley,* was not something that Denny said very often. Like *never.*

Wiley and his superiority were a source of annoyance to her; she felt like he talked in riddles, that he monopolized my time. I thought she was really a little awed by him, a little frightened by what she perceived as still waters running deep – she knew that Wiley could release the sharks at any minute. She'd heard his blazingly insensitive remarks in high school, had been the butt of his derision more than once, when he just couldn't keep his mouth shut about some dumb comment she'd made.

But once I'd started going with her, Wiley had backed off. Now he just talked to her like he would to a six-year-old. If she said, "I saw the tornado damage on the internet," he'd reply, *"You did?"* just like he would to a child. "And what did you think of that?"

But they were allies on the dietary front. It was the only thing they had in common.

"Come on, Wiley. Leave these pigs to their trough. Let's go back to my house. I'll split a salad with you."

Wiley at last smiled. He stood up, gathered up Bo's things. "We'll see you pigs later," he said, and arm in arm, my best friend, his baby, and my pregnant girlfriend left *Morry's Books* to go have a salad.

****

Tom and I went to *IHOP*. He had bacon and eggs and a Belgian waffle smothered in whipped cream, and three cups of coffee. I had a big ol' stack of buttermilk pancakes. I was surprised that they did seem to cure my hangover, but I did feel a little sleepy afterwards.

Tom gently made fun of Wiley, said again that he was a hippie. I told him that Wiley just wanted to be sharp, that he did yoga and Tai Chi, that he wanted his body to be as quick and toned as his mind.

Tom shook his head. "Exercise is overrated. *I felt sorry for the guys packing into gyms, trying to look like Calvin Klein and Tommy Hilfiger said they should. Self-improvement is masturbation.*" He grinned. "You guys are young, healthy. You don't need to work out."

"Wiley wouldn't be caught dead at a gym."

"I didn't think so. No sheep is Wiley Royce. Besides, it's unnecessary, Nate. If you eat right, you don't get fat, so you don't have anything to work off. It's all about diet."

Tom told me that the body was just like any other machine, with boilers and filters, temperature regulators, pulleys and levers, a substructure. Good food kept the mechanism functioning properly. Additives and chemicals and too much junk clogged the filters, threw the connections out of whack.

"We're just meat and chemicals and electricity, Nate; and, literally, figuratively, *unequivocally* – you are what you eat. And anytime you overindulge – have too much to drink, eat shit like this–" he indicated his demolished, billion-calorie breakfast "– you just have to eat right again. Clean the machine. Unclog the filters. You don't need a pill for every ill, you don't need to sweat it out. Just eat right again. Put the imbalance back in balance again."

I thought that he and Wiley were actually pretty much in agreement. "Except Wiley doesn't believe in getting unbalanced in the first place."

"All work and no play makes Jack a dull boy," Tom said again. "He's never gonna appreciate his intellect and his health and youth until he spends a few days dumb-drunk and feeling old, like something the cat dragged in."

"I don't know about that, Tom. Nobody appreciates Wiley's intellect and overall swellness more than Wiley himself." I frowned. "He's just been uncharacteristically serious lately."

There was Brendee and motherhood, and his dad bitching at him; and then there was Brendee and her video, and now, "I think you've really freaked him out with this food additives thing."

155

"It's something to be freaked out about, Nate. Like I said, you haven't even heard the half of it yet. But you can't just *stop*. Civilization has progressed too far. There isn't any untouched wilderness, no untainted air, no pure, spring water, anymore. It's no longer like Thoreau said: *The very timber and boards and shingles of which our houses are made grew but yesterday in a wilderness where the Indian still hunts and the moose runs wild.*

"All that's gone now, irrevocably. You have to live in the here and now, work with what's available. Dionne can't go back, and neither can Wiley. We have to pick and choose, try to find the best, accept that there are a few chemicals in everything. *Every goddamn thing.* And I'm telling you, a little isn't going to hurt you. And even a lot–" he nodded at his plate again, "– isn't gonna hurt you every now and then. You have the longest life expectancy in the history of mankind."

"But we still gotta die."

"Indeed. And there are men that are seeing to it." When I looked curiously at him at this remark, he just shook his head. "Let's blow this pop stand. You didn't take a day off work to spend it with me."

****

When I got back to the apartment, I found Wiley and Denny, with Bo on her lap, seated across from each other at the kitchen table, with a sea of groceries between them. They looked at me when I walked in, and Denny got up and gave me a little kiss. Without comment, she handed Bo to me, then sat back down; like I was his father instead of the guy sitting across from her.

"What was the last one?" she said to him.

"Polydextrose." Wiley read from his phone. *"Polydextrose is an indigestible synthetic polymer of glucose. It is frequently used to increase the non-dietary fiber content of food, to replace sugar, and to reduce calories and fat content. The FDA approved it in 1981. Polydextrose is commonly used as a replacement for sugar, starch, and fat in commercial beverages, cakes, candies, dessert mixes, breakfast cereals, gelatins, frozen desserts, puddings, and salad dressings.* And bread." Wiley nodded at the bread package. That's where Deneen had read the ingredient. *"Polydextrose is frequently used as an ingredient in low-carb, sugar-free, and diabetic cooking recipes. It is also used as a humectant, stabilizer, and thickening agent."*

Deneen shook her head. "What do all those words mean? Is it good or bad?"

"Put it in the *Maybe* column."

I watched Denny painstakingly write *polydextrose* on a yellow legal pad, in a column with a question mark at the top of it. She picked up the bread again. "The next one is *cellulose fiber.*"

"Fiber's good for you," I said.

They both looked at me. "Maybe," Wiley said suspiciously. "What's next?"

"Datem."

Wiley consulted his phone. *"Datem is an emulsifier primarily used in baking. It is used to strengthen the dough by building a strong gluten network. It is used in crusty breads, such as rye bread with a springy, chewy texture, as well as biscuits, coffee whiteners, salsa con queso, ice cream, and salad dressings."*

"This is so hard, Wiley! What's an emulsifier? What's gluten?"

"Didn't we have *emulsifier* yet? Gluten is a protein found in grains."

"No. We have *stabilizer.*" I looked over her shoulder at a column entitled *Definitions*. A stabilizer was *any of various substances added to foods, chemical compounds, etc., to prevent deterioration, the breaking down of an emulsion, or the loss of desirable properties.*

"Ok. Hold on a minute." Wiley typed. "Jesus. There's a ninety dollar book about it. *Food Emulsifiers and Their Applications."* Wiley scrolled. "Emulsifier. Noun. *An agent that forms or preserves an emulsion, especially any food additive, such as lecithin, that prevents separation of sauces or other processed foods."* He looked at Denny. She nodded and only wrote *non-separator* on the pad. Her fingers must've been getting tired from all the writing.

"Okay, here's the rest about datem." Wiley scrolled. *"The exact chemical mechanism is not understood . . . its main function is as a softener . . . datem is generally recognized as safe by the FDA."* Wiley looked up. "Put it in the bad column."

Under a column entitled *BAD*, followed by three exclamation points, Deneen wrote *datem*.

"But–" I began. Wiley just looked at me. He was already convinced. I said to Denny, "If it's recognized as safe . . ."

"Generally," she said darkly. "Wiley told me about all *that* shit, Nate." She looked at me accusingly, as if to say, *Why didn't you tell me?* "You heard Tom. Ignorance is the enemy. I'm eating for two

now. Wiley and I are gonna find out just exactly what's in this stuff."
She gestured at the groceries.

Wiley was looking at his phone again. "Tom says cellulose is
sawdust. He says, if you want some extra fiber, eat some beans."

Denny made a face, but poised her pen over the pad. "What
kind of beans?"

Wiley texted, waited. "Navy beans, pinto beans, kidney beans.
Split peas." He grinned up at me. "Sounds like it's time for some of
Wiley Royce's Famous All-Bean Chili."

I rolled my eyes. *Wiley Royce's Famous All-Bean Chili* was
awful. Bland. Tasteless. *Meatless.*

Denny looked at the bread ingredients again. "The next one is
sodium propitionate (preservative)."

"Just write that one down under *BAD*. Preservatives can't be
good."

Deneen complied. "Monoglycerides, calcium sulfate, *citric
acid.*" She said *citric acid* like she'd read *cyanide.* Wiley had been
busy, filling her pretty little head with all of Tom's bullshit. She was
a convert.

*"Together with diglycerides, monoglycerides commonly are
added to commercial food products in small quantities. In these
applications they are useful as emulsifiers, helping to mix
ingredients such as oily materials and water that otherwise would
blend poorly,"* Wiley read. *"The commercial raw materials . . . may
be either vegetable or animal fats and oils . . . also may be made
synthetically."* Wiley and Deneen exchanged a glance. She wrote it
down in the *BAD* column.

"What's the next one?"

"Calcium sulfate."

Wikipedia told Wiley that calcium sulfate was a desiccant, also
called gypsum, also called drywall. Before I could stop her, Deneen
threw the perfectly good loaf of bread in the trash.

This just went on and on. Deneen read off the ingredients in my
favorite Heart-Healthy brand of *Trader Joe's* Instant Oatmeal.
Dipotassium phosphate (also on the GRAS list), which was used as a
stabilizer and acidity reducer. It was also used in fertilizers. Silicon
dioxide, or just plain silica, was a primary ingredient in
diatomaceous earth and in the production of glass. In food, it was a
flow agent.

"More fucking *sand,*" Wiley said.

Guar gum was mixed with nitroglycerine in explosives – it was a waterproofing agent. In my oatmeal, it was a thickener and stabilizer. It had uses as a cholesterol reducer, also, so Deneen wrote it down in the *Okay* column. Ferric orthophosphate was used as a rustproofer, to kill snails and slugs, and as a source of iron in my oatmeal. It was GRAS in the good ol' US of A, "But it's prohibited as a food additive in Europe," Wiley noted.

Deneen shook her head and went to throw the box in the trash. I objected.

"Leave my oatmeal alone," I told her from the living room, where Bo and I, ignored, were watching television. "You don't have to eat it. I like it. I don't care what's in it."

"Knowledge is the treasure of a wise man, Nate," Wiley said.

"You know what, Wiley?" I got up, leaving his sleeping son on the couch. "Maybe I don't want any more knowledge. I've lived this long, dumb – I'm healthy enough. Who cares? I'm not buying this FDA conspiracy bullshit.

"Anyway, what can be done about it? Just like your new guru said, chemicals are everywhere. I know not to eat too much sugar and fat and sodium. Jesus Christ on a crutch, haven't you preached to me enough about all that? Maybe I don't wanna know any more about this other shit. Maybe it's all okay."

Wiley raised his eyebrows mildly. "Or maybe Red #40 causes cancer. Maybe sulfites trigger asthma." He turned Denny's pad around and consulted it. "Maybe diacetyl, used in margarine, causes Alzheimer's. Maybe if you inhale it in the fumes from microwave popcorn, you'll get–" he read from Deneen's notes, *"bronchiolitis obliterans, also called Popcorn Lung, a rare and life-threatening form of non-reversible obstructive lung disease."*

"Or maybe I won't. I haven't yet." I looked at Deneen. "Did you throw my popcorn away, too?"

She nodded. Wiley grinned. "Why risk it?"

I went back and sat on the couch with the baby. I tried to concentrate on the television, but mostly I listened to them. Denny continued to read off the ingredients from the boxed, bagged, and canned foods; Wiley would look up the awful truth, and Denny would write it down on the yellow notepad, then mostly toss the food in the trash.

I feared a minute for the spaghetti – for all her anorexia-spawned, Wiley-advised healthiness, Denny loved her some spaghetti – she ate it plain, with just a little butter. But it had niacin, iron, thiamine, riboflavin, and folic acid, which was good for the baby. It was fortified. It passed the crazy test.

It amazed me to see Denny and Wiley so in sync. She had always been neutral toward him, if not downright annoyed; and he'd always been appalled by her ignorance, at her blithe unconcern about all the things that had been so important to the shaping of the world, at least to him: history, art, literature, science.

But now – I thought that if they were sitting out there talking about sex instead of chemicals, I would've been jealous. They were copacetic, they were in harmonic synchronicity; they were simpatico. If I didn't know what they were talking about, if they were strangers to me and I'd just walked by and seen them sitting there, it would've seemed like they were attracted to each other, in love – so perfectly in agreement and understanding were they. Partners, *equals,* in this new insanity.

At lunch time, they made mashed-up avocados and mashed-up pears for Bo. They were gonna give him cottage cheese, too, until Deneen read the label. It had modified food starch as a thickening agent. Calcium phosphate – they had a hard time deciding on that one – the web was confusing as to just exactly what it was – Deneen finally just wrote down *calcium supplement.* Calcium carbonate, customarily found in blackboard chalk, was also a calcium supplement, so it was okay at first, until *Wikipedia* informed Wiley that *excess calcium from supplements, fortified food and high-calcium diets, can cause the milk-alkali syndrome, which has serious toxicity and can be fatal.*

It wasn't looking good for this cottage cheese. It also had acetic acid, which turned out to be just vinegar; guar gum again, and Vitamin D3.

"Oh, fuck this," Wiley said, and threw it in the trash. "First it says that there was a study that said this D3 prevented colon cancer. Then some doctor says the study's methodology is ridiculous. The next paragraph says that they use this D3 in rat poison. Write this down, Den. It's also called *cholecalciferol."*

She complied, then they looked at each other, and cut up pears and avocados for themselves for lunch.

"I'm calling your wife," I told Wiley. "You people make me want a cheeseburger."

****

160

I told Brendee about the health nuts' blowing Tom and me off for breakfast, about them throwing away a pantry full of perfectly good food.

"What's wrong with him, Nate?" she asked, tucking into a big, chemically-made-to-taste-delicious *Western Bacon Cheeseburger* from *Carl's Jr.*

I shrugged. I couldn't stay mad at Wiley for long. "He's just looking out for Bo." *And Denny, and my just-made baby*, I thought.

"He's been distant," she insisted. She didn't know that I knew exactly *how distant* he'd been.

"You know," I said, sipping my lethal *Cherry Coke* through its landfill-busting plastic straw, "even Tom thinks he's going overboard with it." I dipped a grease-bathed French fry into the little cup of stabilized, emulsified, sugar and salt infused, red-dyed ketchup, and savored it when I ate it.

"Tom set him up there on the railing."

"I think he'll be able to talk him back down. It's all about moderation, you see. Even Tom knows that all this shit Wiley's suddenly so frantic about is inescapable." I remembered the raspy little song Tom had sung. *"No one he-ere gets out alive."*

"I hope you're right. He's starting to piss me off. Making your own baby food."

My phone beeped. *Come home, I miss u,* Deneen texted. *Wiley went back 2 Morry's.*

"See?" I said. "He's gone back to the Master. Tom'll set him straight."

BRENDEE

The rest of the week passed uneventfully. I discovered that I was still wrung out from my tummy troubles, so I went to bed early. Bo was a little fussy: I thought maybe he'd caught my sickness. But he didn't spit up, so next I thought that perhaps his little system might be unaccustomed to this sudden influx of fresh fruits and vegetables, and I jokingly suggested as much to Wiley. He didn't even smile; he just told me that Bo was all right.

Wiley himself spent the evenings at the bookstore. He had a phone and a tablet to fix, he said, and then some friend of Janae's had dropped off a laptop, and Dionne had lugged in some old dinosaur of a desktop and asked him if he could recover some files from it. He'd taken all his tiny little tools - what I called his *jeweler's screwdrivers* – and his little suction cups and strange wiry things to *Morry's.* Tom had found him a table, and he'd set it all up in the office. Whatever. I was glad he was keeping busy.

I felt as good as new when I got up to go to work on Friday, mostly because I was looking forward to our little party. Bo would be going to stay with Wiley's parents – Aunt Amy was thrilled to have him – and Wiley and I, and Deneen and Nate, and of course, *Tom,* were going to sit around at our apartment and have a good time. Deneen would be designated driver, and Wiley volunteered to be designated drinker.

Another simple plan: I went to the store after work and bought assorted liquors. I got a veggie platter for the health nuts. And I bought a giant bag of *Cheetos* for me and Nate. Fuck Wiley if he couldn't take a joke.

But when I arrived at the store to pick him up, he wasn't ready to go. Aunt Amy had already stopped by and taken Bo home, so that delay was avoided, but I wanted to get on with the party. I wanted to *go.* I found Wiley, Nate, Tom, Dionne and Janae all standing in a circle in the office, looking at the big monitor that Wiley had installed on the wall over his new work table. It showed the feeds from the security cameras.

"Someone could just walk in here off the street and rob this place," I began.

"Shush," Wiley said. "We're trying to prevent just that."

"Did you just shush me, Wiley?" I replied. I was only half kidding; mostly, I was half annoyed.

He nodded at the monitor. One of the camera feeds was enlarged: it showed two young men, about our age, and a woman, a little bit older. They were lounging against a blank brick wall. The woman was smoking a cigarette. Their features were quite distinct, even though it was already dark outside, and the only light seemed to be coming from a streetlight, somewhere off camera.

"Well, hell, Wiley. They can't hear me." They all continued to watch the trio on the monitor. "Where is that, anyway?"

"It's right on the other side of that wall," Tom said, and pointed at the back of the office. "They've just been standing around out there for about ten minutes."

"They don't look like readers to me," Janae said ominously. Then she looked over and smiled at me. "How are you, Brendee?"

"Shush!" Wiley said again.

"Brendee's right, Wiley," Tom said. "They can't hear us."

Wiley waved his hand and studied the monitor.

"I'm fine, Janae," I whispered. "I was a little under the weather this week, but I'm better now."

"Why don't we just go out there and run 'em off?" Dionne suggested softly.

"It's a free country," Tom said. "They're not doing anything wrong."

"And besides," Nate said, "they might be–"

"What?" Dionne said. "Armed?"

"You never know," Janae said. Again she smiled at me. "I hear you're having a little party tonight."

"Yes. Would you like to come?" I wondered if Wiley had already invited her. I touched Dionne on the arm. She was wearing a military fatigue shirt with the sleeves rolled up. "And you, too, Dionne?"

"That's so nice of you, Brendee!" she exclaimed, and Wiley glared at her. "I would definitely enjoy a party," she whispered.

"Why don't you people just go then?" Wiley said tersely. "Don't go around the back–"

"I never park in that lot," Dionne said. "I got my car broken into back there once. I'm parked on the street."

"Me, too," Janae said. I also nodded.

"Then why don't you guys just go?" Wiley said again. "This might be–"

"Dangerous," Nate suggested.

163

"Ah, what would we do without men?" Dionne gestured at the screen. "To protect us from all the dangers of city life? Loitering kids?" Wiley glared at her again. "Okay. I'm going. Ladies?"

I didn't even attempt to kiss Wiley good-bye. He was sleuthing.

I paused outside the office to text Deneen. I told her to just walk on over to the house, that Nate and Wiley would be a minute.

Is Wiley keeping him again?

I started to type *They're watching* . . . But it was too much to explain in a text. So I just said *Yes.*

Fucking Wiley! I could see Deneen stamping her foot in anger.

They won't be long.

I peeked back into the office. "Don't be long, Nate," I said. He glanced over at me. "Or you're gonna piss Mama off." He nodded and went back to watching the ne'er do wells on the monitor.

Janae and Dionne said they'd follow me, and we left.

NATE

After the ladies departed, Wiley went out and locked the door, turned off the lights. He moved one of the folding chairs closer to the table, gestured at the other two by the desk.

"Sit, my friends. Let's see what they do now. Now that we appear to be closed."

Tom and I each pulled up a chair and sat down. We watched. Waited.

BRENDEE

Deneen was sitting on the steps that led upstairs to my apartment, looking at her phone. "They're still at the store," she told me. "Watching the criminals."

I nodded down the street as Dionne and Janae pulled up. "I invited more for the party."

Deneen brightened. "That's great, Brendee! Who knows how long it's gonna take the crimestoppers to show up?"

I was glad that she wasn't going to bitch about Wiley *keeping* Nate again. She seemed in an unusually good mood – it was undoubtedly because she felt that all her dreams were coming true. *Let's see how dreamy you feel once that morning sickness starts,* I thought.

Deneen made us each a drink. She couldn't have any, of course, so she told us to drink for her, and made ours extra strong. She set out the veggie platter and the *Cheetos* on the table, along with an empty bowl. She didn't open the *Cheetos,* but that wasn't unexpected. Deneen didn't eat *Cheetos,* and what with her new additive awakening, she probably didn't want us to, either.

The four of us sat there and stared at each other for a few minutes. We didn't know each other, didn't know what to say. The party wasn't off to a very good start.

"What a beautiful bracelet!" I said to Janae.

"Thank you." She took it off and handed it to me. It had delicate links and all kinds of cute little silver charms: a kitten, a martini glass, a parrot; a tiny set of dice. They all clinked together pleasantly. "It's one of my favorites. Tommy gave it to me." I showed the bracelet to Deneen and Dionne, then handed it back to Janae. She laid it down in front of her on the coffee table, arranged all the charms on one side with her fingernail.

The conversation died again.

Then Deneen clapped her hands together. "I know! Let's play *Who Am I Gonna . . .*" she looked a little nervously at Dionne, then shrugged. *"Who Am I Gonna . . . Do Next?* Remember, Brendee? From high school?"

Janae slammed half of her drink. "I don't think you have to be shy because of Dionne, Den. She's not our mother. It was actually called *Who Am I Gonna Fuck Next?"*

Dionne grinned in surprised delight. She wasn't shy. "How did it work?"

"It's kinda self-explanatory," Janae said. She got up to make herself another drink. Even though she and Tom weren't actually blood-relations, fondness for drinking seemed to run in the family. But what the hell? We were gonna have a little fun. I slurped my own drink. "Just bring the bottle out, Janae," I told her. Dionne smiled at me.

Janae brought the bottle of rum and the two liter of *Coke* back with her. No one had opted for the gin I'd bought for Wiley and Tom. No one had touched the whiskey I'd gotten for Nate, either. Janae poured another little shot of rum into our glasses and sat down on the couch next to Deneen.

"It worked like this. If you broke up with your boyfriend, and you were over it . . ." She mimicked rubbing her eyes in sorrow. "Then you'd tell all your friends about who you'd like to *do* next, and we'd have to guess who you were talking about. Remember that one time, Den? At Bev's?"

Janae told Dionne, "Bev was such a slut. She went into great detail about how she wanted to blow this guy – it was disgusting." Janae wasn't disgusted at all. "And we guessed Lyle What's-His-Name. She said, 'I wasn't talking about him, but he'll do.' Somebody guessed someone else, and she said, 'No, but he'd do, too.'" Janae laughed and sipped her drink.

"I don't think I was at that party," Deneen said. "But I believe it. Bev really was a tramp."

I remembered Bev, too, even though I'd only met her once. She'd walked up to me at Deneen's graduation party, looked me insolently up and down, then asked, "Aren't you going with Wiley Royce?" Then she'd made some filthy comment, alluding to homosexual activity between Wiley and Nate. They hadn't shown up at the party yet, and she intimated that in addition to being gay, it was because they were afraid of her brother.

When they finally did show up, the brother – Neal – said something about me – what had he called me? Something pretty tame. A bitch, a dog – something like that. Before his friends got a chance to finish guffawing at his cleverness, Neal swung on Wiley, just for fun. But to my eternal surprise, Wiley ducked and tripped Neal, dropping him to the stone floor beside the pool. At the same time, Wiley tapped a beer bottle on the concrete, and held the jagged glass to Neal's throat. Then he calmly suggested that it would be in Neal's best interest to apologize to me.

That was the night that I'd learned that Wiley's superiority wasn't all talk. He was lightning fast and just as fearless as his smart mouth had always proclaimed him to be. After Bev's brother apologized, Wiley and I had left the party and went back to his parents' house. They hadn't been home, so we'd taken advantage of their absence . . .

Deneen had been frightened of Wiley for months after that. As Nate said, she'd never seen a real broken-beer-bottle-wielding bad-ass before. I hadn't either, had never guessed that Wiley could display such violence, all in the name of my honor. Nate had found the whole thing hilarious.

Deneen and I had played *Who Am I Gonna Fuck Next?* just between the two of us. Before Nate, Deneen had been a little bit of a tramp herself, and she'd really gotten into telling me the plans for each new conquest. I didn't have anybody to talk about except for Dave, but she'd coax me into describing our latest adventures.

"Of course," Deneen said now, "you guys know who Brendee and I would talk about, although . . ." she looked at me, at a loss for words. She knew about the lack of stories I had to tell at the moment. I had to talk to someone about it, didn't I?

Deneen continued quickly, changed the subject. "Did I tell you guys that Tom helped me get pregnant?"

All eyebrows flew up at that one. "It's true!" Deneen said. "He gave me this magic book. It said that all the fertility spirits – they like flowers and candlelight, so if I surrounded the bed with flowers and candles, they'd enjoy it, and they'd bless me with a baby!" When we looked dubious, she said, "I'm telling you guys! It worked!"

"You might've already been–"

"No." Deneen shook her head. "I took a test that day. It was negative. I took another test two days later, and it was positive. I got pregnant from that night! The spirits helped me!" She grinned mischievously; she didn't really believe in fertility spirits. "Either way, Nate liked it. He was so surprised that I wanted him to do all the other things he likes to do, those things that aren't necessary for actually conception. It was great. I hadn't really been concerned with the quality for a while before that, because I was just concerned with making a baby, but it was so much better, slowly. I'd almost forgotten how *good* he is." She grinned at me. "I'll never rush him again. And it worked."

"Good fucks make good babies," Dionne said, quoting Norman Mailer. Quoting Tom.

"You guys don't know the one I'd like to do next," Janae said. "He's in my Macroeconomics class–"

"You know mine," Dionne interrupted. She topped off her drink and composed her thoughts for a minute.

NATE

"How long are we gonna watch them, Wiley?" I asked. "Maybe Dionne was right. Maybe we should just go out there and run 'em off. There's three of us, so I don't think–"

"Wait!" Tom said. "What's this?"

The girl made a sudden move: she threw her shoulders back and took off the short-waisted denim jacket she'd been wearing and tossed it against the wall. She was wearing a long skirt, and – it was now revealed – a thin white tank top. She had short, dark hair; a tattoo of a dragon graced her shoulder.

"No bra," Tom observed. He was right: we could see the girl's nipples, high and proud. "Damn, Wiley! These cameras are amazing."

Wiley grinned, put his feet up on the desk and crossed his ankles.

The girl suddenly turned and threw herself against the guy standing to her left. He stumbled back against the wall, and she ground her body against his, kissed him hungrily.

"Hot damn!" I said in amazement. "Dinner and a show."

"But what about Joe there?" Tom asked, and pointed at the other guy.

Joe was looking at his companions with interest. His buddy smiled at Joe when the girl started kissing his neck.

"I think it's clear what you have to do, Joe," Wiley said, speaking for the guy that was getting his neck gnawed. "Is it clear?"

"As an unmuddied lake, Fred," Tom answered for Joe. *"As clear as an azure sky of deepest summer. You can rely on me, Fred."*

BRENDEE

Dionne took a deep breath, let it out with a luxurious sigh. "I'd talk him into coming up to my place, in the mountains. I tell him we were gonna go camping. There's this little meadow, behind the cabin . . . very secluded, surrounded by trees. It's a little nippy this time of year up there, but I have this huge comforter. It was my grandmother's. It's old and soft and warm. I'd wrap it around us, and we'd walk out into the field. I'd lay it out in the tall grass, and then there, under the clear sky and the bright stars . . ." She sighed again.

"Tommy hates nature, Dionne," Janae said harshly. "He likes the city. You'd do better to invite him up to the best hotel in town."

"But it's beautiful up there, Janae."

Janae shrugged. "I don't care how beautiful it is. I'm telling you – *Tommy hates nature.* He likes streets and pavement. Lights, noise. Civilization. Room service. He wouldn't want to be out in the weeds, getting mosquito-bit, rolling around on the hard ground." She frowned in distaste.

"Really?"

"He'd never go camping with the family when I was little. When we went to Disneyland, and stayed in a nice hotel, he was down for that. But not camping. 'If I wanna sleep in the dirt, I'll sleep on the sidewalk in front of the store,' he'd say."

Dionne looked at Janae for another moment, considering it, then grinned at us. "Maybe I'll just have to move the whole thing back inside the cabin then." She winked.

"You guys have to come up and see my place sometime. Bring the babies. The cabin has three big rooms, and there's a bomb shelter underground. My late husband, may God have mercy on his soul, left me a lot of money. He avoided the inevitable end of civilization as we know it, but just like me, he was convinced it was coming. So I've prepared." Dionne paused, sipped her rum and *Coke*. "I'm pretty much set, come what may. Although, I would like to put in a bigger, better garden–"

"Then there's your ticket, right there," Deneen said. "Tom told me he has a garden. Right, Janae?"

"One of the best in the country."

"Ask him up for the weekend. To help you *plow* that garden." Deneen giggled.

"Too late for this year," Janae shook her head sadly.

She wasn't sad at all. She was jealous! I saw it all at once. She didn't like Dionne because Dionne liked Tom! Wasn't that cute? Wasn't that . . . odd? Wiley had convinced Tom to consider Dionne's obvious desire for . . . *friendship,* a little more seriously. Dionne was clearly down for Tom to take Wiley's advice, and Janae wasn't liking the situation. Not one bit.

"So I'll just have to go back to my original plan," Dionne said. "In the cabin. Like I say, nights are getting a little chilly up there. We could build a big fire in the fireplace, light some candles . . ."

"For the fertility spirits?" Deneen grinned and Dionne grinned back.

NATE

The three of us watched in amazement while Fred undid his pants and the girl dropped to her knees. Joe continued to observe.

"You got any popcorn, Tom?" Wiley asked.

"And this is right out in broad daylight?" I said in astonishment.

"Right on the other side of the fucking wall," Tom said. "If you go in and flush the toilet, they'll hear you."

"Don't do that," Wiley said. "You'll spook 'em." He grinned at us. "Amateur porn. My favorite."

"*Live* amateur porn," I said. "Right out in broad–"

"It's not broad daylight," Tom said. "It's dark. It's not like anyone can see them from the street . . . Well, someone could see them from the parking lot, I guess . . ."

"How long do you think this kinda shit's been going on, Tom? Right outside your place of business?" Wiley asked. "Aren't you glad we put these cameras in? Hell, this is better than–"

"Wait!" I said. "It looks like Joe's gonna make his move."

BRENDEE

There was a moment of silence; an ice cube broke up in my glass and made an audible tink. Deneen said, "Tell us about yours, Janae."

She smiled deviously, and downed the rest of her drink. "Mine, like Dionne's, is brilliant."

Deneen shot me a glance. "What does he look like?" she asked, holding my gaze.

Janae poured some more rum into her glass. "He's tall, slender. Broad at the shoulder, narrow at the hip, blue-eyed. He's got a very nice ass."

Deneen's own green eyes widened. *Is she describing Wiley?* her expression asked me. There were lots of blue-eyed, tall, slender guys, and even Deneen had not failed to notice Wiley's ass. But Janae didn't have to be talking about my husband. But she could be . . .

"His name is Tyler." Janae paused, looked at us. "I know, right? But I don't care about his awful name. I don't want to marry him. He's got the most incredible blonde hair. Straight, long – all different colors of yellow, like some throwback rock star."

I watched Deneen relax. Janae wasn't talking about Wiley.

"He's so cool," Janae said. "Not cool, like hip, like you thought cool was in high school. He's too intelligent for all that."

Again Deneen looked at me. *She said Tyler's a blonde,* I thought. *She's not talking about –*

"It's just the way he looks at me. Not coldly, not hotly . . . *coolly.* Like he knows what I'm thinking, but . . . I dunno.

"I'm a little bit afraid of Tyler, but . . . oh, my God, deliciously so." Janae shivered theatrically. "It's just the expression on his face when he looks at me. The sparkle in those depthless blue eyes – he's amused with me, but not amused at all. I'm a challenge, but – no, he's convinced; he's smug, he *knows.* When he looks at me – there's always just the tiniest ghost of a smile on his face. It says it all to me, and it says nothing." Janae sipped her drink.

Deneen grinned. "And what do you want to–"

"No." Janae again sipped her drink. "Not this time. Not this one. I've almost always been the initiator in these things. Sometimes they stand too much on ancient proprieties, sometimes they're shy. They think they might offend me if they move too fast. But I don't wanna wait around all night. *An old cat sports not with her prey.* I don't care what they think–"

"Can I get an amen?" Deneen said, and she and Janae high-fived. Dionne grinned.

"I'm not gonna marry 'em. I don't want to wait around all night," she repeated firmly. "So usually, I make the first move. I know what I like, and they don't complain if things happen a little quicker than they'd planned.

"But not with Tyler. I'll respond if a man sends signals to me – but Tyler's signals – they've been subtle. I don't want to just up and make a pass at him . . . What if I'm mistaken about these signals? I'm fascinated to know how he thinks: will he? Damn right, he will, or . . . is he just pretending he will? I want Tyler to come to me, to show me that he wants me, that I'm not imagining it.

"Just from that little smile – I feel like he sees right through me, like my face is an open book, *where men may read strange matters.*" Janae sighed, shrugged. "Like I say, I usually make the first move, if for nothing more than expediency's sake. But with Tyler . . . I find that I want to . . . *submit.*" She grinned mischievously. "I want to just let him do whatever he wants . . ." Janae winked at me and I grinned back. Now here was some good, old-fashioned, girl-talk. "Although I do have a few suggestions for him . . ."

NATE

Joe stood behind the girl, put his hands on her shoulders, effectively blocking our view of the happy ending, if there was one, to what she was doing to Fred. But then she stood up, and turned around. She was taller than Joe, so we could see her head over his shoulder. She smiled at him, bent forward a little bit at the waist to kiss him –

"Oh, yuck!" Wiley said, grinning.

– and at the same time, she hiked up her skirt and leaned slowly back into Fred; he arched his back, looked heavenward, closed his eyes.

"I'll be *damned,"* Tom said. "I may need a moment alone after this."

"Dionne's at my house." Wiley closed one eye and squinted at Tom. "I won't be offended in the least if you guys leave early."

My phone beeped and I took it out of my pocket and looked at it. "Deneen wants to know where the fuck we are." I showed Tom her text, so he could see that she'd phrased it just that way.

"Tell her we're watching the live porn channel," Wiley said. He was perfectly willing to stay and follow the show through to its conclusion, but I'd seen enough.

"I don't wanna piss her off, Wiley," I said, feeling a little bit *whupped,* like my dad used to say.

Wiley didn't comment. "All right." He looked back at the monitor. "I guess they weren't planning to rob the store, after all."

"Yeah, let's go," Tom agreed. "I don't want to run into them. It would be . . . uncomfortable. Wiley might feel compelled to comment."

"To critique," I added.

Tom grinned. "Where'd you park, Nate?"

"Oh, shit!" I looked at the back wall, picturing the parking lot on the other side. "My car is . . . Shit, my car's gotta be right on the other side of the camera." I looked at the happy . . . trio, still locked in embrace, trying to figure out where I'd left the car, in relation to the wall, in relation to *them* . . . "Yeah, it's gotta be a few spaces over from the light."

Wiley giggled. "What should we do, wait 'til they're finished?"

Tom shook his head, pointed at the screen. Joe and Fred and the girl were changing positions. "They're liable to be here all night. Go flush the toilet, Nate."

I complied. My phone beeped again. Denny wanted us to come to the party *now*. I walked back over and looked at the screen. "Joe looked up for a minute," Wiley reported. "But as you can see, he's *involved . . .*"

"I've got an idea," Tom said. "I'll go open the side door and then slam it." It was a metal security door. "Maybe the noise . . ."

But that didn't work, either. Like Wiley had observed, the three were *involved.*

"Okay. Let's try this," I suggested. "We'll go out the front door, walk around the block, approach from the other side. We'll talk loudly –"

"How 'bout this?" Wiley pushed something on the keyboard that was hooked up to the security cam console. A spotlight speared the lovers. They blinked up at it for a moment, then, while quickly redoing buttons and zippers, they dispersed immediately.

"Why didn't you say something about–" Tom began.

"You didn't ask, my son. The lights are only on the outside cameras. Should we go see the ladies? I don't know about you, but after this . . . I think I'm gonna be damn glad to see them."

JANAE

"Say something about Wiley," Deneen said to Brendee. "Just because he's been . . . Just because you guys . . . That doesn't mean . . ." She winked at me. "She loves to talk about him. I've been hearing about him since high school. Go ahead, Brendee. Tell Janae and Dionne about Wiley's . . . trapeze."

Yes, Brendee, I thought. *You tiny, hot little thing. Tell Janae all about Wiley's . . .* Had Den really said trapeze? *Yes. Definitely tell me about* that.

It was only fair. After all, I'd just told *her* about Wiley, about what I wanted him to do, how I, Janae Rossmore, who was always the aggressor – I'd just told her how much I longed to *submit* to her husband's whim. How much I wanted to find out if that promise that seemed to be in his eyes – if it was real or if I was just wishing it there.

No, that wasn't exactly right. It was real, all right. Wiley flirted with me, audaciously, openly, brazenly. Guiltlessly. But that didn't mean shit. He wasn't irresistible to me. He was smart, and he was clever, and he was tall and lean and blue-eyed. And he had dark hair. There was no Tyler. I didn't even like blonde men. I was telling Brendee about her own husband.

But like I say, I didn't pine for Wiley, like a helpless character in a romance novel: my feeling was not all encompassing, burning. It was just a little warm, but it was different than the usual. *He* was different than the usual. It was just as I'd told them – I didn't desire Wiley, so much as I wanted him to show that he desired *me.* And once he demonstrated that desire – it would have to be something a bit more expressive than just putting a filthy hand on my face – then the little warm I had for him would start to boil.

But I wouldn't be tricked again. I wouldn't make an out and out play for him; that would give him the opportunity to turn me down, to hide behind propriety. I didn't want to hear him say, "I love my wife, Janae. I'm sorry if I gave you the wrong impression." I didn't want him to look at me with embarrassment *for me,* as if I was a deceitful homewrecker and he was the last honest man. I enjoyed flirting with him and I very much enjoyed thinking about what it would be like to submit to him; but my small lust for him was still quite at my command. I wasn't gonna let him make a fool of me.

Brendee hesitated. Then after a moment, she said, "The trapeze is something better imagined. I guarantee that it's just as awesome as you'd think, and much more awesome than I can describe."

Brendee grinned at that cow Dionne – why had she invited her, anyway? She wasn't like us – she was old, a weirdo. She was wearing fatigues, for God's sake. How did she think she was ever gonna get a man dressed like G.I. Joe? It was obvious that she liked men, from the way she looked at Tommy, even if she dressed like a dyke. And she'd had the nerve to talk about wanting to do him in front of me. What kind of a whore was she, anyway? Tommy would never . . . She was homely, she dressed like a dude, and she was crazy, with all this end-of-civilization bullshit. He'd never get *that* lonely.

Brendee still hesitated. Maybe she wasn't the kind to kiss and tell. If Wiley was mine, I'd surely brag him up, but maybe she was one of those shy women, the type that could *do it,* but just couldn't talk about it. They were sometimes a whole great big lot of fun, I reflected, once one ascertained that they were willing. I wondered if Brendee had ever . . .

"I'm not like you, Janae," she said, as if answering my unspoken question. I blinked in wonderment, and waited for her to explain. "I mean, about . . . *submitting."* She faltered, stumbled over the words. "Well, that's not exactly true, either . . . Just, not at first . . . But then, later . . ."

Brendee stopped, took a deep breath. Then her words, lubricated by an ample amount of rum, eddied out of her beautiful mouth – slowly, but not haltingly; softly, but not with shyness. I immediately knew that Deneen was correct: here was something that Brendee loved to talk about.

"The thing that I like best is just to touch him. He'll wait – he won't say anything; it'll be like we're brother and sister for the longest time. And when I can't stand it anymore, I'll just touch him . . . on the collarbone, on the shoulder . . ." She actually reached her hand out, and I realized that I was holding my breath.

"And then he'll smile at me, and just lie there, perfectly still, and let me touch him . . . It's the biggest turn-on, *ever."* She grinned craftily, and it was beautiful. "Wiley has a phenomenal amount of self-control. He is fucking *Zen* in his amount of self-control. But eventually . . . Once again, right about the time when I can't take it another second . . . then he decides that he wants to touch *me."*

"And then?" Dionne said.

She was such a stupid cow! Didn't she have any imagination? I could surely imagine *and then,* especially with Wiley. I imagined that Wiley's *and then* was spectacular. Someone who displayed so much smart-mouthed self-assurance could no doubt back it up with performance; that was the main thing that was so attractive about him.

I didn't need Brendee to draw me a picture. But on the other hand, if she wanted to, I would surely pay close attention to it. *Tell me what your husband's like, Brendee. What he does, what he says* . . .

Brendee blinked rapidly for a second, looked down at her drink. Blushed a little bit. "This is silly," she said. "You guys don't wanna hear about . . . This is supposed to be *Who Am I Gonna Fuck Next?* Not, who am I . . . Not my husband . . . You guys don't want to hear about Wiley."

She seemed a little bit disoriented for a moment, and I knew that she was done talking about Wiley, whether we wanted her to continue or not.

BRENDEE

And this is why I don't drink. Beautiful Janae – and she was beautiful – had just sat there and listened to me say the most intimate things about Wiley. Things I remembered more than had been allowed to experience for *so long* . . .

And I was blathering on because I was already about half in the bag, and because Deneen had suggested it. Telling these kinds of stories – Deneen was my friend; she wasn't remotely interested in Wiley. Hell, she didn't even particularly *like* Wiley, past their recently reinforced dietary alliance. But she didn't mind hearing a few details now and then. It was the same thing with me. I was in no way attracted to Nate, but a little salacious tale about him occasionally was still fun.

But I shouldn't be mentioning this stuff to Dionne, someone I didn't even know. I'd never revealed such things in front of a woman her age. I wouldn't ever dream of discussing them with my mother or Janae's or Deneen's mother, and Dionne was a little past *their* age. It would just be embarrassing.

And I certainly shouldn't be confessing them to Janae, a beautiful, *young* woman that I didn't know either. It was just none of their business; I didn't want them reflecting on Wiley in any way, so I shouldn't have opened my big mouth. I really didn't care about Dionne: she was too old for Wiley, and she only had eyes for Tom. But Janae . . . Yeah, I definitely shouldn't have been talking about my husband to Janae.

The door opened and the men walked in, these men that we'd just been discussing. I wondered if their ears burned. Somehow, from the looks on their faces, I thought that maybe it was so: the three of them each sported big, round, eyes; blank, innocent expressions – and the clichés played through my mind: they looked like the cat that ate the canary; like a kid caught with his hand in the cookie jar. But that was just silly. They couldn't know that we'd been talking about them, had been *describing* –

Wiley said, "Can I have a brief word with you? In the bedroom?" He looked at Tom. "Make me a drink, would ya? I'll be right back." He beamed that irresistible Wiley smile at Deneen and Dionne and Janae, then grabbed my hand and practically yanked me from the couch.

I couldn't imagine what it was he had to say to me that had to be said right then, when we had company. Something that was so important that he had to drag me into the bedroom.

Wiley closed the door and, pausing for neither words nor even breath, he roughly pushed me up against the wall. He kissed me brutally, and I was so completely surprised by it that I didn't even think to kiss him back. He paused, murmured against my neck, *"A speedier course than lingering languishment must we pursue, and I have found the path.* Come on, Brendee. *This is the latest parle we will admit."*

I was so surprised that I didn't even have time to realize that he'd said, *Come on, Brendee.* It was never like that, it was always me saying, *Come on, Wiley.* When I hesitated another second – we had a houseful of people, just on the other side of the thin wall, for God's sake – he started to pull back.

I hesitated no longer. I pulled him against me and kissed him, ravenously, pouring out all the deprivation of Christ-only-knew how many months upon his mouth, his face, his neck. He put his hands on my hips, lifted me up; I wrapped my legs around him, and we fell back onto the bed.

After a moment's fumbling – I never realized before how difficult it could be to get my pants off – Wiley and I took each other. Hard, fast, brief; glorious, wonderful, surprising, *amazing.*

He grinned at me, kissed me quickly on the forehead. "I love you, Brendee. Surprise!"

"I love you, Wiley." *Surprise, indeed.* He never *ceased* to surprise me.

It had been a whirlwind, a tempest – I wanted to do it again, immediately, our guests be damned. But he just kissed me hastily on the mouth and leapt up, swift and graceful as a cat. He found his jeans, stepped into them, pulled them up with a little hop.

Mimicking a synthesized voice, he sang, *"Work it, make it, do it, makes us – harder, better, faster, stronger."* He smiled. "Again. Later." He did up his fly and padded quickly out of the room, closing the door behind him. Where did he come up with these weird old songs?

Goddamn you, Wiley, I thought, but didn't mean it. Janae could have her rock-star blondie; Dionne, her nature-hating health nut; Deneen, her big, strapping, daddy-to-be. I pitied them, actually: in my mind, none of them could hold a candle to my flawless, incomparable, always surprising husband. I sighed, sat up. I got up and found my hastily discarded jeans. My underwear was hanging from the corner of the dresser. I put them back on, straightened out the rest of my clothes, ran a brush through my hair. I looked at myself in the mirror. *Hot damn!* He was just downright unbelievable sometimes. Later, indeed. *Again.*

I went back out into the living room. Wiley was sipping a drink, standing with Tom and Dionne, outside the open front door. He blinked innocently at me, almost the same expression that he'd worn when they all walked in. What *had* they been up to? Where *had* this come from?

Tom grinned slyly and waved to me, a cigarette in his hand. He'd guessed the subject matter of the conversation that Wiley had so *briefly* had with me. I might've blushed. I waved back and quickly walked away from the door.

Deneen was sitting on Nate's lap in a chair beside the couch. He blinked blankly at me, smiled. Nate had always been as easy to read as a child's book, with large print and small words. Nate didn't know, nor did Deneen.

Janae smirked at me over the rim of her glass. Her expression communicated so clearly that *she* knew, that it was if she could smell it on me. *"Now,"* she said, affecting a German accent, *"what shall we talk about?"*

Wiley came back into the apartment. "Ask me no questions and I'll tell you no lies, Janae," he said. He smiled at me and I couldn't help but smile back. He looked at Janae again. "I'll tell you no lies, regardless."

"My mama always told me not to ask any questions to which I didn't want to hear the answers."

I wondered for a moment what exactly it was that she might dare to ask Wiley, but then Deneen asked her own question. "Did those people try to rob the store?"

"Not in the least," Wiley said. "In fact–"

"After a little while, they just . . . went on their way." Nate exchanged a grin with his fellows, but when he looked at me, I saw a flash of bemused guilt. What *had* they been up to?

"Who needs another drink?" he said. He gestured for Deneen to get off his lap; he took Wiley's glass, then quickly stalked out to the kitchen.

Tom and Dionne sat next to Janae on the couch. She frowned and moved all the way over against the arm, as far away from Dionne as possible. Her dislike for the older woman was plain, and I thought that Dionne had no trouble at all returning Janae's unfriendliness. I wondered if Dionne knew *why* Janae disliked her. Wiley sat on the arm of my chair.

"I was thinking about telling our friends about the good doctor, Janae," Tom said with a big smile. "And more about how what he peddles is killing us."

Jane rolled her eyes. "Oh, God, no, Tom! Nobody wants to hear your character assassination of Dr. Hutchins. What did he ever do to you?"

"Hutchkiss," Tom corrected firmly. "Hitler never did anything to me personally, either, but I still wouldn't have lunch with him. He was still an enemy to mankind."

"I don't care all that much for mankind," Dionne said. "Mankind has made a mess of my world. Mankind is circling the drain. I only care about myself, and those that are close to me." She patted Tom on the knee. "The rest of 'em are on their own."

"I don't care about anyone except those people that I feel are worthwhile," Wiley said.

"And damn few they are," Deneen said and smiled at him. "Some of them aren't even born yet."

I was absolutely flabbergasted when Wiley leaned over and patted my friend on her still flat stomach. I don't think I would've been much more surprised if he would've suddenly stood up and dragged *her* into the bedroom this time, instead of me.

Wiley was not generally a physically demonstrative person, at least not in public, and especially not toward women. In other words, he was not a hugger, not a shoulder-toucher, and certainly not an unborn-baby-belly-patter. Wiley touched women only for a purpose. It was a familiarity that he wouldn't have attempted, and Deneen certainly wouldn't have allowed, had their food philosophies not so recently moved into such perfect cosmic alignment.

"I don't care, period," Nate said, returning. He handed Wiley a fresh drink.

"You have to care, Nate. For our baby." Deneen got up and sat in his lap again.

Nate shook his head, then nodded at Tom. "He was too persuasive in the first part of his argument. We're the healthiest population in the history of the world. I just can't believe that a little sand, even a little glass, is that detrimental. I think that it's inert, it just passes right on through."

"Maybe," Tom said, smiled. "Maybe that's what they want you to believe."

Wiley said, "Or maybe it clogs things up, or it sticks in your guts, or it irritates your tissues. Maybe all that clogging and sticking and irritation leads to disease, disease that otherwise might've passed me by. What was that disease that the old-timey miners used to get? I bet they thought that coal dust was inert and harmless, too."

"Breathing something's not the same as eating it," I said.

Wily glanced mildly at me, didn't comment on my opinion. He said, "Maybe my body has to work so hard to rid itself of these inert things – things that shouldn't be in there in the first place – maybe resources better served in keeping me healthy are used up with those processes. I've never been sick a day in my life–"

"So you really have no room to speculate," Nate said.

"It's a free country, my brother and only friend. I can speculate on any goddamn thing I wanna speculate on."

"But you're probably wrong," Janae said. "If you've never been sick in your life, then you're proving Nate's point more than Tom's. All these demon additives probably aren't that bad – you've been eating them, and you're okay."

"Wiley doesn't eat that shit," Tom said. "He is almost naturally chemical free. He doesn't eat processed foods, not because of the additives, but because of the fat and the sugar and the sodium."

"And the simple unnecessity of all that garbage," Deneen said. She and Wiley high-fived. It was adorable.

"The Romans believed in *miasma,* that there were evils in the night air," Tom said. *"Malaria* literally translates as *bad air.* They stayed inside as much as possible at night to avoid what they believed caused the disease – the air itself. Mosquitos came out at night, so by one misbelief they avoided the true cause. Not entirely, of course . . ."

Nate reached for the bag of *Cheetos,* and Deneen snatched it away from him, consulted the label. Nate rolled his eyes.

"Wiley eats healthy to begin with, so he avoids . . ." Deneen read the label, "disodium phosphate."

Wiley already had his phone out. *"Used as a food additive to enhance a food's texture, increase shelf life, or to keep a dry mixture uniform during storage."* He looked up, then back at his phone again. "It's also *used in cleaning products, in some pesticides, and as a corrosion inhibitor."*

"Or . . ." Deneen continued, "sodium diacetate."

"It's *a colorless solid that is used to impart a salt and vinegar flavor.* It's also *a fungicide and bactericide registered to control molds and bacteria, and thus prevent spoilage, in stored grains.*"

"Or . . . sodium caseinate."

"*A milk protein used in paint and glue.* It was greenlighted as GRAS in 1979. *It may cause kidney damage and cancer.*" Wiley scrolled, frowned. "It's in everything. Spinach dip, those little lunch things you're supposed to give to your kid, *Hot Pockets, Claim Jumper* pies, liquid coffee creamer, *Cool Whip.*" He scrolled. "The list just goes on and on and on."

"Nor does Wiley eat the rainbow of red and yellow dyes that combine to make that awesome orange color," Tom said.

Nate took the bag from Deneen, tore it open and defiantly stuffed a handful of *Cheetos* into his mouth. "I don't care," he repeated with his mouth full. "I don't want to know."

"There's a big difference between *I don't care* and *I don't wanna know,*" Wiley said.

"*I don't wanna know* gets you an atom bomb in your front yard," Dionne said.

"*I don't care* gets me that, too," Nate said, crunching. "There's nothing I can do about that."

"That's the attitude that gets us a government that tells us what days we can build a fire, what kind of light bulbs we can use. And we just follow along like children." Dionne frowned. "Remember incandescent light bulbs, Tom? The kind that didn't have mercury in them?"

"There still might be a few in the store."

"The store could use a little cleaning, then," Dionne said and patted Tom's knee. "It lacks a woman's touch."

"Light bulbs. Atom bombs. There's nothing I can do about all that," Nate said again.

"Right," Wiley agreed, "except maybe vote." He grinned. "But you can do something about *what you fucking eat!*"

"*I don't want to fucking know!*" Nate repeated obstinately. "These *Cheetos* taste great. That's all I need to know."

Wiley shook his head, appalled. "You're paying for what you think is food, and you're getting sand and sawdust and glass and drywall. Indigestible synthetic polymers of glucose. You're paying for food, and you're getting shit. How can you be so ignorant as to not want to be aware of that? I can *make* you know–"

"But you can't make him *want* to know," Tom warned.

186

"Sometimes ignorance is bliss," Janae said.

Wiley looked at her incredulously. "I thought you were smarter than that."

Janae shrugged. "I'm not like Nate – it's not that I don't wanna know. *I already know.* It's been harped on me since I was ten years old." I thought she would smile at Tom, but she didn't. "I don't care. I am unaffected by it. Just like Nate said – we're the healthiest, longest-lived population in history. So I'm just trying to live my long life. I don't worry about the atom bomb." She sneered at Dionne.

"And you'll be sorry some day for that," Dionne sneered back.

"That's all you do is worry about it!" Janae shouted. "You live your whole life under this cloud of suspicion, waiting, fearing, hating something that might never happen! And if it does happen, you can't do anything about it!"

"I can prepare for it. And it's gonna happen."

"It hasn't happened yet," Nate said conversationally, licking the chemicals, the red and yellow dyes, off of his fingers.

"Sometimes it's difficult *knowing* about things," Janae said. "When I was in high school, sometimes I wished that I wasn't smarter than everybody else. At times, I envied the carefree, dumb girls, the ones that didn't care about anything more than how pretty their clothes were, when shoes were gonna go on sale again." She grinned at Deneen and Deneen grinned back.

Wiley glared at her. "My . . . *Our* children aren't gonna be sheep."

Janae shrugged. "It's hard to be different."

"Not only different. *Better.*"

Harder, better, faster, stronger, I thought.

"I was up above it," Tom said.

Wiley grinned at him in pleased surprise. *"Now I'm down in it."* He looked at Janae again. "But I'll be good and goddamned if I'm gonna wallow in it with the dumb, pretty people."

"Maybe they're happier," Janae suggested.

"Happier?" Wiley cried in disbelief. "What have you got to be unhappy about? Are you unhappy because you care about . . . No – are you unhappy because you *understand* something more about life than the next cute kitty video that goes viral on the internet? *The people that once bestowed commands, consulships, legions, and all else, now concerns itself no more, and longs eagerly for just two things - bread and circuses!"*

"Be gentle with the young," Tom said and winked at Wiley.

187

"All the sheep are happy, too, Janae," Wiley said. "Right up until they're forced down the chute to the slaughterhouse. I imagine that they have a great big surprised look on their little wooly faces then, once it's too late, right before the hammer falls. They live as if they're never gonna die and then die without recognizing that they've been led down *the way to dusty death* all along, by people that paid just the tiniest bit more attention than them. Just like Tom says, it's not like it's a secret." He gestured at the *Cheetos* bag. "It's all written right there on the side. But the sheep are too dumb to notice that they're being had. Because they don't observe, don't look up from their phones for ten minutes; because they don't care . . ."

"I aim to avoid the slaughterhouse," Dionne said.

Wiley ignored her. "I've never been unhappy about not being a sheep. They're a constant source of amusement to me. How could I possibly *admire* someone who puts the ring in their own nose? I've never had a moment's sadness from knowing I'm smarter than everybody else."

"You're a legend in your own mind, Wiley!" Janae said in amazement.

"And you just want to fit in. You lack the self-confidence that should be the most pleasurable outgrowth of all this intelligence you say you have." Wiley smiled at me, then looked back at Janae. *"Baa."*

"You're all going to pay for your complacency . . ." Dionne said portentously.

"And who of you by being worried can add a single hour to his life? Observe how the lilies of the field grow; they do not toil nor do they spin . . . They don't squirrel away shit with a thirty-year shelf life, against the end of the world," Tom observed. When Dionne frowned further, Tom patted her on the knee. Again Janae scowled.

"I'm not gonna be led by the nose to this sand and glass and sawdust-filled slaughterhouse anymore," Wiley said. "And neither is my boy."

When no one spoke for a moment, Tom said, *"You have displaced the mirth, broke the good meeting with most admired disorder,* Wiley."

Wiley frowned, then looked at everyone for a moment. There we sat. The convinced: Tom and Deneen. The unconvinced: myself, Janae, and Nate. And Dionne, who seemed to accept that she was a sheep, but planned to do something about it only after the ranchers had burnt the farm to the ground. The discussion had reached a stalemate, threatened to actually escalate into an argument. An idea seemed to strike Wiley, and out of the blue, he said, "You guys wanna play cards?"

"Since you think you're smarter than everyone else, I'd imagine that you cheat at cards," Janae said.

"God save us from what you'd imagine, Janae," he replied, though not unkindly.

"It's true, though," Nate said.

"Who told you I cheat at cards?"

Nate sipped his whiskey. "You did."

They smiled at each other, and the cloud of disagreement dissipated. Their friendship was stronger than damn near any difference of something so fleeting as an opinion.

"What about you, Tom? Do they play poker on . . . Where you're from?"

"No, Wiley. That's one of the reasons I came here." I noticed that he now had his arm draped loosely around Dionne's shoulders. She positively beamed. Janae glowered into her drink. "I'm down. But I like to smoke when I gamble."

"There's a table on the balcony. Come on, Nate. You can throw me over if you think I'm cheating." Wiley kissed me lightly on the cheek. "We'll play a few hands, and leave the ladies to talk about . . . whatever it is that ladies talk about." He smiled at Deneen. "Babies and such."

Wiley found a deck of cards in a drawer in the kitchen, and a dusty, battered wooden box containing poker chips. He flipped on the lights on our tiny balcony, and he and Nate and Tom and Dionne – Dionne was thrilled to the bone by Tom's unwonted attention, and she wasn't leaving his side – went out and sat at the round table.

"Okay," Tom said. He took the cards out of their box and shuffled them. Expertly, I noted. "How about a little five card draw? You guys all know how to play that one?" They nodded. "What are we gonna call these chips, Wiley? Blues are a quarter, reds fifty cents, whites a buck? How does that sound?"

Wiley grinned at me. "Sounds good," he said. He was obviously not the only poker player in the group.

I smiled at them all and shut the sliding glass door.

"So much for the party," Deneen said with a pout.

"We don't need them, Den," Janae said. "They're just men." She looked out at Dionne. "And half a man. Let 'em have their fun. This party's for you, anyway. Tell me about babies."

JANAE

Deneen started to talk about babies, just like I'd suggested. We discussed names, and after a moment, Brendee busted out her laptop. They Googled what all the names meant, then segued right on into baby clothes, and baby furniture. I contributed to the conversation, but . . . *meh.* It held but limited interest to me.

I went out to the kitchen to get fresh ice for our drinks. On a whim, I texted Wiley. I wouldn't want him to think I was angry with him for his superiority, for his slavish devotion to Tom's – though I hated to use the term – craziness. *Baa,* indeed.

Who's winning? I asked, then went back out to the living room, and poured fresh liquor and *Coke* over the ice for his wife and for myself. She and Deneen were now completely absorbed with baby stuff on the internet. My phone beeped.

Do u want 2 play? Please't ur highness 2 grace us w/ur royal company.

The table's full.

Here is a place reserved – u can sit on my lap.

Before I could stop myself, I looked through the window at him. He was smirking at me: that maddeningly blank, barely there grin. Did he really want to play this dangerous game? He looked down at his cards, then said something to Tom and didn't look in my direction again.

Maybe later, I texted.

2morrow & 2morrow & 2morrow creeps in this petty pace from day 2 day . . .

I'm talking 2 ur wife.

He didn't respond to that for a moment. The cards held his attention. Then he texted, *What r u talking 2 her about? Is it a tale full of sound and fury? Told by an idiot?* ☺

Signifying nothing ☺ I looked out at him again, but he was laughing at something Nate was saying. I texted, *What would we talk about? If I came out there?*

I watched him look down at his phone, smirk, consider. *Y, the first thing that popped up, of course. But may b ur right. Now's not the best time. I need 2 concentrate on taking these peeps' $.*

I read his text, then watched him put his phone back into his pocket. I had been dismissed.

"Only blue and pink?" Deneen said. "Janae?"

"We're boring her," Brendee said. "She's texting her blondie."

I looked at them. "He's done with me for tonight," I said, and dropped my phone into my purse beside the couch. "What did you say, Den?"

NATE

"Let me tell you a little story," Tom said as he raked in the first pot. "What've you got that I can use for an ashtray, Wiley?"

Wiley reached into a cardboard box full of recycling that stood beside the railing of the balcony, and extracted a Budweiser can.

"You don't drink–"

"Don't ruin Budweiser for me, Tom," I said.

"He beseeches you," Wiley said and dealt the cards. "It's his brand."

"I wouldn't dream of it." Tom grinned and lit a cigarette.

"Who wants another drink?" Dionne asked brightly. We all held up our hands. She got up, gathered up our glasses, and practically skipped back into the house.

"Looks like tonight might be her lucky night," Wiley opined.

"Maybe," Tom said. *"Drink, sir, is a great provoker of three things."*

"Don't *equivocate* with me, Tom. You're not that drunk. I wouldn't think you'd tease the old gal."

"Unlike yourself," Tom said.

So he'd caught the little wordplay between Wiley and Janae, just like I had.

"All in good fun," Wiley said. I noticed that he wasn't defensive to Tom.

"I doubt you not, my son. Not for a moment. You know which side your bread's buttered on, as the poet says. And Janae is–"

"Janae is beautiful," I said, before I had a chance to stop myself.

Two pairs of blue eyes blinked at me in surprise. "What's on a drunk man's breath is on a sober man's mind," Wiley observed.

"But I don't talk to her to way you do," I recovered. "I don't make her think–"

"She's gonna think what she wants to think, whatever he says," Tom said.

"Give thy thoughts no tongue, nor any unproportioned thought his act," Wiley said, then laughed to himself and looked out onto the dark street.

"And Janae's mind is *full of scorpions,* on the best of days, Nate. She's a cagey one. Trust me. You have no idea." He said to Wiley, *"Stanley, look to your wife,"* and nodded in at the women.

Denny was standing up, pouring more rum into her friends' glasses. Brendee and Janae were sitting close together on the couch, their heads bent over Brendee's laptop. As we watched, Janae put her arm lightly around Brendee's shoulder, gave her a little squeeze. Wiley and I looked back at Tom, like spectators at a tennis match.

"There are more things in heaven and earth . . . But you know how that one goes."

Dionne opened the slider and stepped back out onto the balcony, handed us each a fresh drink. "What's the game, Wiley?" she asked.

"Same as before." We all considered our cards.

"What's this story you want to tell, Tom?" Dionne asked, smiling happily at him. I exchanged a grin with Wiley.

"Once upon a time, there was a man name Oskar Renfro Hutchkiss." Wiley reached for his phone, but Tom held up his hand. "Dr. Hutchkiss isn't on *Wikipedia.* He's past president and CEO of the *International Food Information Council,* and I've found his name linked to the more shadowy *International Food Additives Council.* These two groups are the pretty faces shown to the public by the food conglomerates. *Cargill, Hershey's, Yum Brands, PepsiCo, the Coca-Cola Company, Heinz, Kellogg's, General Mills. Dannon. Kraft. Dow-Agro. McDonald's. Monsanto. DuPont.* If it's a giant brand name on your local supermarket shelf, chances are it's one of the supporters of the IFIC.

"They claim that their mission is to help keep us informed about all of the things that are going on in the food industry, to scientifically answer all our humble questions, such as, *Why are you motherfuckers poisoning us?"*

I called, Dionne called; Tom looked at his cards, folded. "Before running the IFIC, Dr. Hutchkiss was a butcher, a baker, a candlestick maker: he worked in sales for *Tyson, Dunkin' Donuts,* and *3M.* He worked for the Department of Agriculture, the FDA. He's a medical doctor; he also has a degree in sociology, psychology, history, economics, and chemistry."

"A jack of all trades," Wiley suggested. He asked for no cards, called.

"A Renaissance man," I said, and threw a white chip into the pot. No cards for me, either. I was willing to bet that my hand was as good as Wiley's.

"A man for all seasons," Dionne said. She called my white chip and raised me a blue one. She also took no cards.

Wiley looked at his hand, then considered me and Dionne closely for a moment. "I figure you're too dumb to bluff," he told me with a grin, "and Dionne's too smart." He folded.

"Dr. Oskar Renfro Hutchkiss, polymath, man about town," Tom said. "He just might be the Antichrist."

I saw Dionne's blue chip and called. Dionne beat my three of a kind with a full house. She raked the pot to the space on the table in front of her, then we all looked at Tom.

"You're familiar with the term *eugenics?"*

"Nazis," Dionne said, stacking her chips.

Wiley reached for his phone again, and again Tom stayed him. "Allow me. I'll just read you the salient points." He looked at his phone; typed, scrolled. *"Eugenics is a social philosophy advocating the improvement of human genetic traits through the promotion of higher reproduction of people with desired traits (positive eugenics), and reduced reproduction of people with less-desired or undesired traits (negative eugenics). Eugenics, as a modern concept, was originally developed by Francis Galton.*

"He wasn't German. He was . . ." Tom scrolled. "An Englishman. Cousin to Charles Darwin. The irony of that overwhelms me." Tom sipped his drink, then consulted his phone again. *"As a social movement, eugenics reached its greatest popularity in the early decades of the 20th century . . . was practiced around the world . . . promoted by governments, influential individuals and institutions. Many countries enacted various eugenics policies and programs . . . Most of these policies were later regarded as coercive or restrictive, and now few jurisdictions implement policies that are explicitly labelled as eugenic or unequivocally eugenic in substance."*

"Just like I said: Nazis. Are you gonna deal, Nate?"

"How's your drink, Dionne?" Wiley asked.

"Damn near empty." She drained it.

Wiley grinned, drained his glass, and held it out to her. Tom and I followed suit. We were all in the fast lane to Drunktown. She smiled and got up, went back into the house to make us all another drink.

"Proceed," Wiley said to Tom.

"Dionne is a picture of the average American. If you say *eugenics,* anyone who thinks they know what it means immediately says *Nazis."* Tom looked at his phone again. "But *eugenic policies were first implemented in the early 1900s in the* United States. It says

194

that the scientific reputation of eugenics started to decline only *after* the Nazis used it to justify their atrocities. *Nevertheless,* it says, *in Sweden, the eugenics program continued until 1975.*

"They used to sterilize poor people. Right here in the good ol' US of A, my boys. To help to strengthen the race." When we looked dubious, Tom quoted Wikipedia again. *"The methods of implementing eugenics varied by country; however, some of the early 20th century methods involved identifying and classifying individuals and their families, including the poor, mentally ill, blind, deaf, developmentally disabled, promiscuous women, homosexuals, and racial groups (such as the Roma and Jews in Nazi Germany) as 'degenerate' or 'unfit;' the segregation or institutionalization of such individuals and groups, their sterilization, euthanasia, and their mass murder."*

"Nobody . . . No government does anything like that anymore," I said.

"Nobody would dare call it that anymore," Tom said. He dropped his cigarette into the empty beer can. There was a sizzle. He read, *"At its peak of popularity, eugenics was supported by a wide variety of prominent people, including Winston Churchill, Margaret Sanger, H. G. Wells, Theodore Roosevelt, George Bernard Shaw, John Maynard Keynes . . . Its most infamous proponent and practitioner was, however, Adolf Hitler, who praised and incorporated eugenic ideas in* Mein Kampf *and emulated eugenic legislation for the sterilization of 'defectives' that had been pioneered in the United States.*

"In other words, Dionne's right. The Nazis gave eugenics a bad name. There's a list of people, here at the bottom of the *Wikipedia* page. *Individuals,* it says, without comment. They're mostly all dead, these proponents of the betterment of mankind. Except this guy right here." Tom held up his phone. The name he pointed to was *Oskar R. Hutchkiss.* "And, as you can see, Dr. Hutchkiss is the only one on the list whose name isn't linked. No *Wikipedia* page for the good doctor."

This seemed much more ominous to Tom and Wiley than it did to me. "Maybe he's just not as famous as the rest of them," I suggested.

"He's also an economist."

Wiley frowned. "That sounds like math."

"Baa," Tom bleated at Wiley's legendary mathematical ignorance.

195

Wiley shook his head. "Where's Dionne with my gin? If you're gonna subject me to math, I'm not nearly drunk enough." We looked in: Dionne had paused to speak to the other ladies. She'd set our empty glasses on the coffee table. Janae still sat close to Brendee; I noted that the length of their thighs touched. After the things I'd witnessed this evening, I noted such things.

"I'll put it in simple terms for ya, Wiley," Tom said. "No formulas, I promise.

"What if, like I suggested the other day – what if you fed Bo as few chemicals and additives as possible? You can't keep him totally pure, but what if he avoided all the sand and sawdust, the colorings and the preservatives, the stabilizers, the emulsifiers – as much as possible? How long might he live?

"Where I come from, all that shit doesn't exist. It's not uncommon for us to live to a hundred and thirty; hell, a hundred and fifty's not unknown.

"But what would happen to the economy of the first world – what would happen to the economy of the *whole planet* – if everyone here lived that long? What kind of a job would you guys be able to get, if I was in the workforce, hale and hearty, for another fifty or sixty *years?*"

I smelled that conspiracy again, and it still stunk. "What are you trying to say, Tom?"

"You're saying that it's population control," Wiley said. He narrowed his eyes, considering, knit his black eyebrows together in concentration.

Tom laughed. *"Soylent Green is people!* Atta boy, Wiley!"

But Wiley frowned. "You're saying that they're poisoning us so that we don't live as long as we *could,* so that the next generation has room to grow, to expand. So they have jobs. So the economy doesn't . . . falter."

"What started out as a good thing – food fortification – has led to a population that just might live forever, so–"

Wiley shook his head. "They fortify everything so that we're healthy enough to *work.*" He didn't see anything good in it. All he saw was the ignorance, the chute, the slaughterhouse. I wouldn't have believed that my brilliant friend could be so paranoid, but here it was. "Then they poison us with all these delicious, processed foods, so we die, so we don't take up space in the workforce that should be utilized by the young . . . Then they poison them, too, to keep it all going."

196

"And then there's the negative eugenics," Tom said. "The people that eat this shit all the time, exclusively – they're gonna die before those of us that avoid mac and cheese and *Hamburger Helper* only because of the fat and sugar and sodium. We smart guys – we know better. Isn't that right, Wiley? We buy that good-for-you, organic line – it's a triumph of advertising: all that heart-healthy, low cholesterol bullshit – and that shit has additives in it, too. So all of us smart people aren't so smart, after all, my sons. And we'd realize it if–"

"We read far enough down the label," Wiley said.

I shook my head. Poisoned food as a social program. Killing off the ignorant. It was just insane.

But Wiley looked as if the completeness of a horror was dawning on him. Like he might look if he came home and discovered Brendee in bed with geriatric Wes Thomerville – I grinned to myself at the idea of that. He looked as if things he'd just been led to suspect had now gelled into an awful certainty.

Tom smiled wickedly at Wiley's realization. *"It is the wine that leads me on, the wild wine that sets the wisest man to sing at the top of his lungs, laugh like a fool – it drives the man to dancing . . . it even tempts him to blurt out stories better never told."*

"But who are *they?*" I asked. It was just too ridiculous. "I work for the government, Tom. In my office, they can't keep which secretary the boss is screwing a secret, nonetheless something as complicated as a global, population-controlling, food-poisoning conspiracy. It would have to involve *thousands* of people." I looked at Wiley, who was still thinking, still frowning. "Somebody would squeal. It would be impossible."

"Why do you think so, Nate?" Tom asked. *"Two may keep counsel when the third's away.* Why do you think thousands of people would have to know? You don't even know what you're eating, and it's not a secret. It's right there on the label. You said so yourself. You don't care. It all tastes good, so what else matters? You're young and healthy now, so what difference does it make what kind of cumulative effect eating all this garbage might have on you in the long run?"

"The long run isn't really that long, after all," Wiley reflected.

"And you're only miserable at the end of it, right?" Tom grinned, then continued. "People are concerned with their own lives, today. Not the big picture of tomorrow. If you're working on the assembly line at *Kraft,* and they tell you to put sawdust in the

197

Parmesan cheese – *if* they even bother to tell you that's what it is, which I doubt – what do you care? You just do what you're told. Collect that paycheck."

"It wouldn't take too many people," Wiley agreed. "Two, three. A committee."

"You're telling me that only two or three people control what goes into our food?"

"How many people run the FDA?" Wiley asked.

"I'm telling you that only two or three people know *about the ramifications of what goes into our food,*" Tom said.

"The population control part," Wiley said. "The economics of it."

"It's propping up the medical industry, too. Sure, they've still got a few inherited things to try to cure. Social diseases to treat. They've eradicated polio, but the clap's still with us." Tom grinned at a still solemn Wiley. "And of course, there are injuries; car wrecks. You gotta put that assembly line worker back together when he falls in the wood chipper that supplies all that sawdust. Help revive him when he falls in that million-gallon vat of . . . of Christ-only-knows what." Tom lit another cigarette.

"But the main money-makers in the first world for the medical profession are the diseases of affluence: heart disease, cancer, diabetes. High blood pressure. Obesity. And all of those can be traced back to diet."

"Because we eat *too much,*" I insisted, remembering all of Wiley's rants. "Not necessarily because of what they put in our food."

"While our benevolent healers are treating all the diseases of affluence, brought on by diet, making billions, there's plenty of time for research and development for discovering things to help the illuminati live longer. If we all ate right, eventually doctors would be as unnecessary as paper boys. As librarians." Tom grinned, then said, "I'm sorry I keep using your boy as an example, Wiley. But he's the only baby I know." Wiley still wouldn't smile. "Like I said, Nate – what if Bo's palate was never industrialized? What if he never ate all the additive-laden junk that the rest of his peers are going to eat? What if he just ate *good food?* You don't get heart disease from just eating fruits and veggies. Enriched grains. Not even if you throw in an occasional steak."

"Can you prove that?" I asked.

198

Tom nodded. "I can. Pretty much. A good diet leads to a long, healthy, disease-free life."

Wiley looked cautiously at him. "Can you prove the rest of it, though? The conspiracy? Can you name names, point out the people who are in charge of all this?"

Tom smiled in faux offense. *"Behold, I cry out of wrong, but I am not heard: I cry aloud, but there is no judgment. O, ye of little faith!* I've been looking into all of this for some time, gentlemen. I'm convinced that our friend Dr. Hutchkiss is a key player. The kingpin, actually, I think. He's listed there on *Wikipedia* as a eugenics proponent–"

I shook my head. "I wouldn't base my paranoia about a global conspiracy on something I picked up on *Wikipedia,* Tom. Jesus. They wouldn't even let us use it as a research source in college. Not even in high school. *Wikipedia* is not exactly the *Encyclopedia Britannica.* "

Tom smiled. He was not offended by my disbelief; in the short time I'd know him, I'd gotten the impression that it would be difficult to offend Tom with anything I chose to believe or not to believe. Damn near impossible, in fact. He wasn't a crusader as much as just a simple *purveyor.* He'd tell us; he didn't care one way or the other if we believed him. He wasn't trying to convince us of all these evils any more than he was trying to convince us that he was from another planet. He just wanted to let us know.

"And the doctor himself doesn't even have an entry. But I've seen his name in other places. Like I say, he was once the president of the *International Food Information Council,* the mouthpiece of our industrialized palates. No one knows for sure just who backs the *International Food Additives Council* – but I found out that Dr. Hutchkiss gave a lecture at their mid-year meeting."

"How did you find that out?" I asked.

"I called them." Tom grinned at our surprise. "I asked if the meeting was open to the public – it was – and I asked who would be speaking. He gave a talk entitled simply, *Emerging Markets.* Promoting the great cornucopia of US agricultural commodities to our downtrodden brethren in the beleaguered third world."

"Did you go?" Wiley asked.

"No." Tom grinned again. "They were preaching to the choir. Patting each other on the backs. What would I have said?"

"How about *why are you motherfuckers poisoning us?* "

"I already know why, Wiley."

"But you don't have any proof," I insisted.

"All I have are a few pearls, Nate. No string with which to put them together. Hutchkiss is a eugenicist – but I can't find anything he's written about it. He's worked for several food conglomerates specifically, and headed their public relations organ. He's spoken before all his old cronies at the *International Food Additives Council.* He was a wheel for a few years at my most favorite of incompetent government agencies, the FDA.

"Wearing his economist hat, he wrote a treatise called *The Impact of an Aging Population on Future Workforce Opportunities.* It ends on an upbeat note – he's not suggesting that you take all of us old folks out and abandon us on ice floes – but if you read between the lines a little bit . . . If you extrapolate the statistics . . ."

"There are three kinds of lies, Tom." Wiley looked at me and smiled at last. *"Lies, damned lies, and statistics."*

"I'd find the paper for you, Wiley. But it's all math."

"I trust your interpretation." Wiley's smile faded again.

"Like I say, I've got pearls, beads, but no way to string them together. I have his name, his bio, and a few of his papers and lectures. I know where he works now–"

"You know where he works?" Wiley repeated.

"Yeah. It's another non-profit, a think-tank. Combining, I suspect, the worst of both worlds. It's called *The Food and Medicines Research Foundation.* They claim that their mission is to *effectively coordinate information and research from the world of medicine in general and nutrition in particular and disseminate it to the medical profession, government, teachers, the media* – and us, the sheepish consumers."

"You know where he works," Wiley said. It was a statement now. No longer a question.

"Yes, Wiley," Tom repeated. "It's just another propaganda-spewing–"

"And I would imagine that this center for nutritional and medical research has a website? Their own web *server,* I daresay?"

"What difference does it make? They're just a front–"

"For a minute there, you had me worried, Tom, with all your talk of loose pearls, beads with no strings. Bites, but no hits. No proof. No *evidence."* Wiley chuckled, a low gleeful sound, so out of place after his earlier seriousness. "Where's your woman with my drink?"

Tom knocked on the glass to the sliding door. Dionne looked over, realized that she'd forgotten about us and our thirst, and scurried out to the kitchen with our glasses. Tom tilted his head curiously at Wiley.

Wiley smiled at him. *"Be just and fear not;* the day of reckoning is at hand. Picasso said, *When I was a child, my mother said to me, 'If you become a soldier, you'll be a general. If you become a monk, you'll end up as the Pope.' Instead, I became a painter and wound up as Picasso.*

"I'm neither general, monk, Pope, nor painter." He grinned now, that toothy, merciless, shark's smile. "I am simply – but ever so thoroughly, my son – Wiley Royce. *Hacker.* At your service."

BRENDEE

Dionne stopped in mid-sentence when Tom knocked on the sliding glass door; she then snatched up their glasses and hurried out to the kitchen.

"Her master's voice," Janae said contemptuously. For all of her claims about wanting to *submit* to her blondie, Janae was a thoroughly modern girl. Let 'em get their own drinks.

But I'd learned by watching my mom – one of her greatest pleasures in life was waiting on my dad, making him a plate, fetching him a drink. She made my dad feel like a king, and in kind, he helped with the chores, helped take care of the kids. Theirs was one of the happiest, most *equal* marriages I'd ever seen.

Wiley never asked me to do anything for him: he was as thoroughly modern as Janae. He'd certainly fetch his own drink, I thought, now that he'd taken up drinking. But I enjoyed fixing him a plate when he was taking care of Bo. I didn't feel that it diminished me in any way.

And Dionne was from my mother's generation, at least; I was sure she liked waiting on Tom. If Janae wanted to *submit* to her blondie, maybe she should start by being a little bit more *submissive*. I smiled to myself.

Tom underlined my thoughts: when Dionne handed him his drink, he stood, put his arm around her shoulder and gave her a little kiss on the cheek in gratitude.

I saw Janae grimace in annoyance. "Oh, fuck this," she said under her breath. She looked at Deneen and me. "It's been a great party, guys," she said. "But I gotta study."

Deneen had seen Janae's furious expression also. She didn't look at me, but I knew she wanted to. "What are you studying?"

"Whaddaya got?" Janae grinned tightly. "I haven't really decided on a major. I just like going to school." She glanced out at the balcony again. They weren't playing cards at the moment. They were smiling, laughing. Tom reached over and squeezed Dionne's hand. "Yeah. I gotta go. Thanks for inviting me, Brendee. It was fun." She stood up abruptly, picked up her purse and left, slamming the door.

"Jeez. Bye, Janae," Deneen said. "What was that about?"

I noticed that Janae had forgotten her cute little bracelet. I snatched it up off the coffee table and staggered a little unsteadily after her.

Janae had her head down on her arms on the roof of her car. I said her name and she looked up at me. She wasn't crying, or anything like that, but the jealousy was still plain on her face. "You forgot your bracelet."

"I know I'm nuts, Brendee," she said. "But he can do so much better . . ."

She sighed and I felt pity for her. Sure it was odd, but maybe if she had a man of her own, she wouldn't so keenly feel that Dionne was monopolizing Tom's company, taking him away from her.

I reached forward to comfort her, maybe give her a little pat on the shoulder. She anticipated my gesture – she put her arms around my neck, gave me a hug; a *squeeze,* really, hard against her body. She murmured, "Thanks for understanding, Brendee," in my ear.

Then, before I could object or even react, she slid her cheek across mine, and kissed me on the mouth. Slowly, softly, *teasingly* . . . She ran her tongue lightly across my parted lips, let it linger there.

I was no less surprised by her gentle kiss than I'd been by Wiley's brutal one earlier, and just like with him, I didn't kiss her back. I don't *think* I kissed her back. But it was nice, languid and sexy, *so soft* . . . If I hadn't been so surprised . . . Maybe I did kiss her back a little bit there at the end.

She grinned, looked down at her shoes. Then, still grinning, she kissed me quickly again, just a little peck on my astonished mouth this time. "Call me. We'll do lunch." She opened her car door and slid in, shut the door. Still speechless, I handed her bracelet in through the window.

"You can borrow it for a while, if you want. I'm not too happy with the giver right now." She took the bracelet from me, gently attached it to my wrist. "Thanks again for inviting me. I had a great time."

I searched for something to say. "Any time, Janae," I mumbled at last. "See ya."

She smiled again. "You know it." She started her car and drove away.

I walked up the stairs, feeling light-headed from the rum, from Janae's kiss, from Wiley's glorious attack earlier. Deneen was again sitting on the top step, consulting her phone. She looked up, considered me for a long moment. "Well," she said at last. "At least we don't have to worry about her making a pass at Wiley."

I glanced back at the street, realized that she had witnessed the strangeness. "Did everybody . . .?"

Deneen shook her head. "They're still out on the balcony."

"It didn't mean anything . . ." Deneen glanced sharply at me. That was the wrong thing to say. Of course it didn't *mean* anything. "I mean, just because she kissed me, it doesn't mean that she's . . . She talked about wanting to *submit* to that blonde guy."

"Have you looked in the mirror lately? *You're* a blonde. Maybe she was talking about *you.*"

"I'm not *brilliant.* I don't give her sly looks."

"That you're aware of."

"Don't be ridiculous, Deneen. She's just drunk."

"I've been drunk, and I've never kissed another girl. Not once." She noticed Janae's delightful jewelry jingling on my wrist. "She gave you her charm bracelet? What are you, going together?"

I frowned in annoyance. "She's mad at Tom, so she said I could borrow it."

Deneen looked at me curiously. "Did you . . . Did you like it?"

"It was . . . surprising." I thought about it. I hadn't *not* liked it. It was . . . unexpected. I couldn't really examine it much beyond that. I was drunk, too.

Nate came out on the landing. He said, "I've kinda had enough partying for one night, Denny. Tom and Dionne are taking all our money. I think we're being hustled." He took her hand, pulled her lightly to her feet. He hugged her, kissed her on the forehead. "I was thinking we might stop by the florist on the way home."

Deneen winked at me, giggled, stood on tip-toe and kissed him quickly. "Whatever you want, Daddy."

We went back inside to find Wiley and Tom and Dionne standing in the living room. Tom and Dionne were holding hands, and I got the impression that they were anxious to depart, too. Maybe it was something in the air – maybe the announcement of a new life in the offing had made everybody want to have a go at the act that had produced it. I smiled to myself. No matter how unproductive it would be in the end for all of us, it would sure be fun in the attempt.

Wiley and I bid farewell to our guests. Cleaning up could wait 'til tomorrow.

It was drunken and sloppy and quick, but we laughed and giggled. It was playful, affectionate fun more than serious, monumental passion. There would be time enough for that again soon enough, for *harder, better, faster, stronger.* I was just glad to have my beautiful, loving husband back.

JANAE

The next morning I went to the store for my portion of the miracle hangover cure. Tommy and Wiley had already had their share, and after a few minutes, I was just as bright-eyed and bushy-tailed as they were. The stuff was amazing. I'd asked what was in it one time, and Tommy had told me, "A little green tea, a burr called burdock – it's said to be the inspiration for Velcro – dandelion, milk thistle, spirulina."

"The fish food?"

Tommy just grinned at me. "Eating fish food is the least of your worries."

Wiley was setting up the ladder beneath the camera that spied on the counter; he said it needed to be adjusted. Tommy went into the office to look at the feed.

"Do you want to hold this for me?" Wiley asked.

I grinned at him. "Hold what for you?"

An answering grin bloomed on his face. "It's a little rickety–"

"How big of you to warn me ahead of time."

"I said I believed in monogamy, until she said it weren't bigamy . . ."

"What's that from?"

"I haven't the foggiest. Something my grandfather used to say." He indicated for me to hold the ladder, and I watched him nimbly climb up it. He was barefoot, as usual.

"Aren't you afraid you'll catch something?"

His eyebrows went up at that one, and he looked down at me. "I'm always safe."

Oh, Wiley, you clever bastard. "I mean, from going barefoot in this filthy store."

He looked at the camera. I noticed that he didn't touch the dusty beam. "Wanna lick my toes, do ya, Janae?" He wiggled them. "How forward of you." He paused. "I haven't caught anything yet." He called to Tommy in the office, "How's that?"

"Move it up a little," came the muffled reply. "The cash register is at the top of the screen."

Wiley adjusted the camera. "Better?" he shouted.

I felt a sharp pain in my finger and said, "Shit."

"What's wrong?"

I looked at my hand. "Splinter."

Wiley breezed down the ladder. "Lemme see it." He took my palm between the thumb and index finger of his left hand, and before I had time to react, he put the tip of my finger into his mouth, licked it, then examined it closely. He licked my finger a second time, then ran his right thumbnail quickly over the splinter – it came out. He licked his own finger, then passed it over the sliver of wood, transferring it to himself. He held his finger up for me to see, then flicked the splinter away. I blinked dumbly at him, astounded by this unexpected intimacy.

Now he smiled impishly at my surprise. "Should I worry about where your fingers have been, Janae? I'm not gonna catch anything, am I?"

He still held my palm between his thumb and forefinger, and he increased the pressure of his grasp just the tiniest bit. He held my gaze and I thought that I would kiss him then, just like I'd kissed his wife the night before. And I was sure he'd kiss me back, just like she'd done; that had been *very* nice.

But I caught a little motion out of the corner of my eye, and instead of kissing him like he surely wanted me to, I looked over his shoulder instead.

Nate and Deneen were standing there, aghast. They'd seen the whole thing. Wiley followed my gaze, looked over his shoulder at them. He dropped my hand and turned around. "What's up, Mom and Dad?"

They just continued to stare at him, and he looked back over his shoulder at me, then back at them. "Old farmer's trick," he explained. "For splinters. I can't tell you how many times my grandma told me, 'Just lick it, Wiley. Run your fingernail over it. It'll come right out.'"

They weren't buying it. I don't know if Wiley realized it or not, but I could see it in their eyes: they'd seen him grab my hand, *lick me*; they'd seen us looking at each other. Maybe I'd even started to lean forward a little bit, aiming to kiss him. Maybe I hadn't, but it didn't matter anyway. Nate and Den had seen what they thought they'd seen, and they didn't believe it had anything to do with splinters.

Tommy came out of the back, and said, "It's just right now, Wiley. Now you can see who's behind the . . ." He glanced at the four of us, standing there in silent tableau. He took in my no doubt guilty look: I *had* intended to kiss Wiley – he'd just licked my finger for Christ's sake, *twice,* and if that wasn't a come-on, I didn't know what was. Tommy considered Wiley's blithe insouciance, Nate and Deneen's shocked suspicion. He tilted his head curiously. "What brings you to my humble establishment so early on a Saturday, my friends?"

Deneen blinked once, looked at Tommy, then looked back at Wiley. Nate just kept staring at me. "I dropped my phone in the sink," Deneen said. "The water was running. I turned the phone off right away, just like you told me I should do, if I ever got it wet."

"Lemme see it," Wiley said. "Wet is not the worst thing that can happen." He had the nerve to glance over his shoulder at me: he *had* caught their damning looks, but he didn't care. I watched Nate blink as if someone had slapped him. As if he'd just seen his best friend lick someone's finger, someone who wasn't his wife . . .

Wiley crossed the room and looked at Deneen's phone. I continued to hold Nate's stare until he looked away. I didn't care what he thought he'd seen, any more than Wiley did. It hadn't been anything. They'd interrupted anything that it might've been *going to be* . . .

Tommy said, "I have a surprise for you, Wiley." He ducked back into the office, and I thought, *Sweet Jesus, I don't know how many more surprises I can take today.*

He came back out with what appeared to be a large piece of cardboard, about two feet tall and maybe three and a half feet long. He laid it on the counter and I crossed the room to see what it was. Nate and Deneen didn't look at me. Tommy pulled a strip of tape off the side of the cardboard and lifted it up – it wasn't one piece, but two, and sandwiched in between was a plastic sign. In bold black letters on a white background, it said, *Wiley's Electronics.* We all looked at Tommy for explanation.

"I figured it was about time you started paying some rent." Now it was Wiley's turn to gawp. "It was actually Josh's idea. He called me the other day, and asked if you were still around. He's got some more customers for you. I guess bikers are hard on cell phones." Tommy grinned. "Josh said, 'You should put a sign in the window, Tom. Take your cut.'"

Wiley ran his hands over the sign.

"Speak, count," I said, *" 'tis your cue."*

"Silence is the perfectest herald of joy: I were but little happy, if I could say how much." Wiley looked at Tom. "You want to go into business with me?"

"Fuck, Wiley!" Tommy said. Deneen blinked. "There's been more people in here to see you in the last week than have been in here in *months.*"

Nate at last spoke. "Maybe it's time you went legit."

"It's not all roses and lollipops," Tom said. "You're gonna have to get a business license. Pay taxes."

"Math."

"It's all online, Wiley, for Christ's sake. You just plug in the numbers." Tommy nodded at the sign. "Whaddaya think?"

"I think it's awesome," he said quietly. "That you would offer me this opportunity–"

"He's only in it for the money," I said, and grinned at Tommy. Tommy had more money than God. He was doing it because Wiley was his friend.

"Thanks, Tom. Thanks so much."

Tom picked up the sign and stood it in the front window. "Janae's right. I'm only in it for the money. The bookstore biz has been dead for decades. Sam could've had me locked up for the insanity of keeping this place open for all these years, if for nothing else." He looked at me. "I'm surprised he never tried it. But *I am but mad north-north-west: when the wind is southerly I know a hawk from a handsaw.* You're the wave of the future, boy."

"How 'bout you fix my phone now, *Bidnessman?*" Deneen said and smiled.

"Time is money," Wiley said and took it back into the office.

NATE

Wiley disassembled Deneen's phone and put it in a bag full of something that looked like cloudy glass beads. I asked him what it was and he said it was a desiccant.

"Like what was in the bread. Maybe it's the same stuff, eh, Wiley? Calcium sulfate?"

Stunned, we both looked at Denny; she smiled proudly. I thought unkindly that she had plenty of room in her pretty, empty head: I shouldn't be surprised that she could remember all the bullshit that Wiley had poured in there. He held out the bag. "You wanna taste it?"

She giggled. "No, but maybe Nate might want to pour it over his oatmeal, if it's too soggy." Not only did she remember the name of the chemical, she remembered what *desiccant* meant. I reflected that Denny wasn't really dumb. It was just as Wiley had always maintained: she'd just never cared to educate herself about anything that he thought was important. But she believed this food additive knowledge was important to the health of our unborn child, and now she aimed to study it as thoroughly as she had the processes for getting pregnant in the first place.

"We're going to look at wedding rings," she told Wiley, and squeezed my hand. She still loved me, even though I wasn't buying her new religion. She wasn't like Wiley, she wasn't going to try to *make me know.* She was like Tom – she didn't care whether I believed it or not. Our baby was inside *her,* so it mattered not in the slightest what I thought. It was up to her and no one else to see that it got the best pre-natal care possible. And then, after it was born . . . I sighed, picturing the rest of my life filled with *Wiley Royce's Famous All-Bean Chili.*

Wiley smiled fondly at her. "You kids have fun. I'll text Nate when this dries out."

****

As soon as we were out on the sidewalk, Denny said, "What do you think's going on with Janae and Wiley?"

I frowned, suddenly feeling trapped. It was usually okay with me when Deneen wanted to discuss what was going on in our friends' relationship. Denny would tell me what Brendee told her –

girls loved to talk, and the way they related to each other, the secrets that they shared, the way they gossiped with other women about these same secrets – telling me about it was just a natural extension of the original conversation to Denny. I didn't claim to know about the innermost workings of their minds the way Wiley did, but I knew this one thing. I was sure that Brendee knew just as many intimate details about me, about my relationship with Denny, as I did about her and Wiley. They talked. They shared. It was just how women are.

But when Denny talked about Wiley and Brendee, it was a one-sided conversation. I'd listen to what she said – it was seldom a surprise to me – but I didn't share the things that Wiley and I discussed on the same subject. In the past, I'd always felt that letting Wiley's secrets out of the bag would be a kind of betrayal. Nothing could be gained. He loved his wife, and she loved him; they had a beautiful baby, and telling Deneen about all of the little machinations that Wiley had used to ensure that Brendee would be his – I considered it all none of Denny's business. Wiley was my best friend – he told me things with perfect trust that they wouldn't get back to his wife.

But maybe the situation was different now. His flirting with Janae – all that was a darker kind of secret than Wiley's watching Brendee through her webcam, than setting it up so he knew that she would watch him. The end result of all that was the happiness that they shared now.

But this . . . I remembered Wiley's uncharacteristic defensiveness: "Who's gonna tell Brendee? Her? Tom? *You?*"

I wouldn't tell Brendee anything. It wasn't any of my business; I was not my brother's keeper. If it turned out that there *was* something going on, I would tell *him* what I thought of it. If there was something going on, Wiley and I wouldn't be friends for much longer. But I wouldn't tattle to his wife.

I figured that she'd hate me as the bearer of such news, anyway, that she'd be embarrassed that I knew. But on the other hand, I figured that when she found out – and she *would* find out – I'd seen this kind of shit go on enough in high school, in college. If someone was cheating on someone else, the someone else *always* found out. The someone always got caught. It was as inevitable as the sunrise.

And when Brendee caught her husband and Janae, she would still hate me, because she'd know that I'd known. She'd hate me, and

I'd hate Wiley, and all of us, Wiley too, eventually – would hate Janae.

But I wasn't gonna tell Brendee how I'd seen the two of them flirt, and I wasn't gonna tell Denny, because that would be the same as telling Brendee. What I'd seen didn't really mean anything. Not yet.

Denny wanted to discuss this thing that we'd *both* witnessed – what *had* they been doing? Who'd ever heard of finger-sucking as a method to remove splinters? That was just crazy. Such activities had another purpose, and it didn't have anything to do with first aid. Yet . . . Wiley hadn't looked guilty in the least, and Tom was right there in the other room. It wasn't like they could just start going at each other in the bookstore. But then I remembered the big, dusty bed, just upstairs, remembered Wiley saying how cozy and private that conveniently located space was. Maybe we'd walked in on the precursor, the opening gambit, the *foreplay* . . .

But still, I wanted to believe him, wanted to believe that he was a better man than that, that he wouldn't risk everything just for a meaningless romp in the hay with Janae. *Goddamn you, Wiley!* I thought. *What the fuck are you doing?* Just like in high school, he was putting me in the position of knowing things that I couldn't discuss with anybody but him. Certainly not with his wife's best friend.

All ignorance, I looked at Denny. "He said something about a splinter."

She considered me for a minute, suspiciously. Just like they were free in their secrets with each other, I believed that women knew that we were not as free with our own secrets with them. Wiley and I were like brothers, and Denny knew that if there was something going on, I'd know about it. But she knew I wouldn't betray him with idle gossip – yet, once again, we'd both seen this thing. She wouldn't ask me to tell Wiley's secrets, because she knew I wouldn't, but I couldn't escape a discussion of what we'd both witnessed.

"I'm not so sure it was as innocent as all that," she said. "But Wiley's my friend." Here was a declaration that I'd never heard from her before. Prior to her crusade to protect our baby at Wiley's urging, she had merely tolerated him.

"I want to believe him. Maybe it just looked bad, but wasn't bad at all. Wiley's always said the most outrageous things, and he did grow up on a farm. Maybe we city folks don't know about such country remedies. And maybe Janae . . ." A grin suddenly lit her face, twinkled in her big green eyes. "I know something about Janae that you and Wiley don't know. Something I bet you wouldn't even imagine."

We'd reached the car. "I saw her *kiss Brendee*. Like this." And she kissed me, right there in broad daylight, standing up on tip-toe and wrapping her arms around my neck, pushing me up against the car, just like she used to do when we were in high school. The only thing that was different was that she didn't jump into my arms and wrap her legs around me.

"Well," she said, her arms still around my neck, "maybe not *quite* like that." She smiled and released me. "But I did watch them kiss."

She walked around to the passenger side and got into the car, leaving me to consider the idea of Brendee and Janae kissing. I slid into my side. Here was some news.

"What are you saying, Denny? You women hug and kiss each other all the time. It doesn't mean . . ." What didn't it mean? That Janae was flirting with Wiley *and his wife?* As far as I knew, Wiley had never kissed her. That would be crossing the line, that would be —

"Brendee said they were drunk. I said, I've been drunk on many an occasion, but I've never felt even the slightest inclination to kiss another girl."

I still maintained that girls kissed each other all the time; they hugged, walked around arm in arm, held hands. It was acceptable in the world. But I was aware that deeper things than just childlike affection could exist between them. I didn't know any lesbians personally, but . . . I'd seen pictures. *Movies*. Was Denny saying that Janae . . . that *Brendee* . . . that Brendee and Janae were . . . This needed to be explained, dissected.

"When? *Where?*" I babbled.

Denny looked at me smugly. "Last night. Janae left in a huff, because she's jealous of Tom and Dionne."

Here was another revelation. "Tom's her grandfather, Den!"

"Jealousy doesn't have to be a sexual, man-woman thing, Nate. You only children don't know about all the shades of jealousy. Trust me. Sometimes a person gets jealous because Mom's paying too much attention to their sister, or because Grandma's paying too much attention to Grandpa, and not enough attention to them.

"Anyway, Janae took off in a huff. She'd been showing us this cute little bracelet, and she left it on the table. Brendee ran it down to her. I went out on the landing for a little air, and I saw them. Janae put her arms around Brendee's neck and laid a big wet one right on her mouth. It was not the kind of kiss that a heterosexual woman gives to another heterosexual woman," Denny said firmly.

"So . . . Janae kissed *her?* Did Brendee kiss her back?" I suddenly pictured Brendee and Janae eagerly making out on the dark street, and it was quite the entertaining scene . . . But I thought about it just for a moment. I looked blankly at Denny. I didn't want her to see that considering such activities would entertain me.

"Brendee said that Janae was drunk, that it didn't necessarily mean she was gay. When I asked her if she liked it, she said it was a surprise. That's all she'd say." Denny paused. "I don't know if Brendee kissed her back, but she didn't push her away." She looked at me shrewdly. "I think maybe Janae's trying to play both ends here. Wiley, Brendee . . . Any port in a storm. Whichever one she can get to bite first."

"Jesus, Denny." That's all *I* could say.

"Well? What do you think?"

"I don't know anything about girls kissing girls," which was true enough, "what would constitute friendship and what would constitute . . ." Well, maybe that wasn't entirely true. I *had* seen those movies. "And Wiley's not gonna–"

"Brendee wouldn't either. Not with a woman, not with another man. Wiley's everything to her. He always has been."

This, unlike the other revelations, was not news. I knew about how much Brendee loved Wiley, and why, more than Deneen did. Here was a secret that Brendee had kept: if she'd ever told Denny about her fantasies about Wes Thomerville, about how much Wiley looked like him, I would've heard about it. And I hadn't.

"Wiley loves her, too. I'm not worried about him and Janae," I told her. "There *is no* him and Janae."

Another thought struck me: what about him and Janae *and Brendee?* And then that thought suddenly metamorphosed into Janae and Brendee and *me,* and even though it was just a thought, one that had never occurred to me before, it was not something to be thinking about with my pregnant girlfriend sitting in the car next to me. Not that there was anything wrong with it – it was just a thought, it wasn't like I'd ever dream of acting on it – we still can't be convicted for what we might think, fleetingly, just for a moment, but

214

I didn't want Denny to know that such a thing had crossed my mind, and the look on my face just might've given it away.

I started the car. "Which jewelry store to you want to go to first?"

Denny picked out a moderately-sized, though not moderately priced, diamond. It cost an arm and a leg, but I had good credit, and the payments weren't gonna be that bad. Nothing was too good for her, anyway, as far as I was concerned. She tried to get me to go for some big platinum monstrosity, with diamond chips and swirly designs on it, but I put my foot down. I would not wear such a thing – it didn't even look like a wedding ring. It looked like something a riverboat gambler would wear on his pinkie. I picked out a plain gold band. "It communicates the message that I'm married," I told her. "That's all it needs to say."

The jeweler smiled and sized my finger. He wrote a notation on the receipt, and I just had enough time to think how that one little piece of paper represented the expenditure of quite a bit of my take home pay, when Wiley sent me a text.

Are we goin' to the chapel yet? ☺

Oh, God, there was still all of that to undertake. It would have to be soon – now that she actually was pregnant, Denny wanted to get the wedding out of the way before she started to show, just like Brendee had done. Thankfully, she was not extravagant, and she didn't want me to have anything to do with the planning. She assured me that we would be wed by the end of the month, and that was all I needed to know.

I have news for you, my son. I told Wiley. *Ur not gonna fucking believe it.*

R u pregnant 2?

Hardy-har-har.

Brendee wants me 2 ask u guys if u want 2 go 2 the park w/us. U can tell me then.

U don't have 2 work?

Josh & his buddies came in 2 get their stuff. Brought more. I'm set 4 a few days.

Ok. C u by the big swing set. Say an hour?

C u then.

215

BRENDEE

I sat on a swing, and taking a cue from my always barefoot husband, took off my shoes and wiggled my toes in the sand. Deneen sat on the one next to me, and gently swung Bo back and forth. It was a beautiful day, and I was as happy as could be: I was with my best friends and my beautiful baby, and my intelligent, resourceful, just-decided-to-go-into-business-for-himself husband. Even Uncle Alex had applauded the news, once Wiley told him that it was going to be a real business, not just a sideline, hobby kind of thing anymore. Tom was going to show him what kind of licenses he needed, how to pay his taxes; they'd even drawn up some kind of profit-sharing agreement. That was all bullshit, Wiley told me. Tom didn't want any of Wiley's profits – it was all just another ploy to make them look good to the IRS.

I noticed that Deneen was studying me carefully. "What?" I said.

"Tell me about this licking thing Wiley does. For splinters."

"He didn't lick your finger, did he?" I asked, appalled. "The first time he did that, I told him I could've licked my own finger. Or just ran it under the tap."

"So it's a real thing?"

I nodded. "It works, if the splinter isn't in too deep. If the licking thing doesn't work, then he wants to get out a needle and operate." She still studied me closely. "Where did you pick up a splinter?"

"I wasn't me. It was Janae." She paused, bounced Bo. He giggled. "At the bookstore this morning. I told Nate that it was nothing. Wiley said she had a splinter."

"Wiley–"

"Licked Janae's finger. Yeah. Twice. We walked in and saw them."

Deneen waited for my reaction. To avoid giving her one, I looked over my shoulder at Wiley and Nate. They were down by the lake, skipping rocks like little boys.

Deneen followed my gaze. "What do you think about it?"

"He does that. It's his splinter cure. What do you want me to say?"

"She kinda had the same look on her face that you did, after she kissed you. Surprised . . . but not . . . offended."

"What do you want me to say?" I repeated. "I trust Wiley," I added, then immediately regretted it, when I saw her eyes widen just a little bit. If I trusted him so much, why did I feel it necessary to say it?

"I just thought you might like to know." She kissed Bo's head and stopped staring at me.

I didn't know if I'd given her the reaction she wanted. Sure, it was a little bit familiar, and Wiley wasn't usually the touchy-feely type. But he'd taken to patting pregnant women on the belly lately, and he'd done the splinter thing to me before, and to my mom at the Fourth of July picnic, just last summer.

She'd been smoothing the table cloth on the wooden picnic table, said *ouch,* looked at her finger. Wiley had hopped up, said, "Allow me," and before she could react . . . I thought about it for a minute.

Wiley knew that my mom possessed what could only be termed as just the tiniest little bit of a *crush* on him. Licking someone's finger who found you very attractive . . . It was his unconventional way of removing splinters, true, but . . . He'd done it just to see her reaction, also. He *studied* people's reactions, especially women.

Mom had been stunned, dumbstruck; not so much because Wiley had licked her finger, but because it had been *Wiley* who'd licked her finger. If it had been anyone else, it might've seemed only a slightly disgusting backwoods remedy. But because it was black-haired, blue-eyed, Wes Thomerville-looking Wiley, after a heartbeat to realize what had just occurred, Mom had gotten a totally inappropriate, totally obvious thrill from it. It was as plain as the nose on her face. Wiley had grinned at me, grinned at my dad. My dad had grinned back, shook his head. Dad knew why his wife was so fond of their son-in-law. Hell, my dad might've actually *met* Wes Thomerville, back there in the dim reaches of time.

So now I wondered . . . Had Wiley been out to give Janae a little thrill, too? I'm sure he wouldn't lick Dionne's finger; nor his new BFF Deneen's, even. He would surely tell them how to do it, might even scrape the splinter out for them, but he would just as surely tell them to lick their own fingers first.

I'd noticed his appreciative smile when he'd first saw Janae, had seen him respond to her cutesy movie quotes. I'd watched them argue and call each other names last night – but it hadn't been an actual argument, and such spirited discussions between men and women often led to . . . Was Wiley considering things he shouldn't be considering with beautiful, strawberry-blonde Janae? He was already chummy enough with her to let her watch my son, and now he was licking her fingers.

A cold breeze of something blew through my mind; I didn't want to call it jealousy, or even suspicion. It was more like *awareness*. It told me that I should perhaps be a bit more observant of future interactions between my husband and the *single girl*.

NATE

Wiley was finally cheerful again. Tom's offer, his suggestion that my friend run a real, legitimate, grown-up, tax-paying, electronics repair business out of *Morry's Books* had set things in balance again, with his wife, with his dad, with himself. And because he was in such a good mood, because he was back to his irrepressible Wiley self, I found myself in a mood to kid him, to fuck with him a little bit.

"I heard Janae was making out with your wife last night," I told him. "Seems you're not the only one of the finger-lickin' persuasion."

He smiled at me in mild confusion. "What *are* you talking about?"

"Know anything about lesbians, do you, my son?"

His grin widened. "Only what I've seen in movies. Although . . ."

"Don't tell me you're convinced that you can turn 'em, Wiley."

"Oh, no," He shook his head. "I'd never claim that.

"Kitana asked me once why it was that men liked watching two women so much. She was taking a poll, you see. She said she'd received a lot of different answers, and she wanted to know what I thought. I said that it was not to my particular tastes, overly, but . . . I've never been much for porn, as she already knew, except as an instructional tool. She insisted on a plainer answer to her question, so I said–"

"It's two women." I recalled my earlier thoughts about his wife and Janae. "If one woman is great, two women would be even better. And *three* women . . ."

Wiley blinked at me in delighted amazement. "The things you say, Nate. What would you possibly do with *two* women?"

"Ah, come on, Wiley. You're not telling me that you've never thought about having–"

"Kitana was always a very-hands on kind of person."

My mouth dropped open. "You're not telling me that you . . . That she brought over . . ."

"No, Nate! What an evil little mind you have! She found some site on the internet, and there were these two girls, doing their thing, and she said, 'Okay, Wiley. What's your impression of this?

Rorschach me, baby. What's the first thing that comes to your mind?'

"I thought about it for a second, and when she prompted me again, I said, 'Pity.'"

"Pity?" I repeated. "You felt sorry for them?"

"Well, obviously." Wiley gestured at imaginary lesbians on the surface of the lake. "Because they're so desperate for me, they've had no other recourse but to turn to each other. That was the first thing that came to my mind."

I gaped at him. "Do you really think that?"

He nodded his head back and forth, considering. "Maybe. It's as good a reason as any."

"What did Kitana say?"

"She was letting her feminism show a little bit on this particular occasion. She told me that I didn't know anything about lesbians – which was and is indeed the case. She said that they'd just laugh at me. If they were enjoying each other, then it wasn't me they wanted."

"Do you think she could've been . . .?"

"Such a thing never occurred to me, my son. But who knows?" He shrugged. "I've no doubt that's how it is in the real lesbian world, that they wouldn't want me. But Kitana expected me to say something, the first thing that came to my mind, so . . . that was it." He looked at me curiously. "What did you say about Janae and Brendee?"

"Denny says she saw Janae kiss Brendee. Last night."

He looked over at his wife and Denny and Bo on the swings.

"Perhaps my former thought isn't too far off the mark, after all. Perhaps Janae's frustrated by a certain lack of attention on my part." He smiled smugly. "But I don't think Janae's a lesbian, Nate. And I know Brendee's not."

"How do you know?" When he just grinned at me, I repeated the question. "No, really, how do you know, Wiley? What women might want to do with each other – that's really not your area of expertise, is it? By its very nature, it kind of excludes us, right? Didn't you just say that? You don't know what Janae likes–"

"I can guess what Janae likes, Nate. *Trust me.*"

"But maybe that's not *all* that she likes. And maybe Brendee . . . Maybe it's not *all* that she likes, either. Maybe she just doesn't know it. Or maybe's she *does* know it and has just never told you. Maybe

Janae aims to find out. Maybe Janae thinks she can . . . turn your wife." I grinned in glee at him.

He smiled at my smile. "I'll worry about that right after I start worrying about Dionne's atom bomb."

"But Brendee didn't tell you that Janae kissed her?"

"No. But I didn't tell her about removing Janae's splinter, either."

Now I looked over at the women and the baby on the swing set. "I'm sure she knows by now."

"Yikes," he said, not concerned at all. "That may've been a little over the line. But it seemed like the thing to do at the time."

"Yeah, maybe. Sticking another woman's fingers in your mouth might give her the wrong impression. And your wife."

Wiley's phone beeped, and he looked at it, grinned from ear to ear. "Indeed." He showed me the text. Janae had asked, *What 'cha doin?*

"I wouldn't be worried about her. I'd be worried about Brendee. How are you gonna explain it to her?"

"It's just an innocent trick, Nate."

"An intriguing turn of phrase, my son."

Wiley grinned at my use of his own expression. "I showed it to Brendee when we were still in school. I showed her mom–"

"You licked Brendee's mom?"

"It works every time."

"It works for what?"

Wiley looked at me with wide-eyed innocence. "For removing splinters, of course. Although . . ."

"You licked Brendee's mom."

"She had a splinter. I was a little drunk. She likes me, so I thought . . ."

"You are absolutely unbelievable, Wiley."

"What? I got the splinter out of her finger!"

"I'm sure she was thrilled."

"To the bone." He giggled. "What point have I in living if it's not to keep Wes Thomerville's memory alive for all the Comstock women?" He grinned, squinted at me. "I was drunk; I thought, *Why not give the old gal a little rush?* It was harmless. Brendee thought it was funny. Brendee's dad thought it was funny." He paused. "I was drunk, she was drunk. Everybody was drunk. It was harmless."

"You weren't drunk this morning." His phone beeped again. "I don't think that this is harmless."

221

"You may be right, Nate. I think I may have led Janae to feel a little froggy with my perhaps just the tiniest bit suggestive first aid, and now she's got a mind to jump."

He showed me her text: *Would u like 2 come over 2 my house tonight?*

"What are you gonna tell Brendee?"

"About this?" He gestured at his phone. "I'm not gonna tell her anything about this."

Sure, he texted, *what time do u want me & Brendee 2 b there?*

"I mean, what are you gonna tell her about the splinter thing? The thing that led to this?" I pointed at his phone.

"I think the best path is not to even bring that up, either. If I was doing nothing wrong when I did it, why would I even mention it? 'I hear Denny told you that I was at the bank today when it was getting robbed.' No. I'm not saying shit about it. If Brendee asks me, I'll cop to it – how can I not cop to it, with the witness for the prosecution over there? If she accuses me of something more than just a little harmless first aid, I'll defend myself. I'll promise I'll never do it again."

"Will you ever do it again?"

"I told you, Nate. I don't want Janae. I was just fucking around. And now . . . Sheesh! Can't anyone take a joke anymore?"

He showed me his phone. Janae had responded immediately. *Just u.*

"I seem to be hoist with my own petard here." When I looked at him blankly, he said, "It means to be blown up by your own bomb."

"Why don't you just say that, then?"

"Where's the fun in that?" He looked down at his phone again. "What am I gonna say to her? I feel like I'm in high school again. No, that's not even right. None of them ever responded then . . . None of them ever had the guts to say anything back . . ."

"You're not in high school any more, Wiley."

His phone beeped again. He showed it to me. *What great thing would u attempt, if u knew u would not fail?*

"Who said that?"

"I have no idea." Wiley read her text again. "Holy shit, Nate! What am I gonna say?"

"How about, *Not tonight, dear, I have a headache?*" Wiley started to type that, and I said, "I was just kidding, Wiley. Jesus. That'll just encourage her."

"What should I say?"

222

"I need to write this down. The day Wiley Royce asked *me* what he should say."

"You're not a lot of help."

"I didn't lick anybody's fingers. How about – no?"

Wiley typed, *How about no?*

JANAE

This was the result of day-drinking with Tommy: drunk texting a married man. Wiley had left to celebrate their partnership, his new entrepreneurship, with his wife and baby, and Tommy had decided to close up shop early and celebrate it with me. Dionne had driven up to check on her prepper compound, and I was happy that she was gone, that I could have Tommy all to myself. I was happiest when I had him all to myself.

She'd be back by sundown – I didn't want to think about where she might possibly be sleeping tonight – but the inescapable truth of *all that* had made me concoct our drinks a little bit stronger than they needed to be so early in the afternoon.

I was sitting in the garden, watching him while he barbequed veggie burgers: they were so exquisitely spiced that you couldn't tell that there was no meat in them. He was a phenomenal cook. He didn't need a woman to look after him, and he certainly could do *so much better* than some hardscrabble nutcase like Dionne. The woman for Tommy should be a poetess, a savant, a queen, like Liz had been, yet he was settling for this mannish crazy person. I couldn't believe it. *The difference is wide that the sheets won't decide,* I thought and drained my drink. Fuck it. His choice in bedmates was none of my business.

Even though we were both more or less wrecked already, I made us another drink. And if I had to testify in a court of law, I would declare under oath that it was the liquor that had set me on to texting Wiley.

That, and the fact that he'd *licked me. Twice.* I'd had all day to reflect on it, and these reflections, aided by copious amounts of gin, had led to the idea that it was perfectly obvious that Wiley would like to lick me further, and, since I would definitely like to lick him further, after such a showing – there was absolutely nothing wrong with simply sending him a text to that effect.

How about no?

Best safety lies in fear, I texted back. How about them apples, bitch? *TTYL*

Anon, the nervy bastard replied.

Well. Well, well, well, well. He'd certainly put the kibosh on all *that,* hadn't he? Finger-licking notwithstanding? Well. Such was what I could expect from drunk texting. Wiley, as I might've seen all along, if I'd only let myself see it – was all talk. Wiley would grab my hand, *lick my finger twice,* walk right up to the precipice, invite me to consider the height, the depth, the glory of the fall – *Darest thou, now leap in with me into this angry flood, and swim to yonder point?*

Now I'd *plunged in and bade him follow.*

How about no?

Sober Janae might've praised his loyalty. Sober Janae wouldn't really have wanted to get involved in any kind of a sordid affair with him anyway. *The body sins once, and has done with its sin, for action is a mode of purification. Nothing remains then but the recollection of a pleasure, or the luxury of a regret.*

But the regret would've lasted a lifetime. Wiley and I having an affair would've thrown a monkey wrench into the workings of more than a half dozen lives. Sober Janae would've never even considered such an act.

But it hadn't been sober Janae that had been ruminating, steeped in gin, upon Wiley's come-on. No. While Dr. Jekyll might've calmly taken Wiley's actions as nothing more than a little friendly familiarity, Mr. Hyde considered them a proposition. Lick my finger, would he? I thought I could still feel his tongue, hot, wet, slick; the quick scrape of his fingernail as he deftly removed the splinter; the subtle, insistent pressure as he held my palm between his thumb and forefinger . . .

And while Dr. Jekyll might've considered Wiley's flat turn-down as the proper response to drunk Janae's own proposition, Mr. Hyde was not amused. Mr. Hyde and drunk Janae were in agreement: Wiley was nothing but a tease. All show and no go. All smoky, blue-eyed, smoldering embers, but no fire.

Thou shalt not suffer a tease to live. No. That was a witch.

Sober Janae might've sheepishly admitted that she'd been a little bit of a tease herself, once upon a time. In that same court of law, ol' Nate could've testified to that. But we were adults now, and drunk Janae thought that Wiley's mouth shouldn't be writing checks that, on presentation to be cashed, bounced rather rudely on she whom they'd been promised to *pay to the order of.* Drunk Janae decided that she was more than a little bit offended by his *choice* of bankruptcy.

Sober Janae would've considered that Wiley would behave in one of two ways, now that I'd tipped my hand. He'd henceforth treat me with a little more respect, realizing that it'd been his smart mouth that had led me to believe him capable of an adulterous trespass that he was in no way actually willing to undertake. He would be chastened by my reaction to his thoughtlessness. He'd stop talking dirty to me, refrain from *licking my fingers.* Sober Janae could accept this as suitable recompense for his misstep.

Or, and far more likely – we were talking about foul-mouthed, superior Wiley Royce, here – he'd continue his flirting patter, maybe even ramp it up a notch, now that he was assured of my willingness. Sober Janae might answer this with derision, might call him a gutless chicken. But that response would be sour grapes, wouldn't it? If I made fun of him, then it would only demonstrate that I'd taken seriously what he'd only been kidding about. It would show me to be someone willing to become a treacherous homewrecker, someone who but awaited his command.

Hell, my drunk texts had shown me to be that.

The final mistake had been mine, in jumping at Wiley's bait. But the initial mistake had been his, in fucking with me in the first place. *Stronger than lover's love is lover's hate,* thought drunk Janae melodramatically. Just who did he think he was that he could toy with me like this, drunk or sober?

BRENDEE

I woke up with a start to the sound of Bo crying. Wiley wasn't there beside me, and I waited for a moment, waited for Bo to stop crying, as he always did as soon as his dad picked him up. But Bo didn't stop crying, so I got up and went in to him.

I peeked in as I passed the open bathroom door. No Wiley. As I changed Bo and got him dressed, I listened for noises from the kitchen – maybe Wiley was out there, *making his own baby food.*

I took my freshened son out to the kitchen. *What would it be today?* I wondered. Mashed avocado with a sprinkling of *Cheerios?* Blended cherries and bananas? God, what a bitch it was de-pitting those cherries!

But Wiley wasn't in the kitchen. Wiley wasn't in the apartment anywhere, and he hadn't even left a note. A small shiver of fear ran through me. Wiley always left a note.

I put Bo in his high chair and recovered my phone from the bedside table. No missed calls; no word at all from my husband. I texted him: *Where r u?* I quickly fed Bo a jar of *Gerber,* wiped his face and hands, gave him a bottle of water. No response from his father.

I called. *Tell me something that I don't already know,* Wiley's voicemail message suggested.

Where was he?

The previous afternoon and evening had passed idyllically. We'd come home from the park, and Wiley had made some kind of lasagna – the noodles were fortified – from a recipe that Tom had given him. It had seemed a little bland to me, but I hadn't mentioned it. I didn't want him to start in about how my industrialized palate, raised on chemically-enhanced *Prego* and *Barilla* and *Bertolli, would* find it bland.

We'd had a perfect, happy little family dinner, and after the baby was in bed, Mom and Dad did what Mom and Dad should've been doing all these long months. Mom and Dad were getting back to their normal, unspeakably awesome routine on that score.

But just as I'd been about to drift off to a contented sleep, Wiley got up and told me that he was going back to the store. He said he had some research to do for Tom, and didn't want him standing around waiting for results while he did it.

It was a little odd, but it wasn't that late, only about ten minutes after nine. Mom and Dad, old married folks rediscovering each other that we were, got to bed early these days. "I thought Tom was the researcher," I said sleepily.

"It's a hack, Brendee," Wiley confessed. "After hours is the best time for this kind of thing. It's when all the data dumps occur, and . . . It's gonna take a little bit of concentration. I'll be able to work on it better when no one's there."

"You can't just do it here?"

Wiley shook his head. "Tom's actually got a printer." Wiley did not; he never felt the need to print anything. "Who knows? Some of this stuff . . . might not bear keeping, electronically. He's gonna wanna see the hardcopies, regardless. I'll be back in a couple of hours." He kissed me. "Sleep tight."

My husband, the hacker. Thief of information. Author of notorious webcam-spying apps. Thinking that I probably didn't want to know any more about it anyway, I drifted off to sleep.

But Wiley had been more than a few hours. Apparently, he hadn't come home at all. I called the store, and after a dozen rings, it went to voicemail – no, it was called an *answering machine,* Tom had told me. It was some throwback tech that he'd had since before we were born. I said, "Wiley? Are you there?" I'd heard the thing in operation when I was in the store, and I knew that if he was there, he'd be able to hear me. Tom had told me that the line would remain open as long as I talked, so I said it again. No response. I paused for too long and the thing beeped, then disconnected me.

Where the hell was he? Disasters flocked to my mind: he'd been in a car accident; someone had broken into the store when he was there all alone and murdered him.

I called Nate. "Is Wiley with you?"

"No. I haven't seen him since the park yesterday."

"Do you know where he could be?"

Nate's almost imperceptible pause spoke volumes. Maybe Wiley was somewhere he shouldn't be, and Nate knew it. Where could Wiley be that he wasn't supposed to be? Wiley wouldn't be . . . with . . . Janae. That was just ridiculous.

I let concern crowd out suspicion again. "He's not picking up, Nate. He went back to the store last night. I'm worried."

"Do you have Tom's number?"

"No." What did I have to say to Tom?

228

"Me, either." Nate hesitated again, and suspicion pushed its way back into my mind. "I'll . . . run by the store. If he's not there, I'll run by Tom's house. He's probably over there. Wherever he is . . . I'm sure he's all right."

NATE

I told Denny that I was going out to look for Wiley, that he wasn't picking up his phone, that he hadn't come home last night, that his wife was worried about him.

"You don't think he's with . . ." she hissed, a stage whisper.

"No. No, I don't. I think he's probably over at Tom's, passed out."

"I hope so. Let me know what's going on." Denny rolled over and went back to sleep.

OMG, Wiley, I thought as I got into the car, *if you've changed your mind, if you went ahead and did this thing . . .* But it was too common, too cruel. He wouldn't just stay out all night with Janae. If Wiley had decided that he was gonna do this thing, I thought that he'd try his best to hide it.

But maybe Janae'd gotten him drunk . . . But Janae lived with her parents. It wasn't like she could be smuggling married men into her bedroom late at night. But maybe her parents were out of town . . .

I didn't want to think about all that, so I considered the other not-good alternative: maybe something bad had happened to him. Maybe he'd wrecked his car, maybe the sex-trio had been replaced by real criminals . . .

I went to Tom's house first. That seemed like the best place to start.

No one answered when I rang the bell, but the front door was open behind the screen, so Tom was obviously up. I walked around to the backyard. Tom and Dionne were standing in the middle of an impressive garden, kissing. Geriatric love birds. I ahem-ed and they broke their kiss, looked at me in surprise.

"I don't suppose that Wiley's here?"

Tom's eyebrows went up.

"Not hardly," Dionne said, laughed and hugged Tom to her.

Tom smiled fondly at her, kissed her on the forehead, and quickly disengaged himself from her embrace. He crossed the yard and said to me, "I talked to him last night. Late. Early, actually. Like two in the morning."

"Where was he?"

"He was at the store. He was babbling about Dr. Hutchkiss, said he'd hacked the foundation's computers. He was drunk. Incoherent almost. I told him that I was a little . . . busy at the moment, and he said he understood, that he'd talk to me in the morning."

"He didn't come home last night."

"Did you call the jail?" Dionne had crossed the yard, put her arm around Tom's waist again. "The hospital?"

"He wasn't in any condition to drive, I don't think," Tom said. "He's too smart for that anyway. He would've called a cab. He's probably still at the store."

"He didn't answer the phone. He'd not picking up his cell."

"Maybe he passed out on the floor," Dionne suggested. We both looked at her. I thought I hid my annoyance better than Tom did.

"That doesn't sound like Wiley," he said and once again disengaged himself from her arm. "Come on, Nate. Let's go over there."

****

Wiley had been at *Morry's Books* at some time, and he'd been there for a minute: there was an empty bottle of gin on his worktable, beside an empty glass. Paper had overflowed the printer's out tray, and page after page was scattered across the floor. A red light blinked: there was still more to be printed, but the machine was out of paper. Some kind of computer code inched relentlessly up the screen of the big monitor, repeated in miniature on the laptop that was hooked up to it.

I picked up a line graph from the floor. It was entitled, *Obesity Rates by Country, BMI of 30+*. I was not surprised to see that the United States topped the list, nor was I surprise to see that 39.9 percent of my fellow Americans were big, fat slobs.

The next page I picked up was just text. I scanned a few lines: *The use of carrageenan as a food and food additive stretches back nearly to the dawn of civilization: it was used in China as early as 600 BC and in Ireland as early as 400 BC. It has been with us on an industrial scale since the 1930s.*

A charming local recipe in Scotland and Ireland calls for the seaweed to be boiled in milk and strained, before sugar and other flavorings such as vanilla, cinnamon, brandy, or whisky are added. The end-product is a kind of jelly similar to tapioca. Research creation of such a product for US markets.

In technical terms, carrageenan is to be considered a dietary fiber. The assertion that any type of fiber would cause

231

gastrointestinal malignancy and inflammatory bowel disease must be laughed at by the scientific community. Studies that may be extrapolated to show it as an inflammation and tumor-producing carcinogen must be downplayed. Gastrointestinal disease in laboratory animals, including ulcerative colitis-like disease, intestinal lesions, and ulcerations must be demonstrated to have developed due to other influences. State that rat and baboon physiognomy differ too much from that of humans to be used as comparisons.

Clinical studies have shown coating the insides of the nose with carrageenan to be a preventative against common cold virus infections. This use must be promoted. Carrageenan production is a $700 million a year industry . . .

"What did you say about carrageenan, Tom? In the rice pudding?" I gestured at him with the paper.

He looked up from the one he was reading. "It causes colon cancer. It's in anything that they want to have a smooth texture. Look at this chart, Nate. It's called *Aspartame Distribution by Area/Heart Disease Deaths by Income Level."*

The stats showed plainly that the more aspartame was distributed to your area, and the poorer you were, the quicker you died of heart disease. I looked at Tom.

"This one's even more to the point," he said. It was a simple pie chart, showing that 67.4% of LA schoolchildren ate fast food at least once a week. Someone had written, *Bravo! We should shoot for 70%!* across the middle of it. Wiley hadn't done it – the script was part of the printout. "Care to guess whose handwriting that is?"

"What is all this stuff?"

"Apparently clever Wiley has hit the mother lode." Tom picked up a memo on the *Food and Medicines Research Foundation* letterhead. *"Please see the informative and entertaining study on BHT supplements as a herpes treatment, attached. Promote.* It's from Dr. Hutchkiss to his staff."

"Where is Wiley?" I suddenly imagined a black-clad, ninja assault team from the *Food and Medicines Research Foundation* discovering Wiley's hack and kidnapping him in the middle of the night. But that was just silly. My friend knew what he was doing; his snooping was no doubt undetectable. And if the SWAT team had descended, surely they would've taken the time to gather up all this evidence, to abscond with the computer as well as the hacker.

There was a thump above us and I jumped, again imagining the food additive storm troopers, come to make us pay for our nosiness. Tom looked up at the ceiling and smiled. "I daresay our mystery's solved, Shaggy."

Both the security door that led to the storage room upstairs and door at the top of the steps were ajar. I hesitated in the doorway for a moment, again thinking of assassins, but Tom walked right on in. He located a cord behind the brocade curtain and tied it back.

Wiley, shoeless, shirtless, was passed out on his stomach on the bed, one arm hanging over the side. Just beyond his reach was another bottle of gin, half-empty, knocked over, most of its contents puddled on the floor.

"The king, sir, is in his retirement marvelous distempered," Tom murmured.

"Wake the fuck up, Wiley!" I said, and shook him. When I drew back my hand, it felt gritty, and I discovered that it was coated with a thin layer of sweaty dust, just from touching him on the shoulder. Wiley rolled over and blinked bloodshot eyes at us. He was absolutely filthy from sleeping on the dusty bedspread – his arms, his chest, his face were covered in fine, sandy Riverside dirt, ground in from what must've been a fitful slumber. He sat up and sneezed, which sent another cloud of dust airborne from the wooden headboard.

"Jesus Christ, Wiley," I said. "You're a mess."

Wordlessly, he got up and went into the bathroom, looked at himself in the mirror for a long moment.

I called Brendee. "He's all right. He passed out in the storage room above the store."

"What the hell, Nate?" she replied angrily. "Everything was fine yesterday. Who the hell did he find to get drunk with in the middle of the night?"

Oh, no, I wasn't gonna examine that one too far with her. "He's all by himself. It's really dusty up here. He looks like a chimney sweep."

"What the fuck is wrong with him, Nate?" she demanded furiously. "All this drinking all of a sudden. . ."

I walked out of the room, onto the first step of the staircase. "It appears that Wiley uncovered some shit last night about the whole food additives thing, and–"

"Oh, for Christ's sake, Nate! I'm getting so tired of this!"

"Listen, Brendee. This is not just *Wikipedia* kind of information. This is like . . . secret. Internal memos and stuff like that. Studies. Charts and graphs. You would not believe–"

"Is this some kind of mass hypnosis with you people? Is Tom the pied-piper of Hamelin? First Wiley, then Deneen, now you, too?"

She was getting a little hysterical, but on the other hand, Wiley hadn't ever gone missing before, stayed out all night; he'd never had to be hunted up. He'd never been much of a drinker before, wasn't one to pass out on a filthy bed, not letting anyone know where he was. She'd never before suspected that her husband might be with . . . I wouldn't even let her name form in my head.

"Look, Brendee. These studies – all the shit Tom has been talking about – Wiley found proof. It's obviously upset him a little bit. I just wanted you to know that he's okay. We'll clean him up and bring him home."

She heaved a big sigh of relief, got a hold of herself. "Thanks, Nate. See you soon."

****

Wiley didn't say a word as we walked down the steps; he waited outside while Tom turned off the lights and locked up the store, as if he didn't want to go back in there and look at the flowing code, the *evidence* all over the floor. He'd washed off his face and chest and arms as much as best he could in the bathroom upstairs – I was gonna kid him about getting the inside of my car dirty, anyway, but I didn't. From the pensive, preoccupied look on his face, I knew it would've fallen flat.

His silence continued while I drove the short blocks to Tom's. Dionne blinked in astonishment at his filthiness, but at a glance from Tom, she kept her mouth shut.

"Go take a shower, Wiley," Tom advised. "I'll get you something to put on. While I'm not as stylish, of course, I think we're about the same size." Tom smiled fondly at him and Wiley smiled back gratefully.

I went out and sat on the front porch with Tom while he smoked a cigarette. Dionne busied herself with making us something to eat. Evidently, she was new to cooking at Tom's house, because she had to come out several times and ask him where he kept various kitchen gadgets. "Don't you have any non-stick pans?"

"No," he replied evenly. "Polytetrafluoroethylene is poisonous."

234

Dionne rolled her eyes and went back into the house.

Tom and I sat on the porch in silence and waited for Wiley. At last he emerged, wearing a T-shirt, a pair of Tom's jeans, and one of his signature, long-sleeved, button-up shirts. But he remained barefoot. He flopped down into a deckchair and sighed. "I've lost my phone."

"It was on your worktable at the store, my son. Along with your shoes." I gave his phone back to him. His shoes were still at the store.

He said thanks, looked at the calls and texts from his wife.

"Did you call–"

"Yeah."

"Is she pissed?"

"I think she was more worried than pissed. I'm sure you'll be able to–"

"Without a doubt." He smiled faintly.

"What the fuck happened to you, Wiley?" I asked. "Why did you decide to go on a drunken bender and not let anyone know where you were?"

"It wasn't intentional. It was cumulative." Wiley looked at Tom, who just watched him silently, inscrutably. "I intended to just have a little nightcap while I poked around the foundation's server. The joke was definitely on me."

"But – all those papers . . ."

"Oh, I got in. For a group so evil, their security is shit. Maybe they shoulda hired *Securi-Comp.*" Wiley grinned humorlessly.

"It's all there on the laptop at the store. I've seen things that I can't unsee, gentlemen. I'm afraid it drove me to drink." He looked at Tom again, expectantly. Tom remained silent. "It's all true. There were studies on fortification, folic acid, eradication of neural tube defects. Just like Hitler – they don't want any incurable birth defects sopping up the Federal funding. They want us to be born healthy, to grow and thrive while we're babies. There was a giant study about all the benefits of breastfeeding up to one year. I'm sure Brendee would have plenty of arguments to give 'em against *that.*"

Dionne came out on the porch and said, "Let's eat, boys," and we trooped obediently after her into the house. She'd made Denver omelets, had heaped us each a big plate. "Except there isn't any ham in them. Or cheese. Tom's pantry is a little bit . . . lacking in staples." She smiled affectionately at him. "I'm sorry they're so broken up, but the pan – all I could find was butter, and I'm afraid they stuck."

Tom took a big bite. *"They're grrreat,* Dionne," he said.

I also took a bite. Tom was right. Dionne's omelets were great.

Wiley looked down at his plate as if it was full of yellow scorpions.

"Dig in, Wiley," Dionne encouraged. "Nothing worse than cold eggs."

"Nothing worse than . . . I don't know if I can ever . . ."

"Hoes gotta eat, Wiley," Tom said, without his customary humor. "The eggs are unbleached; the vegetables are from the garden. No fertilizers, herbicides or pesticides. Just pure California sunshine, air and water. It's as safe as you're gonna get."

After another moment's hesitation, Wiley picked up his fork and ate his omelet.

****

Tom and Dionne sat together on the loveseat; Dionne hung on his shoulder like they were in high school. I sat beside Wiley on the couch. We waited patiently for him to regale us with whatever world-shattering information it was that had driven him to drink.

Tom had whipped up a quick batch of miracle hangover cure for him, but Wiley just sipped it. He didn't seem in a hurry to shed what I knew must be the standard, slightly dizzy, sickly feeling, that pounding headache. He had a haunted look to him, and it seemed as though the discomfort was somehow welcome, like it was helping him concentrate. Whatever. I'd never, ever known Wiley to be any kind of a martyr, but he seemed to be wallowing in it right now.

He was about to begin the sermon when Janae turned up, like a bad penny. I was surprised at the sudden feeling of dislike I felt, the sudden thought of *Why don't you just leave him alone?*

I was able to clearly read the silent conversation that passed between them, and I was sure Denny and his wife could've read it too, had they been present, had they been as unwillingly aware as I was of the flirting that had been going on.

Janae looked sheepish. *Sorry that I drunk-texted you, Wiley. It was over the line.*

Wiley brightened a little, picked up his green drink, looked at her over its rim. *S'okay, Janae. You're only human.* Not even the psychological pain of seeing what could not be unseen, not even the physical pain from his hangover, could dim Wiley's superior smugness.

236

Janae went out to the kitchen, no doubt to pour herself some of the green potion. She looked more than a little hung over herself. Wiley's phone beeped. While Dionne whispered something into Tom's ear, he looked at it, smiled, typed, then handed it to me.

Janae had said, *But shall I live in hope?*

Wiley had replied, *All men, I hope, live so.*

When I looked sharply at him, he shook his head serenely. "It's from a play, Nate. It means nothing."

I opened my mouth to say that it most certainly did mean something, but before I could do so, Janae reappeared. She looked pointedly at me until I scooched over, so she could sit next to Wiley. She didn't press her thigh to his, didn't sit on his lap, didn't take his hand, didn't *lick him;* but I still thought it was a damned possessive gesture for someone who had no right to be in the least bit possessive. There were two chairs. She could've chosen one of them.

"Like I said," Wiley began, "the first thing I found was their archived studies." He leaned forward and set his glass on the coffee table, then eased away from Janae a little bit. I'd once seen him make the exact same little sliding-away gesture, when we were still in high school. He'd been attempting to avoid Brendee that time, who had also sat entirely too close to him. I'd still had a crush on her then, still thought I might have a chance, and Wiley had promised me that he wouldn't make a move on her, even though it was clear from the way she looked at him that she wanted him to. She didn't even care that I was sitting in the same room with them – Brendee had never looked twice at me.

Janae was more in control of herself; she didn't let it show as much. Of course, Wiley wasn't the walking, talking embodiment of her secret fantasies, like he was to Brendee at the time. At least I didn't think he was. No. It was just as Denny had said: Janae was just seeing if she could get a bite. And it irked me to see that Wiley was telling her to keep right on fishing.

BRENDEE

I felt like a rat in a cage, waiting for Nate to *clean Wiley up and bring him home.* A rat in a cage, walking back and forth, bouncing my fretful little blue-eyed, black-haired rat-ling. He missed his daddy: *King Rat.* What exactly had he been doing, with whom had he been doing it, that he couldn't send me a text, that he needed to be *cleaned up?*

I called Deneen. She answered sleepily and asked me if Nate had found Wiley.

"He was at the store," I told her tersely. "Drunk. He had to be *cleaned up.*"

"Who was he – where is he now?"

"I'm assuming he's at Tom's house. I still haven't heard from him."

"Do you want to go over there?"

"I love you, Deneen. You can read my mind."

"Come get me. Nate's got the car."

****

I decided that I wasn't going to march up the steps and pound on Tom's door, not going to demand of my husband just *what the fuck* was going on. That would solve nothing and make me look like some kind of paranoid, jealous idiot. Wiley was a big boy – I wasn't his mom, his parole officer, his confessor, his *conscience.* While it wasn't like him to stay out all night, he wasn't under a curfew. He was allowed.

And he hadn't done anything wrong, according to his *accomplice*; his accessory, his confederate, his conspirator, his brother, his best friend. He'd been alone, and he was just upset about more bad news from the food additives front, another shock to his system from digging up dirt on his new obsession, and it had led him to drink a little too much. Maybe I should be glad that he hadn't tried to make it back home. I'd be calm. It was bad enough that I showed up over there, anyway, uninvited, dragging Deneen with me.

I rapped on the door, not too stridently, and Tom told me to come in. He was sitting on the loveseat with Dionne coiled around his arm like some kind of camouflaged boa constrictor. She smiled gleefully at us. Just like Deneen, apparently all her wishes were coming true.

I smiled back. I was happy for her in the achievement of her crush: nobody knew the glories of *all that* better than me. But it was just a fleeting smile. I had other things to concentrate on at the moment, such as all these recent changes in my husband's behavior, and what they might mean for the future of my marriage. The thought sped quickly through my head that maybe my life was less complicated when he was just my crush.

Nate, who was sitting at the end of the couch, arose and crossed the room to hug Deneen. I couldn't help but notice that Janae was sitting beside Wiley – there were two perfectly fine chairs – why did she have to sit next to him?

I didn't want to answer that question, but it was unavoidable: Janae wanted to sit next to Wiley for the same reason that any other red-blooded American woman, even a perhaps bisexual one, would: *Wiley was fine.* Fit, beautiful, blazingly intelligent, scandalously witty; it suddenly occurred to me that Janae couldn't help but find my husband attractive; a kindred spirit, even. He was not a whole lot different than herself. Even I couldn't help but see that, so how could she not recognize it also?

And Wiley must seem not unlike Tom to Janae, too, I thought suddenly. There was a revelation – and it was something that would make him even more attractive to her. Janae worshipped Tom; but time and age and reality prevented any kind of physical culmination between them . . . What other situation did that sound like? Wiley didn't look as much like Tom as he looked like Wes, but then again Wes was twenty-five or so years older now than he was in that frozen three minutes and thirty-five seconds that I was so fond of.

If I saw Wes walking down the street today, I imagined that he might bear a passing resemblance to Tom. The black hair would be gone – Wes was no doubt just as gray as Tom was these days, or perhaps as bald as Wiley's dad. But all four of them were tall and lean; all four of them shared the same blue eyes. Uncle Alex was kind of shy, but Tom and Wiley and Wes all rocked the same killer smile. The genes for black hair and blue eyes were not uncommon in the world – didn't my own son also have them?

I wondered if Janae was aware that here was another reason why she was so clearly attracted to Wiley, why she wanted to sit next to him: not only was he as smart as her beloved, unattainable grandfather, he even looked like him a little bit. At the moment,

239

Wiley was even wearing Tom's clothes. *Observe,* that icy wind whispered to me. *Here is someone who is not really your friend.*

But my friend Janae smiled at me – all was welcome, all was *damned glad to see ya* – there wasn't a trace of guilt in her eyes at my catching her sitting next to my husband. And after all, what guilt should be there? They were friends. It wasn't like she was sitting in his lap, wasn't like she was wrapped around him like kudzu, as Dionne was with Tom.

Wiley was attractive; Janae was attracted to him. There was no sin in that. Wiley was my husband, my darling baby's father. He couldn't help it if this stunning strawberry-blonde wanted him. It wasn't like he was encouraging her, just by letting her sit next to him on the couch, just by talking to her and smiling at her, by trading obscure quotations and lines from movies with her, by licking her fingers . . .

Janae leapt up immediately, said hi. She put her arm around my shoulder, gave me a little hug, kissed Bo's cheek. She gestured for me to take her place, there beside my husband. *My place.*

Sitters and seating rearranged: Deneen and Nate sat on the loveseat now, and Tom took one of the chairs. Dionne slid the other one over so she could be next to him, hold his hand. I thought she might kiss it or him at any moment. Janae ignored her, like she wasn't even there. She now sat down on the other side of Wiley, an appropriate distance away. Had she been sitting closer to him than was appropriate when I came in? I mentally shook my head. Observation was one thing. Suspecting things that weren't readily observable was something else entirely.

Wiley held out his arms – Bo mimicked his gesture and said, "Gaa!" I thought that this baby noise would evolve into "Dad!" long before it would become "Mom!" Wiley kissed and hugged his son as if they'd been separated for days instead of just overnight. I sat down beside them, still a little annoyed with the whole scene.

Wiley kissed me in the same manner, as if I'd just returned after a long absence. Was it from guilt? Just what had he been up to that had summoned forth this outpouring of familial affection? I studied his face. He was drawn, tired-looking: exactly the sort of countenance one gets as a result of staying up all night partying. But just like Janae, his eyes held no guilt. Their summertime blue was marred with a dejected look for a moment, a hopelessness, but this sadness was quickly replaced by an almost overwhelming love. I thought for just a second that Wiley might cry. Then he blinked, and if there had been sentimental tears, they remained unshed.

He set Bo down between him and Janae on the couch and embraced me, *squeezed me*. "Sorry I didn't call, Brendee. Sorry I got drunk."

"It's becoming a habit," I said, with more sternness than I felt. What was wrong with him? Why was he acting like his wife and son had been long lost to him when he'd just been gone overnight? What had he been doing?

Everyone looked expectantly at him, as if he was some potentate holding court, about to enact laws and issue proclamations, perhaps. I tried not to think *King Rat* again, but the term slid through my mind anyway.

"As far as drinking goes, I've discovered that I enjoy it, so I won't say *No more* or *Never again–*" there was a little glimmer of a smile, "– but I will say, *Not for a while*. Not 'til I have something to celebrate." He looked at Tom. "Such as Dr. Hutchkiss's fall."

Tom's eyebrows went up at this declaration, but he didn't comment.

"I hacked the server for a place called *The Food and Medicines Research Foundation* last night, Brendee." Wiley again looked at Tom; Tom offered no further reaction.

Now Wiley looked at me, then at Deneen. "You guys didn't get to hear Tom hold forth on the talented Dr. Hutchkiss, and I won't bore you by repeating his whole bio, like Tom bored Nate and Dionne." Wiley winked at Tom. Tom remained expressionless.

"And me," Janae piped up. "For years."

Wiley continued. "Suffice it to say that he and his whole crew are some very bad people." He picked up a glass of a vile-looking green concoction – some healthy recipe of Tom's, no doubt. He sipped it, set it back down and continued.

"The public face of the foundation included a lot of studies promoting nutrition and health. They claim that this is their goal, to tell us all about health and good medicine, exercise and well-being. There was a rehashing of the food pyramid that we've seen all our lives; recommendations on supplements and pre-natal vitamins for moms, breastfeeding studies and so on. Suggestions for exercise programs. Not a whole lot about what you should eat when you get back from race-walking around the park – there seemed to be an odd disconnect between the exercise and the nutrition – but there wasn't anything groundbreaking; nothing that hasn't been preached to you before.

"I didn't spend much time on what everyone can see. Instead, I scared up what they had that's not intended for public scrutiny."

Wiley winced as if someone had stuck him with a pin. He picked Bo back up and sat him in his lap, held him tightly against his chest, buried his nose in his hair. He peeped at us over his son's head like a sad little boy clutching a teddy bear. A black-haired, blue-eyed teddy bear that looked just like him.

"There were psychological studies that demonstrated that people will overlook a higher fat and sugar and sodium content if something is labeled *organic* or *all natural* or if the term *100%* is listed. For example, *100% Grated Cheese* is understood to mean just that, that one hundred percent of it is cheese. It's a monumentally simple, yet colossally deceptive triumph of incorrect grammar. There should be a comma in there. To be accurate, it should say *Cheese and other shit, comma, 100% Grated.*

"Because that's what it is: one hundred percent *grated;* it's not one hundred percent *cheese,* not by a long shot. Because of the way the label is worded, the fact that it also contains *cellulose powder to prevent caking* and *potassium sorbate to preserve freshness* is overlooked. Completely."

Deneen took her phone out of her purse, typed on it quickly. *"Potassium sorbate is a preservative used to inhibit molds and yeasts in many foods. While sorbic acid is naturally occurring in some berries, virtually all of the world's production of sorbic acid, from which potassium sorbate is derived, is manufactured synthetically."*

Wiley smiled gratefully at her for the explanation and continued. "There were studies showing the ratios of the chemicals we ingest from commercially packaged foods versus what we get from other environmental factors such as air and water, and even from pesticides, herbicides, and fertilizers. Overwhelmingly, the chemicals with which we are bombarded, with which our systems must daily cope are *put into the food.* Environmental exposure is negligible.

"The studies revealed that a veritable Noah's Ark of animals have perished in the name of food additive testing, and the results are incontrovertible. Taken cumulatively, over our long, apparently healthy lifetimes, *this shit is killing us.* The foundation's true mission is to discount these findings, to spin the data to debunk the

242

inescapable statistics. No, it wasn't the additives that did them in: rats are naturally prone to tumors, baboons are always getting cancer; stuff like that.

"I found a discussion regarding all the whistle-blowers and the harbingers of doom: the enemy, in other words. The hundreds or even thousands of papers and articles and websites out there that've been attempting to warn us about this all along. In it, doctors are discredited, accused of having un-American agendas. Laymen are just dismissed as kooks. The author likened these people to ancient alien theorists," I noticed that Tom grinned and looked at the floor, "presidential-assassination conspiracy nutjobs, and racial purity advocates. He compared them to the chirping of crickets during an outdoor symphony performance: miniscule, puny – not really heard, and if heard, considered merely annoying, and thereby ignored. These concerned citizens are not, it was concluded, anything for the good men and women whom the foundation serves to worry about.

"There was a compilation of anti-tobacco studies. It would've been almost funny if it wasn't so damned sinister, how they harped on the evils of smoking. The foundation's bottom line was that no matter how much glass and drywall, detergent and sand they put into our food, it was of the utmost importance to stress that tobacco was still the most horrible plague to ever afflict mankind. They've spent millions to put this point across, to support those public service announcements against tobacco."

Janae grinned. "You remember the one that said, *Imagine a world without cigarettes?* Tommy used to yell at the TV – *Imagine a world where people aren't telling me what to imagine!*"

Tom smiled and Dionne patted his knee.

"What the foundation is doing . . ." Wiley said. "What d'ya call that? When someone says, *Hey don't consider that, look over here at this instead?*"

"Misdirection," Dionne supplied. "It's a tried and true government ploy."

"But these people aren't the government," Wiley replied insistently.

"But I'm sure the government's in bed with them," Dionne insisted right back.

Wiley shook his head. "It just went on and on and on." He laid his cheek against Bo's for a moment. Bo frowned at its roughness, lifted his hand and touched Wiley's mouth. Wiley kissed his fingers.

"High school athletes are dropping dead from something called *sudden cardiac death;* it can be traced directly to MSG, hydrolyzed protein, soy protein isolate, sodium caseinate and aspartame. The kids eat a bag of chips, down a diet soda, go out on the field in the heat for practice; all these chemicals cause their hearts to seize up and they *drop dead.* That sound like your routine in high school, Nate?"

"I never was much for diet soda." But from the look on his face, it was obvious that he'd had his share of chips before football practice.

"Maybe that's why you're still with us," Deneen said and kissed his cheek.

"And it's not just the kids – if you're over forty-five you're liable to keel over from this *sudden cardiac death,* because the bad diet of a lifetime is exacerbated by this garbage. *The oldest have borne most; we that are young shall never see so much, nor live so long.*

"And acesulfame – it's another artificial sweetener – there were two studies showing that it affects prenatal development. Thanks in part to the foundation's lobbying, it says right on the side of Tom's cigarettes that you shouldn't smoke for the baby's sake, Denny, but there aren't any warnings on that *Diet Coke* or that *Yoplait Light.*

"When they give it to the mama mice, it's passed to the babies from the amniotic fluid and breast milk – when they grow up, the babies show a marked difference in their sweetness preferences."

Wiley hugged Bo, as if by sheer force of love, he could keep his son's *sweetness preferences* – whatever that meant – in line.

"Acesulfame's not cleared away very well by wastewater treatment, according to one of their shorter studies. In one of the more comprehensive ones, it was shown to cause tumors: lung tumors, breast tumors, rare types of tumors of other organs. Leukemia. Chronic respiratory disease. Impaired cognitive memory functions. Not to mention that it's derived from *E. coli.* I don't even have to draw Nate a picture of what that means." Wiley smiled tightly. "Then there's carrageenan–"

"I know about that one," Nate spoke up. "The printout was on the floor."

Wiley nodded and left off of an explanation of carrageenan. "But the most horrifying study of all concerned poor people. *Corruption begins when knowledge of how things work is intentionally used to exploit those who have no idea they are being exploited."*

"Who said that?" I asked.

"I have no idea. Just something I picked up on the internet somewhere." Wiley squeezed my hand and continued. "The statistics showed that poor people are more likely to buy fast food, and cheap grocery store food – macaroni and cheese and *Hamburger Helper* are a lot less expensive than blueberries and sirloins, and a whole lot more filling.

"And simply from eating all this shit their whole lives, the poor are less healthy than the more affluent. Sure, they get *enough* nutrition – very few people are actually starving in this country, rich or poor. Thanks to fluoridation and fortification, just like Tom said – we all have basically the same good teeth, the same full bone growth.

"But by the time they reach adulthood, the poor are sicker than the rich, because they eat more of this shit. Plus, they get less exercise, have more stress. The study indicated that more additives can make cheap, unhealthy foods even cheaper, and thereby even more appealing to low income families.

"But the kicker was this – even poor people want what's best for their children. Even though it was shown that they don't read the labels, don't know that trisodium phosphate is detergent, any more than do those who are more affluent, more educated – they still want to try to eat better. So in order to keep selling them the shit they've been eating their whole lives, to keep them just as sick as they've always been – the *Food and Medicines Research Foundation* has encouraged manufacturers to throw a little 'healthy' shit in with the garbage they peddle. They even demonstrate how that word – *healthy* – should always be coupled with the word *choice."*

"Then people believe it's their decision," Deneen said.

"But they've been led to it!" Wiley cried, and hugged his son again. "The best decision is to just *not buy this shit! Kraft* took the *Kool-Aid* out of *Lunchables* – what is *Kool-Aid,* except sugar and dye? They replaced it with *Capri-Sun,* as if that was any more nutritious. It's got a little real fruit juice in there in addition to the high fructose corn syrup. No pictures of a fat, grinning pitcher on *Capri-Sun* labels – instead there are cartoons of surfers and skateboarders, bicyclists, soccer players – so it's just gotta be great for your children, right? They took out the *Reese's,* put in some less fattening candy. Put in something called *real-fruit smoothies.* But the food part is still just sodium-saturated, chemically-enhanced poison.

"Then someone got the brilliant, nefarious idea to sell *Lunchables* to teens. Kids are only kids for a while, subject to Mom and Dad's dietary choices. Pretty soon they think they're grown and wanna pick out their own poisons – no cheese and crackers for the cool crowd – how about subs and pizzas, instead? Both excellent sources of protein and calcium, according to *Oscar-Mayer*. How many *Lunchables* did you eat in high school, Brendee? Nate?" Wiley didn't wait for us to reply. "All along, they've been marketed as a well-rounded, convenient meal to give to the young. And they've made billions.

"And the foundation urged *McDonald's* and all the other fast-food giants to throw a little fresh, unadulterated items in with their junk. Give the health-conscious poor some choices, damn it! We can't have them running to the Farmer's Market!" Wiley took his phone out of his pocket. "Here's what they've been saying for years to the people dumb enough to eat there – *Because we all have the same goal: making sure the food you and your family love is something you can feel good about.*

"Not that it's good *for* you – you can still get some fries with your boneless, skinless, chicken sandwich, and there's still a universe of sugar in the dressing for your side salad – but hey, you're trying to do better, right? We want you to *feel good about your food,* so here's some apple slices and milk to go with the *McNuggets* in Junior's *Happy Meal.*

"They're saying – *we know ya'll have been hearing about how bad our food is for ya, so here ya go – we're making it a little bit better. Ask for some unsalted fries with that five hundred and fifty calorie Big Mac! Knock ninety calories off your Fillet-O-Fish by skipping the tartar sauce!* And it works. People are still buying this shit.

"And then there's–"

"What's your point, Wiley?" Dionne asked quietly.

I shared a glance with Janae over Wiley's head. *That's what we all want to know,* we said to each other. *Why has all this caused a shadow of madness in you?* Janae glanced at Tom, then back at me. I looked at Nate – he seemed to be thinking the same thing. Why had Wiley so surpassed Tom in his passion about this? Tom blamed what they put in our food for his devastating loss – what had Wiley lost?

A wave of impatience broke across his features. I could tell that he wanted to exclaim, to rail – he didn't do it often, but once you got him started – it was usually about the ignorant, obedient, sheepishness of the world around him. But he took a deep breath instead of lashing out – Bo was sitting on his lap after all. He exhaled, spoke steadily, almost softly. "My point is, something has to be done about this. These people know what all this shit does to the human body. They're killing us, in an organized, consistent manner. They're doing it on purpose. Just like Tom said – it's economics; fucking *eugenics*. Keep the poor sick and they'll never rise above their poverty. Reduce everyone's lifespan, rich and poor, and there will always be some kind of a tax-paying job for Bo, and for Deneen's baby."

I wondered if the expectant father noticed that he didn't say *Nate and Deneen's baby*.

"Somebody has to be told," Wiley concluded resolutely.

Tom spoke for the first time since we'd arrived. "Who ya gonna tell, Wiley?"

Wiley took another deep breath, exhaled again. I'd never seen him so worked up about anything, never seen him have to make such an effort to maintain his inestimable cool. "I'm gonna tell everybody, Tom. The internet. The w-w-w, worldwide fucking web."

"Add your voice to the crickets?"

"I've got proof, Tom."

"Proof of what, Wiley?" Dionne asked. "Another government conspiracy? I've got proof of so many conspiracies! The government knew 9/11 was going to happen; just like Churchill knew about Coventry, and Roosevelt knew about Pearl Harbor. It was all because each wanted to go to war or continue a war. Wars make money for the military-industrial complex. People, individuals, be damned.

"How many false flag conflicts have there been?" When we all looked stupidly at her, she said, "That's where it seems like Country A starts a war with Country B, but Country C is really behind it. Usually Country C is the United States.

"And whatever happened with global warming? That never did pan out, did it? We were all supposed to roasting in our own juices by now, weren't we? But the government got another step closer to controlling our every waking minute with that one, didn't they? Weak, *electric* cars! How many bazillions of our tax dollars went into development of that – how much of our disposal income is sunk into repair of them nowadays? Can't shade tree those hydrogen cells too well. And you're *still* not supposed to build a fire in your fireplace on certain days, 'cause it's supposed to contribute to global warming. Hell, they stopped even *building* houses with fireplaces!

How much money does that make for *Southern California Gas* and *Southern California Edison?*

"A million conspiracies: there's no gold in Fort Knox. Not a bar of it. Don't even get me started on the Kennedy assassination."

"And there was no moon landing in 1969," Janae said, grinning. "There's a big face sculpture on Mars, so that means there's gotta be Martians . . ."

"Human beings' DNA is indistinguishable from Sirian DNA," Tom said. Wiley and Nate blinked at him.

"Do you remember when you could get your television signal through the air, Tom?" Dionne asked. "For *free?* That was before you kids were born. Then they made it so you had to have cable, or a satellite receiver, if you wanted to soak up the opiate of the masses. Then the government had them start putting microchips and webcams in the new sets, so Big Brother could watch you in your living room."

Wiley blinked innocently, first at me, then at Nate, then at Tom. A ghost of his normal grin appeared. "How does that work, Dionne?"

Dionne noticed his smile, believed he was making fun of her. "How the hell do I know, Wiley? You're the hacker. I'm just saying – there've been a million conspiracies – our government has always been out to control us, mind, body, thought; will, spirit. You think this food thing is *new?* It's just the latest iteration. And from what you're saying, it's working."

"But I have–"

"Proof. I know. That's what you said. But just like Tom said: who're you gonna tell? Who's gonna hear you? Not to even mention, *who's gonna believe you* – who's even gonna *hear you?* "

"I'll use the *Freedom of Information Act,* make them cough this shit up."

"That's only for government documents, Wiley," Tom said. "Corporations, think-tanks, individuals – they're exempt. That's why they create these foundations. The government might be involved, but only peripherally; they're still private institutions, beyond the reach of the *Freedom of Information act.* "

"And even if they weren't exempt," Dionne said, "why do you people think that anybody really adheres to that? *Gee, Dad – could you please give me a written record of all the things you and Mom have been keeping track of, regarding my hopes, dreams, ambitions, peccadillos, dirty little secrets?*

"*Sure, son. Here ya go. You caught us.* That doesn't even *sound* plausible, does it?"

"I'll send these studies to the media."

"The media isn't going to publish them, Wiley," Tom said. "Because–"

"Because they're all in bed together!" Dionne interrupted. She was getting a little bit worked up herself. "The media, the government. They're all in it together, to pull the wool over our eyes, to keep us in the dark, to make us all into obedient little–"

"Sheep!" Deneen said.

"And that's why this foundation has to be exposed," Wiley said.

I understood then: that was it, right there, in the proverbial nutshell – why Wiley was so vehement, so enraged. Wiley Royce, never a sheep – he'd discovered to his chagrin and embarrassment that he'd been led by the nose, right along with the rest of us. Wiley Royce, vegetarian, healthy eater – he'd had his share of cottage cheese with rat poison in it, consumed enough of that oatmeal with sand in it, the same as Nate. Wiley had been in the chute with the rest of us, and had never suspected it until Tom had showed him the label on a jar of baby food.

He wasn't really concerned with the downtrodden poor, with the tragedy of young athletes dropping dead – as long as that stuff happened to someone else. Go ahead and eat your *Cheetos* and get fat – Wiley knew better than that. But he had been duped, too. He'd been unknowingly industrializing his son's palate; he and his wife and child, his friends, had been eating sand and sawdust. And he hadn't known about it. And that just couldn't be allowed to stand.

"What I was going to say, before I was interrupted, was that the media won't publish your evidence, Wiley," Tom said. "Because it was obtained illegally."

"Oh, so what?" Wiley cried.

"Bet me," Tom replied. "You're gonna have to post it yourself. And they'll probably–"

"They'll probably *what?* Sue me?"

"I was gonna say, they'll probably just deny it. Say you made it all up, falsified it somehow. They don't have to prove you're lying. You have to prove that you're *not* lying – prove that you got this information from *them*. They'll just say you didn't. More probable than that – the foundation will just ignore you. Not qualify your insanity with a response."

"Then why did you tell me all this, Tom?" Wiley cried, exasperated. "Why did you sic me on it?"

"I knew you'd find the proof, Wiley. I'll admit it: I wanted to see it in black and white, all the charts and graphs. The numbers, the statistics. I wanted to see the comprehensive whole. I knew that you'd find it for me. But I didn't think you'd wanna save the world."

"I don't wanna–"

"But that's just what you say you're gonna do," Nate said. "Tell everybody. Bring these people down."

"You're not gonna bring anybody down, Wiley," Tom said gently. "Nobody's gonna listen."

"But there have to be regulations! Laws!" Wiley insisted.

"There *are* regulations," Nate said. "What was that one from the FDA? About *a history of consumption?*"

Tom consulted his phone. *"General recognition of safety through experience based on common use in foods requires a substantial history of consumption for food use by a significant number of consumers.* That equates to, *we've always done it this way, and everybody's fine."*

"There ya go." Dionne gestured at Tom's phone. "Red tape. Loopholes. Everything is always in their favor."

"Habit rules the unreflecting herd, Wiley," Tom added. "People suspect change. Fear it. Resist it."

"I am not prone to weeping," Wiley said, *"but I have that honorable grief lodged here which burns worse than tears drown."*

Tom smiled; his affection for Wiley was evident. "I say, head on, my son. I'll help you any way I can. No one would like to see Dr. Hutchkiss and his band of demons sweat more than me. But don't think you're gonna make a difference. Promise me that it's not gonna make you bitter."

"In the final analysis, the only people we can save – the only people worth saving, are ourselves." Dionne squeezed Tom's hand. She smiled at Wiley. "Your son, your wife – your friends and their baby." I noticed that her largesse didn't extend to Janae.

"We'll see," Wiley replied.

****

There were a few more minutes of small talk. Janae left first – it was obvious that she couldn't wait to escape Tom and Dionne's newly established, physically demonstrative relationship. *She'd better start getting used to it,* I thought.

Nate and Deneen were also anxious to leave. Wiley's falling off of the world had cut into their weekend morning routine – something that was already gonna change forever in about nine months, I knew, irrevocably, in ways that they couldn't even imagine. There were also wedding plans to be made. Deneen asked me if I wanted to come over later and help, and I said I'd give her a call.

I took Wiley back to the store to pick up his car and his shoes. He was silent, pensive. It was a mood I was used to, far more than his emotional sentimentality, more than his strident righteousness. When Wiley was cogitating, it was best to not disturb him with the inanities of daily life, unless I wanted to hear him say, "Look, Brend, could you just leave me alone for a minute?"

He came home from the store immediately, although I noticed that he brought Tom's laptop along with him. That was where all the *evidence* was stored. But he didn't open it.

He changed into his white sweatpants, the same old, worn pair that he'd had since high school, and did his Tai Chi, his yoga, and I sat on the couch with his son and watched him. There was nothing more enjoyable to me than watching Wiley do his exercises. It was still the sexiest thing I'd ever seen. He concluded with a spectacular handstand, as always, then asked me if I'd like to take a nap with him and Bo.

We all snuggled together in the bed, and for some reason I thought of a caveman family in their cave. Had life really been better when the only thing you had to worry about killing you was saber-toothed cats and other cavemen? When thirty would've been considered a ripe old age? I didn't think so. The world really wasn't so bad now, despite all of Wiley's revelations.

I knew that my life expectancy was supposed to be into my mid-eighties, barring some debilitating disease. Bo would live even longer. I just couldn't quite accept Wiley's claims, couldn't understand his anger. Even if it was true, didn't he feel like he could just avoid these traps that he was so sure had been set for us? Regardless, did he think he could live forever?

I foresaw the rest of my long life filled with waiting while he read every label in the supermarket. I was sure he'd insist on doing all the grocery shopping from now on. Making my own baby food, grating my own cheese. I hoped that he'd come to terms with it, eventually; that his new belief that the government and Big Food were trying to kill us all wouldn't make him bitter, like Tom had predicted.

Now that he was once again aware of something that the rest of the populace was too ignorant to concern themselves about, I hoped that his normal Wiley superiority would once again assert itself. I hoped that he'd just remind himself that he was smarter than his fellow man, and give up this campaign to educate them, to save them, to topple the wrong-doers. I felt that this was likely – Wiley was no crusader – but I wondered how long it was gonna take.

Drunken revelations and the formulation of plans to justly smite the wicked had taken it out of him: he fell asleep immediately. Bo grinned at me mischievously from beneath his father's encircling arm, and he kicked and wriggled to be free. He wasn't in a mood to sleep. Dad was home, that was great, but it didn't mean he wanted to nap with him at the moment.

I released him from Wiley's protective embrace, then packed him and his stuff up again, wrote Wiley a note, and went over to Deneen's to help her plan her wedding.

JANAE

Day-drinking two days in a row was not usually my style, but life had been tossing me a couple of curveballs lately. The good news was that I was up to speed on all my classes – there wasn't any rocket science on the schedule this semester, so I could goof off a little bit.

The other things maybe couldn't be termed exactly *bad news,* unless I was feeling sorry for myself. There was Tommy and Dionne. She didn't like me any more than I liked her, and while I *tried so hard* to *try* to like her – I attempted to convince myself that there must be *something* redeemable to her, if Tommy liked her – my logical mind pointed out to me that what Tommy liked about her didn't have anything to do with her personality. Tommy was demonstrating, for the first time in my life, that he was a man, just like any other, and the thing that he liked about certainly-accommodating Dionne was the same thing that any other man would like about someone so unmistakably willing. Once the lights were doused, her skewed worldview certainly didn't matter to him. *Proclaim no shame when the compulsive ardor gives the charge.*

It amazed me, sickened me, that he would so besmirch Liz's memory with someone like Dionne. *Could you on this fair mountain leave to feed, and batten on this moor? But a sickly part of one true sense could not so mope. O shame! Where is thy blush?* It was enough to drive anyone to day-drinking.

And then there was Brendee, who danced through my dreams like Salome, lasciviously dropping her veils at each gate. Brendee *had* kissed me back that night. Not eagerly – she'd been too surprised for that – but there had definitely been a little reciprocation there at the end. I replayed the scene over and over in my head, convinced that if I kissed her again, she would succumb; she would entreat me to show her what she'd been missing.

I had to admit that I objectified her: if I started to think of her too much as a person, all the inconvenient truths smothered my fantasy. She was Wiley's wife, and in real life, she wasn't going to spoil her happy little family scene with extra-marital adventures, no matter how much she'd kissed me back. But I liked to think about her as if she was only a tiny, sexy creature whose charms I might enjoy without repercussion, if only I could set up the opportunity to kiss her again. It was nothing more than that – *I look'd upon her with a soldier's eye, that liked, but had a rougher task in hand than to drive liking to the name of love.* As with any and all similar attractions, it wasn't as if I felt that we had anything in common on an intellectual level. It wasn't as if I thought I would enjoy conversation with her for very long, unless she was talking about . . . *Wiley.*

Ah, Wiley! Reclining on my narrow, cold bed at home, looking out at the waning afternoon sunshine dappling the back yard, I poured myself another drink and thought about Wiley. The pique that yesterday's incarnation of drunk Janae had felt at his denial was transformed. Today's drunk Janae saw it as just a continuation of the hot wave of his enjoyable flirting. How sweet would culmination be after this superbly arousing tide?

I would never admit it, but Wiley had gotten to me a little bit. It was his looks, true – I am always a sucker for dark hair – but there was more to it than that. It was just as I'd told his wife and her friend – I'm usually the aggressor. Not in a dominatrix kind of way – but if I like a person and they give me a signal that they're interested, then I don't usually wait around for very long to let them know I'm interested, too. Wiley had let me know he was interested, and I had responded. Now it was his turn, and I discovered that I could picture it clearer with each passing day.

But I didn't want to throw Wiley down on his back and just do him; that was my usual style, and it had well served. But not with Wiley. I wanted him to throw *me* down, to show me how much he wanted me. I wanted to see the beast that his cute little wife saw. I wanted to see him lose that fiery, incredibly sexy intelligence for just as long as it would take, and it wouldn't take very long. I imagined a passionate Wiley would be animal grace distilled, all instinct and action. In my present state of mind, he might just have to lick my finger again . . . Nah, who was I kidding? It would take more than that.

He was always in control, and I wanted to see him lose it. *Be what thou wouldst seem to be, Wiley,* I thought. I wanted to see a helpless desire in him, one that would compel him to act on all the filthy little things that he said. His brilliant mind thought them up, but it was also the governor that kept him from acting on them. I'd like to see him, in the throes of lust, lose that mind.

He *had* been a little rude – *how about no?* – but had it really been so rude in the face of my clumsy, ham-handed, ineloquent proposition? Just inviting him over for a little interlude was obviously too base for Wiley Royce. I was sure, thanks to a new, fresh coat of gin-colored paint applied to my mind, that Wiley required a little bit more cunning from me, a little bit more frisky innuendo. *Nice shoes, wanna fuck?* was simply not gonna do it for him. Words were Wiley's playthings. He wanted me to intertwine them fancifully into *what a tangled web we weave,* before he'd practice any deception.

His wife had said that he'd hold still while she touched him, and only when her desire and anticipation reached its zenith would he act. Maybe that's what he wanted from me. A kind of direct ingenuity; if not poetry. It could be dirty, outrageous – perhaps the more outrageous the better, as long as it wasn't mundane. Wiley wanted me to prove to him that there was more to my interest in him than just a physical yen. Hell, he had that waiting patiently for him at home. He wanted a spot of intrigue first. He wanted me to talk him into it, before he allowed himself to loose the beast.

He wanted me to show him that my repertoire of filthy come-ons was just as comprehensive as his – and that I could sprinkle a little literature and ageless movie wisdom in there, just for variety. I knew I was up to the task – I was Tommy's granddaughter, was I not? I'd seen more classic cinema than Brendee even knew existed. I'd grown up in a bookstore. I'd listened to Tommy's not always age-appropriate sense of humor my whole life. I was up to wordplay with Wiley; I was more than adequately equipped for a battle of wits with him. And the gin told me that once I proved my mettle, he would amply reward me.

By five o'clock in the afternoon, my mind was more than adequately oiled for the task at hand, the neurons and synapses lubricated with gin. *'The time has come,' the Walrus said, 'to talk of many things.'*

All right, Wiley, I thought. *Let's play. First, let's see exactly where you are.* Maybe his wife was looking over his shoulder and he wouldn't be able to unleash his clever lust at the moment, so I started off innocently enough.

R u feeling better? Do u live?

After a moment, he replied, *I have been long a sleeper; but, I hope, my absence doth neglect no great designs, which by my presence might have been concluded.*

I would very much enjoy the honor of ur presence 4 great designs. R u free 2night or will it cost me?

Freedom's just another word 4 nothing left 2 lose.

Feelin' good is good enuff 4 me.
Have mind upon your health, tempt me no further.
The surest protection against temptation is cowardice.
What u would work me 2, I have some aim.
Let it work; 'tis most sweet, when in 1 line 2 crafts directly meet.
I would not, so with love I might entreat u, b any further moved.
U protest 2 much, methinks. Am I gonna c u, or do I have to lie to my diary?
U with those curves, and me with no brakes . . .

Now we were getting somewhere. *What else have u got 2 do 2night?*

I was thinking about goin over 2 the store. Pick up the mess in the office. Tom said I could use the storage room, but it needs a good cleaning.

I haven't been up there in years. U say the bed's still there?
Yeah, but it's filthy.
Ur filthy.
Better men than u have said so.
I could help u w/the cleaning.
Anon.

Anon we'll drink a measure the table round. It now draws toward night . . .

Come, seeling night, scarf up the tender eye of pitiful day . . . Anon with this. I gotta go. C ya.
Not if I c u first.

I dropped my phone back into my purse, toasted my good fortune, my resourceful cleverness. Wiley had agreed to meet me at the store, *anon.* In a little while. Shortly. *Soon.*

I pictured the bed in the room above *Morry's.* My own little bed here at my parents' house was just a twin, suitable for nothing but sleeping and virgin's feverish dreams. But Tommy's old bed was a huge California King; it dominated the tiny space. It could be a playground for sportive tricks, a veritable world to bustle in.

My mom and dad had the same kind. I would just borrow a set of their sheets, and some kind of cleaner to wipe the dust off the headboard. Once the bed was freshened . . . We could worry about cleaning the rest of the place later. *Anon.*

BRENDEE

When I returned home at six o'clock, I found my husband in a much better mood than that in which I'd left him. A little rest had cleared away the remaining cobwebs of over-indulgence, and his rancorous resolution to topple the wicked and save mankind seemed to have dissipated into the air. He was barefoot as always, dancing around in the kitchen, whistling, singing to himself. He was making veggie tacos, one of his mother's healthy, additive-free staples.

"Wow," I said. "It's amazing what a little sleep does for your attitude."

He kissed me and his son, smiled. *"Sleep that knits up the ravell'd sleeve of care, the death of each day's life, sore labor's bath, balm of hurt minds, great nature's second course, chief nourisher in life's feast . . ."* He grinned at Bo's blank, rapt attention. Whenever his father held forth in such a manner, quoting some long poetic passage, Bo would just stare at him, mesmerized. The sound of Wiley's voice, the lyrical cadence of the words . . . I hoped that his boy would always pay so much attention when his father spoke. Wiley kissed him on the forehead. "Dr. Hutchkiss *shall sleep no more."*

So the campaign was not forgotten. "What are you talking about?" I asked slowly, warily.

"Be just and fear not, my wife. Nothing earthshattering. I just emailed the *Health and Wellness* reporter at the yellow *Press-Enterprise.* I told her that I had some rather eye-opening statistics, obtained from the server at the *Food and Medicines Research Foundation.* I told her that I'd give her the opportunity to bust this barrel of rotten monkeys right the fuck open. Told her there'd probably be a Pulitzer in it for her."

"And what did she say?"

"It's Sunday, Brendee. I don't expect to hear back from her before tomorrow. So!" He took Bo from me and put him into his high chair. *"Go thy way, eat thy bread with joy, and drink thy wine with a merry heart; for God now accepteth thy works."* Wiley had set aside a small bowl of the taco filling for Bo, cooked but not seasoned. He proceeded to feed it to him, while I made us a couple of tacos.

We weren't cavemen. But life was still great.

JANAE

I took a bath, shaved my legs. I sobered up a little bit. I stuffed a set of my parents' sheets into a small overnight bag, and added some sexy underwear, a sheer robe, some sexy outerwear. Wiley could unwrap me like a Christmas present, uncover my secrets layer by layer, like a nested doll. I threw my make-up bag in there, various perfumes. A towel. The rest of the gin and a fresh bottle of tonic. Tommy would have ice in the little fridge in the office, as well as a couple of limes from the tree in his back yard. I found a bottle of *Windex* and a roll of paper towels in the kitchen. Dressed in an old pair of jeans and a sweatshirt, I headed on over to *Morry's Books.*

The office was a mess: papers covered the floor, the *Out of Paper* light on the printer blinked. Apparently Tommy had been too busy entertaining Dionne to even come in to work today. I rinsed out the glass from Wiley's worktable, stole a few ice cubes from the tray in the fridge. The hell with this; this mess was Wiley's. He could clean it up himself.

I went upstairs and squirted *Windex* on the horizontal surfaces of the bed's headboard, wiped off the dirt. I stripped the bed; billows of dust arose, as if I was changing the linen at the *Motel 6* that had been put up for the workman who constructed King Tut's tomb. I put the fresh sheets on it, then stripped myself, and went in to take a shower in the tiny bathroom.

There was no hot water. It hadn't occurred to me that the pilot for the water heater that served the tiny apartment might've been shut off. Why should Tommy pay to supply hot water to a place that hadn't been used for decades? Needless to say, my shower was brief – I didn't wash my hair, and hoped that it didn't smell too dusty.

I dried off, dressed. I put on my face, primped, perfumed. Then I freshened my drink and sat down on the bed to wait for Wiley.

BRENDEE

Sometimes, when I watched Wiley interact with his son, I felt like I was in some kind of a Norman Rockwell painting. Never had even a shadow of annoyance crossed Wiley's face when it came to Bo – not through all the diaper changes and spitting up, not through all the late night feedings, the messy meals, the slippery baths, the constant picking up of the toys he liked to throw on the floor from his high chair. I could not say the same about myself. I loved my baby, but his babyhood was something that I regarded with a *this too shall pass* mentality: I longed for the day when he could *tell me* what he needed, when he could walk over and get what he wanted for himself.

But Wiley, just like my mom, relished every detail of being a slave to this little inchoate tyrant. All of Wiley's curiosity, all of his awe and patience, he lavished upon his son. I knew Wiley had always been a loner; he'd never had a friend in the world before Nate, except for that physical therapist that had taught him the ins and outs, the ways and means of females and what they liked. And I'd always secretly believed, and with a resigned despondency (on my sadder days), that Wiley would have no trouble whatsoever going back to his solitary lifestyle, if the need arose. He might miss me and Nate and Deneen; but it wouldn't be for long.

But Wiley couldn't live without his son. A woman could wish for no better father for her child.

At about eight o'clock, Wiley was lying on his back on the floor, tossing Bo lightly into the air and catching him. Bo giggled and smiled, and Wiley giggled and smiled right back at him. His phone rang, and he laid Bo on his chest and reached up to retrieve it from the coffee table.

He said, "Shello," then paused. "I'm at home. Where the fuck are you?"

JANAE

"I'm at the store," I told Wiley. "Waiting for you."

"Why would you be doing that?"

"Didn't you tell me that you would meet me? To . . . to clean the upstairs?"

"I didn't realize that you meant *today.*"

Oh, Wiley, you chickenshit son of a bitch! I thought. "Did you not say *anon?* Does that not mean *later? Soon?*"

"That's exactly what it means." He paused, and I thought he might've lowered his voice a little bit when he added, "But I meant it as in some undefined future timeframe. If I would've meant tonight, I would've specified, *tonight.*" I took this to mean that he couldn't make it tonight because of his familial obligations. At least that's what I thought he meant, until he said, "Hey, Brendee, do you want to go over and clean the storeroom?"

"No, Wiley!" I hissed. "Don't bring her over here!" I had attended only to the bed; I was dressed not as a maid – not even as a *French maid* – but as something perhaps akin to a streetwalker. It wouldn't take any genius-caliber leaps of logic for Brendee to intuit that they only thing I had intended to *clean* further was her husband. I could change back into my jeans and sweatshirt, rinse the make-up off; but she'd no doubt smell my perfume, and she couldn't help but wonder why I'd changed the sheets on the bed in a room that Wiley was intending to use as part of his repair shop. I might as well hire a plane and have a skywriter proclaim, *I'm trying to seduce your husband,* across the heavens.

"Why not?" Wiley said. He paused when I didn't answer, then said, "Oh." I could see him look at Brendee. His snappy misuse of the Bard had once again scored at the very bulls-eye of my innermost, sinful thoughts, but what was he gonna say to his wife? "It's a little late for . . . cleaning, tonight, Janae. We were just about to put Bo down to sleep. Maybe . . . some other time."

"Fuck you, Wiley," I said and hung up.

BRENDEE

Wiley blinked at his phone thoughtfully for a split-second. He hit the disconnect button and put it back on the coffee table, sat up with Bo in his lap. Two pairs of identical blue eyes looked expectantly at me.

I would oblige them. "What was that all about?" I asked. I knew who Wiley had been talking to, because he'd said her name. The fact that Janae had his number was news to me. She didn't have my number, and she'd *kissed* me. What had she been doing with Wiley, that she felt she could just so cavalierly dial him up at eight o'clock on a Sunday night, like they were old buddies, pals, friends, *intimates . . .*

When he still just looked at me, obviously searching his nimble brain for an appropriate response, I thought I might just lay my suspicion out a little more clearly for him. "Where did Janae get your number?"

Now we were apparently on solid ground, because Wiley answered immediately. "I . . . *looked up* her number, actually." He grinned – not because we were talking about another woman's phone number, but because he knew that I knew that if he *looked up* someone's number, there was not a power in the universe that could keep him from finding it. Wiley had once told me that this was the easiest hack of all. "Nate and I went over to her house last week."

I tried to disguise my surprise at this news, but failed. Wiley's eyebrows went up in reaction to the look on my face.

"Remember when you said that Tom's theories about food additives might all just be a reaction to his wife's death? That he needed something to blame?"

I nodded, unable to make a connection between this and why he felt it necessary to go over to the single girl's house without telling me about it.

"I considered that this was a legitimate point, so I went over to ask Janae what she thought about it." I must've still looked skeptical, because just the minutest shade of defensiveness crept into Wiley's voice. "We didn't even talk to her. Her dad told us that Tom was crazy, and Janae got offended and left the room. Slammed the door."

Though I didn't particularly care at the moment, I said, "Why does Sam think Tom's crazy?" I had noticed an undercurrent of tension between them on the one occasion that I'd seen them interact

– maybe Sam did think he was crazy. So Wiley wasn't lying. Not yet.

Wiley paused, and I thought if there was gonna be a lie, it would be coming next. "I guess Tom dragged his wife to Mexico, right before she died. Something about healing waters there. Sam thought it was nuts, desperate. I guess Liz didn't live too much longer after that. Sam blames Tom for hastening her death."

I couldn't tell if this was a lie or not, but Sam and Tom didn't really concern me at the moment. "What did Janae say about it?"

"Like I say, we didn't talk to her." Again that hint of defensiveness. "I don't think Tom's crazy. He's never said anything to me specifically about the additives giving his wife cancer. He's just talked about how we're being duped." He paused again. "Anyway, that's why I've got Janae's number."

"What did she want now?"

"She texts me all the time." Here was a confession; but by his innocent expression, he either didn't think it was, or didn't want me to think it was. "We were talking earlier about cleaning out the storage room. I can't be monopolizing the whole office, and Tom said I could use the space upstairs, too. But it's filthy . . . I guess she thought I meant that I wanted to clean it immediately. You know how things can get misunderstood in texts."

When we were still in high school, Nate told me how he'd once reached for Wiley's phone, sitting on the dining room table in his parent's house. Nate told me that Wiley had actually grabbed his wrist, grinned, and said, "Don't ever touch my phone, Nate. It might blow up in your hand."

"I couldn't tell if he was kidding or not," Nate told me. "But couldn't you just see him, installing little worms of plastic explosive in there? You know how devious he is. Needless to say, I withdrew my hand."

I knew Wiley's phone wasn't rigged to blow now. He had a baby; I'd seen him allow Bo to hold it, maybe even gnaw on it for a second every now and then. I'd never really believed that it had truly ever been explosive, but Wiley's phone was Wiley's phone, and what's contained in a person's phone is their own private business, so I'd never looked at Wiley's phone. I was sure that he had it locked down anyway, encoded – not so much to hide damning texts from strawberry-blondes, but because he no doubt had apps on it that might not be of the strictly legal sort.

So I'd never had a mind to peruse Wiley's phone. Not until now. What else had Janae had in mind besides just cleaning the storage room, that might be obvious from her texts? Had Wiley, quoter of quotes, *licker of fingers,* led her to believe that there might be something more to be gained from helping him than just a little dusting? Had he done it on purpose, and just changed his mind when she actually called his bluff? *Had he changed his mind?* Or had he just put her off for the moment, because he knew he couldn't just be traipsing out of here for no reason? Tom's laptop was here. He had no excuse to go to the shop tonight.

"I think Janae likes you," I said neutrally.

Wiley grinned. He didn't break eye contact with me. "I know Janae likes me." Now he looked down at Bo, tickled him. "Mommy's jealous," he told his son.

"Does Mommy have a reason to be jealous, Daddy?" I asked for Bo.

Wiley didn't answer the question I'd put into his son's mouth. Instead, he looked up at me, nodded at the bracelet on my wrist. "Maybe Daddy should be jealous."

He hadn't asked me where the bracelet had come from, hadn't mentioned it at all, so I thought that he hadn't noticed it. That was a mistake on my part: Wiley noticed everything. The bracelet made a pleasant tinkling sound, and he'd no doubt noticed it on Janae's wrist before he'd seen it on mine.

My wearing Janae's bauble wasn't enough to prompt such a statement, however. I realized that there were three ways to disseminate information in our little circle of friends: telephone, telegraph, and tell Deneen. She'd been gleefully anxious to let me know about Wiley's performing his little wet splinter removal trick on Janae. I pictured her telling Nate about Janae kissing me, imagined that she might've even spiced it up a little bit in the telling, might've made it sound like it had been a mutual thing. And just like Deneen had told me about Janae and Wiley and that little sliver of wood, Nate had told Wiley about that little kiss.

I saw that Wiley knew that I knew about the splinter thing, too. Nate and Deneen had both witnessed it, and Nate had no doubt warned Wiley that Deneen would tell me about it. Men look out for each other. I wondered what tying Nate to a chair and giving him a shot of sodium pentothal might reveal about what was going on between Janae and his best friend.

263

So there was no sense in guilelessly asking Wiley, *Whatever do you mean?* Instead I said, "Don't be ridiculous."

"I dunno," he said. "I don't know how I feel about another woman kissing my wife . . ." He smiled blankly, that familiar *I'm not giving away shit* Wiley smile. From it, I couldn't ascertain how he felt about it, one way or another.

This was a ploy to get me to defend myself, to say, *It didn't mean anything*, or *She was drunk*, or even, *I was drunk*. But I was smarter than Wiley took me for. I came from a big family, where blame for childhood missteps – *who broke this lamp? Whose turn was it to take out the garbage and why didn't they do it?* – was often laid at the feet of the one who jumped to defend themselves the quickest. Vagueness was always the key, if not downright evasion – *the lamp was all right the last time I saw it; lemme take a look at the garbage-taking out schedule.*

Wiley was an only child – I understood it made them poor liars, because there wasn't anyone else to blame but them: nobody else could've broken the lamp; it was definitely his turn to take out the garbage, because it was his job alone. On the other hand, I thought, perhaps being an only child could lead them to be *exceptional* liars, because they would have to be more inventive in their excuses than just blaming their transgressions on an absent sibling.

I knew how to be cagey. He didn't know how he felt about *another woman* kissing his wife? "Especially not one as lovely as Janae," I replied and returned his blank smile. I wasn't copping to anything.

"Perhaps this is my fault," he suggested. "Perhaps I should remind you what it is you enjoy about being a heterosexual."

I grinned at my beautiful husband, all suspicion fled. Now he was speaking my language, and Janae was left to clean the storeroom by herself. "Vive la difference."

"Time for you to go to sleep, my son," he said to Bo. "Mommy and I have a yen to compare anatomies."

JANAE

Oh, I was pissed now.

I tore the fresh sheets off the bed, stuffed them back into my overnight bag. The next time he came up here, Wiley wasn't going to be able to see just how much I'd prepared, how much I'd fallen for his suggestion. *Anon. As in some undefined future timeframe. If I would've meant tonight, I would've specified,* tonight. *It's a little late for . . . cleaning, tonight, Janae. Maybe . . . some other time.*

Oh, no, Wiley, you slick, lying son of a bitch. Not tonight, not in some undefined, future timeframe. Not ever. Fool me once, shame on you, fool me twice, shame on me. He wasn't gonna fool me a third time.

I wouldn't believe him now, if he came right out and asked me. He'd never intended to meet me tonight – but I was just as convinced that he *had* intended for me to think he was gonna do it. It wasn't a misunderstanding – it was intentional. He thought it was funny that he could manipulate me this way.

I shoved my make-up bag in with the sheets, changed out of my sexy clothes. Someone was sure to ask me if I was looking for a date if I walked out on the street in them. I put my jeans and sweatshirt back on, took one last look around the room. It appeared only as if cleaning had begun: there was no way to tell that someone had planned an adulterous tryst here.

Oh, Wiley, you conniving, teasing *bastard,* I thought. You have just whacked the wrong hornet's nest. *I never wish'd to see you sorry; now I trust I shall.*

When I got home, I called Tommy. "You wouldn't happen to have Deneen's phone number would you?" He'd found baby books for her – I thought maybe he would've taken down her number in case he found any more. He had no reason to have Nate's or Brendee's; and wild-fucking-horses couldn't get me to call Wiley again.

I was right. He gave me her number. "I saw a sale on baby clothes at *Target,*" I told him by way of explanation. I knew it was a liar's flaw, to give clarification where none had been requested, but I couldn't help myself. Details seemed to be necessary.

I thanked him for Deneen's number, and called her. I told her where I'd obtained her number – all bases must be covered – then I supplied the same excuse for calling her, about the sale at *Target.*

She exclaimed her simple-minded thanks for that, and then I said, "I was wondering if you'd like to have lunch sometime this week?" *Anon. As in some undefined future timeframe.* Like that arrogant bastard Wiley, I did not specify. Den said that would be great. "Could you give me Brendee's number? So I could invite her too?"

NATE

On Monday, I was surprised to hear Tom's voice on the other end of my office phone. "Sorry to call you at work, Nate, but I didn't have your cell number."

"It's okay. But you could've just asked–"

"I have a surprise for Wiley. I thought you might want to be here to see the look on his face when I give it to him."

"What–"

"Then it wouldn't be a surprise would it?"

"I'll stop by right after work."

"Great. See you then."

****

Tom grinned at me, winked even, when I walked into the store. As usual, there were no customers. "Wiley?" he called. "Could you come out here a minute?" When Wiley emerged from the office, Tom said, "Catch," and tossed a medium-sized padded envelope to him.

Wiley of course caught it deftly. "What's this?"

"Note the name there on the return address."

Wiley and I noted it. It said *Thomerville,* with a street address in nearby Corona. Wiley peered cautiously into the already opened envelope.

"You're too damned slow, Wiley," Tom said, and snatched it back. "The anticipation is killing me." He shook the envelope over the counter. A thin plastic box fell out – something they used to call a *jewel case;* my parents still had a bunch of them. They used to store movies and music on plastic disks in them in the old days. On the front was a picture of a high-rise office building, and *Rolling Blackout's Hometown Debut* ran across the middle. Wiley picked it up, turned it over, scanned it briefly. He handed it to me. The back showed a picture of some bar called *Mickey's* and a brief description of the band's start there. The last sentence caught my eye – *featuring the video to My Disgrace.*

"We've seen this, Tom," Wiley said, with what I could only describe as relief. "The whole thing – the documentary and the horrible video – they're on *YouTube.*"

"Not so, my son," Tom said. "This one's a little bit different." He shook a folded piece of paper out of the envelope. *"Dear Mr. Bastion,"* he read. *"Thank you so much for your interest in my husband's music. Even though it was a very long time ago, I remember the days when he and the band played in Riverside. I even remember his fans, and I'm sure that I'd recognize your friend if I saw her. Please find enclosed, a copy of* Rolling Blackout's Hometown Debut – *I'm sure your friend already has a copy of it, if she was as big a fan as you say. Also enclosed is a disc of Jason's raw footage – what he talked about in the interview you mentioned. The rough-cut of the video for* You Can't Be Shy *is on that disk, the last file. I hope your friend enjoys it as much as I always have. Sincerely, Madeline Thomerville."*

Wiley's mouth dropped open. I almost went for my phone to take his picture; it was not often that I'd seen such a flabbergasted look on his face. "How?"

"First, I tried to get a message through to big Mr. Hollywood Oscar-winning director, Jason Whitsun. No luck. He probably gets millions of emails a day. I did get an auto-response thanking me for my interest – whatever it might've been, because no human being read my email – and a coupon for two free tickets to his studio's next release, however." Tom grinned.

"So, I decided to go a little more low rent. I Googled the man himself, got an address right there in Corona. I sent him a nice letter, explaining how a friend of mine had been a big fan back in the old days. I was referring to your mother-in-law, of course. I said that I'd heard that there was lost footage, another video . . .

"I knew he'd have a copy of it somewhere, Wiley. Artists never misplace their art. Every office building in this town would just float up into the ionosphere, if it wasn't for all the unpublished novels in all the bottom drawers of all the desks to hold them down. People keep what they've created, even if no one else ever sees it. I await the day when some archivist somewhere uncovers Jefferson's first draft of the Declaration of Independence.

"And if the artist himself doesn't keep all his works, you can bet the one that loves him best does. Sometimes, it's his mom . . . In this case, it's his wife."

Wiley opened the case. Sure enough, there was a mass-produced disk, with a picture of blue skies on it. Brendee's favorite video was on *that* one. But there was another one, with *Raw Footage* written across it in *Sharpie,* in a neat, feminine hand. It wasn't the original,

I'd bet my life on it – Thomerville's wife had just made a copy for the enjoyment of one of his biggest fans.

Wiley looked at it like it might suddenly fly out of the case and wound him. "Did you watch it?" he asked Tom, and I remembered that I'd asked him the same question after he'd hacked Brendee's computer and copied Wes's original video.

Wiley had given me that ol' shark's grin. "Of course," he'd replied. He'd already known by then that he looked just like Brendee's favorite from-before-she-was-born singer. He'd already known that he'd soon have her in his hip pocket.

But things were different now; Brendee was out of his pocket, in the world. She wasn't a high school girl anymore – she was a grown woman, with a job and a baby and a beautiful woman giving her wet kisses on the street corner. Just as I'd already been considering for a while now, perhaps Wiley wasn't so sure about his absolute control over her anymore. And this new video of old Wes Thomerville – from the look on Wiley's face, maybe he wasn't so sure that this search and its finding were the best ideas, either. But he was in it now. Against all odds, Tom had found it for him. He had to at least *watch it.* Whether he would give it to Brendee as originally planned . . . That was another matter entirely.

Tom grinned. "No, my son, I didn't watch it. This is all your deal, Wiley. I wouldn't even know what I was looking at."

"Oh, you'll know," I told him.

"I can't watch it, either, anyway," Wiley said with renewed relief. "I don't have anything that'll play it."

Tom blinked at him in amazement. "Are you kidding? Wiley Royce, boy genius, can't figure out a way to play a DVD?"

"I need a DVD player, Tom," Wiley retorted, offended. "Genius doesn't have anything to do with it."

"Ah, is that all?" Tom winked at me. "I took the liberty of going home and retrieving this for you." He brought a dusty black box out from under the counter.

"I need an adaptor cable for the laptop. . ."

Tom held one up.

Wiley, sighed, defeated. "We might as well watch it on the big monitor."

The bell over the door tinkled, and Janae walked in. I had spoken to Wiley earlier in the day, and he'd filled me in on their little texted misunderstanding. He told me she'd told him to fuck off because he wouldn't rendezvous alone with her to *clean the store*

269

room. Yet here she was. *Hot damn!* I thought. *She just doesn't know when to quit.*

But her special-smile-just-for-Wiley, the one that she was careful never to display in front of Brendee or Deneen, was absent. She just looked blankly at him. *Oh, this isn't gonna just go away,* I thought.

"Know anything about old-timey bands, Janae?" Wiley asked.

She tilted her chin defiantly. "Yes. As a matter of fact I do." She looked at Tom for confirmation.

He shook his head. "Not this one, I don't think. They were local. Circa 2011. Unknowns." He grinned at Wiley. *"Shall we about it?"*

JANAE

Goddamn him, anyway, I thought. *Why was he still here? Didn't he have his happy little family to go home to?* I'd hoped to have a few words with Tommy before he locked up, before he no doubt went off to meet ugly Dionne and commit more homemade sin – but I'd expected Wiley to already be gone.

Damn him, I thought again. Seeing him drove home to me that I was becoming like Tantalus, locked in the Tartarus of my own mind. I was never going to be satisfy my hunger with this ripe and no doubt delicious fruit that always skated just out of my reach; never would I slake my thirst on the waters that always receded – *if I meant tonight, I would've specified,* tonight – whenever I inquired about them. But just like the Greek king, doomed for his appetites – it seemed that I would always want to try *just one more time.*

But my will was like iron at the moment, even if its impurities might make it bend in his direction again someday. But not tonight. I held onto my anger tonight, and it dispersed Wiley's attractiveness a great deal. But not completely.

We went into the office, and Wiley sat down and busied himself with hooking up some black plastic box to the laptop that was linked to the monitor for the security cameras. I recognized it as a player for those old fashioned plastic disks on which movies used to be kept. He plugged the thing into the wall, then looked at Tommy.

"No remote?"

Tommy went back out into the store, then returned with the player's remote control. Wiley pointed it at the box, pushed buttons. Nothing happened.

"You got any batteries, Janae?" Wiley asked innocently, as he took the back off of the remote.

Tommy rolled his eyes. "Just push the fucking buttons."

Oh, Wiley was pushing buttons, all right. They were neither my *Amused* nor my *Attracted* ones, right at the moment, however. Wiley was proving just how much of a bitch he could be.

He looked at the box for a moment, tentatively pushed a button. A plastic tray slid out. Wiley grinned at his own skill in the use of ancient technology. Tommy dropped a round piece of shiny plastic onto the tray. Wiley gingerly pushed it shut.

A list of files appeared on the monitor. "Let's just copy all this into the modern world, shall we?" Wiley said. "So we don't ever have to deal with all this–" he gestured at the box and the wires and the dead remote, "– again?" I got the impression that he was stalling for some reason. What was in these files that Nate and Tommy were so anxious to see, but Wiley was not?

Since there's *neither good nor bad but thinking makes it so,* what did Wiley think he was gonna see that he thought he wasn't gonna like? I was intrigued by his reluctance.

"What is this, anyway?" I asked Tommy.

He opened his mouth to speak, but Wiley interrupted him. "It's a music video of an old local band. Tom found it for my mother-in-law. She was a big fan."

Yes, Wiley, I know you're married, I thought. *I know you've got a mother-in-law. Didn't you drive that point home yesterday? Do you think you're gonna get by with continuing to rub my nose in it?*

"Jason Whitsun directed it," Nate said.

"Really?" I replied in amazement. "Did you guys see *Eileen's Mother?"* The three of them looked blankly at me. "Jesus. Really? You people are Philistines. It was amazing!" It was a bittersweet tale of star-crossed love; of overwhelming passion, and ultimately – I looked at Wiley – of revenge.

"Did you know he was from Riverside?" Nate said and smiled at me. I looked at him in surprise. Was Mr. Deneen flirting with me now? Oh, no, honey. You're not nearly clever enough – I looked at Wiley. Was he telling tales out of school? Or course he was! *The bastard.* He was leading his buddy to believe I was a homewrecker, down for any married man I thought I could get. But Nate was even more gutless than Wiley. I could tell that just by looking at him. Yet still he thought he could smile at me.

"No," I told Nate, and didn't return his smile. "I didn't know that."

Reputation depends more on what is hidden than on what is seen. If you can't be good, be careful. I hadn't been careful, and hadn't gotten the chance not to be good. And Wiley and Nate had no doubt had a good laugh at my expense. *Life being what it is, one dreams of revenge.*

Wiley sighed. The files were done copying. "Here goes nothing."

The video started; a little drummer behind a sparkly black Zildjiian kit counted off. The camera pulled back, past a giant bass player wearing a cowboy hat, a guitar player with a big nose. The singer was wearing a tight, dark blue t-shirt that accentuated his wide shoulders – he had his back to the camera. He was wearing black jeans, also form-fitting; the camera moved back a little more, and I admired his exceptionally fine ass. He had black hair, curling to just below the nape of his neck. He turned around slowly; he was wearing *Blues Brothers'* style *Ray-Ban* sunglasses. He leaned in toward the mike, breathed.

I said, "I didn't know you played guitar, Wiley."

Wiley hit a button on the keyboard and the video stopped, before a note was sung. He looked at Tommy. "What did I tell you?" He looked at me, didn't smile. "This is from before I was born, Janae."

He hit another key and the singer put his finger on the corner of his sunglasses, gazed into the camera with the bluest eyes I've ever seen, strummed his guitar and sang:

> *Come on over, baby*
> *I know you can't be shy*
> *You looked over twice now*
> *Done looked me in the eye*
> *I know you've heard the rumors*
> *That I'm that kinda guy*
> *Come on over, baby*
> *I know you can't be shy*

The singer's lip curled ever so slightly – *he* certainly wasn't shy. I reached over Wiley's shoulder and hit the same button on the keyboard. "That's not you?"

Wiley shook his head. "Just watch it." He pushed the button again.

> *I know what you're thinkin':*
> *'I wonder if he'd tell?'*
> *You looked over twice now*
> *You're buyin', will I sell?*
> *You're thinkin' you might do it*
> *Aw, damn, you might as well*
> *I know what you're thinkin':*
> *'I wonder if he'd tell?'*
>
> *Now you're walkin' over*
> *I kinda knew you would*

273

You looked over twice now
One, two more than you should
I know you've heard the rumors
And bad news must be good
Now you're walkin' over
I kinda knew you would

They'd reached the bridge in the song, and the singer discarded his shades, danced around a little bit, smiled at the other guitarist while they played together. He was incredible: tall, lean, black-haired, blue-eyed; charismatically, *awesomely* sexy. I couldn't believe he was from my hometown, couldn't believe I'd never heard of him, never seen him before – how could a singer so sexy have never become famous? His voice had a little yelp to it, just the slightest bit of a put-on, country twang. I could see how maybe his voice alone might not be to everybody's tastes, but combined with those blue eyes and that come-hither smile, I found that I liked his voice well enough.

So that guy that brung ya
Is thinkin' what he might
Wonders where you're goin'
Now this just can't be right
Maybe he's even thinkin'
It's time to start a fight
Fuck that guy that brung ya
You changed your mind tonight.

Let me pay my bar tab
And then we'll blow this place
I know what you're thinkin'
It's written on your face
Those stories you been hearin'
That I'm all style and grace?
I'm that fast horse, baby
That always wins this race.

The camera pulled back to let the viewer get a look at the whole band again as the song drew to a close. If I really studied the singer – such a task wasn't difficult – I could now see that it wasn't Wiley at all. He was older, maybe just a shade stockier. He was just as sexy as

Wiley; more so, really – those extra years only added to his confidence, and of course, nothing is sexier than a self-assured musician. From the way he smiled at his bandmates, I thought that he might be a little more easygoing that Wiley: he was obviously the star of the show, but he didn't display an insufferable superiority about it. But still, his resemblance to Wiley was uncanny, inescapable.

The song ended and the big monitor went dark.

Wiley looked expectantly at Nate, who shrugged. "It's better than *My Disgrace.*"

"You think so?" Wiley squinted at him in disbelief. "Just sounded like more inane, poppy crap to me."

"I doesn't matter what you think, now does it? It only matters what–"

"What do you think, Janae?" Wiley asked. He'd effectively, cleanly cut Nate off.

"Who is this guy?" I asked.

"The story goes that once upon a time, my mom and my Aunt Darlene – Brendee's mom – used to go see this band." At my shocked expression, he added, "They're not really sisters. They were just good friends, and when we were kids, Brendee and I called each other's mom *aunt.* Then we moved away . . ." Wiley shook his head. "All that's not important.

"The story goes that Mom and Aunt Darlene used to go see this awful band." He gestured at the screen. "Rolling Blackout. Aunt Darlene had a huge crush on the singer."

"What's his–"

"Down, girl," Wiley said and grinned wickedly at me. "He's pushing sixty by now." Wiley looked appraisingly at Tommy. "I doubt if he's as well preserved as my health-conscious friend here, and besides, he's married. Although that apparently never stopped–"

"His name is Wes Thomerville," Nate said, just as effectively cutting Wiley off, before he could finish his unkind thought about me. *Thanks, Nate,* I thought. *Maybe you're not so bad after all, despite your choice in friends.*

"He lives in Corona," Tommy added. "Damn, Wiley!" he continued. "You weren't just a'whistlin' Dixie."

"Yeah," I said. "Why do you look just like him?"

Wiley shrugged. "A curse of genetic coincidence. Like I said, Mom and Aunt Darlene used to go see this guy – Aunt Darlene was entirely smitten with him. But he was older than them, married, not interested. My mom couldn't understand why her friend liked him so much, when the guy wouldn't give her the time of day." I thought that Wiley paused significantly. *What a bastard he is!* I thought.

"My dashing father came along, swept Mom off her feet. Mom always claimed that ol' Wes didn't do a thing for her – she wasn't the yearning-after-married-men type . . ." Again that significant pause. "But as luck would have it, Alex Royce just happened to bear a striking resemblance to Wes Thomerville. And so does his son."

"Brendee's mom loves him," Nate said. He opened his mouth to say something else, but at a glance from Wiley, he thought better of it and shut up.

Now Wiley looked appraisingly at me. "So tell us, Janae. I already know my mom's opinion, and Aunt Darlene's. I'd like to hear a younger woman's thoughts." He exchanged a look with Nate. "You're obviously taken with our now geriatric crooner. No offense, Tom."

Tom grinned. "None taken, my son."

"What, besides his resemblance to me, do you find so intriguing about Wes Thomerville, Janae?" Jesus, he was arrogant – *beside his resemblance to me*. He didn't wait for me to answer, but said, "I mean, the band's okay, I guess, but those little whimpers in his voice – what the hell is all that about?"

There was some weird undercurrent here, an oddness that I just couldn't fathom. Why would Wiley go to all the trouble to find this video of some forgotten singer for his mother-in-law, then waste his time bad-mouthing the guy? Why did he care about how the guy sang? Why did he care about a *young woman's* opinion?

He wanted me to agree with him, that this old guy couldn't sing, that his band was just ho-hum. In my present state of mind, I wouldn't agree with Wiley if he said that the sky was blue.

"Ah, Wiley, that's little yelp's sexy," I told him. "It displays a little vulnerability. Sure, he's telling this girl about how hot he is, how much he knows she's going home with him. And that's sexy as hell, too, that confidence. But that little waver in his voice let's her know that he wants her, too . . . I dunno. But he *is* very attractive. I would've gone to see him play, too. I would've–"

"Whatever." Now Wiley cut me off, annoyed. I liked his annoyance.

"I'm sure your mother-in-law will love it. A walk down Memory Lane and all, a remembrance of her youth, before all the mundane realities of marriage and kids and all that." Wiley didn't smile and I looked curiously at him. This was just odd. "But what's her husband gonna think of it? Won't he be jealous?"

"It was a long time ago, Janae. It was just an unattainable fantasy." Again that significant pause. "Aunt Darlene found Bo – my son's named after him – and then she forgot all about Wes Thomerville."

NATE

"And you've decided to bring all of her old fantasies back to life for her," Janae stated. She looked curiously at Wiley, as if she sensed there was something more to his finding Wes's old video than just an unusually thoughtful gift for his mother-in-law. Wiley had picked up on her suspicion, her curiosity. That's why he'd looked sharply at me, cut me off when I was about to mention Brendee. He didn't want Janae to make any association between Wes – and Wiley's resemblance to him – and Brendee's opinion of all that.

"I don't know if dredging up all of her past fantasies would necessarily be a good thing, Wiley," Janae continued. "Maybe she might take a look at her life and decide that there's something lacking *between the promise of her greener days and these she masters now.* Maybe she'll decide that life is short, that she wants a change, a new adventure. Maybe she'll dump your father-in-law and head on over to Corona."

"I sincerely doubt that," Wiley said, and I caught a whiff of the condescension he used to use when speaking to Deneen. "Not everyone is down to be a homewrecker."

Janae's eyes widened a little bit at this obvious slam, but then she grinned, shrugged. "Her husband can't do anything about what she *thinks about,* though, can he? You bringing all this back into her mind – she might not actually go out and find this guy – but she might become dissatisfied with the old man, just because of the memories." She shook her head. "I dunno if it's such a good idea, my son."

"Whatever," Wiley repeated. Then to my astonishment, he took his phone out of his pocket and started scrolling through it. This was something that Wiley never did; he often bemoaned the sheepishness of looking at one's phone when there were live people in evidence. For Wiley to start it was tantamount to an utter dismissal. Wiley telling Janae to *fuck right on off* couldn't have been ruder, coming from him.

Janae, modern girl, didn't notice, didn't perceive it as the insult that it was. She looked at Tom. "I just stopped in to say hi, Tommy," she told him. She kissed him on the cheek. "See ya."

She smiled at me, ignored Wiley ignoring her, and left the store.

I shared a glance with Tom, then we both looked at Wiley. "She's gone," he said.

Wiley looked up at us absently, glanced around. "Oh. Bye, Janae." He looked down at his phone again. "Syd Caraway answered my email."

Tom looked at me, and we shared a thought – Wiley didn't want to talk about Wes Thomerville, his video, or his attractiveness to *young women* anymore. Janae might've been talking about Brendee's mom – *Maybe she might take a look at her life and decide that there's something lacking . . . Maybe she'll decide that life is short, that she wants a change, a new adventure . . . Her husband can't do anything about what she thinks about, though, can he? You bringing all this back into her mind – she might not actually go out and find this guy – but she might become dissatisfied with the old man, just because of the memories . . .* Janae couldn't possibly know anything about Brendee's fantasies about Wes. But I knew, and to a lesser extent, Tom also knew.

Wiley had been feeling doubtful about the future of his marriage lately, ever since his son had come into the world. This whole quest for the lost video had been a product of that doubt: *maybe she'll like it,* he'd said to me. But maybe that doubt had returned with a vengeance, storming into Wiley's mind on the back of Janae's words: *maybe she wants a change, a new adventure.*

Brendee wasn't going to high-tail it to Corona and look up elderly Wes Thomerville, any more than her mom would. But maybe the memory of what he'd once meant to her, her inner fantasy life . . . Wiley wasn't the only black-haired, blue-eyed game in town. Not by a long stretch. Maybe he was thinking that he oughta just leave Wes frozen on the little plastic disk that Mrs. Thomerville had so thoughtfully provided to Tom.

But whatever Wiley's thoughts, the subject was now closed; he'd changed it.

"Who's Syd Caraway?" Tom asked. He still held my gaze for a second – he was thinking about Wiley's doubt, too.

Wiley looked up from his phone. "She's the *Health and Wellness* reporter at the yellow *Press-Enterprise*. I emailed her about the stuff I got off the foundation's server."

"What'd she say?" Tom asked with palpable interest. He forgot all about Wes with this new development on the food additive front.

"Let's find out," Wiley said and grinned. It was one of Tom's favorite expressions. *"Dear Mr. Royce–"*

"You gave her your real name?" I asked in astonishment.

Wiley regarded me mildly. "Who am I, Deep Throat?" When I looked at him blankly, he said, "He was an informant. Watergate? Nixon?" When I remained ignorant of the reference, Wiley shook his head and looked at his phone again. *"Dear Mr. Royce: Thank you for contacting me regarding the information that you have on* The Food and Medicines Foundation. *And thank you for saying that you believe my journalistic skills merit a Pulitzer."* Tom's eyebrows went up at that. Wiley grinned. "I told her the info that I had was gonna make her famous." He consulted her email again. *"However, I regret to inform you that, due to other obligations, I will be unable to write a story based on your findings at this time. Perhaps you might contact* The New York Times. *They're always winning Pulitzers."* Wiley frowned.

"Neither Woodward nor Bernstein is Ms Caraway," Tom said.

"And the yellow *Press-Enterprise* surely ain't the *Washington Post.*" Wiley looked up at us. "She's thinks I'm a nut."

"I told you," Tom said gently.

"Maybe you shouldn't've mentioned the Pulitzer."

Wiley looked at me, narrowed his eyes humorlessly, thought a moment. Then he smiled. "The *Health and Wellness* reporter for this dying local rag thinks *I'm* a nut? Well, we'll just show her how much of a nut I am." Wiley disconnected the plastic disc player from the laptop, stacked the cable and the worthless remote on top of it, and handed the entire pile of old technology to Tom. He waved his hand. "Make that disappear will ya, my son?" Tom complied, sticking in unceremoniously on the desk across the room.

"Now . . ." Wiley began to type. I saw *Skype's* website flash on the screen for a minute, then it disappeared behind a wall of fast moving code. "I'm sure even an intrepid journalist like Ms Caraway isn't still at her desk. It's the shank of the evening, after all, so . . ."

A few more keystrokes and a window opened up on the laptop. A few more keystrokes, then Wiley viciously tore off the strip of masking tape that he used to cover up the webcam on the monitor. There was such a contrivance on every piece of electronics Wiley used, or even came in contact with: his own, Tom's, Brendee's, Denny's. TVs, laptops, tablets, monitors. Wiley knew he could be watched, and took this precaution against it.

A woman in her early forties blinked at us in surprise, larger than life, from the window. She was heavily made-up, a little overweight, and from her gray-streaked hair and peacock-feather earrings, I got an immediate hippie/earth-mother vibe.

"Hello, Ms Caraway. I'm Wiley Royce."

"How did you get this—"

"A mere bagatelle, Ms Caraway. I felt a little snubbed by your email, so I thought I'd get in touch with you directly." The reporter just blinked in surprise, and Wiley told her his name again. "As easily as I hacked your *Skype* account, I hacked the *Food and Medicines Foundation's* server. Yet you seem to think I'm some kind of nut."

"Oh. You're the Pulitzer kid."

"I'm a little bit offended that you'd so off-handedly dismiss the info I have for you. I wouldn't have expected such disrespect of the newspaper-reading constituency from a discerning journalist such as yourself."

I couldn't help but grin. Wiley wouldn't read the *Press-Enterprise* if you told him that he'd won the lottery, and the numbers from his ticket were listed on the front page. Wiley didn't play the lottery, either. "It's for the odds-impaired," he'd say.

Now the reporter smiled. "All right, kid. I'm impressed. This is supposed to be a secure line—"

"There's no such thing as a secure line, Ms Caraway." Wiley grinned, still without a trace of levity. "Not to me."

"It's a good thing that I don't surf the internet in the buff."

"You'd be surprised at how many people do," Wiley replied.

"Who's that with you?" she asked.

"This is Tom Bastion. My business partner." Tom nodded at the webcam. "And this is my friend, Nate Osbourne. He works for the government."

"In what capacity?" she asked.

I blanched. I was still on probation, *working for the government.* I couldn't get mixed up in anything that would get me fired. Not with a baby on the way . . . I looked at Wiley in alarm, then back at the webcam. "Not in any . . . official capacity. I'm just Wiley's friend, Ms Caraway."

"Please." She smiled winningly at me. "Call me Syd."

"I just work for the Assessor's Office, Ms – Syd. My job doesn't have anything to do with this—"

"Ms Caraway understands, Nate. I understand." Wiley inclined his head a little bit, indicating for me to step out of camera range. Then he looked at it again. Waited.

"I imagine that you'd like a more . . . secure manner of speaking to me?"

"Oh, this is secure enough. Now. Trust me." Wiley narrowed his eyes again. "I get the impression that you still think I'm a nut, Ms Caraway. Perhaps a paranoid one. Nobody can . . . intercept us. I'm not afraid of anyone overhearing the secrets I have to tell, anyway. That's why I contacted you. I'm not afraid of reprisals. Not yet." He brightened. "But I would like to see you in person, if you can fit me in between exposing pesticide use at the Farmer's Market and whatever other not-illegal, not-surprising, breaking news you're working on at the moment."

"Shall we meet in a public place?"

"I said I'm not paranoid, Ms Caraway."

"You can come to my house," Tom volunteered. "At your convenience."

Wiley was looking at his phone again, scrolling the screen rapidly with his long index finger. "I'll text you the address," he said, not looking up. "Say, seven o'clock, Thursday evening? I see your schedule's clear then."

Again Syd Caraway smiled. "I said I was impressed, kid. Don't hack my diary. It'll make you blush."

Wiley's eyes flickered up toward the camera, but he didn't grin. Wiley was not in the mood to fuck around with some old hippie. "I sincerely doubt that, Ms Caraway."

"Your young friend, then."

Wiley ignored this remark. "I'd never dream of such an invasion of your privacy. I'm sure your diary is . . . imaginative. Enchanting. Yet still none of my business." He squinted at me for a split-second. "Or either of my friends'. I can expect to see you at seven on Thursday then?"

"Text me the address. Apparently you have my number." She disconnected from *Skype*.

BRENDEE

I was surprised when Janae called me at lunch time on Thursday. After a big, long, involved explanation as to how she got my cell number, she told me, "I was going through my closet, Brendee. I have a bunch of stuff – I know we're not really the same size, but I've got several outfits that were just too cute to pass up, even though they didn't fit too well. So they're practically brand new. Can I bring them over? See if you want any of them? It seems like a shame to just donate all these new clothes just because I forget my own size sometimes."

How delightfully girlish of her, I thought suspiciously. It was something Deneen did all the time. That cute dress might be just a little too big, or just a little too short – simply the wrong size – but Deneen would buy it anyway, because she liked the look and figured that she would make it work somehow.

It seemed an uncharacteristic frivolity on the part of the modern, intelligent, studious, *single girl,* however. But I liked the way she dressed, and I didn't think that we were that different in size. She was just taller. I surely wouldn't be able to wear any of her pants. Besides, I was curious to see what else she wanted – I couldn't help but wonder if this sudden friendliness was somehow another play for Wiley, just like I'd suspected her willingness to help take care of his boy.

I couldn't make up my mind about Janae: Deneen had said that she hadn't been at all offended when Wiley licked her finger. She obviously liked my husband – who wouldn't?

And Wiley liked the attention Janae paid to him. It suddenly occurred to me that Janae was the first women that I'd ever witnessed actively admiring Wiley, except for my mom and Aunt Rae, of course. Deneen was now his best buddy, but it wasn't because she found him attractive. Even if she'd just met him, even if she wasn't pregnant and in love with Nate – Wiley just wasn't her type. He was too skinny for her, she'd always told me. And despite her thin, green-eyed beauty, despite their newly strengthening friendship, I knew that Wiley would not ever be attracted to Deneen: she just wasn't smart enough for him.

But Janae was smart as well as beautiful, and I could see that she liked Wiley. She hid it masterfully, but I could still see it. He was usually polite and aloof to women, even though I knew that hadn't always been the case. But either way, polite and aloof or filthy and denigrating, the way he acted didn't usually garner snappy movie-quote-exchanges, didn't make attractive young women want to sit next to him. Janae's attention stroked Wiley's limitless ego. He *liked* that she was attracted to him, just like it amused the hell out of him that my mom had a crush on him.

The question, of course, the unavoidable, sixty-four thousand dollar question was this: just how *much* did he like it? What might he do, what might he risk? I'd never doubted Wiley for a second – but this was a brave new world. I'd never seen Wiley ever so much as look at another woman before, but he'd looked at Janae; and this was the first time I'd ever really seen another woman look at him, talk to him, smile at him. Argue with him, sit next to him on the couch.

Now she was actively cultivating my friendship. What was the true agenda here? I was curious, wary, suspicious. So I said, "That sounds great, Janae."

"I'll come over when you get home from work. What time will you be there?"

"Five's good."

"I'll see you then."

****

Janae was sitting at the top of the steps, waiting for me. She had two shopping bags with her, stuffed full of clothes. "Someday I'll have a job like you." She smiled. "I'm sorry I'm here already – you haven't even had a moment to relax. Go on in, change out of your work clothes. I'll make us a drink."

How nice she is! I thought. *Just what exactly does she want?*

I did as she suggested: I took off my work clothes, and put my robe on over my underwear. No sense getting dressed if I was gonna be trying on all these hand-me-downs she'd brought. As I stepped out of the bedroom, Jane met me in the short hallway. She passed me, dumped the shopping bags out onto the bed, then went back out to the kitchen and retrieved our drinks.

I pawed through the clothes – they were all lovely. Janae had great taste. I found a long, slinky black dress. It was obviously too big for me: it would've almost dragged the ground if I put it on. But I held it up, anyway. "This is so pretty, Janae! Why would you want to give it away?"

She shrugged, held it up to herself, looked in the mirror. "Maybe you're right."

"Let me see how it looks on you."

While she slipped out of her clothes, I sipped my drink, then selected a little teddy from the pile. It would be short on Janae, but would probably hit me about mid-thigh. It was dark green, shiny, slick; not too revealing. I saw that it was really more of a fancy slip than lingerie, once I picked it up. But it would have the same effect, I thought. Wiley liked me in green, so I doffed my robe and slipped it on. It fit perfectly.

Janae was holding the black dress up to herself, trying to decide if she wanted to bother trying it on again. She looked at me in the green slip. "That's so cute on you!" she exclaimed.

Janae tossed the black dress onto the bed. She took a step toward me, adjusted the straps on the slip. Her hands rested, *lingered* on my shoulders. I looked up into her green eyes, almost the same color as the silk robe I'd just taken off, the one that Wiley had given to me when we first moved in together, so long ago . . .

Janae leaned forward slowly; she hesitated. When I didn't flinch, she kissed me again, and her kiss was slow, hesitant at first. I found that I liked it, so I kissed her back. Emboldened, she pulled me against her, kissed me harder. It seemed so strange to be embraced by another woman, the both of us standing there in our underwear. It seemed so odd for me to be kissing beautiful Janae . . . But I liked it very much, and I wrapped my arms around her neck and went right on kissing her. I discovered that I was *digging it.* Her body was molded against mine, her tongue probing, warm, wet, soft . . .

God only knows what would've happened next if she hadn't heard the front door open and hastily broke the kiss. I surely hadn't heard it.

She released me immediately, and just had time to step away from me, before Wiley was standing there in the doorway, holding Bo, looking curiously at us.

The Golden Rule suddenly bludgeoned my mind: *do unto others as you would have them do unto you.* How would I feel if I walked in to find Wiley standing here with Janae, both of them in their underwear? Guilt assailed me; I was sure it was plain on my face.

I shouldn't be kissing Janae; I shouldn't be liking it so very much. It wasn't just a little friendliness between girlfriends as I had been thinking while it was going on. It was *sex,* or at least the precursor to it, and just because our equipment was the same didn't make it into any less of a betrayal of my beautiful, blue-eyed husband, standing there in the doorway with my beautiful, blue-eyed son. No, I wouldn't want Wiley kissing Janae in his underwear, and I shouldn't be doing it either. It was wrong.

I noticed that Janae just smiled at him, but didn't make any maidenly moves to cover up. Wiley didn't make any gentlemanly moves to avert his eyes, either. They just looked at each other, for way too long, I thought. At last she said, "We're trying on clothes, Daddy. Do you boys mind?"

Wiley narrowed his eyes for a split-second, blinked at me. "But of course," he said, then turned and left the doorway.

Janae grinned at me, gave me a quick peck on the forehead, a little squeeze of a hug before I could react. Oh, no, this wasn't good at all. She thought I was down to continue this . . . this . . . *adultery.* Everything was all good with her. I needed to say something, needed to tell her that we couldn't be doing this anymore, but I was speechless. Wiley had seen it on my face. This wasn't just two women innocently trying on clothes, and he knew it.

Janae threw on what she'd been wearing and quickly left the room without saying anything. Before I could follow suit, I heard the front door slam, and then Wiley was standing in the doorway again.

He nodded at the clothes on the bed. "What's all this?" he asked expressionlessly.

"Janae told you. We were trying on clothes. They're hers. She thought that some of them might fit me." I realized that it sounded like a lie, even though it was the simple truth. If *I* had been trying on Janae's clothes, why was *she* standing there in only her bra and panties? Why was I wearing a sexy negligee?

It was too much to explain, and if I started to explain it, I'd just look guiltier than I already did. If it was such an innocent thing, if I hadn't been standing there making out with Janae, about to let myself do God-only-knew-what, why would I feel the need to explain it? So I shut up, didn't elaborate any further.

But I couldn't look him in the eye either. To avoid having to do so, I picked up the shopping bags and started sweeping the clothes off the bed, back into them.

"Trifles light as air are to the jealous, confirmations strong as proofs of holy writ," Wiley murmured.

I looked up at him. "What?"

"Nothing." He squinted at me again, studied me. "I just stopped home to drop Bo off. I have a meeting at Tom's, with the reporter from the *Press-Enterprise*. It shouldn't take very long. But if it does . . . I'll text you."

"Okay."

He crossed the room and kissed me, slowly, lingeringly, just as Janae had done. I realized then that I'd kissed Janae back simply for the novelty of it. It was nice, it was different . . . But this! This was what I really liked, the one thing that I could never get enough of. Kissing Wiley.

I put my arms around his neck, my ardor arching up a notch. Yeah, Janae was all right, but Wiley . . . Nobody, nothing would ever do it for me like Wiley could.

But my husband stopped kissing me after a moment, again studied my face. "I gotta go, Brendee. I don't wanna be late for this meeting. But you look great in that." He ran his hands down my back, paused with them on either side of my hips. He squeezed me a little bit with his thumbs, just enough to ascertain that I wanted him to continue. As soon as he was sure of it, he released me. "I'll be back as soon as I can." He kissed me on the forehead, then turned and departed.

I dressed quickly and went out to the living room. Bo said, "Goo!" when I picked him up out of the playpen. I squeezed him, kissed him, told him, "Mommy just almost messed up. Big time." He was unmoved by my confession.

I put him into his highchair and was just about to uncap our very last jar of baby food when my phone beeped.

Janae texted, *Did Wiley say anything?*

What did she think he was gonna say? He hadn't caught us; he'd only *almost* caught us. He hadn't seen us making out; he'd only seen the guilty look on my face. If she hadn't heard the door open . . . I thought that maybe this wasn't a new thing to Janae, kissing married . . . *people.* I could now see that Janae played for both teams. She clearly liked my husband, and she had now twice demonstrated that she also liked me. This was somewhat of a revelation to me, as well as was the fact that it didn't seem to matter to her if either gender was married, so maybe she was used to having one ear cocked for the sound of imminent discovery.

No, I texted back.

That's good.

287

Why was it good? Again, I thought: we hadn't gotten caught . . . I looked down at my phone for a moment and was suddenly aware that an undeleted text conversation was evidence. Where had that thought come from? Evidence of what? Wiley hadn't caught us doing anything, but what if Wiley hadn't come home when he did?

I'd never felt the urge to kiss Janae or any other woman before, but once she started kissing me, it had seemed like the most natural, most enjoyable thing in the world. At what point would I have stopped her? If Wiley hadn't come home when he did, if seeing him in the doorway hadn't made me realize that I wouldn't have appreciated it if the situation had been reversed – no, I wouldn't have appreciated it one little bit – how far would I have let Janae go before I realized that I was cheating on my husband?

And Janae was down for it. Apparently, she either didn't believe or didn't care that *forsaking all others* didn't just mean other men. I'd found it to be nice and all, something different – but it wasn't overwhelmingly exciting; when Wiley kissed me afterwards, my priorities reasserted themselves.

I *had* enjoyed kissing her, however, and I might even have let her go ahead and do whatever she wanted, had we not been interrupted before things could go any further. I just wasn't thinking. It hadn't seemed to be wrong at the moment; Janae was not a man, out to cuckold my husband – she was just *friendly.*

Thank Christ Wiley came home when he did. Such *friendliness* was not allowed – how would I feel if Janae had decided to be *friendly* with him instead of me? I'd just been caught up in the moment, my guard down – you didn't expect your girlfriends to suddenly start kissing on you. I wouldn't have allowed myself into such a compromising situation with another man – it was obvious that a married woman standing around half-clothed in her bedroom with a man was just not done, but . . . I had been taken by surprise. I'd just gone along with this enjoyable, unexpected thing.

I looked at Janae's text on my phone, and decided that I didn't have one thing to feel guilty about, anyway. I hadn't been the one flirting with her, the one licking her fingers. That had all been Wiley. I hadn't been basking in her obvious adoration – she'd just caught me off-guard. I wondered if she'd ever attempted . . . Had she ever caught Wiley off-guard, too?

She'd bragged to us that she liked to make the first move. That was now patently obvious, whether the object of her desire was male or female. She liked Wiley – I wondered if she'd made a similar move on him? Wiley, ever observant, wouldn't have let himself be taken unaware, as I had been. I was sure of that. If Janae had been of a mind to kiss my husband, he would've seen it coming a mile away. The question was what he would've done about it. Would he have just gone with it, like I did, saw it as just a little harmless friendliness?

Maybe I was projecting my guilt onto Wiley. Maybe Janae had never made a pass at him, although it was clear that she was attracted to him. She was an instigator, by her own admission, and I was still not quite sure what exactly that *cleaning the storeroom at eight o'clock on a Sunday night* business had been all about.

But regardless, the question of the moment didn't concern Janae and Wiley; the question concerned Janae and *me*. No matter how much I told myself that her kisses were harmless and innocent, no matter how far I would've gone with it, all in the name of a little girlish fun, it was a good thing it had been stopped when it had. And I needed to explain that to her. However she felt about it, it was a betrayal to my husband. It couldn't happen again.

We need 2 talk, I texted.

Great! Janae replied without hesitation. *I'll b back in a little while.*

JANAE

I fled to Tommy's to regroup after Wiley caught his wife and me in their bedroom. It wasn't like he'd seen anything, but Brendee's expression had broadcast that something else had been going on besides just a girlish fashion exchange, and Wiley had caught the look on her face as effortlessly as if she'd announced it to him.

He'd smiled curiously at me when I left. Not accusingly by any means, but he hadn't said a word, either. I was sure he knew he had interrupted something. Whether it had just begun or had already concluded . . . He wasn't so sure about that.

"Tell your wife goodbye for me, Lover," I said as I walked out of their apartment. I couldn't resist.

Tommy was surprised to see me; he mentioned that he'd been seeing a lot of me lately. He tilted his head curiously at me. "He's on his way over here right now, by the way."

I just blinked in amazement. "What?"

"I said, Wiley's on his way over here right now. We're meeting with a reporter from the *Press-Enterprise.* She's gonna do a story on Dr. Hutchkiss."

Oh, was that all? Well, I didn't want to get in the way of any of *that.*

"I hope it turns out just the way you want it to."

Tommy shook his head. "I doubt it. She ignored Wiley at first, but he . . . insisted."

"I imagine he can be . . . persuasive."

"I bet you do."

I grinned at him. *"Do not, as some ungracious pastors do, show me the steep and thorny way to heaven; whiles, like a puff'd and reckless libertine, himself the primrose path of dalliance treads."*

Tommy looked steadily at me. "Dionne's not married, Janae."

"I told you before. I'm not a homewrecker, Tommy. And Wiley is as pure as the driven snow. There's nothing going on between us."

"I know that. Yet–"

"O, fear me not." I kissed him on the cheek. "I gotta go. Good luck."

****

As I strolled down the walk in front of Tommy's house, Wiley and Nate pulled up. Nate said hello, but hurried on into the house, no doubt at Wiley's bidding. I realized this because once Nate was inside, Wiley said to me, "So . . . are you trying to seduce my wife? I won't give you any play, so . . . You're trying to . . ."

I leaned in close to him, as if I might kiss him. Just like his wife, Wiley didn't flinch. "Just like yourself, *I do . . . or do not. There is no try.*" I took my phone out of my purse. I read over the brief conversation I'd just had with Brendee.

Did Wiley say anything?

No.

That's good

We need 2 talk.

Great! I'll b back in a little while.

I handed the phone to him so he could read it. "This isn't exactly a Sapphic confession, Janae. This doesn't tell me anything," he said and handed it back.

I shrugged, dropped it into my purse. *"Amidst the dust, and the falling things, and the flapping scenery, Cincinnatus made his way in that direction where, to judge by the voices, stood beings akin to him.* I have been summoned." I started to walk away.

"I'll be sure to make a lot of noise when I come home," he called after me.

I gave him the thumbs up over my shoulder, but didn't look back at him.

NATE

"What the fuck, Wiley?" I said to him when he came into the house. Watching them through the window in the door, I'd seen Janae lean in close to him; it was already dark, and I couldn't tell if she'd kissed him or not. But he'd said he had to have a few words in private with her, so . . .

He held up his hands. "It's not what you think, my son. Turns out she's not interested in me in the least." When I rolled my eyes at that one, he said slowly, pointedly, "She's on her way over to see Brendee."

My mouth dropped open. "Are they? What are they? How do you know? *What?*"

Wiley shrugged. Tom came out of the kitchen, handed us both a drink.

"I think Janae's trying to seduce my wife, Tom."

"It takes two to tango, my son," Tom replied mildly, with absolutely no surprise whatsoever. "Where I come from, bisexuality is virtually unknown. But neither is monogamy, so I'm really not in a position to comment. I found my true love here. Anything else, before . . . or even now . . . it's just a way to pass the time."

"It's not like it's another man, Wiley . . ." I began, but then the picture of Denny with anybody else, even a woman, came to mind, and I realized that that would be devastating. "I'm sorry," I said immediately.

Wiley grinned. "Seriously, gentlemen. You have got to be fucking kidding me. I'm not worried about this – really? I didn't say that Janae *had* seduced my wife, or that I was worried about it. I just said that I thought she was *trying–*"

The doorbell rang, and this discussion of domestic drama was put on hold.

BRENDEE

I answered the door and Janae immediately tried to embrace me again.

I shook my head. "This is what we need to talk about."

She grinned. "You can't blame a girl for trying."

I found that I couldn't help but grin back at her.

"Are you sure?" she asked. "It's a lot of fun."

And just like that, the spell was broken. I'd been worried that there was going to be some kind of a problem here, that she would be angry with me, or hurt, or . . . I didn't really know. But it wasn't anything like that. Janae didn't want me desperately, longingly. She didn't have some helpless crush on me. She just wanted to see if I'd go for it. Sport-fucking. Since she was also clearly attracted to my husband, I wondered if Wiley had hit at the same bait.

"I'm sure," I said. I paused, removed her bracelet and handed it back to her. She took it without comment. I paused for another heartbeat, then blurted out, "I want you to know that I liked it very much, though. But . . . Wiley . . ."

"You didn't say anything to him, did you? You didn't . . . confess?"

"No," I replied. "I don't think that we did anything that I needed to confess. But I can't do it again, Janae. It's . . . It would be a betrayal."

"I understand, Brendee. You're right. We didn't do anything wrong . . . But eventually we would've." She paused. "But I wouldn't say anything about it to Wiley. If you tell him something happened, however harmless, then he'll be looking for it to happen again. Why make him . . . suspicious?"

I nodded, considering. Wiley was observant. It was what he did. He already knew that Janae had kissed me once, and he knew something had been going on in our bedroom today. But suspicious was not something that he would allow himself to be. He knew what he knew. He didn't suspect what he only *supposed* he knew. It was just how he was. Wiley knew Janae had kissed me, and whatever he thought about that, well . . . He would let me know when he wanted to discuss it.

"Still friends?" Janae said.

Again I nodded. She gave me a hug then, a sisterly one this time, but damned if Wiley didn't walk in at just that precise moment and catch us again.

I watched the two of them look at each other for another long moment, just as they'd done earlier. Janae smiled at him, perhaps a trifle defiantly, and Wiley remained expressionless. I couldn't help but wonder, as I did every time I saw them interact – what, if anything, was between them?

Janae said that she'd talk to me soon, smiled, and left.

"It seems like she always takes off as soon as I arrive," he said. "Was it something I said?" He went over and looked at his baby, asleep in his playpen. When I didn't answer right away, he looked questioningly at me.

"I dunno, Wiley. What have you said to her?"

He ceased looking at his boy and said, "That's the rub, isn't it? It's not so much what I've said to her, it's how she's interpreted it."

"That's not really an answer."

He shrugged. "Did you like it? Kissing her?" He gestured toward the bedroom. "Whatever else you were doing–"

"There wasn't anything else." I watched him carefully. "I didn't not like it," I said, noncommittal. "Do you like her . . . misinterpreting what you say to her?"

"Yes," he said without hesitation. "I do. She's clever. Fun. It's enjoyable to be desired."

"And so obviously."

He wasn't copping to anything more. His admission stung me a little bit, even though it wasn't really a surprise. So Wiley enjoyed Janae's desire, did he? Maybe I'd just add a little bit to what he thought he knew. It wasn't true, and it was childish to want to make him think that it was. But his easy admission that he enjoyed Janae's desire had been too easy.

I glanced toward the bedroom for a second. "I don't know how clever she is. But I'd have to agree that she's fun."

Expressionlessly, he said, "Does that mean you want to . . .? Does that mean you want me to say it's all right with me if you and Janae . . . ?"

Ah, the inimitable Wiley Royce, at a loss for words. It was a first. But I wanted to hear him say it.

"If me and Janae *what*, Wiley?"

"Since you think she's so much fun, does that mean you want me to say that it's all right with me if you and Janae . . . have sex?" He paused, the expression on his face totally neutral.

"I could ask you the same–"

"Not really," he said, and grinned. "It's not really the same thing at all, now is it? It wouldn't hold the same kind of novelty for me that it would for you, now would it? I've already had sex–"

"With Janae?"

"No," he replied mildly. "Nor would I, even if you gave me permission to do so. Unlike Nate, I have absolutely no desire for more than one woman at a time."

"What are you talking about?"

"Nothing that bears repeating. He just let a little bit of the inner monologue out the other day." Wiley shrugged. "It's a common fantasy. But not for me. I have no desire for two women. Not separately, and certainly not at the same time. I'm familiar enough with the territory that I have absolutely no desire to explore a different neighborhood of exactly the same city. You, on the other hand – I could see how perhaps you might be curious to find out about–"

"Can you describe for me exactly how all that works, Wiley?" I asked ingenuously. "What women do together? If I was curious?"

His eyebrows went up. "You want me to Google it for you?"

I grinned at him. "I wasn't disgusted when Janae kissed me. She caught me by surprise both times. But neither was I turned on by it, Wiley, not like when you kiss me. There is no comparison. I am a heterosexual, my son – *your* heterosexual, actually. I don't want anybody else but you. I'm not even curious." I arose and crossed the room, put my arms around his neck. "Allow me to prove it to you."

"I have to ask you to hold that thought, Brendee. I have to go back to Tom's. The reporter said she was gonna be delayed for about an hour, so I came back home to see if I could catch you and Janae." Wiley grinned.

But I discovered that I was offended, and quickly removed my hands from him. "Did you really think you would catch us? That I would . . . cheat on you?"

Wiley shrugged. "Things happen. People change. Life goes on. I didn't know what I was gonna find."

My admission of wanting no one but him meant nothing to him, because he knew implicitly that it was true. Neither did he really care, one way or another, if I was attracted to Janae. *People change.*

Had he changed? He'd said that Janae didn't interest him, but she was beautiful. . .

"I told her never to touch me again. Because–"

"I love you, Brendee," he said and kissed me quickly on the forehead. "But I gotta go. You wanna come with me?"

NATE

The caller at the door hadn't been Syd Caraway after all. It was Dionne. Either she didn't yet have a key to Tom's house, or she'd misplaced it. Tom let her in and she exuberantly hugged and kissed him, not concerned at all that Wiley and I were standing right there.

A few minutes later, the reporter texted Wiley to let him know that she was running late; she assured him that she would be there, however. Wiley told us about the delay, then abruptly said, "I'll be right back," and left without a backward glance.

I kept expecting Janae to turn up again at any minute. She knew Wiley was here, and she always seemed to want to be his shadow. But Wiley said she'd been on her way to his house, to see his wife. It was just as my discerning Denny had said: Janae was playing them both, and apparently now Wiley knew it, too. She hadn't gotten a rise out of him, but maybe Brendee had decided . . . It was all too sordid. That was the only word I could think of to describe it: *sordid.*

I wouldn't call myself a prude, but – seriously? Just what was going on here? Wiley said that he thought that Janae was trying to seduce his wife, and then he'd run out of here – was he trying to catch them? Stop them? *Join them?* I shook my head. It was just too much. Dionne made us a drink, and I discovered that I needed it.

Syd Caraway arrived before Wiley returned from his . . . errand. Tom made introductions and the reporter accepted the drink he offered. When he went out into the kitchen to confer with Dionne on liquor selection, Ms Caraway sat next to me on the couch. *Right next to me.* Now I knew how Wiley felt. But why was it that he always got young, sexy blondes sitting too close to him, and all I got was middle-aged hippies?

Ms Caraway grinned at me like I was on the menu and said, "Tell me about you, Nate. What did you say you did for the government?"

Unlike Wiley, I discovered that I couldn't surreptitiously slide away from her, either literally or figuratively. I was more or less pinned against the arm of the couch, and I didn't want to talk about *what I did for the government.* I blinked stupidly at her for a moment, then finally stammered, "I'm not here in any kind of official capacity . . ."

"That's right," she said, and smiled brilliantly at me. She was wearing large, hoop earrings today and they swung gently back and forth. "You're just the hacker's buddy. And–"

"I don't know anything about all that, either," I said hastily. It seemed like a chickenshit thing to say, but it was the truth, wasn't it?

She patted my knee, then left her hand there. "It's okay, Nate. I'm not here to grill you on your friend's methods of acquiring information. But I'd like to know a little more about it. He went through *Skype's* security like a knife through butter. How long has he been doing this kind of work? You guys can't be a day over . . . ."

"Twenty-three," I supplied. "Wiley's twenty-four."

"Ah! What a delightful age!" She squeezed my knee. "Just out of college are you? No wonder you don't want to talk about your job! You must be new there!"

I thought that her hand inched up on my thigh, but I didn't dare look down at it. Again I wondered why Wiley got the willowy strawberry-blondes, as well as the tiny, pixie blondes, the *spinners,* while I now had a woman almost old enough to be my mother sliding her hand up my leg. It just wasn't fair. Not that it wasn't nice . . . But still.

"What exactly does Mr. Royce officially do for a living?" she asked, and gave my leg another little squeeze. Yes, her hand was definitely moving upwards. Another couple of minutes, and she would be squeezing my –

"I'm sure he'll tell you all about it, as soon as he gets back, Ms Caraway," Tom said. He watched the reporter remove her hand from my leg – none too quickly, I might add – and take the drink that he offered her. He grinned at me.

Dionne, behind Tom, also took in the whole scene. She didn't grin.

"And you, Mr. Bastion? What do you do?"

Tom and Dionne sat on the loveseat, just as close to each other as this woman was to me, and I reflected that they were allowed. They actually *were* lovers. I suddenly found myself wishing that Denny was there, or maybe even Janae . . .

"I own *Morry's Books,"* Tom replied. "It's been in my extended family of a very long time." He paused, then returned to the subject under discussion. "I first started looking into the food additives phenomenon after my wife passed away."

"Excuse me just a moment," the reporter said. She reached into her bag and brought out a tiny portable audio recorder. She said,

"Please, continue," pushed a button on the device and set it on the coffee table. Dionne regarded it with distrust, if not downright alarm. I wasn't too happy about it either, but I figured it was all part of telling one's story to the media. I reminded myself to keep my mouth shut. This was Tom and Wiley's show.

"I've been researching this for many years, and one name has kept popping up – Dr. Oskar Renfro Hutchkiss. He's worked for the Department of Agriculture, the FDA, headed the *International Food Information Council.* He spoke at the most recent mid-year meeting of the *International Food Additives Council.* Are you familiar with these groups, Ms Caraway? They're the public relations organs of all the chemical and food manufacturers that set America's table."

"Big Food," Dionne threw in, then put her hand over her mouth, looked in horror at the audio recorder.

Her comment attracted the reporter's attention to her, something Dionne clearly wanted to avoid. "What's your take on all this, Miss – ?"

"Never mind," Dionne said. "I don't want my name in the paper. You don't even need to know my name."

Tom patted her knee consolingly and continued. "Dr. Hutchkiss is also a physician; he has a degree in sociology, psychology, history, economics, and chemistry. He's a eugenicist. Currently, he's the director of the *Food and Medicines Research Foundation.* I've suspected for some time that the good doctor is the ringleader of a cabal that's responsible for slowly but surely poisoning the first world, through food additives."

"A cabal?"

The doorbell rang. Tom arose and admitted Wiley and his family. He made introductions, and after everyone was seated, he said, "Would you say the *Food and Medicines Research Foundation* is a cabal, Wiley?"

"Fucking A, Skippy, I would."

"You're being taped, Wiley," Dionne warned, nodding at the recorder.

"I doubt that it's the first time," he said and winked at his wife. Then he sobered again when he looked back at the reporter. "I have proof, Ms Caraway. I have it on paper," he reached into Bo's diaper bag and removed a thick, wrinkled sheaf, held together by a large black binder clip. He set it on the coffee table in front her. "And I can email it all to you, also.

"There is a global, first world . . ." He glanced briefly at Dionne, then back at Syd Caraway. "All right, I'll use the word. There's a global, first world *conspiracy* afoot here, Ms. Caraway. At its center, we believe, is Dr. Hutchkiss and the *Food and Medicines Research Foundation.* There are no doubt others, in other countries, but all the proof we need is right here." I noticed that the reporter didn't pick up the stack of papers that Wiley offered as proof. "They are poisoning us. It's one big eugenics experiment, one big economic plan. Our foods are fortified, so we grow up to be strong, able to work. Then they're slowly poisoning us with deadly chemicals, masquerading as emulsifiers and stabilizers, colorings and preservatives, so we don't live overly long. Don't overstay our welcome, so to speak. So there are still jobs and housing and a future for the next generation."

"These additives cause cancer, heart disease; they compound diabetes," Tom said. "They counteract the effects of the vitamins that are added to our food – the fortification."

"It's all right here," Wiley pointed to the stack again. "If you're poor, they're trying to wipe you out, and they're succeeding, because you eat more of this shit – cheap processed stuff from the supermarket, and fast food. If you're more affluent, and you think you're healthier – you buy oatmeal and granola bars and cottage cheese – you're still gonna die quicker than you should, because you don't read far enough down on the label to find the glass and the drywall and the sand that's put in your food." Wiley paused. "Drink coffee, do you, Ms Caraway?"

"I just read a study last week that said that a little caffeine is good for you," she replied with a shade of defensiveness.

"Moderation is the key," Tom said and blinked innocently at Wiley.

Wiley shook his head. "I don't drink coffee, so I haven't explored all that. Do you use milk in your coffee?"

"Milk's for cows," Ms Caraway retorted. "Besides, it's full of hormones."

"Milk's also fortified with Vitamin D." Wiley shrugged, glanced at Tom again. "One picks one's poisons, I guess."

"Besides, I'm vegan," the reporter said with a proprietary sniff. Dionne rolled her eyes.

"I'm somewhat of a vegetarian myself."

"The way they treat animals in this country . . ." Now Ms Caraway thought she was preaching to the choir, that she'd found in

Wiley another believer. "All kinds of animals, not just the ones that are slaughtered for our overflowing tables – the way we treat them is obscene. Meat is murder."

"We need protein to live, Ms Caraway," Tom disagreed mildly.

"Protein is available from other sources, Mr. Bastion. I eat nothing that had parents, that had a face. It's a philosophical choice."

Wiley touched his tongue to one of his canine teeth to indicate he was a carnivore, and grinned at me. He said, "My choice of vegetarianism is strictly a dietary one, and it flees in the face of one of Tom's exquisitely grilled T-bones . . . But the martyrdom of our delicious animal friends is a tiresome argument for another day, Ms. Caraway." He smiled politely, and since she didn't know him, I was sure Ms Caraway didn't detect the shade of annoyance in his tone.

"So, since you don't believe in milk, I'm assuming that you use some kind of creamer in your coffee?" When she nodded, he said, "The liquid kind contains carrageenan, to give it that smooth, slippery, milk-like texture. It's in there simply to make it *seem* like milk. Carrageenan has been demonstrated to be a tumor-causing carcinogen; a source of inflammation. It causes gastrointestinal malignancy, colitis-like disease, intestinal lesions, and inflammatory bowel disease. Yet you're pouring it into your coffee." When she made no reply, he said, "Perhaps you use the dry kind instead. It contains sodium aluminosilicate – essentially, sand – for no other reason than to make it pour out of the container efficiently.

"Like I told my friend –" Ms Caraway turned away from Wiley and smiled at me. "You're paying for food and you're getting shit. And it's killing you."

She looked back at him. "But not you."

"Not anymore. And not you, and not your readers, either, after you break this story."

"What exactly do you think the angle to this story should be, Mr. Royce? That would make it Pulitzer material?" Clearly, the whole idea that some twenty-something had uncovered information that would win her a Pulitzer amused the hell out of the *Health and Wellness* reporter. "The evils of Americans' dietary habits has been done and redone. We're all a bunch of fat, lazy slobs, and it starts in childhood." Ms Caraway smiled and waved at Bo, and he smiled back. "What do you think you have to say that hasn't been said before – that hasn't already been ignored?"

"You don't understand, Ms Caraway," Wiley said, and I detected an intensification of his annoyance. "It doesn't have

301

anything to do with our dietary choices. We're being had, regardless. If I offer you a bowl of *Doritos* or a bowl of instant oatmeal or cottage cheese, it doesn't matter which one you choose. I'm not talking about fat and sugar and salt. I'm talking about additives. There's just as much poison inserted into the stuff you think is healthy as there is in the snack food. You're just too dumb to know it."

Ms Caraway's eyelids fluttered a little at his more or less direct insult. I exchanged a glance with Brendee: Wiley's superiority was showing again. We silently agreed that this might not be the best stance to take with the somewhat-superior-herself reporter.

Tom, ever the diplomat, jumped in. "What I think Wiley would like to accomplish is this, Ms Caraway. He'd like you to do a story describing what some of these multi-syllable compounds really consist of, and then perhaps pointing out how unnecessary they are. The worst offenders are there just to make processed foods appealing to the industrialized palate." She blinked at his use of this unfamiliar term, and I wondered with a grin how I had lived so long, grown and prospered, was about to reproduce, without ever having known before that my palate had been industrialized.

Tom explained. "It means that you've been give processed foods since birth, and therefore, you've come to believe that what you've been fed – this cavalcade of additives – that's what food's supposed to taste like. You'd be appalled if your oatmeal was suddenly lumpy, so they put silicon dioxide – which is a primary ingredient in the production of glass – into it, so it pours nicely out of the envelope. You don't want your grated cheese sticking together – and you surely don't have time to grate it yourself – so they put a little sawdust in there, so it shakes out nicely for you.

"You have neither the time nor the inclination to bake your own bread. And you surely don't have the time to be running to the store every other day to buy a fresh loaf, either. So they put calcium sulfate – essentially, gypsum–"

"Drywall," Wiley said.

"– into your bread, as a desiccant; to keep it dry. They put propitionate in it, to prevent it from getting moldy. Propitionate has been deemed toxic by the *Pesticide Action Network of North America.*

"We learned the evils of hydrogenating – that one was uncovered by some intrepid reporter such as yourself, I'm sure – so the health-conscious avoid hydrogenated oils. Now they process the palm oil in your healthy energy bar with a procedure called *fractionalization* – without going into too much detail, it makes the oil less healthy for you – and the sole purpose of the oil being in there in the first place is only to keep that delightful chocolate icing from melting in your hand. It's unnecessary for anything other than to make your healthy snack *look* appetizing."

"There are hundreds of these chemicals," Wiley said. "They're put into what we eat for no other reason than to make processed foods look better: to retain color, to melt or not melt. To have a better texture: emulsifiers, stabilizers. To have an incredibly long shelf life: preservatives, chemicals to *retain freshness*. To make them pour conveniently out of the packaging: flow and anticaking agents. To make you think they taste better: citric acid. All synthesized, artificial, unnecessary. Poisonous. To industrialize your palate. To make you buy more of this shit." Wiley glanced at me. "There's no flavor enhancers in a real banana.

"So there you are, conditioned from birth to like the taste of this shit. You say you're a *vegan?*" Wiley said the word with the same inflection he might use if he said *sociopath.* "You would not believe the poisons that are in your salad dressing, just to make it pour out of the bottle efficiently, just to make it smooth, creamy – there's no cream in it; you have to torture a cow to get that, and that costs money, takes time, doesn't keep as well."

"But salad dressing tastes good," Ms Caraway protested.

"And so does baby food and rice pudding and everything else you buy at the supermarket. It's tasty, creamy, soft or crunchy; it doesn't stick to the packaging or your Teflon pan." Wiley grinned at Tom. "It doesn't melt in your hand, it keeps on your shelf. But it's not real, Ms Caraway. It's artificial, synthesized poison, being passed off as nutritious by a group of people that are seeking to control you, to control how long you live, how healthy you are while you're living. They know how soon you'll die, based on how much of this shit they've conned you into eating." Wiley again nodded at the stack of papers. "All of the proof is right there."

"And how did you obtain this proof?"

Wiley smiled his shark's grin. "The same way you did. From an anonymous source."

Ms Caraway took a deep breath and reached for the sheaf of *proof.* She thumbed through it with little interest.

"Now that I've told you about these vipers in our midst, your eyes are opened." Wiley at last loosed his killer smile, and I thought

Ms Caraway responded to him a little bit, despite herself. "And then, after you tell everybody else, people will stop buying this stuff, and . . ."

"And?" Wiley searched for words – something he rarely needed to do, so she said it again. "And what, Mr. Royce? If I expose this conspiracy, if I tell the world how *Kraft* and *McDonald's* are poisoning them, for eugenic and economic purposes . . . Then what?"

"People will stop . . ."

"Stop what? Eating food that's bad for them? What did you call it, Mr. Bastion?"

"Industrialization of the palate."

"Our entire lives are industrialized now, Mr. Royce. Not just our food, but our cars and our electronics; our, jobs, our houses . . . Our news," she added with a touch of sadness. "We're not going back to unadulterated food, any sooner than we're going back to *Extra! Extra! Read all about it.* It's too difficult. Too much trouble."

"Give me convenience or give me death," Tom murmured.

Ms Caraway ignored him. "You think you're going to get people to give up *Doritos* and TV dinners and instant mashed potatoes and ramen noodles because you tell them that they've got poison in them? That didn't work when it was just fat and sodium and sugar, now did it? And it's certainly not going to work when you try to explain the evils of a bunch of polysyllabic chemicals. Too much fat makes you fat – that's an observable, universal truth; yet it was ignored. People are suspicious – there is always a study this week that is contradicted by another study next week. And the internet is always warning them about shadowy government agencies out to control them."

"But *Frosted Flakes* are always *grrreat!"* Tom observed.

Silence reigned for a heartbeat, then Wiley said, "So you're not gonna–"

"Oh, I'll write the story, Mr. Royce. I wouldn't waste you good peoples' time with an interview, otherwise." She smiled and patted me on the knee, then turned back to Wiley. "But I want you to not get your hopes up too much about the reaction to it.

"People want to believe that they're more concerned with those less fortunate than they are about themselves. They want to feel outrage about things that don't really concern them. Genital mutilation of little girls in foreign countries. Hell, all the terrible things women have to put up with in foreign countries." She looked at Dionne and Brendee for agreement. They both just looked blankly back at her. "That's the kind of copy that sells. Or children. Americans always want to save the poor third world children. However . . . Did you know that children as young as twelve are forced to pick tobacco in this country, Mr. Royce?"

"What I'm talking about here concerns your readers' *own children,* Ms Caraway," Wiley countered. "I believe that they would be more concerned with their own than they are about the unfortunates that have to pick tobacco."

The reporter shook her head. "Maybe. But childhood obesity is rampant in this country, right? That tells me that my readers don't care what their kids eat. It's not entirely your additives that are making them fat, now is it? We're back to the obvious again, the sugar and fat and sodium. People in this country don't care about their diet, Mr. Royce. They are healthy enough–"

"Nobody's skin's peeling off from pellagra anymore," Tom observed.

"– and there are a million other issues, thrown at them constantly, that they have to worry about. The plight of the third world. The idea that the third world might at any moment rise up and start a war, because they're envious of our first world wonderfulness. There's political corruption. Global warming." Again Dionne rolled her eyes. "Taxes. Welfare. Welfare cheats.

"Once upon a time, I worked for *Time Magazine,*" Syd Caraway said.

"I know," Wiley replied. "I read your bio. That's why I came to you with this."

The reporter smiled, flattered. "Then I hope you'll believe me when I tell you that they'd never touch a story like this. Any type of conspiracy angle – the public has had it up to here with conspiracies, Mr. Royce. There have been so many . . ."

Dionne grinned tightly at me, vindicated.

"And Americans have also heard about *so many* shadowy organizations: the NSA, the CIA . . . Paranoia has been assimilated. Another dark group, another conspiracy doesn't interest them, and it certainly doesn't surprise them. They already believe that their government is out to get them, and they've more or less accepted it as a fact of modern life.

"This info that you've uncovered might indeed be the earthshattering *new* conspiracy that you think it is – *to you.* But the man on the street isn't going to be overly impressed." She smiled kindly at him. "No Pulitzer." She reached toward the audio recorder, hesitated. "What is it that you do for a living, Mr. Royce? When you're not saving mankind?"

"I fix electronics," he replied simply.

"His business is called *Wiley's Electronics,*" Tom said. "Out of the bookstore. We're partners." He smiled at Wiley, proud of their partnership, and recited the phone number and address of the shop. I realized that Tom knew that even if the reporter's story didn't topple the *Food and Medicines Research Foundation,* even if it didn't *save mankind,* if she included the address and phone number of their business, they might turn a little trade.

Now Ms Caraway reached forward and shut off the recorder, picked it up and dropped it into her purse. She arose, and Wiley and Tom and I followed suit. The ladies remained seated.

"Thanks so much for telling me about all this," she said seriously, demonstrating that she was, indeed, a professional. "I'll let you know when the story's gonna run." Then she grinned a little mischievously at Wiley. "Although I must admit, I think that sand in the coffee creamer makes it taste better."

She wanted to end the interview on a playful note, but Wiley was not in a playful mood. This was all very important to him. But since she waited for his response, he bleated, *"Baa,"* at her and sat back down.

"Thanks for your time," Tom replied tactfully, and shook her hand. He grinned at me. "Why don't you walk Ms Caraway out to her car, Nate?"

She smiled winningly at me again. "Why don't you, Nate? I've been thinking about doing a story about the roles of recent college graduates in County government. Perhaps after I submit Mr. Royce's story, we could have a little interview of our own." She looked at everyone else. "It was nice to meet you."

Then Ms Caraway, *Health and Wellness* reporter for the *Press-Enterprise,* former correspondent for *Time Magazine,* had the nerve to take my hand and lead me out of Tom's house. I just had time to look over my shoulder at Brendee: she grinned at me with no sympathy whatsoever.

BRENDEE

Dionne looked after the reporter and a quite completely reluctant Nate and rolled her eyes. When the door closed behind them, she said, "Jesus. What a hippie. Wants to save all the little animals. Does she think the animals would want to save her?"

Neither Tom nor I replied. We were looking at Wiley. After another moment, Tom said softly, "I told you, my son. People don't care."

"There's a difference between not caring and not knowing, Tom," Wiley insisted. "There has to be. People want to know. For their kids' sake." He ruffled Bo's hair.

"The sheep don't want to know," Dionne said. "Just like the hippie said, corruption is commonplace. Even the most outrageous scandal – even poisoned food – people just accept it. This thing that you've uncovered is subtle, cumulative, Wiley. You can't demonstrate that eating a *Happy Meal* is gonna cause little Johnny to drop dead immediately, and sustained outrage takes too much energy, too much thought. *I was gonna get mad because this stuff is slowly killing my kid, but . . . Did you see that cute kitty-cat video online today?*

"You can't save anybody but yourself, Wiley, and those that you love." She squeezed Tom's hand. "I keep telling you that."

Nate practically ran back into the house, and we all looked at him. "She asked me if I wanted to . . ."

Wiley grinned. "Maybe you should. Maybe it would get our story told better." Nate's eyes got as round as dinner plates at the very suggestion, and Wiley slapped him on the back. "I'm just kidding, my son. I wouldn't prostitute my best friend, unless there was a little more certainty of the results."

"Wait 'til Denny hears about this," he said.

"There might be a fire at the yellow *Press-Enterprise,*" Wiley opined. He looked at Tom and Dionne, and his expression of defeat cut me. "I'm sorry to have imposed on your hospitality for this charade, my friends."

"It's quite all right, Wiley," Tom said in surprise.

"Still, it's time for us to leave you to the rest of your evening." He smiled at me, but I could see that he wasn't really as blithe as he was putting on. "Come, my wife; my son." He took Bo from me. "Let us to home."

The short drive to our apartment was a quiet one. Wiley was introspective, contemplative. It was as clear to him as it was to me that the reporter from the *Press-Enterprise* was far more impressed with Nate than she was with Dr. Hutchkiss and his plans to control the lifespan of the first world.

****

Wiley didn't forget that I'd been in the mood before we had to go and attend his meeting with the media. But its outcome had been disappointing to him, and it showed in his attention, in his performance. I was there and he was there, but we weren't there together, gloriously, as we were supposed to be. As we used to be.

I wondered for how much longer he was going to allow this conspiracy bullshit to get to him, to preoccupy him. He'd consulted a professional, and she'd told him the same thing that his guru had told him, the same thing we'd all told him: nobody cares. He simply couldn't warn people that ignored his warnings, couldn't help people that didn't want to be helped. It was so unlike him, anyway. Wiley didn't even *like* people.

Then another, more dire thought slunk into my mind. Maybe it wasn't the *Food and Medicines Research Foundation* and the evils of carrageenan that were on his mind at all.

Maybe he was thinking about Janae. I had put the skids to the whole thing between the two of us, but maybe Wiley was still considering allowing it all to roll on between the two of *them*. When I'd told him that I told her not to touch me again, I realized that he hadn't said that he'd stop flirting with her, that he'd correct her misinterpretation of his words. I couldn't help but wonder . . .

****

The following afternoon, when I opened the door to our apartment, I heard Wes's voice. I stopped dead, thinking perhaps I was having a stroke or some kind of brain hemorrhage. Yes, it was Wes's voice, emanating from my bedroom, punctuated with the same familiar, soul-caressing little yelp. But he wasn't singing *My Disgrace*. It was definitely Wes's voice – I would know it anywhere – but the song was unfamiliar.

I walked slowly toward the bedroom, still certain that I was having some kind of brain malfunction. What misfire in my synapses was causing this auditory hallucination? Wes's voice, smooth as glass, soft and sexy as black velvet . . . Since I was hearing him, when I knew he could not possibly be there, would I also see him when I walked into the room?

But of course, there was no Wes. Instead, there was Wiley, shirtless, sitting on the bed with his back against the headboard, his laptop on his lap. I noticed to my amazement that he had busted out my favorite black satin sheets. One of them was gathered demurely at his waist, covering all the important parts, leaving his exquisite legs bare from the thighs on down. As always, I noted the ugly scars on his left one, reminders of the surgery he'd had to repair the bones he'd broken as a teen. He had his ankles crossed.

He looked up at me and smiled blankly. His eyes were just as blue as a summer's day, and wrapped up in that black sheet, he looked good enough to eat. I was spellbound by this unexpected treat, not to mention the sound of Wes Thomerville's voice.

He glanced back at whatever we was watching on his laptop. It had to be Wes, because Wes's voice was coming out of the little speakers. Why was Wiley watching Wes? He looked back at me again and featured me with that familiar tell-nothing Wiley smile; he waited for me to speak. I had absolutely nothing – why was Wiley listening to some-never-before-heard Rolling Blackout tune? Why was he naked, wrapped up in only a slick satin sheet like some kind of naughty Christmas present, in the middle of an otherwise non-descript Friday afternoon? Where was my son? I couldn't begin to speculate, and as the silence threatened to lengthen, he at last said, "Surprise, Brendee. Bo's at my mom's."

That was all I needed to hear. Before the day got another minute older, I kicked off my shoes and climbed onto the bed, up the length of him. I closed his laptop, cutting off Wes's voice. He set it on the bedside table and waited for me to kiss him.

And kiss him I did, slowly, languorously. Ah, there was nothing in the world better than kissing Wiley, except for Wiley kissing me. But his control was Zen, just as I had once told Janae. But I didn't think about her right then. Wiley had stowed our son with Aunt Amy, and I wasn't going to waste a moment of that time thinking about anything but him.

He let me kiss him and responded a little bit, kissing me back the way he knew I liked it. But by the same token, if the phone rang or someone knocked on the door, I knew Wiley could cease what he was doing in a heartbeat. It was not so much that he wasn't into it – it was that he wasn't into it *yet*. He was letting me do what I wanted, what I liked, first: Wiley knew that there was no bigger turn on for me than just kissing him, tangling my hands in his curly black hair, running my hands over his muscled shoulders and exquisite chest, lacing my fingers in his and squeezing his hands.

Wiley was not distracted as he'd been the night before; he was attuned to me, like he used to be, in the old days, before Bo, before *Janae,* before his need to wreak havoc because he'd discovered that he'd been duped by Dr. Hutchkiss and his kaleidoscope of food additives. He waited, patiently, while my desire grew, expanded. He knew the precise moment to act, and would not act before I'd reached it.

But I also knew what Wiley liked, what button to push, what signal to give to release him from his self-imposed bond of passivity. I knew how to loose the glorious beast that he really was. There was really nothing shy, nothing at all passive about Wiley, once he got a mind to act.

I reached down and slowly pulled the black satin sheet away, sliding the slick material across his thigh, pooling it against his side. I raked my fingers lightly across his bare belly, and Wiley gasped beneath my mouth, kissed me back hard. It was always the limit of his endurance – I could touch him *anywhere else,* and he could retain his cool for at least a few more moments. But not his smooth, taut little belly. It was his sexual Achilles' heel. Wiley always lost it, showed me what *he* wanted to do, once I just ran my fingers lightly across his tummy.

And what he wanted to do was of course what I wanted him to do, and for the first time in a long time, it was just as incredible as it used to be; and I suddenly kenned precisely how much I'd missed it. I'd always desired Wiley, from the very first moment that I'd laid eyes on him – except, I realized, for all these stupid months when I had let other things take up space in my mind. How could I have forgotten that this was the supreme pleasure of my life?

He'd picked up on my distraction, perhaps found distractions of his own, and had simply waited, just letting it all ride. He knew I'd come back. He'd sensed that the desire had been returning for some time now, but he'd just let it grow, like some kind of delicate plant that might shrink, might retreat from too much attention from an eager gardener. He'd just let it all germinate, only giving a little encouragement here and there: that brief passionate surprise when we had a houseful of people, a drunken, sloppy romp here, a few friendly, loving excursions there.

He knew I'd find him irresistible, wrapped up in that black sheet, that it would tip the scales, make me forget whatever had been on my mind; like a landslide, the memories would rush back on me. There was not one thing in the world that I wanted to do more than this. Wiley had given me the time to remember that he always knew exactly what I wanted. And now that I had remembered, he was going to expertly show me just what it was.

My husband and I made love all night, over and over; pausing only to eat and take a couple of showers. The things Wiley could do under running water were sublime. He woke me up in the morning, again with his wonderful touch, and we might have gone at each other all day again, like we had the first time we'd ever been alone together in high school – that one had gone on for nearly four days – had it not been for a knock on the door at about eleven-thirty Saturday morning.

Wiley threw his black, dragon-decorated mandarin robe on and went to see who had arrived. I found some sweats and a t-shirt and followed him.

It was Tom. He smiled indulgently at our disheveled state – nothing got past Tom. "I'm sorry to drop in unannounced, Wiley, but you didn't answer your phone."

"That's the equivalent of a *Do Not Disturb* sign in the modern world, my son." He grinned. "What can I do for you?"

"This is called a *newspaper,*" Tom said, and produced a folded one from under his arm. "I'm sure you've heard of them. This particular one isn't much good for anything but lining hamster cages and making your fingers grimy, but I thought you might wanna see it."

Wiley opened the paper and scanned it. "Hot damn, Brendee! We made the front page!"

I looked hopefully at Tom, but he shook his head: Wiley's enthusiasm was premature.

"It's on their website, too, of course," Tom said. "But I thought that you might like to experience it like the Luddite on the street."

"I can't believe that people still buy newspapers," I remarked.

"Nonetheless read them," Tom agreed.

"Local Businessmen Warn of Death in Your Dinner." Wiley looked up at us. "That's clever.

"*If you need your phone or computer repaired, or would like to browse for the classics in print form, look no further than Wiley's Electronics and Morry's Books, housed in the same quaint old building downtown.* Look, Tom. She listed the address."

Tom smiled, but didn't speak.

"*This blending of the very old and the ultra-modern makes for an interesting combination,*" Wiley read, "*and the proprietors of these establishments have a message for their fellow citizens, concerning the multitude of polysyllabic additives that are put into America's food.*

"'*There are hundreds of these chemicals,*' Wiley Royce said. '*They're put into what we eat for no other reason than to make processed foods look better: to retain color, to melt or not melt . . .*'" Wiley skimmed over his own quote.

"*He went on to describe two such chemicals, each found in coffee creamers. Carrageenan, derived from seaweed . . .*" Again Wiley skimmed. "*He concluded by saying that these additives add nothing to the nutritional value.*

"'*The worst offenders are there just to make processed foods appealing,*' Tom Bastion, owner of Morry's Books, added. '*You'd be appalled if your oatmeal was suddenly lumpy, so they put silicon dioxide . . .*'" Wiley skimmed over what Tom had said this time.

"'*The reason that Americans are so unhealthy,*' Royce continued, '*doesn't have anything to do with our dietary choices. If I offer you a bowl of chips or a bowl of instant oatmeal or cottage cheese, it doesn't matter which one you choose. I'm not talking about fat and sugar and salt. I'm talking about additives.*'

"*Their recommendations for a healthier first world? Read the labels, past the nutritional info. The most important aspect of modern food is not the sodium and the fat and the high fructose corn syrup according to Royce and Bastion, but the additives – 'There's just as much poison inserted into the stuff you think is healthy as there is in the snack food,*' according to Royce.

"*All of these dangers can be sidestepped by avoiding processed foods, foods that have been 'industrialized,' says Bastion. 'We've been give processed foods since birth, and therefore, we've come to believe that what we've been fed – this cavalcade of additives – that's what food's supposed to taste like.*'

"*So, just like your mother always told you, eating your fruits and veggies, avoiding pre-packaged food, junk food, and fast food will make for a healthier you.*"

312

Wiley frowned. "That's it? She didn't even mention Dr. Hutchkiss. Or the foundation."

"I told you, Wiley," Tom said gently. *"She* told you. People are tired of conspiracies."

"Fuck it, then," he replied and threw the newspaper on the coffee table. "Dionne's right. The sheep don't wanna be saved."

"You really knew that all along, didn't you?" I asked.

At last Wiley smiled. Just like that, the bubble burst, the righteousness evaporated. He was through with the fruitless, thankless task of trying to save his fellow man. It had all been so uncharacteristic of him anyway, all just an outgrowth of his feelings of being had. He'd given it his best shot.

"Fuck 'em all, big, tall, and small. Only my friends and family really matter."

Thank Christ, I thought. As insufferably superior as he was, I was glad that my husband had at last decided to abandon this crusade. Just like Tom had once said, you couldn't make people *want* to know, and trying to even make them just *know* was equally as pointless.

"Indeed," Tom agreed. He was also relieved that Wiley's save-the-world fervor seemed to have died down, seeing how he had sicced him on the whole thing in the first place. *"And he called his name Noah, saying, 'This same shall comfort us concerning our work and toil of our hands, because of the ground which the Lord hath cursed.'"*

"And every living substance was destroyed which was upon the face of the ground, both man, and cattle, and the creeping things, and the fowl of the heaven; and they were destroyed from the earth: and Noah only remained alive, and they that were with him in the ark." Wiley grinned at my amazement, then turned to Tom. "Was there anything else?"

"Not at the moment."

"I'll be in to the shop a little later, then." Wiley winked at me. "Maybe."

****

Tom left, and at first I expected that maybe a little of Wiley's insouciance might've gone with him. After all, he'd been adamant about toppling the foundation, about exposing what he and Tom saw as a vast conspiracy to poison the first world.

"The ability to reconsider an unsuccessful line of attack in favor of a different plan is basic to intelligence," Wiley told me once. He'd grinned then. "Or, you can just give up. Some things can't be remedied." He now knew what he now knew, and if the sheep couldn't be bothered enough to listen to him, he would no longer bother trying to pave the chute to the slaughterhouse with his good intentions.

Wiley had given up on the sheep; their situation couldn't be remedied. But it seemed to me at first that he'd given up entirely too easily.

On the other hand, Wiley had never been one to beat his head against the wall for very long over his fellow man's complacencies, their lack of indignation at what he saw as the wrongs that they allowed to be heaped upon them. Now that he'd recovered from the horrible discovery of his own ignorance, that status quo had returned. Wiley was smarter than everyone else, and their ignorance was certainly not his problem.

As if to underline his, he didn't even mention Syd Caraway's worthless article. Instead he just grinned at me and said, "Wanna go back to bed?"

Wiley slithered out of his robe and flopped back down on the slippery black sheets. I slid in next to him, but before I could make a move to touch him, he said, "I've got a big surprise for your mom."

"I don't think my dad would be too happy about that," I said immediately. I could make off-color remarks, too.

Wiley looked curiously at me, but let the comment slide. "Did you know that Jason Whitsun directed the video of that singer your mom likes so much?"

"The guy that did *Eileen's Mother?* Really?" *Eileen's Mother* was a romance, full of passion and helplessness – it showed how far a woman might be driven in the name of love, to keep the man that had enslaved her.

Wiley had taken his laptop from the bedside table, opened it in his naked lap. I wondered to what lengths of revenge I might travel to keep him. Because he had just reminded me how much I was enslaved to him, and so thoroughly, so gloriously; body and soul.

"Yeah. Nate saw an interview with him, and he said they showed a little clip of that singer, what's his name?"

I blinked blankly, shrugged, as if I couldn't recall. Wiley also shrugged. "I guess it was Whitsun's first project. From film school. Anyway, he mentioned to the interviewer that there'd been another

314

video, to another song. It's called *You Can't Be Shy*. Whitsun said he hadn't ever gotten around to finishing it, but the rough cut of it used to be online somewhere. So I had Tom find it. I thought it would be a nice surprise for your mom." Wiley looked over at me, again with an expression of mild, somehow expectant curiosity. "Do you wanna see it? Or do you wanna . . ." But he didn't make a move toward me. He just sat there, stock still. Waiting.

I thought that in my present mood, watching a *new video* of Wes, OMG, might just put me completely around the arousal bend. And then there would be Wiley, who looked so much like Wes, waiting for me, in the flesh . . .

Legend has it that the fiery horses of the desert peoples were put to a test before they were deemed trustworthy enough to carry kings into battle. It was said that the warriors would keep the horses from water for a set period of time – not long enough to hurt them, but just long enough for them to understand in their horsey minds that they were thirsty. Then they would release the steeds in the presence of the trough, and at the same moment, they would sound the war trumpet. Only those that turned away before they reached the trough, only those that answered the call to arms instead of their own thirst, were deemed worthy enough to become battle chargers.

Here was a similar dilemma. I could make Wiley wait while I watched this new clip – it would no doubt do untold wonders for my libido – but in the meantime, Wiley might lose interest, might get up and find something else that he wanted to do. Then I would be left all dressed up with no place to go, so to speak. Or I could eschew Wes's video for the moment – I'd certainly get to see it when Wiley gave it to my mom – and avail myself of my husband again. Seeing Wes might add a little something-something, but it wasn't like I actually *needed* one extra thing to heighten my appreciation of Wiley and the things he could do. I could slake my curiosity with this new novelty, or I could answer my husband's call to further pleasures. The choice was as simple as that.

It wasn't like I'd ever pretended that Wiley was Wes. Wes wasn't real. Wiley was Wiley – flawless, impeccable, talented. I couldn't deny that he was also attractive to me because he looked like Wes; this fact had made me notice him in the first place. When we'd first met, Wiley had seemed quite shy and boyish to me – I never would've given him a second thought if it hadn't been for this propitious resemblance, and my secret fantasies about Wes.

315

But after our initial moments alone together – it was Wiley himself, his skill in always knowing exactly what I wanted, that had bound me to him. If it hadn't been for that, all the resemblance in the world wouldn't have mattered. One's imagination can only go so far. Wiley was infinitely attractive to me because he was Wiley, so I'd more or less forgotten all about Wes – I'd only looked at his video once more in all the years I'd been with my delightful blue-eyed husband, and that had been just recently.

So the choice was not difficult. I would see Wes's old-new video later. I wanted Wiley now. We were parents, with all the responsibilities that entailed, and an afternoon alone with Wiley was not something to be passed up, not even three minutes of it.

I took the computer from him, before he even had time to locate the file. I closed it and set it on the table again. I climbed astride him and when he looked up at me, I thought his smile held the slightest hint of surprise. But I had to be imagining it. Nothing I did in this arena ever surprised Wiley.

"Well, alrighty, then," he said and kissed me, just the way I liked it. That was all it ever took. All remembrance of Wes, his old video; even curiosity about this new one – all thought of anything except for Wiley and his touch and smell and taste, fled from my mind.

JANAE

I stopped by *Starbucks* to get Tommy his favorite caramel macchiato, and one for myself. It was always a great way to start Saturday morning. I'd planned to go to the store, have a few laughs with him. Maybe glare at Wiley a little bit; maybe flirt with Wiley a little bit, depending on his attitude. I was curious to see what his mood would be like; I wondered what Brendee had told him about our little not-tryst. I'd tried to text her, but had received no response.

But as I exited the *Starbucks,* a girl, texting herself, was coming into the store. Oblivious to the world around her, she collided with me, making me drop Tommy's coffee. The earth-friendly paper cup hit the ground, sending up a volcanic flume of hot, over-priced, sweet liquid, drenching me and the girl from the knees down.

"OMG, I'm so sorry!" she said.

I looked up, prepared to be furious. Instead, I gaped at her, because she was exquisite: she looked like Snow White, complete with a little red bow stuck into a riot of black curls. But unlike the Disney character, her enormous eyes were just as blue as a summer's day.

She opened her red, bow mouth and exclaimed again how sorry she was. "You have to let me buy you another one!"

It must've been the stupefied look on my face, because one side of her perfect mouth quirked up wryly, and she said, "Better yet, let me buy you breakfast." She linked her arm in mine and led me out of the *Starbucks.* I allowed myself to be led. She was gorgeous.

NATE

I had lunch with Brendee on the following Friday. Guiltlessly, we went to *Arby's,* and a moment's wondering about what might be in my delicious *Beef 'n Cheddar* was the sole influence of Wiley and Tom's obsession. It was a flash of curiosity, but not a second of concern. *No one he-ere gets out alive.* And *Arby's* is one of my favorites.

After Ms Caraway's fluff piece, Wiley had not mentioned food additives to me all week, had not read me the Riot Act about anything I was eating. I had been warned, and now I was on my own. He was done preaching, and I was glad of it. Brendee confirmed, with a big, bright smile, that Wiley was getting back to his old self.

"He seems to have finally let this insanity go, Nate," she told me. "At least as far as the whole saving-the-world-from-the-evil-conspiracy thing is concerned, anyway. He still spends a lot of time reading the labels in the supermarket, however."

"We're stuck, Brendee," I agreed. "Denny does the same thing."

"But at least the crusade is over."

I nodded. "Wiley's back to being the rancher. He's no longer out there with PETA, holding up a sign, trying to save the sheep."

"Thank Christ," she said with a sigh.

"You knew he'd come around, though, didn't you?" I asked with interest.

I'd always believed he would. But on the other hand, I knew Wiley and just exactly how superior he felt to humanity – including her – a little bit more thoroughly than she did. Brendee probably believed that theirs had been a fairytale romance, full of fateful coincidences. Some of the things that had occurred had been coincidental – it was simply kismet that Wiley looked just like her fantasy – but after he'd discovered that he did, he'd played her like an accordion.

"It was touch and go for a while there," she said. "I couldn't believe that he'd stoop to talking to the media – the yellow *Press-Enterprise,* yet."

"He believes in all this, Brendee. He felt compelled to get the word out to the world."

"But the world slammed the door in his face, didn't it? In the person of Syd Caraway?"

I shrugged. "Wiley accepted her take on it. He believes that she's a professional, and even though he probably wouldn't admit it, he respects her opinion. She didn't think it would burn up the blogosphere – *no Pulitzer.* If people cared, there would've been some response by now, even to her little fluffy piece, and she would've let him know about it. Wiley finally saw the handwriting on the wall. Nobody cares."

"Could you imagine, if he would've got people's attention like he intended, though? Just picture it – all of a sudden, a million fat, whiny, sheep start texting Wiley, telling him about their troubles. 'You're right, Mr. Royce! I'm a big, fat cow because of the carrageenan! What should I do now?'"

"You don't think he'd like that?" I said in surprise. Wiley, suddenly the leader of some kind of movement? People suddenly recognizing that he was smarter than them, believing that he knew something that they didn't know? I thought he'd love it.

But Brendee shook her head. "Just go with me on this, Nate. If people suddenly believed him – that it was the additives that are making them fat and miserable and sick – what advice could he possibly give to them? All he could do would be to tell him to *stop eating this shit,* as he so ineloquently terms it.

"But then what? 'So, we all stopped eating additives, Mr. Royce,' his followers would say. 'When are we gonna be svelte and strong and wise and wonderful like you?' Wiley Royce, suddenly a health guru – he would lose his hillbilly mind, Nate, when they didn't follow his advice after that. Even if they all stopped eating additives, he wouldn't want to have to explain to them, over and over, that they still eat too much, that they are still way too much in love with food. All the shit he's been telling us for years. He's an absentee rancher, at best. He wouldn't want to have to actually shepherd the sheep."

"You don't think he'd like helping people?"

Again Brendee shook her head. "People need to help themselves, Nate. Even if they believed Wiley, even if they stopped eating all the chemicals – like I say, then what? Wiley never looked past that. He never had a plan for the world. His plan is only for us: we're going to be the healthiest we can possibly be, because you and me and Deneen and our children now know better. We're going to cut out additives. We're gonna live forever, because we're not gonna fall for Dr. Hutchkiss's eugenic machinations any more.

"But we've always been subjected to Wiley's little-meal health regimen. Don't you think that we're *already* as healthy as we could possibly be? Despite . . ." She looked down at her demolished *Three Cheese & Bacon* and grinned. "Wiley's Mr. Zen Physical Fitness. But he's above going to the gym with the rabble, isn't he? " I thought of his impressive handstands. "He takes care of himself because he loves himself. He doesn't do it to impress other people. Not even me. That's why he wouldn't be caught dead at the gym.

"And if he convinced the world to give up food additives – it would only follow that they'd do it because they'd think that it'd make them all just like him. That's how guru-ship works, doesn't it? Do what I say, and you'll be trim and healthy just like me. And that just ain't the case, now is it?"

"But–"

"But me no buts, Nate," Brendee said and shook her head a third time. "Wiley wouldn't want to be a leader of sheep. Their health problems wouldn't be solved by giving up just this one aspect – he thinks it's gonna save him and us, but we're already fit enough. It's just gonna make us *harder, better, faster, stronger.*" She grinned.

"But giving up additives is not gonna make the world over in Wiley's image, and he wouldn't want them all whining 'Why not?' to him. He wouldn't want to have to take them all back to square one. 'Not additive-free *Cheetos*, people; no *Cheetos* at all.' Where's the fun in that?" Brendee sipped her *Cherry Coke.*

"So, yeah, I guess you're right. I knew he'd come back around eventually. It was never really about saving the world, Nate. It was about saving face – to himself. Wiley discovered that he was just as dumb as the rest of us, and the only way he thought he could make himself feel better was to reveal the awful truth. Then he would be a redeemer, of sorts. A secret kept from Wiley Royce, for his whole damned life – that was an evil secret indeed. He had to tell everyone about that one."

"And since it really is a conspiracy . . ."

"Is it? Is it really?"

"Did you read any of those studies?"

Brendee shrugged. "I skimmed them. I might sound like Deneen, but they're *boring*. I get the point: the stuff they're putting in our food is deadly."

"Yet Dr. Hutchkiss is promoting its use," I replied. Now I was starting to sound like her husband. But it was true. I'd spent an evening with my beloved, poring over all of the information that Wiley had seized from the *Food and Medicines Research Foundation's* server. Denny had insisted that I read the studies with her – she was still a little self-conscious that she wasn't as quick and complete in her comprehension of charts and graphs and data as Wiley was. She'd rather have me explain them to her than him.

And the data was incontrovertible – food additives were killing us, and the foundation was encouraging their continued and expanded use to Big Food. They made recommendations: put some polydextrose in there; call it low-fat. Put some cellulose, some sawdust, in there; call it high fiber. Put some sand in there so it pours out nicely. Diacetyl makes in yellow, No. 40 makes it red. Make it soft, make it chewy, make it smooth; sweet, salty, savory. *Appetizing.* Make it poisonous. Make millions.

I was now just like Janae: I knew, but I just didn't care as much as Tom and Denny and Wiley did.

"But it's not a secret, Nate," Brendee continued. "That's what got to Wiley so badly. These comprehensive studies, the ones on the foundation's site – they may be secret, but only because they're encouraging the continued and expanded use of this stuff. They see a profit margin and are out to help their clients exploit it. They're not in the saving-the-world business, either. They're in the making-money business.

"I think that maybe Wiley and Tom see a conspiracy that isn't actually there, Nate. To want to control all our fates, wouldn't Dr. Hutchkiss and his minions – and even Big Food – wouldn't it indicate that they cared about us? Even if their concern was just to corral and control us, it's still concern.

"I don't see it that way. These people don't care about how long we live, when we die. They don't want to limit our lifespans to ensure that Bo can get a job. They don't want to wipe out the poor, because their money is green. All Big Food wants to do is *make money.* Today. Next week. I don't think there's any conspiracy. It's just about making money.

"And besides, the same kinds of studies are on the internet; enough websites and whistle blowers, telling us about how bad all this stuff is, right?" I nodded. "So it's not really a secret, is it? So how could it be a conspiracy?"

I had to agree with her on that.

Brendee grinned. "And as far as Pastor Wiley and his preaching goes, he doesn't want to save anybody anymore. He's an insider again – it's not a secret, but he's one of the few people that're aware of it. If everyone else is too dumb to figure it out on their own – *like he once was, but now isn't anymore* – then that's their problem."

****

Dionne invited us all up to the mountains for the weekend, so she could show off her prepper compound, and also so she could throw a big family wedding/baby shower for Denny. The ceremony was slated for the following weekend in town, at the same little church where Denny's mom and dad had gotten hitched. It was going to be a simple thing, but Denny had invited the world to it. This gathering was just for our immediate families. Dionne wasn't big on a bunch of strangers, but she'd wanted to do something nice for the bride/mother-to-be, so she'd arranged for this shindig.

I'd begun to re-evaluate Dionne a little bit. Initially, I'd gotten the impression that she was appalled at the idea of our wanting to bring a baby into this vale of tears. Mankind was circling the drain, after all, according to her – why would we want to produce a person that might have to live in the rubbish heap of a once great, but now destroyed society? Her apocalyptic vision was like something out one of those old movies Wiley had made me sit through: dirty ragamuffin children, picking through the skeletal ruins of destroyed cities, living like animals . . .

Now she'd changed her tune, embraced Bo and our baby as the future. Just like Tom, I believed she saw them as people who could be influenced to make our little corner of the world better.

But not the world in general – Dionne was by no means a globe-saving crusader, any more than Wiley was, now that he was back in his right mind. She still believed that society was on the verge of imminent collapse; it was coming any day now. But she was not concerned, because she had her place, above-ground and below, and she aimed to save no one but herself and Tom when Armageddon came. And us, now, if we wanted to live.

The cabin was gigantic: a big bedroom, a huge living room, a more than modest kitchen and a nice-sized bathroom. And then everything was replicated on a smaller scale underground. But the bomb shelter went unused; it was musty and dusty down there. Dionne said something about needing to clean the radiation-proof HEPA filter on the air circulation system before it could be habitable.

The five of us: Denny and me, and Brendee, Wiley, and Bo –
we all came up on Friday night and camped out in the living room,
like a big slumber party.

Tom whispered to me at one point that he was glad that his
granddaughter hadn't shown up for the pre-shower festivities. "She'd
kinda be odd man out, don'tcha think? Unless Brendee and Wiley
. . ." Tom grinned wickedly at me. "Either way, there's not really
enough privacy, is there? What would they do with Bo while they
were . . ."

I shook my head and grinned back at him. "Wiley claims he's
not down for two women, Tom. Not separately. *Consecutively.* And
certainly not at the same time."

Tom looked over at Wiley, who was showing the fireplace to
his son. *"Really?* I would've thought that Wiley, of all people, reader
of women's minds and all–"

"Nope. He says it's not his thing." I nodded at him. "Wiley
Royce. One woman man."

"What about Brendee? Janae wouldn't tell me anything, which
would indicate that . . ."

"There's nothing to tell, from what I've heard. In all his
humbleness, Wiley said that even the offer of a little novel
homosexuality couldn't tempt his wife to stray from his virility."

"I bet he said it just like that, huh?" Tom grinned.

I nodded.

****

The rest of the tribes showed up the following morning. Wiley's
parents and Brendee's parents; my mom and dad; Denny's parents
and her little sister, Delia, who was eleven. I'd known her since she
was five, and I was like the big brother she'd never had. We were
buddies.

It occurred to me that all girls from eight to eighty smiled at
Wiley. They liked him until he opened his mouth. Unfortunately, he
always opened his mouth, and then they avoided him.

But he was always nice to Denny's little sister, and thereby,
Delia *loved* Wiley. He talked to her like she was an equal, an adult –
whatever the reason, Delia always had a little girl's special smile and
a big hug for Wiley. Except when her mom or dad called her over to
help with the cooking, she was his shadow.

I asked Tom if Maxine and Sam were coming. He frowned and shook his head. "Sam avoids me as much as possible, Nate. My delusions and all." He seemed sad for the space of another heartbeat, then shrugged. "But like I said, Janae'll be here. She was just busy last night. She says she has a new friend she wants us all to meet. She's unusually enthusiastic. This one's *a keeper,* she says. It's the first time I've ever heard that from her."

I squinted at Wiley: we both wondered what gender this keeper would turn out to be. I thought that perhaps Brendee might be thinking the same thing when she exchanged a glance with Denny. Dionne was oblivious; she could not possibly care less about any aspect of Janae's life, no doubt because Janae always frowned at her. I wondered if Dionne realized it was jealousy and not just plain old dislike that made Janae so cold to her.

Dionne's cabin was on a little rise on one side of a short, wide valley. She had set up about five picnic tables, widely spaced, around a big barbeque on one side of the tree-shaded meadow. We clustered around one of them, and our parents and Delia sat at another one some distance away, across the small expanse of the meadow. It seemed as if there wasn't another dwelling around for miles, although we weren't too far off the main road through Big Bear.

"How far does your land go, if you don't mind me asking?"

Dionne grinned and described the whole of the little short valley, the other side of the ridge with her hand. "It's a little less than a hundred and twenty-five acres, all in all."

"Damn!" Wiley said. "It must be worth a fortune!"

"My late husband, may God have mercy on his soul – his grandfather acquired it all for a song. A long time ago."

"It's perfect for the commune," Tom said, not looking up from his phone.

"Actually, it is, wise-ass," Dionne retorted. I noticed that she had become comfortable with Tom. She still worshipped him – Tom was far more charming than Wiley – all the girls loved him, too, and they never regretted talking to him, like they frequently did with my always-superior best friend. But Dionne's own curmudgeonly personality sometimes brushed up against Tom's and it produced sparks.

She smiled at me. "I would be willing to subdivide for you guys, Nate." She pointed at the opposite ridge. "You could build a place right there. And Wiley and Brendee – you guys could be just down the valley there."

Dionne, standing behind Tom, looked over his shoulder to see what absorbed him on his phone. She laced her fingers together and put them on top of his head, then put her chin on her hands, and looked down at whatever he was looking at. "We could even build a cabin for you, for those days when we don't get along."

"But we always get along," Tom replied, noncommittal. "Besides, I like the city. All this fresh air – it reminds me of . . . the farm. Of home." He looked up for a moment and winked at me.

"I like the company," Dionne said, and smiled at Bo. "The fresh air would be good for these children, Tom. What do you guys think?"

"It sounds fantastic, Dionne! Absolutely awesome!" Wiley enthused. "Just think, Brendee! A place in the mountains . . .

"I think that kind of thing is a little out of our price range right now," Brendee said, her eye always on the bottom line.

"I'll make you a low interest loan," Tom said, still not looking up from his phone. "Like no percent. You and Denny, too, Nate. Dionne's right. This would be a great place for the kids to come on the weekends. But during the week . . . I like the city," he said again.

"That would be incredible, Tom," Denny said softly, solemnly.

The four of us were dumbstruck with his generosity, and when no one spoke for several moments, Tom looked up at us. He smiled at our disbelief, our gratitude. "It's only money, kids. Once again, we'll all get one over on the IRS."

"You're a piece of work, my son," Wiley said.

Tom shrugged. "You can fill out my sainthood papers later." He smiled at Wiley, and again I could see how proud he was to be acquainted with him. "It's only money, Wiley," he repeated.

Wiley shook his head, then looked across the meadow at our parents. He grinned at Brendee. "I'm gonna give Aunt Darlene her surprise. You wanna come with me?"

Brendee shook her head, which surprised me. According to Wiley, she hadn't yet seen the lost Wes Thomerville video to *You Can't Be Shy,* even though he'd bitten the bullet, or so he said, and went along with his original plan. As much as he'd doubted the smarts of it, he'd made up his mind to show his wife this new clip of her old crush, and let the chips fall where they may.

But her reaction, he said with a grin, had been no reaction at all.

"And why is that?" I'd asked suspiciously. Once upon a time, I'd witnessed Brendee's enjoyment of Wes Thomerville's original video. I couldn't buy that she wouldn't want to see another one. *You*

Can't Be Shy was a lot better than the one she liked so much: it was craftier, catchier; the subject matter was a lot sexier than *My Disgrace*. I was no judge of Wes's attractiveness – he just looked like a slightly older Wiley to me – but considering Janae's reaction, I figured that Brendee would probably enjoy this one as much, if not more, than the original one.

And I suspected that Wiley might think so, too. So I thought maybe he was having me on – maybe he hadn't mentioned the thing to his wife at all.

"I was in bed, all wrapped up in her favorite satin sheets, playing it on my laptop, when she came in." Wiley batted his baby blues at me. "She showed no interest in it whatsoever."

"Maybe she didn't recognize his voice."

His grin only widened at my skepticism. "Oh, she knew it was him, all right. I could tell from the kinda dazed look on her face when she walked into the bedroom. But she didn't ask what I was watching; she just climbed into bed, closed the laptop and attacked me." Wiley squinted at me. "I told you, my son. Just figure out what they want, then make 'em wait for it for a little while. It works every time."

I still looked doubtfully at him, and he said, "You were right all along, Nate. Brendee forgot all about Wes Thomerville the minute she saw me; I'm still more interesting to her than anything from him. I tried to show it to her twice."

"What happened the second time?"

"The second time, I actually told her about it. I told her about how I thought it would be a fun surprise for her mom. I gave her the whole story, about the interview, about Tom tracking the video down. I asked her if she wanted to see it, or if she wanted to . . ." Wiley smirked smugly. "Apparently, there was no choice to be made. She again closed the computer and we proceeded."

"I told you, Wiley: you never had anything to be concerned about. I think you're an asshole, but Brendee loves you. For you. Not because you look like some old guy she's never even met."

Wiley's deepest, darkest fear had been allayed, that one nagging doubt that he'd always harbored. He'd once told me that he could deal with anything, except the idea that Brendee might someday become bored with him. He'd been starting to believe it was happening, ever since their son was born, and her tuning in to Wes's original video again, after all these years, had been quite the blow to his ego. I thought that it had almost driven him into Janae's embrace.

But all was right with the world now. Brendee had ignored Wes in favor of Wiley, just like I knew she would. For someone who *had the world by the short hairs,* like my grandpa used to say, he was really just too sensitive about the whole thing. Hadn't Brendee's appreciation for Rolling Blackout's awful old song been instrumental to Wiley's happy life today?

I watched Brendee watch Wiley as he crossed the meadow and greeted her mom. I smiled with her when Aunt Darlene grinned adoringly up at Wiley – she really couldn't hide the fact that she had a totally inappropriate crush on him. She'd been the original Wes Thomerville fan, after all. Wiley sat beside her on the picnic table bench and took out his phone, handed it to her. Aunt Darlene's mouth dropped open, and Brendee's grin widened.

Of course she was in no hurry to see it, I thought. She could always check it out on Mom's phone later; it held no burning interest to her at the moment. Wiley was all that she wanted, all she'd ever wanted, from the first moment she'd seen him.

He looked at her from across the meadow and they smiled at each other.

****

While Wiley was wowing Aunt Darlene with Rolling Blackout's lost not-hit, Denny's sister escaped for a moment from under her parents' watchful gaze. She trotted over to our table and asked us what kind of drinks we had in our cooler.

"You shouldn't drink soda, Delia," Denny told her automatically, not looking up from her phone.

Delia ignored her and rooted around in the ice. She pulled out a bright yellow can and asked me what it was.

"It's some citrus stuff. I got it at *The Dollar Store.*" Denny glared at me. "What? It was on sale. You're not gonna drink it. What do you care?"

"I'm gonna take one to Wiley," Delia said, and pulled another soda out of the cooler.

"Wiley's not gonna drink that," Denny told her, but Delia was already skipping back across the meadow.

Curious, Tom reached into the cooler and looked at one of the soda cans. *"The Dollar Store* is not the best place to buy food, Nate," he suggested with a gentle smile. *"Hecho in Mexico. Third world* additives. Christ only knows what those might be."

Tom glanced up and I followed his gaze. Wiley was frowning, gesticulating at Delia. Delia looked up at him, a hurt, frightened look on her face. Wiley softened, patted her on the shoulder. She still looked like she might cry, so he kissed her on the top of the head, gave her a big-brotherly hug. Then he scowled in our direction and came marching back across the meadow with the can of yellow soda clutched in his hand.

Tom said, "Uh, oh."

Denny looked over her shoulder, then said mildly, "Looks like we're gonna find out what's in it."

We all looked expectantly at Wiley, waiting for him to blow up. He caught our expressions and got a hold of himself. Wiley would not give anyone the satisfaction of anticipating his mood, his reaction to anything. He looked at Tom, his guru. Tom shrugged, grinned. He looked at Denny, his fellow convert. Without looking up from her phone, she pointed at me.

Wiley now turned the full force of his angry glare on me. I shrugged. "It was on sale."

"Do you have any idea what's in this? What your little sister-in-law is ingesting?"

"No, but I'm pretty sure you're gonna tell us," Brendee said playfully. It was probably not the best idea. Wiley's glare intensified.

"This contains something called *brominated vegetable oil,* children." He took his phone out of his pocket and I caught Dionne rolling her eyes. *"Brominated vegetable oil is used primarily to help emulsify citrus-flavored soft drinks, preventing them from separating during distribution,"* Wiley read. *"It's been used by the soft drink industry since 1931.*

"In the United States, BVO was designated in 1958 as GRAS, but this was withdrawn by the U.S. Food and Drug Administration in 1970," he added.

"Then how can it still be in there?" Dionne asked.

Tom grinned ruefully. "It's called a *substantial history of consumption.*"

Wiley looked at his phone again. *"The U.S. Code of Federal Regulations currently imposes restrictions on the use of BVO as a food additive in the United States. Several large manufacturers ceded to consumer pressure and removed BVO from their products in 2015, but it is still an ingredient in numerous generic citrus sodas, including Dollar General brands."*

I sighed. "And what's so bad about it, again?"

328

Tom grinned, feeling pity for my ignorance, and for how much Deneen and Wiley were going to skewer me for it. "It's a flame retardant, Nate. It can cause skin lesions, memory loss, tremors, fatigue, loss of muscle coordination, and headaches."

Now my fiancée looked up from her phone and glared at me, just like Wiley. "You're feeding flame retardant to my little sister?"

"I'm not feeding anything to anybody, Denny. I just bought some soda that was on sale. You don't drink soda, so I didn't think I'd be poisoning anyone but myself."

If Brendee and I, or even Tom, thought that Wiley had given up on his crusade to eliminate the scourge of poisonous additives from his life, and from ours, we were mistaken. The sheep could remain blissful in their ignorance, but not us. He was pissed, livid. "This is just the kind of shit I'm talking about. Seriously, Nate? You don't feel bad about Delia drinking this?"

"Oh, for God's sake, Wiley! By all means, dump it out! It was a buck for a six pack!"

"You dump it out," Wiley growled and walked back across the meadow. I watched him dig around in the cooler over there. He extracted a bottled water and handed it to Delia, patted her on the head again.

Tom looked at me indulgently. "He'll get over it, Nate. He's already given up on saving the world. He'll stop lecturing you eventually."

I felt dumb. A lot of the chemicals that Wiley harangued us about seemed more or less harmless to me – what difference did a little sand or sawdust make? But flame retardant? And it was in there for no other reason than to keep this shit from separating, to make it look appetizing? That really did sound awful. And besides, whatever the reason – I would never want Wiley to give up on me. I followed him across the meadow.

BRENDEE

I sighed. Tom was right: Wiley was through with trying to save the world. But I knew he'd never led us slide. He would never let up on us, not for a moment. When Wiley was single-minded, he was *single-minded,* would brook no back-sliding. Nate would have to start reading the labels on the food he bought, if he didn't want to listen to his best friend – and his woman, too – bitch at him about it.

I considered the incredibly generous, incredibly phenomenal offer that Tom and Dionne had made to all of us. Such a thing would go a long way to making Wiley happy – he had grown up on a farm, after all, and the idea that he would be able to get back to nature sometimes with Bo – I bounced him in my lap and he gurgled up at me – our own cabin in the mountains! I knew that idea had to be just awesome to Wiley.

Tom and Dionne had walked a little bit away from us, and were pointing at the little ridgeline, discussing where our cabins could be built. It was all just so inconceivably kind of both of them. Deneen was gazing thoughtfully at the ridgeline, one hand on her belly, not yet showing much of a bump. She hadn't been plagued with morning sickness, like I had been. At least not so far. I hated her for it, in a happy way. If she continued to have such an easy time, I thought that the Osbourne clan would probably grow to more than a few as the years went by. Like my mom, Deneen loved babies.

I smiled at her, touched her hand. "How did we get so lucky?" she asked, a little hitch in her voice.

"Oh, for Christ's sake, don't cry, Den," Dionne said, turning around and returning to the table. "You're not the only one that's lucky. I was just a lonely old widow, chasing the bookstore owner." She smiled at Tom. "But he finally came around . . ."

"You grow on a person," he said, and fondly caressed her cheek.

"And you guys . . ." she said to us. "My parents died when I was in my early twenties. My husband . . . He was always very busy, working, making money. And for what? We never had any children – there just never seemed to be time for that, and before we knew it, the time for it was past.

"And then he dropped dead from a heart attack at forty-six, right before construction started on this place. We were gonna wait out the end of the world here, together . . . I went ahead and had the place built, even though it was looking like the end of the world was going to be a damn lonely place.

"Now, there's Tom." She squeezed his hand. "And here's a second opportunity for me to experience family. Not many people are given second chances like that in life. I think it'll be great – like a commune, just like Tom said. I'll get to see your children grow up – maybe they can call me Grandma Dionne." She grinned to disguise that she was getting a little choked up herself. "Even if Wiley is a hippie."

"We're the beneficiaries of those that came before," Tom said. "Like I say, my family's been here a long time, squirreling away money." He grinned. "What's money for, if not to benefit my friends, too?"

Deneen leapt up and ran around the table, hugged them both. "Thank you guys so much! I'm so stoked! I want to learn how to garden, so my baby will never have to eat a single additive!"

"Ah, that's impossible, Denny," Tom said. "I believe we live at the best time in the history of this planet. I don't think it's gonna end anytime soon," he grinned at Dionne, "but still, we can't go back. The advances that have been made are great, even in food – you like cottage cheese, Denny?"

"Yes. I even found a brand with no poison in it. Just milk and cream."

"But it's not made the same way it was in the oldie days. It's still made on an assembly line." Tom smiled. "There are no more cottages in the production of cottage cheese anymore. They used to make it from raw, unpasteurized milk. There's been a movement to go back to raw milk . . ."

"Fucking hippies," Dionne said under her breath and grinned at us.

"Exactly," Tom agreed. "Consuming raw milk is just ridiculous. Pasteurization kills so many bad things – you know one thing you can get from raw milk, Denny?" She shook her head.

"Tuberculosis," Dionne supplied.

Tom smiled at Deneen's look of wide-eyed shock. "I'll teach you all the gardening you can stand. It's really incredibly easy. This place has evolved to be bountiful; the Earth *wants* to produce. You just have to provide the necessary ingredients, and then stand back. But we ain't gonna be milking our own cows anytime soon."

"Chickens, though, maybe?" Deneen said hopefully. "For eggs? Little chickies are just so cute!"

"I'll set you up a little coop at the house," Tom said. "You don't have to come all the way up here to Prepper Heaven to raise chickens. You can do it right there in town."

A car horn sounded, interrupting Deneen's dreams of *chickies* and additive-free self-sufficiency. We looked toward the house, and after a moment, we saw Janae skipping down the short hill.

I wondered if Tom would want to build a cabin on the ridge for his granddaughter, too; if Dionne would be willing to subdivide off a couple of acres for someone who so obviously disliked her. Somehow, I didn't think the clean mountain air and natural surroundings were really Janae's thing – she was a thoroughly modern girl, and like Tom, I imagined that the city was more to her liking.

Janae pranced up to us, threw herself into Tom's arms, kissed him sloppily. Then she smiled at me and Deneen, and even at Dionne. "How are you all on this glorious day, my beloved friends and family?"

"Not as good as you, apparently," Tom said, and she hugged him again. "Where's your new friend? I thought you were bringing her along for the party?"

So it's a girl, I thought, and exchanged a glance with Deneen. The plan with the brilliant blonde rock-star with the beguiling smile must not've worked out. Apparently *submission* hadn't been Janae's forte after all.

"She'll be here in a minute. She went back down to the store to pick up some smokes. Some beer." Janae smiled at me. "I can't wait for you to meet her, Brendee! I think you guys will really hit it off." She released Tom and dug around in the cooler, coming up with one of Nate's third world, flame retardant citrus sodas. "What the fuck is this?" she asked merrily.

"A mistake," Deneen said, just as merrily. Janae's good mood was infectious. "On Nate's part. There should be some beer in there somewhere."

Janae dug through the ice again. "Where's Wiley?" she asked casually.

Even with a new girlfriend, my husband was on her mind. I thought that perhaps there was something more to my earlier assumption that Janae might be a city girl, that she wouldn't like to be up here in the mountains with us. I realized that maybe *I didn't want her up here with us every weekend.* It wasn't a very nice thought, but there it was. Janae was beautiful, she liked Wiley – I admitted to myself that the less the *single girl* was around him, the more *I'd* like it.

I looked over my shoulder, across the meadow. The eight parents were sitting four to a side, all getting to know one another: the *ancestors,* as Wiley liked to call them, brought together in happy celebration of Deneen's pregnancy and the impending nuptials. It was another scene as old as time – the branches of all our family trees allying because their children and soon-to-be grandchildren were inseparable friends.

Wiley was standing a little ways away, talking to Nate, smiling, laughing. Nate's soda faux pas was clearly forgotten. Delia beamed up at them like the beloved big brothers they were to her.

Delia's dad called to her, and she reluctantly went to see what he wanted. I caught Nate's eye, and nodded for him to come back. Janae was here. She wanted to see Wiley. I was not jealous enough to think that I could keep him away from her when she was standing right here. And since things were getting back to the once-upon-a-time awesomeness between us again, maybe he would stop flirting with her now, stop *licking her fingers.* Maybe he would stop allowing her to flirt with him.

When my husband and her husband-to-be were within earshot, Deneen said shrewdly, "Janae's looking for you, Wiley."

He smiled at the strawberry blonde and said, "Well, here I am. What were your other two wishes?"

Silence ensued. It was daytime, so there were no crickets, but they would've been clearly audible had they been singing. Janae smiled wryly at him, amused – *You stepped in it this time,* her expression said. *No one else seems to appreciate your sense of humor right at the moment.* To underline this, she said, *"Wit's an unruly engine, wildly striking, sometimes a friend, sometimes the engineer."*

Nate sat down next to his fiancée, gave her a little kiss on the cheek; then he, too, considered Wiley. He stood at the head of the picnic table, and with everybody staring at him, Wiley looked back curiously at us: it seemed as if we all expected something else from his smart mouth, so he would oblige us.

"Once upon a time, there was a wise and virtuous king," he began. "His kingdom was unfortunately peopled with sheep of the baa-ing-est kind," he grinned at us, "but his inner circle of courtiers was crammed with lords of surpassing skill, strength, intelligence and wit, with ladies of beauty and grace. So the king was happy. His queen, of course, was the most beauteous of all." He cupped my chin for a moment, smiled lovingly at me.

"Now of late – or maybe it had been always so – aspersions had been cast upon this king's virtue. Being master of all he surveyed, all the women in the kingdom admired him. And because he was king, sometimes their ambitions clouded their better judgments, and sometimes they texted the king seditious messages that didn't always reflect well on their honors."

Janae blinked blankly at Nate, who dared to look at her, and at Tom, who dared to grin at her.

"Now it would be an untruth to say that the king didn't enjoy these attentions. Rare was the woman who didn't bashfully lower her eyelashes and remain silent if he spoke to her of country matters." Wiley batted his baby-blues at me.

"He'd discovered this phenomenon while still a prince, when it was rumored that he was perhaps too free and coarse with his suggestiveness." He smiled at Deneen now, and she did just what he'd described: she looked down and busied herself with plucking non-existent flotsam from the table cloth. Deneen had never been able to withstand Wiley's steady gaze for too long.

"Leave jesting while it pleaseth, lest it turn to earnest," Tom commented.

Wiley shook his head. "'Twas not the case. Perhaps because of a determined lack of finesse on the young prince's part, his jests never received any positive response. From the vast garden of eager high-school womanhood, he'd only picked one flower before he met she that was to be his queen."

The look of shocked disbelief on Janae's face was unmistakable. She couldn't believe that a) Wiley had been with only two girls; b) that he was admitting it; and c) since Wiley had only been with two girls, she couldn't believe that he hadn't been, married or not, therefore ripe to pick a third. One so beauteous and worldly as she so obviously was.

I was just like Bo – I loved to listen to Wiley talk, and since he was in Olde English fairy tale mode at the moment, even my own inner monologue was filling up with therefores and similarly florid phrases. His boy looked raptly at his father, and Wiley ruffled his hair before continuing.

"This first flower that the prince picked was queenly in her own right. Wise, scholarly, skilled, adroit – since she was the prince's first, it must truly be said that the prince was the one that was *picked.*

Broken off at the stalk, plucked from the garden of boyhood. All boys should be offered the apple in such an unspeakably incredible and thorough fashion." Wiley grinned at his own poesy. Tom and Nate grinned back. Encouraged, he added, "Thus would we all, like the fortunate king, become masters of the Tree of Knowledge, or at least this branch of it.

Wiley sighed theatrically. "But, alas, the prince's dalliance with this other queen was like the best horserace: fast and hot and utterly exciting. It left both bettors profited, satisfied. But just like that horserace, it ran its course. The worldly mare left for foreign tracks, and accepting this without regret, the prince turned his attention to local and more elegant fillies." Again Wiley smiled fondly at me.

"But still, the prince, now grown a king, couldn't forget all that his first queen had taught him. Women fascinated him. He loved to watch them – all the different shapes and sizes, the multi-levels of beauty and years – a slut, here; a friend as loyal and as undemanding as a playful puppy, there; a darling, pretty gem, as unconcerned as a summer breeze; a wondrous and contemplative diamond-in the rough, nearly the king's equal." My husband winked at me.

"Yet, by virtue of his instruction at the feet of his first queen, the king knew the inescapable truth – as different as all women appear on the surface – you're all so exactly, precisely, unwavering *the same.*" Wiley grinned smugly at us. "That first queen, you see, was a traitor to her gender. She let the tender prince in on all those secrets that you endeavor so mightily to hide. The king knows," Wiley tapped his temple, "what it is that women want.

"A favorite book is no less enjoyable, even if the reader knows the ending. And as such, understanding what women want, how they think, didn't make the king any less apt to talk to them, to interact with them–"

"To tease them," I interjected.

Wiley feigned surprise. "And perhaps out of this aspect came the aspersions cast upon the king's virtue. At the base of all paintings is a substructure – the canvas, the wooden frame it's stretched over. But just because we're aware of this, does it lessen our appreciation of the paint skillfully applied, the composition, the beauty, the meaning of the artwork?"

Janae spoke up. "Charlie Chaplin said, *What do you want meaning for? Life is desire, not meaning!*"

Wiley ignored her. "But women aren't only the art; they're also the artist. And sometimes, unlike with his appreciation of a colorful painting, the king discovered that his appreciation for a colorful woman was returned back to him, manifold."

I thought that Janae might be sorry she'd opened her mouth. Wiley was obviously talking about her.

"Unfortunately, the king was unmoved by this returned appreciation. If I may once again return to the analogy of women as flowers – imagine a vast conservatory of loveliness – all the world of buds and blossoms, pruned and watered and grown to ripeness, strictly for the king's appreciation. Because that's how he viewed them. A world of women, placed here by a munificent deity for no other reason than for him to look at them, to smell their heady fragrances, to study them as if he were the most resolute botanist.

"But from this garden, the king plucked only one more, after that first ravishing bloom. And while he knows that all flowers are the same at heart – he understands the workings of their roots, he knows just want they want to be nourished, to thrive – this blossom he has picked is like no other. *Man is one world, and hath another to attend him.* The king's queen is utterly unique, different than every other woman that has ever lived, alone, separate from any that breathes and lives today. Because this queen is the mother of his child."

"The king can make other children with other queens, Wiley," Dionne observed.

"Thou know'st 'tis common," Janae said.

"Ay, madam, it is common," Wiley replied, pleased. "But there was a story of some renown in the kingdom, that touched on just such matters. And while I will beg the pardons of those of you with brothers and sisters, and would wish to make no judgments on your sainted parents–" he glanced over his shoulder at our sainted parents, laughing and talking across the meadow, oblivious to his pontification, "– the king ascribed to the moral of this story as a great truth. So I'll relate it to you.

"Once there was a fox and a lioness, that, for reasons that don't need exploring at this juncture, had thrown off their natural enmities. One day, they were having a pleasant conversation, and the subject of children came up. The mama fox, proud of her litter of many kits, remarked upon how happy she was with all the Lord's largesse.

"'So many do I have!' she said proudly, then looked in pity at the lioness. 'Thereby, you must be saddened, that you have only the one. Yet still, with just this paltry showing, you see yourself as the King of Beasts, and scarce deign to speak to the rest of us.'

"The lioness smiled. ''Tis true that I am above you, and 'tis true, I have produced just one. But unlike your many, who are but foxes – my one is a lion.'''

Wiley picked his blue-eyed cub up from my lap, bounced him, kissed him, then handed him back. "And so it was with the king. He neither desired nor needed any other children. He didn't think that he could divide his attention between any more – foxlike; he instead preferred to devote himself to just that one and make sure he would indeed become a lion.

"And as he needed no other cubs, he needed no other lionesses. But still, the king lived amid all the flowers of that vast conservatory of roses and daisies, philodendrons and gaudy weeds. And while he liked them all, admired them all, might even smell one occasionally, be amazed every now and then by this one's exquisite beauty or that one's wildness or the other one's poison-ivy-like danger . . . It didn't mean that he ever felt the need to *pick* another one. Like in any other conservatory, picking another one, even by the king, is not only strictly verboten, it's in extremely bad taste.

"The king has made his choice, and not a day has gone by when he has regretted it. Because he was such an apt botanist in his youth, because he was taught by a gardener so forthcoming with her secrets, all the myriad gorgeous flowers of the world hide absolutely no mystery for him. The king's choice has created a melding of itself – his choice and the queen's choice are now a separate person, someone else entirely.

"*The best thing a father can do for his children is to love their mother*. For the king, this love is effortless. Forsaking all others . . . that was the easiest choice of all for him."

Now Wiley grinned. He met everyone's eyes for a moment, including Janae's. "But the queen, in her wisdom, and his noble lords and ladies of the court, and even the flowers themselves, must accept without rancor that the king is always gonna talk to women, always listen and reply to them, always watch and study them. It's his very nature. Thus ends my tale." He sat down next to me.

"*Do well and right, and let the world sink,*" Tom said.

"I'll drink to that," Dionne agreed. She arose, dug around in the cooler and found a beer.

337

NATE

Before anyone could comment on Wiley's excessively elaborate explanation for his own appalling flirtiness – and his unapologetic warning that we'd all better just accept it – a horn honked from the direction of the cabin.

Janae's grin lit up her lovely face. "That would be Tisha!" she exclaimed. She arose and trotted up toward the house.

The seven of us all watched her, curious to see what *a keeper* was gonna look like. Even Bo looked up the hill. Moments later, Janae reappeared, hand in hand with a trim, black-haired girl, a little shorter than her, perhaps a year or two older.

"My best friends," Janae said when they arrived at the picnic table, "I'd like you all to meet my newest best friend. This is Tisha." Janae squeezed her hand and the girl smiled happily at her. Janae was obviously also *Tisha's* newest best friend. Clearly, here had blossomed new love. It made me feel a little poetic myself, just observing it.

Janae introduced us all, and when she got to Wiley, I watched Tisha's smile falter a little bit, as did Wiley's. They looked at each other in amazement for a split-second, then friendly, first-impression smiles broke out again and they shook hands.

Watching them, I again thought about the first time that Wiley had shown me Wes Thomerville's video. I'd asked him to find out what she was watching that turned Brendee on so much, and he had obliged me the very next day.

Suffice it to say that I wasn't impressed with Rolling Blackout's video; their sound was poppy and forgettable, their lyrics inane. But the most annoying thing about the video wasn't their sound or their look. The most annoying thing about the video was the singer.

"What's this guy's name?" I'd asked Wiley.

He'd held up his finger, then typed something on his phone. A moment later he got a text. "Mom says his name is Wes Thomerville." He typed something on his phone again, then exclaimed in surprise. "Well, what d'ya know? They'll let anybody on *Wikipedia*, these days, I guess." When I didn't look amused, he cleared his throat and continued, reading the entry for this ancient, unknown singer, whose video made Brendee – then my crush – into a writhing wildcat. *"Wes Thomerville, born 1980. Riverside's native son, lead singer of Rolling Blackout, one documentary video,* Rolling

Blackout's Hometown Debut, *featuring the video to* My Disgrace. *Married to Madeline Rearden since–"*

"Is there a picture of him?" I'd asked.

"I'm sure there is," Wiley said, and looked down at his phone again.

I'd slapped him on the back of the head. "Is it like looking in a fucking mirror, Wiley?"

Because the main problem with Rolling Blackout, as the luck of the universe would have it, wasn't their sound and it wasn't their lyrics. It wasn't even their singer, really, this Thomerville guy, who was old now, who wouldn't turn Brendee on in the least anymore, not even if she saw him walking down the street, guitar in hand.

The problem, of course, the thing that was going to prevent Brendee from ever looking in my direction, was that Wiley, like his old man before him, *looked just like this guy.* And he already knew it.

"What can I say, Nate?" He'd batted his blue eyes at me. "Don't hate me because I'm beautiful."

And now the whole scene was repeating itself. I wanted to say to Wiley, to Tisha: "Is it like looking in a fucking mirror, kids?"

Because Tisha looked just like Wiley, and Wiley looked just like Tisha. She could be his sister; if it wasn't for the gender difference, she could almost be his identical twin. Wiley was a masculinized version of her, she was a feminized version of him. They had the same dark blue eyes, the same curly black hair.

I glanced over at Brendee, who saw me looking at her and abruptly snapped her mouth closed and tried to erase the dumbstruck look on her face. I grinned to myself. Here was another curious conundrum. Janae was thoroughly bi-sexual, and she had entertained a little yen for Wiley. She had found herself a girl that looked just like Wiley, deemed her *a keeper.*

Perhaps there were other aspects to Tisha that made Janae like her so much – but all I could see was this uncanny resemblance to the married man for whom Janae had so obviously lusted, and after all, Janae had only known Tisha for a little while . . .

And then there was Brendee, who had displayed just a tiny hint of bi-sexuality. Wiley told me that Brendee had admitted that she'd liked kissing Janae, but then went on to claim that it hadn't been a big turn-on for her. Nothing did it for her like Wiley did, according to him. And yet, again, here was a girl that looked just Wiley . . . I wondered if Brendee might not feel a little stirring in whatever part

339

of her that Janae had touched, for a blue-eyed, black-haired *girl* this time . . .

I glanced at Deneen, found that she was looking at me. I discovered that I didn't like the look on her face, probably because she didn't like the look on mine. She could tell that I was thinking about interpersonal interactions that maybe a good husband and father-to-be shouldn't be thinking about – at least not if I couldn't keep the sly look off of my face. I smiled blankly at her, asked silently, *What?*

She nudged Brendee, and Brendee gave her the same blank look.

BRENDEE

Tisha and Wiley looked in amazement at Janae, and she just grinned innocently at them. It was phenomenal – even Bo looked at this beautiful woman in awe. He blinked at me, then back at her. "Goo?" he asked, which I interpreted to mean, *Why didn't you tell me Daddy had a twin sister?*

Tom, Wiley, Wiley's dad, Tisha, Bo . . . *Wes.* There was definitely a deep pool of black-haired, blue-eyed genetics going on in the Riverside area.

"It's so nice to meet you," Wiley said, and I thought, *I bet it is.* Because, other than his son – who also looked just like him – I knew that Wiley loved no one more than he loved himself. I just had time to wonder how much he might be attracted to a *woman* that looked just like him, when Deneen's dad called over to us to come and get something to eat before everything got cold.

Janae and Tisha started across the meadow, hand in hand, and I realized that whatever horticulture Wiley may or may not consider with this newest flower in the king's garden – it was really an unfair thought: Wiley had just told me that I was the only one for him, and so elegantly – but even if he might be just *thinking* inappropriately about this new bloom, he was out of luck. Tisha obviously only had eyes for Janae.

Before the rest of us could answer the call to eat, Delia came back across the meadow with two *Chinet Classic White* dinner plates, filled to overflowing: there were two hot dogs on each plate, loaded; a big helping of store-bought potato salad with a plastic fork sticking out of it; a generous pile of potato chips. She set them down and beamed her adorable, adoring little-girl's smile at her big brothers.

"I made you guys a plate. I didn't know what you'd like, so I just made you what I'd like."

In that aspect, Delia was like Deneen – her big sister had bought me a bedazzled rhinestone phone cover for my eighteenth birthday. It was absolutely hideous, at least to my tastes. But it was something that Deneen would've bought for herself, so she was convinced that I'd just have to love it, too.

"Thanks, Delia!" Nate said. He ruffled her hair, then stuck a big handful of potato chips into his mouth. He chewed, then started in on one of the hot dogs with no hesitation whatsoever.

The rest of us looked at Wiley as he considered the meal that Delia had so lovingly prepared for him. Hot dogs – OMG, I doubted if Wiley had ever eaten a hot dog in his entire life – *lips and assholes,* he called them, *and more chemicals than a sewage treatment plant.* And that had been before he'd discovered just what all those chemicals really were. Delia had topped it with mustard and relish, all full of emulsifiers and stabilizers – I'd bet there might be a little carrageenan in there to make it all smooth.

Wiley had probably never allowed a potato chip to pass his lips, either – they were just salt and fat – his mom, the nutritionist, didn't eat potato chips, so neither had Wiley. And the potato salad: it was a nice appetizing yellow color, no doubt from the dye added to it, and it was probably guaranteed not to spoil amidst the picnic fun, because it was stuffed full of preservatives to keep the microbes at bay.

All this was presented to my hippie husband on execrable, landfill-filling disposable dishware, topped off with a non-biodegradable plastic fork.

Making a plate for a man you liked was an ancient, womanly tradition. With a totally unapologetic sexism, I thought that Delia would make a fine little wife someday, just like her mom, just like her sister. Just like me.

But I knew better than to even dream of serving my husband anything like this. It was a run-of-the-mill, commonplace little picnic meal that Delia had brought to Wiley, all-American. There was no possible way for her to know that her beloved big brother wasn't going to touch any of it.

We all looked at him, waiting. He had frightened Delia earlier, hurt her feelings when she had thoughtfully brought him a soda. I wondered if she had taken his lecture to heart, if she would now stop drinking soda, just because *Wiley said so,* because she looked up to him so much.

But her sister also told her not to drink soda. So maybe she had also dismissed Wiley's advice about it. But he was going to deliver her a preachment now, one for the ages. She would not soon forget the rant big brother Wiley was gonna sling at her now.

But it wouldn't sink in: I didn't think that Delia's eleven-year-old mind would quite comprehend what he was telling her. I didn't think that she could be anything but hurt when Wiley refused her offering of food, so cutely brought. She knew her sister wouldn't eat it, but her sister was weird: her sister didn't eat much of anything.

But the whole rest of the assemblage was chowing down on this – I didn't think she was quite old enough to understand all the explanations that Wiley was about to give her about the poisons in the food she'd brought for him. It was a picnic lunch after all. Why wouldn't he want it?

I knew that Wiley didn't want to hurt Delia's feelings again; he appreciated her little childish gesture of adoration. He knew what women wanted, how they thought, after all, even little ones. And what he was going to tell her was going to be a huge chastisement. Delia was just being nice to a man she loved. Wiley knew instinctively not to criticize any woman for that. Especially not a little girl that looked up to him so much.

But the *shit* she was asking him to eat . . . He hesitated.

Tom at last came to his rescue. "Have a hot dog, Wiley. The buns are fortified." He reached over and took one of them himself, took a big bite. Wiley smiled, followed suit.

"Thanks, Delia," he said, around a mouthful of industrialized poison.

"How's that taste, Wiley?" I asked him.

"It's delicious," he said genuinely. "Just like they want it to be." It wasn't like he could pretend that it wasn't tasty, no matter what he knew it to contain. He grinned at me, then said to Delia, "A little later on, I have story for you about where hot dogs come from." He finished the hot dog with nary a grimace. "Then you'll be enlightened, smarter than the average bear, Dee. Just like me."

Delia smiled. Nothing would please her more than that.

Wiley couldn't save the world, but he could save his family. First Deneen, and now Delia; later Bo and Deneen's baby. One convert at a time would be good enough for Wiley.

****